Eric R. Williams

Copperman

Foundling

The night that I was born the sky exploded. Bits and pieces of it tore across the mountains, shredded in blue white streaks. The Gods clawed along the fields, flung trees like scrap wood, flicked boulders down the ravine and into the new river. The others ran, and in their terror, forgot my mother and her new cub. Left us there in the dark, wet and wounded by hours of struggle. Left us on a blooded blanket, too exhausted to cry out or even care if the world ended before I saw it.

The sky exploded and the others ran, torches flaring out in the storm. They fled along the sheep-trail up to the first of the three caves, holes that weave deep down to the underworld. Then the mountain shifted above them and all thought was gone, the world collapsing, pouring down in a flood of ice and snow. And then a silence as cold as death.

They found me the next day. She had covered me with herself...that is why I lived. They had to pry her ridged arms from around me and nurse me against the fattest woman in the clan. They wrapped me in calf's furs and set me in a circle of hot stones from the fire while the Council gathered to decide what I was: a gift or a curse. They spoke in low tones as if I might hear and judge them for cowards. The spring-valley was unrecognizable now, covered in broken trees and twenty lengths of snow and ice. The village just a memory, represented by the torn hides and few scraps they could dig out.

'Why had the Gods spared him?'

They spoke low about their guilt and I cried out until one of them finally picked me up.

"We will take him down to the Lake-people and trade him for food and tools. We will never speak of his birth and they can take our bad luck."

It was decided and it was done. I was twelve hours old but I remember it…I remember everything.

The Lake

The smell of smoked fish. The sound of women slapping clothes against rocks. The prickling of sunshine against my new skin. And voices murmuring from a hundred villagers doing a hundred tasks, happy as bears climbed out from the ground to find that summer had not forsaken them after all. Winter, suddenly dragged away like a musty blanket, revealing clean colors and sharp lines. There were boats and nets to repair, shoes and clothes to clean, speckled trout schooling in the spring creeks. Here, someone sat sharpening a copper knife on a flat stone; there, a family stuffing mud and old straw into cracks around their hut. Children ran happily, fighting over nothing and men cursed at them good-naturedly, laughing as they scattered and galloped like sheered sheep. In the chaos no one paid much attention to the straggle of survivors from the High-mountain clan as they came in from the north trail and set down their few belongings. There would be traders coming and going all summer now and this lot did not seem to have much to trade anyway. A few gathered in to listen as the mountain Elder stood, holding me out.

"This is a child we found!" he said, wheezing from the effort.

"I want to tell the story properly but I, like my people, am nearly starved and in need of food and drink."

Beggars? This was unusual. Their clothes were well made, the few tools they carried were proper and they were not thin or diseased. Work stopped as the village gathered closer. He has a story? After a long winter, bored of each other's stories, this was currency enough to warrant a bite of food. Small cups of goat-milk were handed around followed by chunks of hard baked bread and strips of smoked whiting. Precious few bites, but enough to get the old man talking. He took off his rabbit-skin hat and smoothed it out before sliding it into his pocket, revealing thin silver hair, greasy from the sweat of travel. He stood proudly and addressed the crowd with the flair of a seasoned storyteller. It felt to the Lake-people like a ceremony. The last of the clamber settled as they waited for their story. The old man was good. He was very good. He told them about our village of fifty, escaping the storm. He waived his arms and paced, voice rising to cries of fear as the storm descended, dropping to a soft quaver as they discovered the village gone. The Lake-people forgot their chores as they listened to the epic tale. The Elder exclaimed that the Gods had punished them for not praying enough, for not working hard enough to appease them. But they had given them a strange gift. On the journey across the mountains to the lake they found a woman alone, in the throes of birth. They tried to help her but she had not survived the labor. They understood that this was a sign. The child would help them. They would bring it to the Lake-people where it would be raised in health and safety in exchange for some food and a few small goods. Then they would follow the river down to green fresh land, find a new home far away from the mountains. The child was their gift to the Lake-people. During the telling of this story, every member of the village sat mesmerized... all save one. Copperman sat cross-legged, slowly shaping and sharpening the blade on the flat stone, a stone covered with the shiny dust of countless hours' use. He never even looked up. In the silence of the story's end he spoke loudly.

"Did you bury the mother?"

"What?"

"The mother...did you bury her?"

"Of course we did. We are poor but we are still humans. "

"With what tools?"

The Elder shifted from foot to foot, thinking hard.

"Tools?"

"Must have been hard to bury a body in the frozen earth in the highlands without tools."

"We"...the Elder paused..."we buried her in the snow the best we could."

"And this 'Gift from the Gods' that you bring us? It is because of your good will towards the Lake-people? A generous gift from a clan who has lost so much already?"

There was an edge to Copperman's voice. The old man looked around, unsure.

"He is clearly meant for your clan. The signs are there to see."

He reached down and brought me up to the crowd, naked, squealing, wet and chapped from the waist down, belly-cord blackened and tied by a piece of twine.

"He has the wrist marks." A woman whispered. I did. A stroke of genious by the Elder: five small cuts on my right wrist, rubbed with soot from the fire to blacken them.

"It is true!" Another said. The crowd gathered to examine me. Copperman sighed and stood stiffly, stretching the blood back into his legs. He walked through the crowd over to me and held my tiny wrist to see the marks; marks like his. He looked between my legs and checked the color of my eyes.

"One bag of eincorn, a lamb and a copper blade."

The Elder shook his head "But that is not enough to..."

Copperman turned and glared at him. He leaned in and whispered, "One more word and you take the child and leave. Or do you want me to expose your lie?"

The Elder slid me back into the calfskin.

"We have done the Gods' will, now we will leave you and the new-born to your warm houses and food. We have land to cross before this day is over."

The others watched as Copperman gave them their lamb, grain and blade. A man spoke out:

"Trading a child? This is not done. At least the Lake-people keep and care for their own."

They left as quickly as they arrived. As if they could not get away fast enough. Then the others came around, one at a time, to look me over. A young girl tickled my cheek with a yellow flower. Then, losing interest, the crowd found their way back to half-done tasks. Copperman was standing alone holding me when his wife came down, fresh from a wash in the creek.

"What is it you have there?" she asked. He smiled and handed me over like a warm loaf of bread.

"It is our son."

Growing

The life of a boy is a fighting life. From the time I could crawl I knew to eat fast when food came, to grip and pinch the children's hands that would reach in to steal it. The adults did not stop the theft... Ever. A child who will not fight his brother for a crust of bread will become a man who will not fight wolves for a freshly killed deer. We all got enough to eat but never as much as we wanted. Over the seasons, I grew into the language and the way of the Lake-people. The summers stretched on endlessly. There were bugs and frogs and other children to chase; there were visitors from distant valleys come to trade and share news. Boats poled out morning and night to chase fish into the labyrinth of reed traps and funnel nets. We browned naked and free, unaware of the adults unless reprimanded. We awoke fresh to the first birds and collapsed into dreams as the sun began to fade. The winters came as a sleepy coziness.

Small games and short trips into the dark day sapped our strength. The summers would soon appear and open up the world again.

And so it went from summer to summer. Winter to winter. Copperman was seldom there in the summers, spending his time in the caves of nearby mountains. He took different assistants with him each season and paid them in a small percentage of the metal he made. They would in turn pay him to shape the blades and spear points from what he made. Copperman said that if he used the same men each year, they would soon steal his secrets and our family would starve from the loss. I knew even as a child that this was not true. He was the most skilled in our clan and could turn his hand at anything he chose. It was his certainty that others would make the metal poorly. And few things repulsed him more than a tool poorly built.

I suppose it would be wise to describe him: A pair of powerful hands, with long, lean fingers. Hands strong enough to twist the bark from a frozen branch but delicate enough to scrawl ink-scars, a hair's breadth apart, into flower patterns on a woman's skin. He was a tall, lean man with a slightly crooked nose, thick black hair and dark brown eyes that always seemed to be staring out past anything we could see. He was my father and I looked nothing like him. Travelers would point this out and I began to avoid them to avoid hearing it. He was my father and I wanted more than anything to be like him. To be him. To be respected and slightly feared. Copperman was one of the Lake-people but always an outsider and this also connected us. The others wanted him to be in the Council and if he had chosen to become our leader it would have been an easy victory. His refusal to join in on any leadership roles amazed and annoyed the clan.

"Who is he to come and go as he pleases?" The day he traded for me made him many enemies for he never even asked the Council for permission. They would most likely have assented…but the arrogance to not even ask? This was against the clan. But who would dare confront him? He was a good hunter and the only artist in branding scars and, of course, his fine tools kept the clan busy with traders, some coming from awkward routes just to buy his blades. When they came, he would ask them about the stone and waterways in their valley and then repeat each new bit of information over and over till it was engraved in his knowledge. He wanted bluestone. Rare veins of it grew into the hillsides and he needed it to make his metal. This was his obsession. The mental map he would use to choose the next season's metal work. Each season, he went further and further afield. I begged to come with him and be his assistant and each year he would give me a new task to complete. Staying a night out in the woods alone. Shooting an arrow into a plum from fifty leg lengths. Chopping two holes in the ice, five long steps apart, then swimming from one to the other. Each new task he rewarded with a new line of ink-scars on my wrists, knees or ankles, until I began to wonder if I would be covered from head to foot before we were done.

Every year I would ask to join him and he would turn his head to the side. And then came my fourteenth spring. This was the year I began. My mother woke me at dark one morning and whispered for me to dress quietly. Copperman was waiting outside fully bundled in his bearskin cloak, his fire-kit belt over thick britches. He had a bundle of well-polished arrow shafts and half a dozen already tipped with flint points of varying size. From his full rucksack I could see the blade of his metal ax. This was the makings for a long journey.

The first day

My stomach felt hollow. I understood the need for quiet as we left the village, going up and out of the steep sunrise valley. He always left secretly before my sister or little brother was awake. Before anyone in the clan could watch the direction he went. I looked back to see my mother latch the door behind us. The snow had melted but it was sharp cold and the trees scratched welts across my face as we stepped from stone to stone in the dim light of the half moon. We avoided patches of snow or wet leaves that might show our path. The village of my youth disappeared from sight. By first light we were farther than I had ever been from the lake and we stopped to rest, looking down on it from the vantage point of a rocky ledge. Could it be that big? I squinted to see the first boats, like water bugs crawling along the edges of still water. Copperman, a sparse talker at the best of times, had not spoken a word on the journey. I tried not to show it but my deepest desire was to be home with my mother. To awake in a few hours to fish and play in the first days of spring. To wrestle my little brother and make my sister laugh. I wanted goat's milk porridge with a chunk of honeycomb in it. I wanted to go back home. He looked at me as I tucked my head against my knees. His eyes softened for a second.

"The first day is the longest," he said... "Bluestone will remind you of why we came."

He stood and threw a small rock down and we listened for seconds before it hit. A deer below spooked and clattered along a hidden trail. He nodded at my bow.

"Keep it strung and ready...keep your eyes sharp. There are more days of travel than we have food for in the packs."

I strung my bow and we walked ahead. The path was open now. We had climbed raw woods and scrub to connect with the goat trail (not in use yet by the shepherds). It would be crawling with sheep and goats in the coming weeks. We were surely the first of the season to cross the hard packed snow and I was happy for my mother's parting gift: a new pair of faun-skin boots stuffed with soft dry grass for warmth. I switched my short moccasins for the boots and with the fur facing down they gripped well. I could feel the warmth of her hands on them. The sky grew until we were on the white tops of the ridge, separating our world from the next. I had only seen it from a distance and it was marvelous and blinding in the full sun. Copperman slid his hood down to cover his eyes. I did the same, using the fur fringe to block most of the glare. We stumbled half blinded, hot from the exertion and cold from the rising wind. I wanted to stop and rest at the saddle between the highest ridge but Copperman refused.

"See your breath? Feel the cold up here? Once you have a sweat you cannot risk letting the body rest and cool." He said there were bodies of frozen travelers scattered across the mountain and most of them "just stopped for a rest." This drove me on past any exhaustion. I could feel them around, staring up with dead eyes. Eventually we were angling down and the fresh air had the delicate smell of trees again; Moist moss and juniper. By evening, we were back into scrub-pine and rocks. By nightfall, we followed a hidden trail to a shallow cave covered over by dry branches. He knew where we were and smiled at the fire pit stacked with separate bundles of tied twigs. I recognized his work. Nobody made as much of a fuss about fire-starting as Copperman did. And nobody could do it faster. He sat crosslegged and unwrapped his fire kit. A long strip of elk-leather rolled up into a pouch in the middle. He used it as a belt over his breeches. He unrolled it onto a large flat rock at the cave's entrance and laid out the pieces. A bundle of mushroom moss, so dry it powdered as he pinched off a clump. Next to that, a chunk of charcoal and a strip of half burnt cloth. He tore off a strip of the burnt cloth and sprinkled the mushroom powder and charcole onto it. He had two fire-stones, long scarred by use. Grey flint from the riverbeds and black flint from the quarry near the lake. Hit together, they sparked well and with a short flurry of well-aimed strikes, he saw the spark hit the charred cloth. It held a tiny spark. He cupped it like a baby chick, folding his hand around it, blowing slowly until a white spot began to pulse. He dipped the spark bundle into a handful of dry grass and began to blow harder. When smoke came dark and thick from the other side of the grass, he set it into the stacks of twigs and with a small whoosh, a flame rose into the pit.

A mouse had set up camp in the twigs. It jumped out, startling us as it disappeared in an offended blur of gray fluff. He laughed, face lit up in the magic of it all, and then glanced sideways at me.

"Wood! Where is the wood?"

I scrambled to gather branches as he set out camp. I felt wind-burnt, sun-burnt and desperately sore from the day. The fire crackled as we chewed a few bites of hard bread and gulped water from the goatskin. I fell asleep to the sound of Copperman repeating sections of his map. Murmuring the path we would follow the next day. I was too tired to dream. Or maybe the dreams kept their secrets even from me.

Brains and ashes

I will not describe the next several day except to say that hardship has its own rewards. My legs (legs that I thought were strong) gave out and would refuse to take the next step. My arms would drop from my side and refuse to balance, letting me topple from the sides of trails like an arrow-struck doe. Copperman would busy himself with arranging his pack or flaking a new edge on his flint knife until I managed to gather myself together and begin the journey again. By the fifth or sixth day we were low on food and in thick forest when I realized that I had walked the day without stopping and still had strength to gather a fire and set camp. The trees were different here. Bigger around and moss covered, with bent arms and thick chunky bark. The soil was rich and black. Good planting soil. Richly rotting around the base of the bigger trees. There were small springs here, pure and safe bubbling out from the ground. We filled our skins and drank deeply. Copperman pointed out hoof prints of a small deer. Its scat nearby was speckled with berry seeds. We found the trees nearby eaten clean from their berries as high as deer can reach. Copperman whistled cheerfully.

"We will stay hear for a few days."

He pulled a cord of strong braided sinew from his pack and began to arrange it into a loop knot. The cord had a hook-shaped root tied to its base. He searched around until he found a strong flexible branch near a trail and tied the cord to it. He stretched the cord down until the branch strained from the weight. Then he carefully hooked the root to fork in a sapling on the other side of the trail. He used twigs to arrange the cord into a loop about a foot high facing the trail. Then he gently set branches around blocking the spaces around the loop. I watched fascinated, knowing better than to pester him with questions. Finally he streached and looked at the snare.

"If it does not rain we might have meat tomorrow."

I lay awake that night pondering the contraption. Just before I dozed off Copperman chuckled. I looked over and he smiled at me.

"Do not worry, I will teach you how it works. This summer you will learn much bigger things than how to snare your supper. Things few other men will ever know."

I lay awake for hours, listening to the strange woods. Bubbling over with excitement. Expanding, learning, becoming.

The snap of a large branch woke us at dawn. Three deer darted past our camp and Copperman rose quickly. I followed him to the snare and half hanging from it, twitching was a small doe.

"Perfect." he said.

He knelt down next to it and spoke softly, thanking it for the food. We skinned it there, cleaning its cavity out with bundles of wet grass, saving the heart, lungs, liver and kidneys. Then the real work began. Copperman was urgent, barking orders as I ran around gathering what would be needed. We carried the doe to a tree near camp and hung it upside down by sharpened branches through the heels. He used a curved piece of antler (one of the many strange tools he carried) to slide between the skin and flesh. He worked with a fury, peeling away the skin down from the legs on the inside until the pelt came away in one piece. While he did this I built a smoke rack from saplings, arranging them like the frame of a hut. This was my favorite kind of work because I got to use the copper axe. It swung so heavy in my hand that a sapling would slice half through in a single chop. In the center of the frame I built a small fire from the hot coal still alive in the depth of the night's fire pit. Copperman was particular about the wood we smoked with, choosing certain types to give the meat flavor and other types to cure it well. He used a thin flake of black obsidian to slice long strips from the doe and I hung them on the branches until they covered the frame completely.

Lazy, thick smoke crawled up around and between the strips of meat. The camp began to smell savory and delicious. By afternoon the doe was a neat pile of bones sectioned and arranged on a clean flat slab of stone.

We ate. We ate without hurry or concern. We ate slow roasted pieces of heart, liver and kidneys cooked on the tips of small sticks. We ate pieces of fat and meat sizzled on a hot flat stone. We hummed with delight, sucking the hot marrow from roasted bones. The rich food flowed through my blood, like courage. The sky clouded over but the rain never came, just the pressure of it, making us sleepy. We tended the smoke rack and napped through the night. By morning the smoked strips were turning hard and shiny. We tended the fire and ate more until bones filled the fire pit. Copperman had me find and split a long arm-thick sapling and bend it into a circle. The doeskin had soaked overnight in a nearby pool. We stretched the wet hide, cutting strips of the outer skin to tie together over the frame like the top to a giant drum. As the skin dried in the sun it pulled tight. I began scraping the fur, a job all children know too well. It is tedious to slowly drag a rounded flint blade against a hide, careful not to slice through the skin.

Copperman washed and prepared the tendons, useful for so many things: binding arrow tips, stringing a bow, sewing a torn pack. He sat braiding them together until he had a legs length. He rolled it into a coil and stored it moist in a piece of cleaned intestine. It would stay waxy and flexible when we were ready for it. I finished the scraping as he came over with his hands full of sticky ashes. He began to smear the hide with it. The goop smelled strange and stung the nostrils.

"Brains and ashes," he explained. "Every animal has the right amount of brain to cure its own hide. Never eat the brains of any large animal, it will cause madness."

He undid the sloppy hide from the frame and rolled it tightly, binding it together with green strips of bark.

"By the time we get to the next valley we can wash it."

We arranged the hard smoked strips of deer into our packs and dismantled the drying rack. As the sun set we were already asleep.

Trade tounge

I awoke to voices. Copperman sat cross-legged making beads from the teeth of the doe. He was speaking softly to someone. I wondered if this was still the scraps leftover from some dream. It looked from the back like a creature of some kind but after a moment I realized it was a woman. An old woman. She sat next to him in a friendly closeness. Her hair was gray-black but braided with different colored strips of black and green and red cloth, the hair was matted and clumped together in parts, long enough to reach the ground as she sat. From the back it was almost all of her I could see. She had on a sheep tunic sewn from different colored pelts in a pattern of stripes. This was a style of dress I had never seen and after our journey alone I was uncomfortable with the idea of the existence of others in our little camp. I lay silent for a while just looking at this strange creature. The skin of her arms was dark yellow and her hands, draped with bracelets of seashells and beads, clacked when she gestured. Suddenly she turned and looked at me. I startled and she laughed. Her face was decorated with scar patterns, swirls of dark lines along her cheekbones and down the side of her neck. Her ears hung with the weight of bird bone piercing, and her flattish face dark from the sun. She spoke loudly, almost a shout.

"Come boy! Good thing! Friend!"

She was speaking trade tongue, a special language used by the traveling peoples. I had grown up listening to it whenever people came to our village from far away lands. I stood and then walked behind a tree to urinate. She peered over, confused by my shyness. Finished I joined them, sitting close to Copperman. She examined me—leaned in until we were face to face. She took the back of my neck in a strong hand and pressed her nose to mine. I knew enough to keep eye contact for a few seconds until she let go. This was her way to test my bravery. If I looked away she would know not to trust me. She seemed satisfied.

"He. Puppy?" she asked, smiling. "Small to travel."

Copperman shook his head.

"No puppy. He is a man," he said and I liked that.

She frowned. "OK trade food…shell?

"Trade what?" He asked.

She raised her skirt and shrugged. He shook his head. I had no idea at the time what she meant and it is probably just as well. She took my arm and examined it for ink-scars.

"Good, good, good," she murmured, counting them with great interest. She pulled back her ragged sleeve and exposed the same markings on her wrist. Exactly the same.

"Family," she said

Hers were fine markings, parallel lines and patterns unique to Copperman's work. So he had met her before and worked on her with the patterns. I did not like the feel of it.

"Do we want to trade with her?" I asked

"Do not speak now," he said. "Just listen."

They bartered back and forth; she searched through hidden pockets and leather pouches in a huge pack next to her. There were dried roots of every kind and mushrooms set on strings of leather. Sculls and bones of tiny animals bleached white, small birch containers of black horrid smelling paste. Copperman met each new offer with interest and offered her beads, sewing pins and jewelry in return from his trade bag. His choices were strange to me. Why trade copper and clay beads for plants we could easily find ourselves. I stood and began to arrange camp to leave. It was rude behavior towards a trading guest and

Copperman gave me a sideways look to let me know. I did not care, I wanted away from this creature of rags and filth. Finally she stood and stretched her arms and legs. Then she struggled to stand under the weight of the large rucksack and she pointed to me one last time.

"Puppy? Trade?"

"No! No trade," I said.

Copperman held out a hand. "Wait!...Puppy?"

She set her pack down reached into it and brought out a lifeless scrawny puppy. She held it out by the loose skin of its neck. We both gasped. It was the first time I had ever seen Copperman thrown off guard. A dog was a prized possession. It would keep you safe, help you protect crops, keep you warm in the winter, and catch injured prey during a hunt.

"How do you have a puppy?" Copperman asked.

"Stole it," she said. "Trade?"

Suddenly the puppy whined and I realized it was alive. I traded her my calfskin hat for the puppy and she put it onto her head. Without looking back she walked into the woods and disappeared. Copperman knelt down to eximane the little bundle of skin covered bones. He shook his head.

"If you can keep it alive, you will be the richest boy in the village."

I looked down at the puppy—all ribs and patchy fur. It sniffed out weakly at the grass and whined, eyes closed to the world.

"Find a piece of meat and begin chewing," he said.

For the rest of the morning I chewed little pieces of meat and fed the puppy, stroking its neck to help it swallow. I dribbled handfuls of water down its throat. By nightfall it was still limp and lifeless. I massaged its belly to start the body eating again but there was no response. Finally I crawled around it and felt no warmth. Just a slight shallow rise and fall as it struggled for breath.

"Please live," I told it. "You will be the top dog in the village. Live."

The next morning I awoke at dawn to a wet tongue licking at my face. The puppy stood on shaky legs staring into my eyes with hunger.

"Feed it again," Copperman said over his shoulder "and then find a place for it in your pack… we have some land to cover."

Moon

I walked with a bigger stride with puppy's weight on my shoulders. He rode slung over my neck like a new lamb and I held his big paws threaded in the fingers of my right hand to keep him from sliding off. He had gained strength as animals do without the thought of earlier trauma. Today was good. A full belly... that was enough. At the first spring I gave him water and more chewed food (my jaws were getting tired from all the chewing) then I massaged his belly again and he yelped as he passed the first scat. A dried, painful looking little poop. I washed him a bit in the spring and then off we went. Copperman was a bit sullen and I could see that the new arrival had slowed us down. Also, the meat would disappear faster now with a new mouth to feed. Still he smiled when puppy gave his first bark at some magpies. It was a pathetic yawl and I told him he would have to do better than that if he was to fend off a pack of wolves.

We walked and I smiled a stupid smile the entire day. There was no hardship or weary trail or hunger or thirst, just a dog...my dog, watching the trail ahead and licking my ear from time to time. We stopped at a ledge of trees overlooking a wide flat pasture valley. The sun bore down now and puppy's fur was wet with my sweat against my neck. It itched. Copperman set his pack down and I did the same. There was a camp already made, well-used stone fire pit and sleeping level worn smooth of grass. A deep creek gurgled nearby.

"It is a common camp. We will have to leave something."

He sounded weary. I knew what he was thinking. We were paying out more than we were bringing in and soon we would be out of trade at this pace. The camp belonged to another clan and if we used it without leaving a suitable fee we risked being stripped of much more if they caught us. I looked at puppy and realized that for the first time in my life I had something to lose. Out of the safety of the Lake-people I felt vulnerable. I understood the importance of following the rules.

"Go get trout," he said. "Do not worry. I know this place. They are sheep people. They will only want a few trinkets."

He strung three bone needles with red clay beads to separate them and set them up in a knothole of a large tree. Under it he placed small stones in a pyramid.

"Go!" he snapped. "We need trout."

I wrapped puppy in my coat and gave him another piece of meat before heading out to the creek. He whined at me as I left, soft nose sniffing in my direction. The creek was perfect for hand fishing and I crept along spooking a few before I got the feel of the hunt.

"Slowly. Slowly. S l o w l y..." I whispered crouching down along the bank. Trout lurk in the undercut of streams, hidden away from predators. They only look forward. The trick is to reach down in from behind until you can cup your hand under its belly. They do not know you are there until you swoop up and grip them. It takes a dozzen tries until you get your first trout and after that its one out of two. I fished this way until I had six trout the length of my foot and one whitefish twice as big. I carried them through the gills on a forked branch hurrying back to camp. There was a fire crackling by the time I got there. Puppy was fast asleep. After days of venison, the trout tasted like home and I felt a pang of longing for my mother, but not nearly as severe as that first day, just a hollow feeling in my chest. We roasted the fish splayed on green twigs over the fire and baked a few small arrowroot in the coals. Puppy ate mashed whitefish suspiciously and I realized it was the first fish he had ever tried.

"Become friends with it," I told him. "You are a lake dog even if you do not know it yet."

That evening I could hear the villagers from down in the valley whistling the sheep and goats into their pens. Dogs barked, probably helping corral the sheep. Puppy pricked up his ears. I rubbed his fur. Copperman nodded.

"Tomorrow you take it down to the spring scrub it with mud and rinse it well. Keeps the fleas down. A dog deserves a name."

I pondered this. Yes. His name. What a feeling of power. Naming something alive. "Buck," I announced.

Copperman laughed. "That was quick. Strange name for a girl."

I could not believe my ears. I grabbed the pup and rolled it over. How had I never checked? How could I not know this about my own dog? It was a female.

"Puppy! How could you?" My image of a broad-chested hound was shattered by the news. A female.

Copperman nodded. "See how lucky you are. A male dog is one dog. A female dog is a whole pack."

Suddenly I understood. Eventually she would breed. I looked at her with new admiration. Her fur was already growing in, silver downy gray along the patches that had been bald. She already looked heavier after two days of

32

food. Her eyes were dark and intelligent; she watched our every move and seemed completely at ease as if she had been traveling like this with us from the beginning. I could not remember how it had been without her. As I looked she yawned and then scratched the ground in a circle dance before finding a comfortable angle. Then she curled down in a tight circle until her nose rested on her tail.

"Her name is Moon," I said.

Copperman nodded. "That is a fine name. She is silver and round. She will guide us if we get lost."

He sat looking out into the night and I lay down to sleep but after a while I realized sleep would not come. There were too many things happening and my mind kept running the possibilities over and over. I rejoined Copperman next to the dying fire and added a few branches to the coals.

"Who was the old woman? She had our markings."

He sighed. "She does not have our markings... we have hers."

I waited.

"Her name is Asha and she comes from so far away it would take two or three seasons to get there. She came across the sea on a boat bigger than ten lake boats put together. I met her when I was your age and she was a full-grown woman. We were slaves carrying bluestone from the mines to the shore. She was once beautiful and proud. She was favored among the workers because of her skills with ink-scars."

I had no idea what he meant by slave or sea or shore or mine, but it was the most exciting story I had ever heard and I wondered why he never spoke of it before.

He talked for hours, telling me more that night than he had over the whole of my life. Maybe he had wanted to wait till I was old enough to understand, maybe he wanted to get me excited about our own hunt for bluestone, or maybe meeting Asha after all these years had opened up a long forgotten path. Whatever the reason he told me everything that night about how he came like me to join the Lake-people.

Copperman's story

He had been born among sea tribes in a dry land a season's travel from our mountains. The sea was a salty lake, so big you could never find the end of it. Lands unlike ours were hidden far out into it. He said there were fish so huge a village could eat from one of them. Fish massive and fierce enough they would sometimes eat fishermen who fell from boats. You could not drink the salty water from the sea and there was little rain and there were few rivers. He did not remember much from childhood until a terrible dry season came and the rains refused to come. Copperman said he used to have another name as a boy but would not tell me what it was. His people (he called them the Kaowri) fished and raised goats. They lived from water in deep caves dug strait down into the earth. They would drop a leather bag tied to a rope and haul the water up each day, saving it in clay jars to sip from. He said wasting water was an offense to the Gods and woe to the child who spilled it. (This was hard for me to imagine having grown up with friendly water in each of the four directions: Water carved our mountains and fed our crops; our water jar was the great lake, steps from where we slept.)

His story made me aware of a dryness in my throat and I thirsted for the gurgling stream near by. In the year of the big drought the cave water dried up. Crops faded, goats began to die. They dropped bags down and retrieved only mud. Those Kaowri with the strength to do so, left their straw homes and traveled along the seaside. They marched through the soft sand for weeks, traveling at night, huddling under sparse trees to avoid the blistering sun, sipping water from jars and praying as they went.

One night his mother was stung by a long-tailed spider. She was too weak to wake the next morning. His father carried her for hours before he realized she was gone. Finally they came upon a bay with a river of clean water pouring into it. This was the first river he had ever seen. His father was the first to reach the water. He knelt down to drink from the bay river. The Kaowri did not know they were trespassing until the arrows came down. His father was hit in the neck and the others fell to their bellies begging for mercy. The Bay-people were tall, broad-shouldered warriors. They had spears with copper tips and shields made from giant water-turtles. They spoke a language the Kaowri did not recognize. They killed every adult and kept the children; tied them by the wrists and herded them like goats out to the mines. They were made to work, climbing down into crevasses in the rock and hammering out chunks of bluestone with rocks and pointed spikes of ironwood. Then they would carry woven reed baskets of the bluestone down to the seashore where it was melted into copper. (I asked Copperman how it was melted…but he ignored me. He was too far back in time and I was not foolish enough to interrupt him again.)

Giant boats came to trade the Bay-people for the copper. He said the ships were 100 paces long and 50 paces wide. They had trees in the center of them with cloth sheets tied between. The sheets would catch the wind and push the boats forward. (I wanted to believe him but it was more than my mind could take.) By spring he was one of only ten children from the Kaowri who had survived. By the summers end he was the only one left. He forgot his old language and what his parents even looked like.

Life was only work and sleep and the dreams of food that never seemed enough to sustain him. They were forbidden to speak to their masters but Copperman learned much of their language by listening to them speak around the dinner fires.

Other slaves always came, a slow steady stream of miserable villagers caught up in the tide of drought and desperation. Some of them dark skinned; some as pale as fish, blue eyed and light haired. Their parents dead or escaped.

One day a boat came and traded foreign slaves for copper. One of them was Asha. She had long jet-black hair and rich yellow skin. Her high cheekbones and black eyes

37

made her fearsome to the slave-herds who left her alone. They said she was evil. She was a wild creature, almost an adult, with a high angry language and she scratched out at anyone who came near her. The camp-master, a chunky, bear of a man, kept her tied to a wooden stake for days in the hot sun but was unable to calm her into submission. For some reason he was afraid to kill her. Copperman thought it was a fear of being cursed for she was surely a witch. They tried to trade her back on the next ship but none would have her aboard.

Asha escaped one night and when they found her she was sitting by a fire with a sliver of flint making an ink-scar on her ankle. This was the first ink-scar any of the slave-herds had seen and as such sealed her title as witch. The camp-master had finally found a use for her. He was a shrewd trader whose greed seemed to increase with each new deal in copper and slaves. He announced to his men that Asha's ink scars were good luck and she would have certainly been killed without them. He ordered one of his warriors to receive the markings on his wrist to prove it. It took some work to explain to the witch what was required of her but Copperman suspected that she understood more of the trade language than she had let on. They led her back to camp and tied her ankle to a post. Everyone gathered as she made the ink scars on the warrior's wrist.

Late that night Copperman noticed the camp master speaking to the warrior in private. The next morning the warrior claimed to find a large lump of pure copper on his morning walk. The word traveled quickly among the Bay-people that the ink scars were luck-magic and soon began asking the camp master for their own markings. Over the next months Asha worked, forever tethered to her post, making ink-scars on the wrists and ankles of his men. They became marks of great status for the Bay-people and the camp master became wealthy that season charging raw copper, dried fish and beads for the scars.

The miners gave Copperman the job of assisting her. He built her a lean-to from branches to keep out the midday sun. He searched the beeches for glass-flint and flaked it into her needles for the scars. He ground powdered bluestone and ashes, mixing them with water in a seashell for her ink. Asha used a body-length stick of greenwood hammered and split at the tip. She would insert a flint needle sideways into the split and pour thick ink onto the roughened wooden fibers above it. The ink would slowly drip down onto the needle. Holding the back end of the stick into the sand with her foot she would arrange it over an arm leg or just above the skin. She tapped the needle stick with a small stone and it would vibrate down into the skin. Her fingers were amazingly nimble, edging the pulsing needle this way and that, achieving perfect thin lines and as she would wipe away the pooled up blood and ink the others were mesmerized by the clean blue-black patterns emerging.

Copperman washed the faces of the men with cool water as Asha tapped the markings into their skin. He was aware of the importance of her ceremony. She would sing and chant incantations as she worked, peering into the sky, calling to the Gods for guidance. The others watched in fascination. Those receiving the scars would look with a mixture of fear and awe as she worked. This was magic that gave the men their story to take to the others. These marks kept her and in turn Copperman from the bone breaking work in the mine. He played the game as well, weeping as she chanted, babbling with mock fear. The others began to bring food and small offerings for Asha as well.

With his new position Copperman began to hope for life beyond the mines. The camp-master took most of their gifts but Asha would hide anything useful in her dress of rags, adding pockets and inner linings whenever a new patch of cloth came her way. The things she kept began to make sense. Flint knife, fire starting flint, dried fish, string… She was planning an escape.

Copperman learned to speak to her in traders' tongue and she began to advise him what to steal and where to hide it. One night he managed to take two water bags of waxed calves leather; another night, a bolt of warm cloth, and three arrows. He waited weeks before he had the opportunity to steal a bow and quiver. He hid them all in a high cleft of rock near camp and could hardly breathe from the terror of what punishment awaited him if he were caught. These thefts caused fights among the slave-herds who suspected each other. Nobody ever thought a slave would dare steal from them.

One of Asha requests took Copperman dangerously close to being caught. On the trail from the camp to the mine there was a fresh spring oasis and its greenery stood out from the distance. In the four seasons he had been there he was never allowed to visit it. The slave herds prayed there and poured its water onto their feet but for the slaves it was forbidden territory. Asha wanted Copperman to go there at night and find a plant with bright blue colored berries. She needed at least twenty of the berries. He waited until a bright moon night and snuck out from camp. It was stomach-curdling business to crawl along the rocks and the night seemed far too bright to escape detection. Within an hour he was along the trail and approaching the spring. Ringed by short trees and tall reeds it smelled dank and oxygen rich. As he crept along its bank strange bugs crawled along his skin and he thought of the long tailed spider that killed his mother. He shivered in the foliage, searching for the plant. The spring bubbled up from the ground and he drank deeply from it. In the moonlight he could see bone-white branches scattered along its bed. Night birds and small creatures rustled in the undergrowth and he spooked at each new sound. He searched desperately for the plant and tried to remember Asha's description: "Broad green leaves, short thick flower buds, fat round blue berries."

He found them at first light, carefully detaching a few dozen berries and wrapping them in leaves. He tucked them in his pocket. The walk back to camp was one long terror, hiding behind rocks, crawling along awkward ridges; ever fearful of the growing morning. He came near camp as three slave-herds approached. Turning, he dropped his waist-cloth and squatted near a rock. They shouted and approached as he pretended to struggle with his bowls.

"Boy! What are you doing away from camp?"

One of them came up to strike him with his staff, recognized Copperman and then thought better of it. This hesitation to strike had never happened before. Perhaps they all wanted to keep good relations with Asha and her helper in case they needed a scar in the future. He struggled with an explanation.

"My stomach is foul. I was sent by Asha. She said others will get sick if they are around me like this."

They backed away. Foul stomach was sometimes deadly and the mention of the witch's name along with the threat of sickness was enough to repel them.

"Do not shit on our trail. Go wash in the sea. Stay away from the water supply until you are clean of it."

He groaned and gasped and they retreated. As the camp awoke he joined Asha under her tiny shelter and handed her the pack of leaves and berries. She smiled.

"Yes," she said. Yes yes yes."

There was a design that he could not see, as is often the case in life. Asha told him to do things and he did them. He felt no closer to escape. The dry season grew to a close with the distant clouds promising rain. Asha had not mentioned the berries again although she sometimes brought them out at night and prayed over them. He began to wonder if she was touched and his errands were in vain. If he would eventually die there of work or sickness or hunger or at the hand of an angered slave-herd.

Asha seemed focused on the bags of red seeds brought in weeks earlier on a ship. The others were skeptical of the trade, but, the seeds, fat and pungent as a bag of beetles, were obviously precious to the traders so the camp master wanted them. He gave them to Asha to prepare. She slightly burned them on a clay plate in the fire until they were dark brown, then ground them in a mortar into powder. She boiled them into a tea. The camp master made her drink a cup and waited for a day until trying it himself. Asha told him it made men stronger. He gave cups of the tea to his men. Bitter and black the drink made the warriors nervous and aggressive. But they wanted more the next day. After weeks of the ritual they seemed to grow used to its taste and would gather insisting that Asha prepare it.

The life of a slave-herd was nearly as boring as the life of a slave. They clung to rituals to pass the time and the stimulation of the seeds Asha called *qui* had become the high point of their day. The camp master charged small trinkets and choice bits of food for the *qui* and grew fatter each day on the earnings. His stomach bulged out shiny with sweat and his cheeks puffed up from the surplus of meat, fruit and goat's milk. He encouraged the nightly ritual and bought cups of clay to keep for the ritual. He often joined in, sitting in a circle of his men telling stories and planning the next trades with coming ships. One day after a successful trade of copper for cloth and a small ox, he brought a slab of honeycomb to Asha and ordered her to make a big pot of *qui* and sweeten it with the honey. Tonight there would be a feast.

The Bay-people were happy with the camp master and had sent lemons and figs, goats and drums. This was to be festival to bring in the rains and Copperman could feel the excitement in the air. The others spoke of the last work for the season and he overheard one of them laughingly say, "Good for us, bad for the little slaves."

He wondered why there were no slaves from the year before. What would happen to them? What happened to slaves when they are no longer needed. Whatever Asha was up to he hoped it would happen soon. That day there was no work. Warriors had contests to gauge their strength. Lifting rocks, throwing spears and shooting arrows at small targets.

Copperman thought of his father kneeling to drink, wondered which of them had shot the arrow. He hated them in their laughing and feasting, hated himself for smiling and cheering with the other slaves, saving his own skin by being their errand boy. Hated the sound of their language in his throat. He could smell *qui* boiling in Asha's huge clay pot.

The winner of the contest was a huge man with dark curling hair. Copperman knew him to be the most vicious of the slave herds. He stood forward proudly and the camp master handed him an ironwood club with intricate carvings on its handle and copper bands wrapped around the head for weight. The club was lacquered dark at the hammer end from the blood of its victims and again Copperman wondered what happened to the slaves after the rains come. The winning warrior stood before the ox, a kind of huge fat deer, slow witted and tame. He postured and nodded to the camp master. The others began to drum slowly and the warrior stretched and bowed to the camp.

Asha motioned to Copperman and he pulled himself away from the spectacle to join her. She motioned him to kneel between her and the crowd. Smiling a demonic smile she unwrapped the dried leaves from the berry plant and waited. The warrior flexed his muscles and slowly, dramatically raised the heavy club. The drumming increased in tempo to a rapid heartbeat as the ox, tied head low, began to bellow. As the drumming reached a rapid blur the warrior strained and brought the weight of the club down in a perfect ark onto the ox's head, crushing its skull with terrible force. It collapsed with a cheer from the crowd. He turned to see Asha innocently stirring the powdered berries as they disappeared into the black boiling liquid. She added the honeycomb and it melted slick and sweet. Asha smiled.

They dragged the ox to the seaside and as they cleaned it out great fish came in, their fins high in the shallow water, drawn in by the smell of blood. They roasted the ox whole over the high fire peeling back the burnt skin to reveal a camp's worth of meat sizzling underneath. The roast oxen was sectioned and shared around. Chunks of it even came to the young slaves who were let rest the entire day. The slave herds were soft to them, even kind and the guilt in their eyes froze Copperman's heart. Skinny and desperate, the mix of slaves from different lands and different languages were united in the celebration.

Cooling winds came from the clouded north and they lounged and ate, happy in the moment. Copperman ate but it was all he could do to choke the food down. It all tasted of death, the festival, the drums, the kindness of monsters, all death. He ate pieces of the ox and swore that if he lived he would never eat it again. He knew the fear of the tamed beast and what it meant for his people.

The night came down dark and moonless; winds whipped the fire into shards of flame and the warriors sent the slaves into their shelter against the Cliffside. The camp master gathered his men in a circle around Asha's tiny camp, a ring of worn earth in a circle around her. They gathered for q*ui* tea and she poured it out as the camp master announced the end of the mining season. He said it had been rich and the Bay-people were waiting with open arms. Wives and children, fresh crops, and no enemies as far as the eye could see. They cheered and drank. He said the next year most of them would have work, Gods' willing, and plenty of copper to trade to the boats. The slaves were worthy and would make a great sacrifice to the Gods to ensure crops and wealth. Each slave herd would be given many the next day to take to the spring. Copperman remembered the white branches in the bed of the spring and gasped at the thought. They were bones. He had drank from the bone spring of the slaves. The guard noticed his expression and smiled at him.

"Death?" he laughed. "No, we have bigger plans for you and the witch. You will be spared. Traded for a high price, I think."

The camp master scowled. "Why do you talk to them?" he said. "They do not understand anything…do you?"

Copperman smiled dumbly, nodded and poured him another cup of *qui*.

The effect of the berry powder was as powerful as anything Copperman could have hoped. The warriors were listening to a story from the camp master when he began to slur his words. He sat down to rest and the others laughed, confused until one of the others simply fell. He shouted that he could not feel his legs. Another stumbled to his feet and tried to throw a spear into the night but staggered to his knees. Then fell twitching. Others began looking at each other for answers but found only panic and fear. One warrior looked at Asha's *qui* cup in his hand and then ran towards the sea. He made it almost to the shore before falling face forward. His legs kicking out franticly. Some merely slumped dead where they sat. The big warrior who killed the ox stood and shouted at Asha, "witch!" He grabbed his club and raised to strike but his right arm seemed to fail him; he dropped the club and tried to retrieve it. Asha, cut free from her tether, was at his side. She slid the flint blade under his throat with such hatred in her eyes that Copperman turned away.

And then they were alone. The wind had died down and the fire showed bodies ghostly scattered along the beach. Asha stood and took Copperman by the hand. She led him to the hiding place and he gathered the bow, arrows and water bags. They walked the path north in numb silence. There was a cry of alarm in the darkness behind them. The slaves must have found the bodies. He prayed they would find their escape as well. They walked the northern path for days and days.

They walked until the hills became mountains, until the desert gave way to shrubs. Until the rivers became creeks. They hid during the day and walked through the night, avoiding habitation, until the trees, green and heavy with sap had finally cleared away the smell of death. They walked the rainy season up into the snowy mountains and eventually to our great lake. There, Copperman stopped and joined the Lake-people. Asha, still heart sick from being trapped, could not accept the Lake people's offer of a home.

Copperman said she has never stopped walking and will live out her days moving, waking each morning with the ache of the leg tether and the thrill of breaking free of it.

By the time he finished his story we were looking out at the growing dawn. He seemed exhausted by the telling of it. Now I understood why we traded the witch in the woods so much for so little. Copperman walked to the sleeping ledge and seemed to collapse onto it.

Chasing the fox

Moon was worth ten men when it came to finding a path or warning us of danger. She had her own body postures to communicate with us. A rabbit would freeze her nose in its direction; a deer made her creep on her belly, ears back. Sometimes she would cower, lips curled, and then later we would hear wolves howling. She fattened up over the days filling out before our eyes. She could keep up with us on longer walks and I began to carry her less and less.

Copperman was silent again and I could see his wild hunger returning for the bluestone. We hunted high and low, followed the tree line over ridges still tipped with snow. We dipped down into swamplands slogging through knee-deep sludge and climbed down into caves with torches and searched the dry beds of sleeping rivers. Once we found a thin streak of bluestone and spent two days digging it out only to find the color fade and disappear leaving us with pale pebbles too weak to be worth melting. The summer lengthened the days and still no sign of it. Copperman grumbled and became quick to anger.

One day sweating and bored beyond knowing, I lagged behind as he crashed through thick undergrowth in a shallow valley of maple wood. Moon zig-zagged, fascinated with each new smell. She was in a mischievous mood and I had to reprimand her constantly. She dug at badger holes, circled trees after uncatchable squirrels, taunted crows from tree to tree. Suddenly a young fox darted out from under a hollow log and she bolted after it. I called and called but her barks faded as she chased it. I whistled a warning to Copperman, left my pack on a high branch and followed. This running away frightened me. It had happened twice before and Copperman's patience, short to begin with, seemed near an end. If Moon did not settle into the journey he would trade her at the next village. I pondered methods to teach her that became more severe as the trail steepened.

By the time I found her I was soaking with sweat, scratched bloody and furious. She barked down cheerfully and wagged at me. She was hopelessly stuck on a high ledge. I called her but she did not have the legs to dare the walk down. I scrambled and struggled, growing angrier each failed decent. By the time I managed to lift up to the ledge I gave her such a shout that she cringed against the wall. Behind her was a wide cave. Light shining in revieled shapes and images against the walls. Red Deer, pale fish, death birds... all painted in various colors of clay, a strange style far finer than anything I had ever seen. I could make out details of fur and horns, shades to show leg muscles and ribs, eyes that seemed to stare out at me. Moons fox huddled in the back of the cave breathing heavily. She had cornered it but did not know what to do from there. She had a bloody mark on an ear where the fox had nipped her. It hissed and looked back and forth for an exit. Behind the fox was a thick layer of bluish green from wall to wall. Like the paintings, it stood out in stark relief from the gray rock. Copperman whistled in the distance and I tried to whistle back but my lips would produce only a dry whisper. I cleared my throat and yelled.

"Bluestone! Bluestone! Bluestone!"

Cracking Rocks

He said it was a place of prayer for a people that lived long before us. We had to be careful not to draw attention to our work. This was unfamiliar territory and the risk of trespass was very real. We would leave gifts.

His eyes shone at the sight of the bluestone, marveled at its purity and depth. More beautiful to him than the art on the cave wall. This was a blessed trip and I must be good luck to find this much on a first hunt. Moon received a chunk of deer and water from his hand. The fox its freedom. We made camp on the outer ledge and prepared to mine copper. I could barely contain the thrill. His dark mood for so many days lifted to jokes and we ate the remaining food that evening next to a fire with the cave at our backs and the lush maple valley shimmering leaves beneath us.

The next morning before first light he woke me with a nudge of a foot, pointed to the bow, strung and ready, "little fauns, rabbit, fish, berries, nuts... anything easy to clean and cook. We do not want to strip and dress a big red buck now...too much to do."

I grabbed the bow and Moon whined as Copperman held her by the scruff of the neck. He did not want any foxhunts getting in the way of our work. I crept down to the wet soft forest floor. The chilly morning smelled lush and promising with a warm breeze weaving in and around the giant maples. There were rabbits in abundance darting in and out of bushes and after missing a few I managed to gain my aim again and take three of them. I broke an arrow pinning a squirrel to a tree and nearly hit a galloping faun. There were acorns, small plums and raspberries by the fistful; I filled the large pockets in my shirt with them. Against the shade side of a giant dead log there were dozens of yellow wrinkle mushrooms (Copperman's favorite, and the only mushrooms I could trust without his guidance.) A shallow gravel creek held sweet-water crawfish. I flipped over rocks to grab ten or so to roast over the coals. By mid morning I returned to find a crackling fire and Moon scratching and grinning wagging her whole body.

We ate a rabbit each and dried the other by hanging it high over the fire on a forked green branch. The mushrooms tasted meaty and rich, the crawfish salty and the berries were so juicy they stained our fingers red. We sat digesting in the growing sun and Copperman sighed with comfort.

"We have time," he said. "If we do this right we have time to get all of it."

I gathered dry branches and he discarded half of them for reasons I could not understand. The ones he wanted were dry and dead but still hard wood, varying in thickness from mere twigs to wrist thick spikes. He sat shaping them with the copper axe and fine tuning the thickness with a hand held adze of black flint. He arranger the spikes by size in a row beneath the seam of bluestone. Copperman was peculiar this way, always arranging tools and equipment in perfect order, always sharpening and cleaning. He could not abide by a tattered cloth or torn arrow fletching and a messy camp would send him into a fury. I did my best to emulate him sensing this attention to detail as part of his magic. By mid day we had fifty or so spikes, several hammer-stones and all five water pouches full and waiting.

He stood and pondered the puzzle of stone before selecting a spike and sliding it into a crack that ran down the top of the bluestone. He began to tap it and when it stuck he unwedged it and chose another slightly thinner. He hammered it until the end stuck out by a few inches. I waited expecting the stone to come crashing down, or the crack to widen or something. He selected another and nodded to me. I chose a small spike and found a crack space to fit it. We began setting spikes into the stone hammering them twenty or thirty times until they reached their limit and began shredding. As the sun reached into the cave we were sweating and sweltering. Moon hid behind a rock from the noise of the hammering and from time to time we would pause as I scampered up to a space above the cave to lookout for others.

The woods were empty. By nightfall the spikes dotted a line along the top of the bluestone looking like more art decorating the cave. My hands were swollen and blistered, arms ached from the hammering. I had bounced a stone against my right pinky and it throbbed with a blackening nail. Copperman caught me nursing it and laughed.

"You are lucky if that is the only nail you loose before the job is done."

I hate to admit it but my doubts were beginning to rise about his methods. A full day of work and not a single pebble of bluestone to show for it. We used the water bag to soak the wooden spikes before collapsing into sleep. Sometime during the night I thought I heard creaking from the cave behind us. At first light there came a shout. I jumped up and ran to the back of the cave. Copperman held up a wedge of bluestone the size of a man's head. In the night it had fallen to the cave floor. He carried it out to the sunlight. The colors were radiant glimmering and impossible in the fresh morning. Behind us a thump sounded as new bluestone separated and fell.

More wooden spikes and trips to the spring for water. New hammer stones, more food and firewood. The days flew by with more work than I could handle. I seemed to always be rushing and just behind what was expected. Copperman worked twice as hard as I, refusing to rest until the light failed each day. Even his trips to the shit pile were resented as unavoidable delay. He spoke to the stone as he hammered, unaffected by the chips of rock that flew out to nick his face or sliver into his hands. After several days I began the miserable task of separating the bluestone which consisted mainly of chipping out the most colorful bluestone from the large stones until I had a growing pile of rocks at the mouth of the cave, one pale blue and the other dark green and rich. The first layer, perhaps a hand's length deep, had come away from the strip of bluestone against the cave wall. Behind it the stone was even darker. Copperman thrilled with each new crack he could use a spike on but soon the cracks disappeared and we were up against smooth rock.

"Now is where the real work begins," he said and I was struck by my own laziness.

"We have so much," I said, looking out to the pile of dark stone I had chipped into fist size chunks. He shook his head.

"That is enough for an axe head, maybe five of six blades. That is ten sheep and a bag of seed. We need more and better if we are going to feed the family and have something to trade on the way back. We need this." He held his hand out to indicate bluestone in a pile thigh high.

"Come."

Moon and I followed, bow and arrow ready. Down along the creek we searched until Copperman found a cone of gray granite, hard and smoothed by the river, so big it was all we could do to carry it back. We made a triangle-frame in the cave with head high branches forked at the top and a sturdy arm-length branch lashed across them with wide, strong strips of bark fiber. It took all of our rope to make a swinging hammock for the granite spike. It was a strange contraption that held the granite suspended next to the bluestone seam. Copperman covered his face with a strip of thin cloth and began to lift and hammer with the granite spike. This was a fine tool; it was easier to swing a giant stone on a hammock than to hold it up with your hands. I could understand why he had the cloth over his face. Splinters of stone flew from the wall as he hammered into the rock.

Soon a chunk fell and he expertly worked the broken edge, sending more to the ground. I darted in and out grabbing sizeable pieces from around his feet trying to avoid the flying chips. I collected handfuls as he worked. Moon, more miserable than ever by this new development, hid out in her rock crevasse as far away from the noise as possible. Day followed day and our pile grew, until one morning hands torn and bloody, Copperman told me to start gathering strips of bark from the bigger trees. He handed me his copper axe (something he had never trusted me with alone before) and I understood we were done. The bark was for baskets to carry the stone. I spent the day making them as he rested. His hands were in no shape to weave baskets anyway. There was no art to my work. I made two ugly and poorly built baskets without handles. They only needed to transport the stone a short way.

We cleaned out the cave sweeping it with branches to remove the broken stone chips; and, we dismantled the stone hammer throwing the branches off the cliff and saving the rope. Copperman made a paste by grinding a chip of bluestone against a flat stone mixed with spit. He made a brush with a green twig, hammered soft at one end, and carefully painted a small fine image of a man, a boy and a dog on the back wall of the cave. Under it he left the coiled rope, a perfictly round copper disk and a pile of polished deer-tooth beads.

Clay oven

It took two days to transport the stone down to a fresh camp in the valley. Copperman chose a sandy bank next to a wide slow bend in the creek. We piled the choice bluestone until it stood in a stack up to my waist. The work in the cave followed by ten trips with painfully heavy bark baskets of stone had me numb with fatigue. Copperman said he had carried baskets loaded twice as high when he was a child slave. I truly do not know how he survived but one thing was certain, I would not insult him by complaining.

There are different types of camps, an overnight with simple fire on a flat stone, a wet camp with light branch shelter to keep off rain. This was a stay-camp; wood frame lean-too with deep branches to handle a storm, swept clean to dirt floor, deep fire pit with a green branch drying rack and a giant stack of wood. We would be here a while. It took a day to set it up and another day to snare and prepare several rabbits and a very small roe deer. I dried trout and gathered nuts and berries until we had a week's worth of food on the racks. A young bear came in the second night and Moon woke us in time to blaze the fire with some dry branches. Copperman said we were lucky it was young and small enough to frighten off. I could smell it and see its eyes in the firelight, standing on its hind legs grunting... it did not look small to me. I struggled to sleep imagining what a big one would look like. The next day we hung the dried food away from camp high up in a tree. We would have to be careful.

I was growing weary of mining and wood living. The adventure had lost its joy and I suffered a wave of homesickness that far outweighed the hollow longing I experienced that first day. Moon could sense the change in me and whined as I trudged through the morning chores of setting the fire. Copperman found me staring into the water after breakfast and sat next to me.

"Are you sickly?"

"I do not know," I said. "My whole body seems heavy, I feel dark and ill at ease."

I felt the hot flush of tears and turned my face from him. He was silent until I regained myself. He smiled.

"I know what will heal you. Follow me and I will show you how to make copper. This is the best part of the journey."

I trudged behind him to the muddy bank at the slow bend of the creek. We gathered slick yellow clay and sat in the warm sun rolling it out and kneading it into long snakes of clay the length of a man's open arms. We rolled them into a circle pinching the ends together and sealing them with water. The next one slightly shorter lay atop the first and that was sealed to the one underneath with water. Inside the dome we made a structure of bent green twigs to hold its shape. Soon we had a growing circle of clay like a giant beehive. Eventually we had a complete clay oven open at the top. Copperman carefully cut a hole in the wet clay on either side of the bottom and inserted a fat dry branch of wood through both holes.

"This will be a doorway for the air to get through," he said, "and the copper comes out the other side."

I understood nothing.

We built a ring of fire around the pot and as the clay began to dry we shoveled coals around its base. We built up the fire all afternoon until glowing coals covered the entire structure. That night I slept, still heavy in my heart but also curious about what we were building. The next day the clay was still hot but it was hard and the wooden branch had burned away from the spaces at the bottom. We cleared away the coals and lifted the blackened structure whole from the pit. Copperman seemed very happy with the results. We carried it to the sandy bank and set it down on a flat base of rolled-out wet clay. We took more wet clay and smoothed it over the ridges until it was as smooth as a bald head.

We searched for the stickiest pinecones and pine knots dripping with sap, gathering them by the armload. Then we brought only hardwood branches. I could not imagine how a small fire pot could eat this much wood but we kept gathering all day until Copperman was satisfied. He wrapped clay around a dry branch. He packed wet clay into many small slabs and pressed copper blades into the slabs leaving their impression in each. He did the same with his axe head, detaching it from its handle, making several slabs with its impression in each half. He heated these strange things in the fire eventually burying them in coals. The next morning the wood had burned away from the branches he had wrapped with clay, leaving a shiny black tube. The slabs were also shiny and he spent the morning carving away at them until I could see the perfect halves of potential blades on either side. He carved out a hollow at one end and a small space for the copper to drain into. I watched every step memorizing them by repeating each step over and over until it held strong in my head. The heavy feeling faded as we worked. This magic was a soothing element to the mind. The process of it. The promise of it.

Moon grew strong on deer fat and rest, sometimes running off to chase rabbits but quickly returning to camp. The week in the cave had cured her of the need to wander.

One morning the space below the hanging food was disrupted and the bark around the tree torn by heavy claws. They reached higher than I could reach and Copperman whistled. This was not the little bear from before. We kept our best arrows notched and bows always near.

The morning of the copper melt, he seemed tense, pacing back and forth, muttering and focused. We had the wood stacked, the molds strung together with twine and sealed with clay, the water bags ready and full…it was time. Copperman knelt and prayed next to the fire pit, lifted a glowing coal with a twig and carried it over to the well-packed clay oven. It started up the sap covered pinecones with a whoosh and began smoking from the air holes. Copperman set up the skin from the deer. We had scraped it clean and thinner than usual. He had sewn it into a giant bag, fur side in, and fitted a hollow reed to its tip. The back end was open and he lifted it to fill it with air and then leaned on it to trap the air. The air whistled from the reed end and he positioned this into the air hole of the clay oven. Fire leapt to life each time he did this and the pot began to radiate heat. It was a big lung.

"More," he said and I piled in sticky pinecones and small chunks of wood into the other side singeing the hair on my arms as a flames shot out from the top. I had never seen a fire eat this much.

"More," he said, pushing air in and out of the deer hide. I began to appreciate the camp's location near the creek. Its cooling breeze made the proximity of the fire only tolerable. We fed it more and more until the red center began to glow white. "Now!" he said, sweating from the effort. I began to drop the chunks of bluestone down into the oven one by one until it was half full, then followed it with a full stack of pinecones and wood. I covered the top with a thin slab of slate singeing myself again in the process. Copperman worked the deer hide bellow franticly whooshing white-hot flame with each push. I wondered if he could possibly keep going as the fire grew hotter and he sweated and heaved. I sprayed water on his blistered hands and down his neck. He had the look of someone in trance pushing and breathing the bluestone into the flaming center. I hurt, watching him suffer. This was magic with a high price and I wondered if I could ever battle flames long enough to match him.

Suddenly he leapt up and scrambled to the back end of the oven. With trembling hands he arranged the first of the molds beneath the exit hole and then tapped it with a long pointed stone. The clay seal crumbled and we watched…nothing happened for a few seconds and then a long pure trickle of golden liquid poured down the funnel and into the mold filling it to the top. He packed a chunk of wet clay against the opening to seal it and then staggered to the creek. With a hiss he dropped it into the shallow water. We waited a few moments and he held his hands into the cooling water. Then he brought up the mold and tapped it with a stone. It cracked and reveled a beautiful copper blade. He cracked away the other side and it came away rough but real and pure. He shouted to the woods, slapped me on the shoulder, and examined the blade. Chipping away the flakes of clay, he rubbed it in the wet sand and it gleamed in the sun. He handed it to me.

"It is yours. Polish it and make a handle from the buck's horn."

I was rich with a dog and a copper knife and the last of the heaviness lifted from me.

"Come on, boy, get the wood going. Let us make another one."

Copperman suffered several burns and blisters on his arms and hands when he worked and the hair on his arms singed away as that first day came to a close. We made five blades that day and three spear-points, blunt tips to be polished sharp for big game or battle. That night I took a dry branch and wrapped it in clay as he had done to make the pipe for the exit hole of the oven. I set it into the hot coals and he shook his head.

"You still have energy for playing in the fire?"

"I have an idea," I said, and he looked at me with interest. He said nothing as I set coals around the clay and built up the fire around it. The next morning the clay pipe was hard and pinged when I flicked it with a finger. The wood had burned out from inside of it and I took it down to the creek to polish it with sand. As Copperman cleaned ashes from the clay oven I brought the pipe up to him and set it into the air hole of the clay oven and fitted the deer hide bellows to its end. He looked for a few seconds nodded and began to smile.

"This is interesting."

I watched nervously as he began to blow the fire to life and with the bellows connected to my pipe he was an arm's length from the fire, the flames and sparks safely away from his hands. He began to laugh.

"The best ideas are the ones you cannot believe you have not thought of already."

I had other ideas for modifications on our clay oven but decided to think them through before trying them out. Things were too good to risk arrogance. I tried not to smile too broadly and focused on the work. It pleased me at the end of the second day to see his hands healing from the blisters without any new ones. We slept hard, ate little and worked from first light till pale dark.

The fire burned in the clay oven for five days. Our camp, tramped down with steps, bed rolls sunk into the padding of soft boughs, fire pit deep with ashes, trails to and from the creek, worn nearly grassless in places. Moon followed my every step holding just out of reach of the heat of the clay oven, sleeping in the crook of my legs at night. We made seventeen blades, ten spear-points and axe head molded from Copperman's very own. This last attempt failed twice; once from a broken mold and once from lack of melted copper to fill the mold. We re-melted the copper each time adding more bluestone. When the third was successful we cheered and threw ourselves into the creek in victory. It was the last of the mining and my face and arms were red and chapped from the continuous heat. Copperman had suffered far worse but said the clay pipe of mine saved him some misery. We washed in the creek, scrubbing with a mixture of ashes and deer-fat. It was a shame to use the delicious deer fat for cleaning bodies that would be dirty again soon but it was another of Copperman's habits and it did feel good afterwards. I had to wash our clothes and Moon wallowed around in the water with me as I did. Her fur was thickening and she rolled in the cool muddy water at the other side of the creek after I washed her till I had to call her over the sandy side and wash her again.

I sat drying in the sun basking in the week of wealth and knowledge and the thrill of being finished with the mining. I imagined Copperman doing this every summer when my family and I played with fishing and food gathering and thought it was work. Now I knew work and realized the summers would never be as carefree again.

He had told me to break up the clay oven and scatter its pieces in the bushes. I took a stone over to it but hesitated. It was such a thing to build, blackened and glassy. I turned it over with a struggle and examined the inside. It had been dangerously thin in a few places and clumpy in others. I memorized these problem areas determined to make an even better one next summer. I sifted through the ashes with a stick finding a few fat beads of copper among the coals. I pocketed them and reluctantly broke the oven with the stone. It shattered, gaping open like a mouth full of teeth. I broke it apart and tossed the many pieces into the bushes, then, raked over the area with a long branch to cover up our traces; finally, I smoothed over the coals with fresh sand. It was not perfect but a few good rains would finish the job.

It was always Copperman's wish to hide our activities. I was to tell anyone asking that we were shepherds following our clan to better pastures. He said a group of hunters could turn thieves if they knew what we carried. And local tribes would feel justified in taking any copper made in their territory. I thought of this and went over the place again finding many things I had missed. By the time I finished there was not a trace of our work left to question.

Moon stopped and pricked up her ears. She grinned, showing teeth, and her hackles rose along the ridge of her neck. Seconds later I heard it. A moan of rage, deep chested and hollow. It grew louder and though it was a sound I had never herd before I knew instantly what it was. A bear. An angry bear in the heat of battle. The sound came from our camp.

Death visits

Terror is purely physical. Blood curdles at the sound of animal rage. Bones weaken and muscles sag as in a slow dream. I stumbled to a tree and hid. Yes! I hid in terror, feeling no warrior's desire to save my father from death. I was alone in the woods and frozen in cowardice like a child. But then not alone. Moon moved forward, eyes blazing, beginning her own growl of battle. She crouched down low and stalked the short trail towards him, towards them, towards death. In her courage I found my legs again and moved after her picking up my bow. It seemed hopelessly puny, like a thin reed in my hands, the quiver of arrows merely twigs with rabbit points. It was a boy's hunting device and I doubted it would as much as pierce a bear's rough hide. With a man's bow, thick and strung with an obsidion point I might injure a bear. With my little bow I might just annoy it.

I began to sprint towards the sound of trauma along the creek to the little trail and there I froze. The bear stood to its full height, clawing at the base of the huge maple next to where our lean-to had been. The bear had smashed the lean-to, snapping its arm thick beams like kindling. He had torn our rucksacks open and chewed their contents to get to the small amount of dried deer meat. It was...how do I describe an angry bear so you could understand the enormity of it? Raised on hind legs it reached far taller than a full-grown man can reach. Fur, thick and rough as barley. Brownish black, its body was round and ungainly, short limbs tipped with shining black claws that ripped bark from the maple in long strips exposing white wood beneath.

Just above the reach of those claws, on a solitary branch, Copperman stood, desperately searching for a way higher up. There did not seem to be one. He was bare backed, bleeding down his right shoulder. His torn leather cloak at the bear's feet. He must have been attacked from behind and the looseness of the cloak allowed him to wriggle free. The bear gripped the base of the tree and climbed towards him but Copperman struck down with his axe and bounced it off the thick slab of the bear's skull. It howled a deafening roar, slipped down, and began to climb again. Copperman struck him, almost losing his balance on the branch. This must have happened several times as the bear had many small cuts on the bridge of its nose and forehead. I notched an arrow and aimed it. Copperman looked over and saw me.

"Climb, you idiot!"

I slung the bow and quiver over my neck, picked a tree and began to climb. The bear was on me before I had grabbed the second branch, closing the space between us faster than anything that size should be able to move. Even faster was the white blur that ran between us. Moon. She snarled and bit up and under the bear's crotch and it rolled, trying to curl in on itself to get to her. I screamed and climbed as the two tumbled. Moon let go and ran free with the bear in pursuit. Copperman dropped and found his bow as the bear ran circles, Moon just inches ahead. It turned and came growling back as Copperman climbed the first branches of a smaller maple. It had better footholds and he made it ahead of the bear. The bear began to climb up after him. I had a good platform of branches to stand on. I notched an arrow. Now Copperman's training with the plums came to good service. I shot with all the bow's power and sunk an arrow into the bear's hindquarters. It bit back and tumbled to the dirt as Copperman shot down and into the bear's neck. It rolled again and I notched a second arrow, shooting into the snarling fury. The bear came towards my tree and Copperman shot it in the side, the arrow nearly disappearing to the fletching. The bear turned and came back towards him and I shot again. Moon came in and I shouted at her to get back. She circled and the bear gave chase but this time only to the edge of camp. She could sense her advantage and waited till it reached my tree before baiting it into another chase. I shot and Copperman shot and again and again the bear chased Moon, growing more tired with each run, more injured with each volley of arrows. Finally it began to climb up the tree after me and could not be dissuaded by Moon clinging to its backside or

Copperman's arrows. I dropped my bow and began to climb. Few things can climb faster than an angry bear. Fortunately a frightened boy is one of them. I scampered up that tree like a squirrel and the beast, dripping blood from a dozen places, kept coming after me. He came close enough for me to feel his hot breath on my naked feet. I screamed as we reached the small branches. My choice of tree was a poor one. An old crooked oak that came out in long angled branches.

There was a shudder, a loud crack and we both came down with the tree as the top half snapped from our combined weight. I spun through the air slowly, grabbing and clinging to branches in motion, the bear above me, next to me, under me. We landed with a thud. The air went out of me and I gasped as the bear reached over and clawed in the air, catching me across the forehead with a front paw. I stumbled to my feet as Copperman stood clubbing the bear with his copper axe as it twitched and flopped. Moon came out and grabbed it by the neck fur, shaking back and forth. The bear exhaled one final time and went limp. I fell to Copperman's feet and wept. He stroked my head.

"Well fought," he said. "That was a battle well fought."

Moving on

Moon snarled and worked over the bear. Copperman said it was good for her. That she would think she killed it. His wounds were painful but not very deep: four long claw scratches from shoulder to ribs. I had scratches and bruises from head to toe; my ribs hurt; and, the blow from that giant paw had me dizzy and confused. We washed the wounds in the creek and Copperman crushed the mushrooms Asha traded us. He sprinkled their powder over our open cuts. Camp was in shambles and any thoughts of leaving were put off by the new events. We had to heal up and repair nearly everything: clothes, rucksacks and broken arrows. In a short time the bear had torn our lives to pieces.

Copperman looked down at the giant pile of stinking bloody fur that nearly killed us.

"At least we have some dinner."

The bearskin seemed to weigh as much as I did and Copperman said it would be the best sleep-robe in the land. We removed its leg-fur intact, to use as boot leggings. I scraped for hours, saving the bear-fat in piles to be melted later. There were hundreds of uses for it from cooking to oiling sunburns and curing fevers. He cut as much of the meat as we could use from the carcass and set it to roast on a spit over the fire. I tried to help but the creature so large and fearsome in life was somehow more monstrous and gruesome in death. A skinned, grinning nightmare. Copperman worked swiftly and without emotion, severing its head with effort and removing its great claws. We dragged the carcass to the creek and I watched, as the body, already beginning to swell, floated gently down-stream and disappeared into the growing dusk.

That night, I watched the stars swirl imperceptibly across the roof of the world and waited for sleep that never came, spooking at the slightest noise, at times crying out at the snap of twigs or rustle of leaves. By morning the bear meat was cooked and smoked nearly hard. Moon ate well from Copperman's own hand but I avoided the meat despite my desperate hunger. Copperman cut a large chunk of it and set it in my lap.

"You will grow stronger from this meat than anything you have ever eaten."
It was a chunk of bear-heart. I bit and began to chew, nearly choking on my own fear. I swallowed and bit off another chunk. It was strange but good, rich, necessary. When I finally finished he nodded.

"Now you cannot hate the bear because the bear is a part of you. I will make you a necklace from his teeth…the claws are mine."

It took three days to repair our equipment enough to dare travel. I stitched the packs back together with strands of sinew and rolled birch fibers from the inner bark. It was poor workmanship and Copperman groaned each time he looked at a new mend.

"You sew like you have broken fingers!"

I scowled and thought of his own terrible sewing. People are usually most annoyed by weaknesses in others that they suspect in themselves.

He cursed and grumbled at our foul luck, at the Gods' dark sense of humor, at our own stupidity. We were prepared for a small bear but we should have been prepared for a great bear. It was a failure to plan that nearly caused our end. I asked him how you prepare for a great bear and he rattled off a dozen possibilities. Pit Traps, pitch covered branches that could be lit into giant torches in an instant by placing them over a smaller fire, spike covered tree platforms with barkless bases to prevent them from climbing. It sounded like a summer's work to ward off a big bear.

His first order of business was a sturdy spear shaft for his largest copper spear-point. He chose carefully and rejected many before finding a half green shaft of ash as thick as he could grip closed fingered. It was half again as tall as he was. He scraped it smooth with a curved sharpened piece of gray flint, then, covered it with beargrease and heated it over a fire, slowly twisting and kneeling on it till it was dark brown and perfectly straight. He sharpened the copper point and polished it with sandstone then fitted it on the tip of the shaft with pine tar and wrapped it solid.

I began to dread the forest we were in and mended the packs' inner frames as quickly as I could. But a good pack is the work of a week to make and that's if a woman who knows how to make one is doing the sewing. After two days we left camp with our tails beneath our legs, bows and spears out, limping, bruised and scratched. Our fortune wrapped in our packs nearly forgotten.

The forest, dark and still, felt choked off from the outside world. Trees, gnarled and broken with age, seemed to menace our every step. It took two days to follow the path and another to cross a rocky valley, slipping down the loose boulders of one side and up the other side. I cared not for copper or my father or even food anymore. I simply wanted rest. Rest and a mouthful of water. Moon whined and followed, head down, sensing our misery. She managed to catch a few mice and munched grass along the way, licking moisture from morning plants.

Copperman never spoke. He had a look of determination in his eyes, an angry drive forward. I could see that his shoulder hurt and he tended it nightly with mushroom powder. One of the scratches seemed to resist healing; it puffed red and puss welled from it at the edges. When we passed a dead rabbit he held Moon back from it, flipped it over and gathered several wiggling maggots, placing them on the shoulder under his tunic. Seeing this I worried he had gone dark in his mind from fever and followed behind, watching for further signs of madness. That night at the other side of the boulder valley, he explained that maggots eat dead flesh but ignore the rest. We searched for more but found none to use. The next morning he was stiff in the shoulder and it bled, sticking his shoulder to his tunic. We descended the other side of the mountain, a gentle slope, soft and grass covered. The dark forest was far from sight now and bears slowly faded from my mind. Moon found a spring and we drank, then we descended further to the base of the mountain. The land seemed new and green, well traveled by men. Copperman nodded.

"It has changed in the many seasons since I came here. Sheep and goats tread here often. I remember this place but have never come upon it from the mountain. Come, let us feel our feet on valley soil again, I am tired of angles."

Old friends

It was in the wide green fields of the Bog-shepherds' valley that we rejoined the world of people. Their dogs came up to us, snarling, and I had to hold Moon over my shoulders as Copperman backed them away with the blunt end of his spear. Villagers came, a group of them, armed with bows and battle-clubs. One of them suddenly smiled and called out to Copperman.

"Brother...I did not know you at first, beneath the mud and filth."

They touched noses and held the gaze between them. There was laughter in their eyes and the others lowered their weapons.

"Come and set yourselves down in my home...are you injured?"

Copperman shook his head but the man saw the blood-soaked shoulder and ushered us forward, calling to his wife to set out food and milk. We followed them with a dozen others at our heels to the front of the man's house.

I marveled at the village. Its cleanliness and design. The Bog-shepherds lived in different dwellings than I had seen before. Square and made of turf and mud riding up above the earth on large beams of wood sunk down into the sod of a wide flat field. The houses were easily three times the size of the Lake-people's houses with well-thatched roofs, fat goat kids and equally fat children. This was a truly fine village. I could not keep track of the number but there must have been four or five dozen houses and the same number of smaller structures. Our lake village seemed thin and poor in comparison. Even the paths between were swept clean and grassless.

In front of one of the largest houses there were low tables formed from half logs where women stopped their wool-work to watch our arrival. I suddenly felt shame at how we must have appeared to them: two thin, filthy, bedraggled travelers, stumbling in with broken packs. I need not have worried, they were all looking at Moon who seemed as fit and thick-furred as any they had. I had her slung over my neck to prevent any of the circling males from trying to mate with her.

The shepherds were big themselves, large limbed and sturdy in the hips and calves. They were dressed in thin leather summer shirts and short cloth britches, curious items of clothing as they gathered around each leg, giving more freedom to move. And, unlike the round skirt of the Lake-people, this showed each individual in size and shape.

This is the first time I noticed there were elements of the female form that were pleasing to the eye. It was to be a lifelong study.

The man who greeted Copperman opened his home to us and I had to set Moon down at the entrance, as dogs are not allowed into a home. I need not have worried about the others mating with her; I found out that if a female is not in her mating phase she simply crouches tail to the ground and bites at the males' softer parts. With a few nips and yelps the other dogs fell into line and sniffed her apologetically. After fighting a bear my young dog was afraid of nothing. Point made, she began to run in happy circles with dogs and children joining in.

One of the joys in life is to watch children and dogs play. But my hunger drove me inside where Copperman sat across from his friend. His name was Lan and he was obviously a man of influence in his clan, one of the main council, who decided on important matters and owned a fine section of the sheep in the village. His wife set out a round clay plate before us with a mound of fresh wet cheese and a chunk of hard dry cheese, cold roasted roots and small round bread from a dark grain I had never tasted before. I forced myself to eat slowly. The wet cheese melted into the crusty bread and the waxy roots were spiced with mint and thin onions and goat fat. I trembled from the effort not to gulp it down. We finished with sour milk, a drink I had never liked as a boy but could not get enough of now. Copperman stopped me after the second cup.

"You will need to let your body settle now."

He was right. After a while my stomach, having been, empty began to struggle with the rich food. Lan's wife, Sola, noticed my discomfort and gave me strong mint tea. She looked at me softly as my mother would have, she must have seen the hard journey in my eyes. As Copperman spoke to Lan, Sola tended his wounds, washing the shoulder with lye soap and patting it dry with a clean cloth. It looked slightly swollen and painful. Lan looked at us both with a keen eye.

"I suppose you are going to tell me you are on a stroll around our mountains for pleasure?"

Copperman smiled at this but said nothing.

"We will talk trade later. You are in good fortune, you have found us at the height of a rich summer, sheep are doubled by their lambs, sun has kept our grain dry and night rains keep our vegetable gardens full. In two days we will hold a wedding for three of the daughters of the village. A full moon ceremony. You have to stay as my guest so you can see the way the bog people celebrate. I insist."

This was a clever way to offer us help without taking away our power. We were no longer desperate beggars, we were wedding-guests. Copperman waited the long silence necessary for an offer to hang in the air before nodding.

"We are proud to be your guests."

Lan stood. "Fine, I will announce the purpose of your visit to the others."
He strode out and spoke loudly to the small crowd gathered outside his house:

"These two visitors, Copperman and Copperson from the Lake-people, have come to honor the wedding. They are to be kept as my own and credit to them for any services are honored by the house of Lan."

The others murmured. One by one, visitors peeked in to welcome us. Lan returned with his two sons. They were smaller versions of their father but with thinner beards—and this I am not exaggerating—They were copies of each other in every way. I had known of double births before but had only seen one and those two were brother and sister. Lan's sons, however, were two of the same person standing next to each other.

Copperman laughed and rose to clap them on the sides of their heads.

"You have grown strong...which of you is Keer and which is Koor?"

One of them stood forward, "Keer...I have redder hair."

Copperman nodded. I could see no difference in their hair, strawberry colored and with a few thin braded coils on either side. They were handsome square-jawed and probably two or three years older than I. I pondered my own hair and fancied having braids like theirs some day. Braids were like ink-scars, earned for bravery. Keer had two more than Koor and I imagined it was hard to compete with yourself. I stood to greet them nose-to-nose and they looked at my features curiously. I knew what they were thinking, 'He does not look like Copperman's son.' But I liked them for not saying it.

Sola took over the situation, scooting her boys out to gather warm water from the fire and other women to help. Our clothes were stripped from us and taken out to be cleaned. Copperman and I suffered what Copperman called a 'wedding-scrub.' Cleaned from head to foot by old women, determined to take my skin off with soap weed and wool-rags. I found it humiliating but did not have the strength to resist as they stripped away a month of travel. Copperman enjoyed it as he did any kind of cleaning and organizing. They rinsed us with water, scented by some kind of stinging oil and then massaged the pure oil into our scalps to keep flies and nits away. Then they used a wooden comb to work the oil through the tangles in our hair, a painful process. One of them noticed the deep scratches on my scalp and looked at Copperman.

He nodded. "He got those from a bear." This made them laugh but then he reached over to his pack and pulled out one of the curved claws, as long and thick as a man's finger. They gasped and looked at me with a mixture of pity and awe.

"He certainly should have a braid in his hair for that" one of them said.

Copperman nodded and the woman began twisting a clump of my hair into three separate ropes and weaving them together, tying small knots along the way to keep it together. It hurt but I did not mind. Halfway through the braid I must have fallen asleep because when I awoke I had no idea where I was. It was dark and I cried out.

"Quiet!" Copperman's voice came from next to me. "We are guests." It took a while for me to remember the day. I was between two furs on a straw mattress, warm and safe in a big house. I dosed and then fell back into dreamless sleep.

The wash and rest seemed to give Copperman the strength to finally fight out the sickness in his shoulder wound. He had a short fever and sweats, groaning lightly as the women scrubbed and treated his wounds. They were herbalists of a sort, different than the witchcraft of Asha. Their methods were not as powerful but they were safer: garlic oil and pinesap, dandelion root and hot water. He suffered their treatments gladly and by that night the fever slackened and his hunger came back. I rested and ate, receiving small treatments for scratches already healing. I did not know enough to be worried about Copperman (though I have since seen smaller animal wounds kill men with the fever of it). The next morning he nudged me awake with a foot.

He had that look in his eyes, the look that said 'come if you want to learn something.' I dressed in the new cloth pants given by Lan's neighbor. Wearing them felt like being naked; the shirt made from the same cloth was thin and soft. In the summer heat I felt free and for the first time in the summer season I walked without pack, bow or cloak.

I followed Copperman through the village with dogs and children in tow. The bog village was a wonder of creativity. It lay in the very center of a valley meadow with sharp mountains on either side. It seemed an easy target for invaders. Copperman explained that the very foundation had been a huge bog generations ago. But when the Bog-shepherds came, they dug channels on either side to drain the water. In one summer the bog had dried and they began to build houses with the surrounding trees, hammering straight birch logs into the soft peat, down three times the height of a man to the hard ground beneath. On these posts they made frames, and their homes, wood- and mud-sided, were chest high, safe from the worst floods and above rats and thieving scavengers. Under the houses, the numerous dogs were safe from weather and wind. They could also sneak out to attack invaders from all sides.

The Bog-dogs were long lanky hounds with darker fur and longer snouts than Moon, and I began to wonder what a puppy from the two would look like. Not good, I decided. If Moon wanted to mate I would have to intervene. One thing I liked about the Bog-dogs is that they were trained to never bark and woe to the stranger who tried to enter a house unannounced.

I marveled at the industrious nature of the Bog-shepherds. Their houses were arranged in sets of five, one log frame attached to the next. This seemed to give the village a sense of stability, as if they were pieces of one giant house that no natural disaster could topple. At the end of the village, dozens of men and women were working like ants, constructing a new home. The two houses next to it were lacking roofs. I guessed they were for the couples to be married. All the logs on the final house had been set but one, and this log, sharpened at the end, was carried by several men. Others waited on the frames of the adjoining house to lift it up and set it into the soft peat. With stones held high, they hammered the blunt end and with each hit the log sunk into the peat perhaps a finger's width. Over and over they hit the log; taking turns they began to sing a work song, using the rhythm of the strikes to follow with their voices. Though they had the same basic language as the Lake-people the bog shepherds spoke it and sang it with more rolling of the tongue, and their voices sang out with the joy building people have when building something.

> *The rocks of the land move the tree of the land.*
> *The tree of the land holds the house of the land.*
> *The house of the land holds the people of the clan.*
> *The people of the clan move the rocks of the land.*

"What are you waiting for?" Copperman said, and I realized that in my fascination I had been very rude. I ran in to join and waited my turn in line on the wood frame. I took the rock and tried not to show how heavy it was. I sang along and raised the rock striking the base of the log over and over to the rhythm. I hardly think I moved it one bit into the earth but the Bog-clan cheered as I finished and handed it over to the next man.

As the sun rose hot, the log finally hit hard dirt. The build-masters began to shout orders, fitting the logs together with thick, braided rope, and carving out half-rounds into other logs to rest on the frame. With so many working, the house seemed to rise before my very eyes. Wood-slats formed floors and separated rooms; stones, packed with mud and grass, became a fireplace; perfect squares of peat, stacked in the places between, built up the walls; and, pure clay and ashes, smeared over the seams, began to dry, brilliant white in the sun. I busied myself, helping where I could, but the Bog-clan had done this before and it was all I could do to keep from stumbling into them as they worked in closely packed quarters.

As the sun began to set, we formed a line and carried heavy strips of peat to a man standing on a wooden ladder who handed them to boys, Keer and Koor among them. The boys, balanced on wooden roof-beams, set the peat over a latticework of birch bark strips. The roofs looked far too delicate to handle a winter snow but soon grass would weave it all together and hold over the house like a warm blanket. And then we were done. Tools and scraps cleared away and paths swept clean with branches. The homes were glorious to look at and I felt pride at having helped build one. That night, Lan sat across from Copperman after a dinner of lamb stew. I sat with Keer and Koor, teaching them how to play drop-rocks, a game every child of the lake knew. The object is to bounce a small pebble from one flat stone onto another. It is a child's game really but the brothers became fascinated and we played earnestly. The competition was strong between the two. When they began to argue Lan forbid them to play.

"Your son is strong and lean like you," Lan said.

Copperman nodded. "It is his first journey and he has done well."

"Is he not young to be on such a journey?"

Copperman did not answer. I sensed he was annoyed by the question. Lan must have sensed it as well. "But the Lake-people are adventurous by nature," he added. "I can see by his ink-scars that he had earned the right."

Copperman examined our boots, well mended by someone while he had been sick. Also, his shirt and our packs. Everything neatly sewed and cleaned. Our arrows re-fletched and tipped with new flint.

"You are building up debt on our behalf."

Lan shrugged off the comment. "It is the week of my daughter's wedding. To have guests come from so far is a great omen."

Copperman smiled. "Your daughter is one of the three? My blessings to her."

Lan laughed. "This is small talk for long lost friends. I have waited for two days for you to heal up and now you owe me a story, a long story."

The brothers sat in close and Sola scooted in and lit an oil-lamp to add to the firelight. Copperman looked at his old friend for a moment.

"Forgive me for being tight lipped. It is an old habit from the nature of my work. If it is a story you want, a story you shall have."

He began with the story of his own marriage to my mother and it was good to hear, as I had never known many of the details. How he knew he must marry her and she ignored him for two seasons before he could win her for marriage. How my brother and sister came into the world and how one more came just months before I did but fell asleep one night and never woke from slumber. He told about my arrival to the Lake-people and of the council's anger at his decision. He described our journey over the last month. (Slightly vague about our location, I noticed.) He said nothing about our good fortune with Asha, Moon and the bluestone. He went into great detail, however, with the story of the bear and our journey to their valley. It was a long tale and the boys followed it intently. When it was over, they insisted on a look at my ink-scars and the bear's teeth and claws. Sola knew of a woman in the clan who made fine, strong jewelry, she would take the teeth and claws over to her.

Now Copperman said: "Why did you greet us with spears and clubs. Is there an enemy of the Bog-shepherds who I should hate as well?"

Lan sighed. "The forest dwellers, the old ones. They came searching a few days before you came, armed and angry. I could not understand even their trade tongue (we rarely see them) but there is one among us who came from their region and she said their sacred cave had been disturbed and food taken without permission. They are usually a peaceful clan but there were twenty at least, all main hunters and ready for battle. I offered them some food and my word that we knew nothing of their intruders and would alert them if we came to that knowledge.

I felt a cold shiver down my spine. The painted cave. I had thought it was older than memory. People still worshiped there. Copperman looked at me and I understood. I was glad he had not burdened Lan with knowledge of the cave. He had given his word and it is a heavy thing to carry your word against the life of a friend. Lan would not have to choose. But I think he knew we had something to do with the trespass. Of course he must have. This is why he immediately clothed us in Bog-shepherd's clothes. If the warriors came back, we would not stand out to them.

The next day the clan buzzed with preparations for the wedding. In a half circle in front of the three new homes, they gathered wood into a giant stack and arranged blankets, low tables and straw enough to seat the whole village. There were torches prepared with pine tar and beeswax, sticking up high from the ground in a circle around the sitting places. Five sheep were slaughtered as well as a goat and many waterfowl. Smoked fish and fruit and nuts gathered from high and low, many kinds of cheese laid out on low tables and clay jugs of milk.

I watched as it gathered and arranged, growing hungrier with each new arrival. Copperman had sat with his tools and I knew enough not to peek over to see what he was working so intently on. The others were equally curious but resisted the urge to ask. This was one of his methods, building mystery around his work by doing it in front of people who were too proud to ask. He knew we all wanted to see it and whatever it turned out to be had our interest already. I knew from the glint of copper and the tools he used (elk horn spike and smooth sandstone), that it was jewelry of some kind. Whatever it was took the whole day to hammer, smooth and prepare.

Nobody eats the day of a wedding, not until the couples are wed. I had been to five or six before and they were long days for a child, sitting through prayers and speeches while food waited in view. Now I was used to hunger and the wedding fascinated me.

As the sun began to set, torches were lit and then the giant wedding fire. As it rose into the fading sky, three young men came out, their hair and beards cut short to represent the new beginning. They looked strange. Bare and nervous, they stood before the Council with the rest of us surrounding them in silence. Then the women walked out, red-cheeked and proud, flowers woven into braids in their long hair. Each one took stance by her man. The elder performing the ceremony was very old indeed, draped in a robe of black sheepskin. He stood (with more than a little help) before the clan, his white hair and beard in stark contrast, appeared to float white against the backdrop of the darkening night. The evening, windless and sweet with summer grass, began to smoke as small bundles of dried herbs, lit by the children, perfumed the wedding ceremony. The crowd, still silent, looked at the wedding couples and they looked back; it was a test like the nose-to-nose greetings. The couples looked at each member of the clan, eyes locked for a few seconds. It was hard to meet their gaze and I wondered how hard it must be to face down a clan of that size, looking for you to shy away, daring you to falter. The old man raised his hands and called to the Gods in a strong voice that shattered the heavy silence.

"Birds, wolves, fish, lambs, deer, trees, earth, water, wind, sun, moon, light, darkness, everything that 'Is' and everything we know but cannot see. Let it be understood before all that these three couples are tonight bonded together and any who seek to disrupt them will be an enemy of the Bog-shepherd clan. Those who have gifts, bring them forward, one by one."

I felt a hollow in the pit of my stomach. I had no gift, how could I be this ignorant, I had been to enough weddings to know better. I looked down in shame. People brought out chairs and furs and clay pots and clothes of every kind, handed one by one to the different couples. As the last of the gifts filed past, Copperman stood next to me and handed me three small rings. They were woven from thin strands of copper and curled into flower patterns where they joined. I could have cried with relief. He motioned me toward the newly married and I knelt before each of the women, in turn handing them a ring.

"A small gift from the Lake-people," I said. They were thrilled with the rings and put hands to my cheek with such affection that I blushed. Then, Copperman gave his gifts, shining round medallions, hammered flat and decorated with a ram's head on the front and barley grain symbols on the back. They were strung with thin leather cord. He gave each to the grooms and they called out, holding them up to the crowd. The medallions gleamed in the firelight. Then the party began.

Wedding

A woman, singing softly at first, started a chorus of women's voices, raising the hair on my arms with the beauty of it. Their calls were answered by the men, deep and melodic. I did not know the song as there were no words, just the tone, rising and falling. Slowly at first, then a drumbeat came in from behind us. Then another and another and another... Someone had a reed flute and another a pair of clacking sticks. The song grew into a fast-paced hum as more and more joined in. The fathers and mothers of the wedded danced, and, after a respectful wait, we all joined in.

Dancing was strange to me and I simply had no idea how to do it. Of course children do it but I did not remember if I had or how. Keer and Koor fixed that in a hurry. They grabbed me, one on each arm and suddenly I was dancing, jumping and bouncing as the drums raised their tempo. The dance seemed to shake off the silence of the wedding, my shame at not having a present, the long journey, the bear, all of it, shaken loose by jumping around to drum-songs. Finally, the drums reached an un-danceable speed and a cheer ended it all. Keer, Koor and I dropped, laughing, to a low table and I knew we would be friends for life. Then came the food and a drink called honey wine, honey and water left in lidded clay jars for months until it bubbles out to become sweet and clear again. I drank a cup of it to be polite but it was not to my liking. After some cheese and roast goose and toasted pine-nuts I tried another cup of honey wine and found it to be more to my liking. Fish and mutton go nicely with the drink as well and then we were dancing again. Keer and Koor began to wrestle and were good-naturedly pried apart by Lan who sent them to opposite sides of the circle to settle down. He sat next to me, offering chunks of dark bread with goats butter and crushed blueberries. I thanked him and we sat together, watching the party unfold. The dogs took every advantage, grabbing bone after bone as we threw them behind us. I was happy to see Moon, so much smaller than the others, racing in from time to time for her share. Lan put an arm around my shoulder.

"Do you want to taste honey wine?"
"Worth a try," I said and held out my cup.

Wine Sick

Under something. Straw stuck to my face, and jaw aching with the pulse of blood rushing to my head. It was dark and late by the arc of the moon, the wedding still in full cry with drums and singing. It sounded more like harpies howling to my sickening head and the drums more inside the skull than out. Keer found me somehow upended behind the straw and laughed, calling out to the others, "The Lake-people cannot handle their honey wine."

I stood and reeled, stumbled to the edge of the swamp somehow shy even in my condition and cleared out my stomach into the tepid water. Others howled in laughter, but it seemed they were animated beyond normal and I suspected honey wine was the culprit. Sola came over to me in the darkness and washed my face with cool water.

"Foolish of them to give a boy honey wine."

She patted my head and held me for a few minutes until the spinning of the earth slowed and finally stopped. I must have fallen asleep there, head in her lap. For when I awoke someone had carried me to the straw bed in Lan's house. Copperman took me by the shirt and hauled me to my feet.

"Now I will cure you and your sickness." He led me out to a deep swimming spot in the stream, eyes squinting from the sunlight that seemed determined to burn its way into my head. There were dozens of men and many of them appeared to be in the same shape as I. We all stripped and wallowed into the icy, clean water. Yelling at cold water does not help but sometimes you try it anyway. I groned and treaded water back towards the bank but Copperman shook his head.

"All the way under. Stay for a bit. Trust me, it is the only cure for what ails you."

Of course, he was right. That water pulled the sickness from my body and improved my mood tremendously. Finally on the bank, I dried, naked in the sun with the others, as more filed down to the water to be reborn in its icy currents. I decided to never try honey wine again. By the time Keer and Koor slunk to the river, I laughed at their sorry state. They raised fists as I cheered their attempts to enter the stream. When they joined me at the bank they were still suffering. Keer shook and gasped.

"It is a good thing there are so few weddings or we would be old before our time."

I nodded. "But it was fun dancing."

The others, sitting on the bank like a naked tribe, were curious about my ink-scars. They had all done things in their lives that they felt earned them an ink-scar or two. I could see Copperman mentally preparing for a busy time in the days ahead. We would repay Lan's debt in short order. Women called down from the grassy bank.

"Out! It is our turn now!"

We gathered ourselves and dressed passing the women who stumbled down to the creek shedding clothes as they went. However I had humiliated myself that night was erased by the state of half the clan.

There were all manner of food left after the feast, and Copperman made me eat and this cured me further. I asked him when we would leave and he answered when we have repaid our debt. That day we set out the ink-scar tools and began adorning the Bog-shepherd clan with symbols. I followed Copperman's every move, memorizing the angles and styles, the way he held his obsidion needle in the green split branch, the mixture of ash and crushed bluestone, the various patterns. He asked each recipient to describe in detail their brave deed and as they told it their fear of the needle subsided. It was clever to take someone back to their bravest time before facing the unknown. He told me in private that men who he had seen charge wolves with a spear could faint from fear at the first touch of the needle. They needed to be led like children to a strong place before they were ready to attempt it. I remembered him doing the same with me before the first ink-scars. After a few scars, the pain is no longer grounded in fear, and then it becomes more of an ecstatic burn, Back and forearms were the least painful; ankle and ribs the most tender, especially around the bones' thin skin. Men sweat and shook by the end of the ordeal and this was the same for all men: they would stare out into the past and sleep long into the next day from the experiance.

The second day of work, six men and three women had ink-scars, ranging from dot flowers around a finger, to thick bands of dark lines surrounding a calf. The thick, red hair of the Bog-men made detail difficult, unless the skin was bare. Copperman used a half round of black glass flint, wedged into a handle of greenwood to shave the hair from around the area on men (a part of the process that took the most caution). Keer and Koor sat with us, fascinated. I knew what they were thinking. They wanted one so bad it caused them to pace back and forth between the houses.

The next morning early, Copperman took me aside. "Do you remember the methods?"

"Yes, of course I do"
"There is no 'of course', you either do or you do not."

"I do"

"Ok." He handed me an apple. "This is Koor's wrist, he is frightened but trying to be brave, give him an ink-scar he will wear for the rest of his life, proudly."

I set out the tools and arranged the ink in its tiny clay jar, mixing it to proper thickness. I sat cross-legged and held the greenstick, stained black with the ink and blood of the others. I inserted a fresh needle and checked its angle, then said, "Tell me about the time that you earned this mark of courage." I held the apple in the crook of my knee and began to tap the lines and dots into it. It was much harder than I had imagined, keeping rhythm with the stick and the depth and lines strait. Every now and then Copperman would bump me slightly or make a sharp sound that took my concentration away. After a short time, my back cramped and calf-muscles twitched, making the steady hand, that much less steady. When the lines met on the other side of the apple, it looked crooked and wavy. I had also missed the pattern, so the line ended with two dots next to each other.

"Would you want that on your arm forever?"

I looked down at the mangled design and shook my head sadly

"No, I would not."

"Well it's a good start. Try another when you get a chance but not around the others. They need to feel confidence in your ability."

I hid the apple and over the next few days my skills improved, as a boy can learn more in a week than a man can in a season. Our days were spent working lightly, eating heavily and each day at high sun, working our copper-blades into shape. Copperman performed seven more ink-scars that week, not only clearing our debt but also adding dried food, beads and oil to our trade stock. I managed to hide away many times with my apples and ink, working out the design-flaws and strengthening muscles needed to hold the positions for a scar. The last apple examined by Copperman received his approval.

"You do this for Keer and I will follow exactly your pattern for Koor." He looked at me proudly. "This is a skill that will feed your family and make you a man of importance among the clans...but with it comes some distrust. It is a magic that will make jealous men speak of you secretly and feel anger at their inability. Once you have gone down this path, it is the one you will walk forever. Like the scars, it will never leave you for good or ill."

I nodded. For me it was never even a question: This was my father's path and I would follow it into my future.

Theft

Lan sent us hunting with several other young men of the clan. I enjoyed the walking after a week of rich food. We moved in two lines of four, twice the distance apart that a man can shoot. This way we could try for anything between us without hitting each other. My legs were faster than the Bog-shepherd boys'. They sweated and panted like dogs in the wet heat. After a summer of mountain hiking, I felt I could out-walk anyone. Our group circled the thick grass surrounding the village and took a dozen rabbits between us. I missed mine as it zigzagged, then missed another that stopped, not thirty paces from me, and turned broadside. A shot a child could have made. One of our group watched me miss the shot, a chunky, pug-nosed kid with long dark hair and even darker eyes. He strode up to me with two rabbits slung onto a loop over his belt.

"Do you not have bows and arrows where you come from?"

I did not like the pitch of challenge in his voice. He was a big kid, my age, but heavier and much stronger. He was trying to pick a fight. I could not back down but I wanted to. I paused and he knew I was afraid. I dropped my bow however and he dropped his. Keer and Koor called over to us.

"Are we hunting or not?"

The others were already fading in the high grass. I shrugged and picked up the bow. The kid grinned and picked his up as well.

"Do not worry Lake boy. I will shoot some rabbits for you to carry."

I missed three more rabbits after that and by the time we stopped for lunch on the outskirts of a young birch-forest, it seemed everyone else had dinner for their family. The one who insulted me was named Okla and he had three rabbits and a female pheasant. Keer took me aside. I could now tell them apart, not as much by hair color but by personality. Keer was more subtle and soft, but only slightly. Koor was usually one to speak first and quicker to anger. Keer handed me some dark bread from his pack.

"What are you doing? Do not be shy with your bow."

I told Keer about my bad shooting and Okla's insults. He looked over at him and spit into the dirt.

"He is a rat-shit, I would knock him over myself but it would not be right to fight him because he is younger."

Keer frowned. "Plus he is bull-ram strong. I would not fight him if I were you. Stick with us. In fact, stick next to Koor. If he hears one word against you he will happily dunk Okla's head into the swamp."

"Thanks," I said. "But I want to hunt next to Okla, to show him he will not back me down."

Keer nodded.

"I think I know why you could not hit those rabbits. Your new arrows are strange to you. Use your old ones."

I thought about it and understood everything. I had been excited to use the newly fletched arrows. They were fine gifts and I wanted to show appreciation by using them, but their feathers were bigger than the used fletching I had in my quiver. Whoever had fletched the arrows made them wider than I was used to. From my small bow they were slow and awkward. I looked at the two arrows I had left with old feathers. They did not look good but I could tell they would shoot where I wanted them to go. I would have to trim the others down with flint when I had the time.

With an old arrow knocked and ready I joined the group. We split off into twos and threes. I stood next to Okla and said loud enough to be heard,

"Let us team up. We can walk the outer edge and flush game towards the center."

I was trying to bait him into the hard walk for those who flush game. Scampering in and around the outskirts of a birch-wood would tire him out and give me the advantage.

"I have a better idea," Okla said. "Let us go to the main trail and ambush what comes through. Just be ready to shoot fast, anything they spook will be running full out."

The others looked around, sensing the challenge in his voice. Koor stepped forward towards Okla but I looked at him and shook my head slightly. He looked around, puzzled.

"Okay, Okla thinks he is the leader today. Let us watch how he leads."

Okla puffed up at Koor's tone. "I am only offering our guest a chance to make a kill today after his ...lack of good luck this morning. It is important to show respect to guests of the clan. But if you want him thrashing the bushes, take him along...I will take him myself if you want."

Koor shook his head. "No, let us give the youngsters a try at the main trail."

The others grumbled at the change of plans since usually they would draw straws to see who got the chance at a kill. There were known to be red-deer in this part of the forest. The others left to surround the section of forest. The plan on a hunt is to move big game along a trail towards waiting hunters. It was a job for men but a group of boys with bows always feel like men and we were ready for anything. I followed Okla along a small deer trail to a large fallen log next to the main path. The trail was well worn. Fresh hoof prints marked wet leaves. Okla crouched down behind the fallen log, an excellent vantage point facing the trail, and a good shooting spot. Deer would not see him as he drew back from behind the waist-high log.

"You take that spot." He pointed to a rock, facing the trail on the other side, a poor shooting place with branches hanging down around it. It would be hard to draw comfortably, and, being right- handed, I would face the wrong way to shoot oncoming game. He was clever. And I began to hate him as only a boy can hate a bully. I could not argue; a good hunter can shoot from any position and my complaints would only show weakness. It was his trail and I would have to make do.

I took position and Okla sneered at me from thirty paces, smug in his spot.

The wait is terrible on a hunt. I had only ever moved game towards the main hunters, jealous of those waiting quietly while we worked. Now I understood the misery of waiting. If we missed, the others would have worked for nothing. It was a heavy responsibility. I steadied my hands by telling myself what Copperman had always told me about shooting. 'It will go as it will go. Do not shoot at the target, shoot at a small place in the center of the target.' But this was going to be a moving target and instinct would have to take over. There would be no time to think.

Flys buzzed, my haunches ached from the bordome of squatting behind the rock. Okla sneered at me from his superior post. Then a branch snapping warned the coming of an animal…several. I could feel them as they crashed through the brush. Wild boar. Several large adult males, followed closely by smaller females. Even the females would be heavier than a boy. The males were something to see, dark hair, raised in hackles on humped backs. They galloped like nimble roe deer, jumping over logs and ducking under low branches, they were moving at speed directly towards us. Okla raised his bow and the lead boar ran directly towards him. He shot wild and high as the beast knocked him sideways. I aimed at one of the younger fat boars and managed to hit him directly behind the left shoulder. He ran full speed with the others but I knew he was hurt. It was over as quickly as it began. The group of boar became a rustle of branches off in the forest. Okla stood and dusted himself off.

"Fool," he said. "You let him maul me."

I knew of nothing to say to this. The others came up quickly along the same trail. Keer shouted to us.

"Did you see them?"
"See them?" Okla said. "I hit one."

At first, I was too stunned to speak up. To claim to shoot another's game? It simply was not done. I looked at Keer with desperation. I could not be the one to challenge Okla on this; it was an accusation worthy of a meeting with the elders. The Lake-people would have kept a young hunter out of the clan hunts all season for such a breach. Koor plowed forward to the edge of the trail.

"Blood! Good job, Okla, you hit him."

We all followed and Okla fell in behind with me.

"You loaned me an arrow. That is what happened. If you say different I will deny it. They all saw how you shoot. Who will believe you?"

Ahead there was the boar, a fat young bull with an arrow fletching sticking out from his ribs. An arrow in the neck from Keer finished him and the others gathered around the boar, arrows out in case the others came in as bore sometimes do. After a few minutes it was clear that we were safe. The time after a kill is far busier than the hunt; you have to move quickly to avoid spoiling meat. A tall boy, the oldest among us, began to order the preparations. We had to act quickly to get the boar cleaned and carry it home before evening. As the others split branches and gathered dry tall grass in big clumps to clean out the cavity with. We slit the belly open and began the gruesome task of gutting the animal. Unlike deer, there is as much weight in intestines as there is meat in a boar. We were red from the shoulders down by the end of the job.

While we washed in the muddy water of a near by ditch, Keer whispered to me; "I saw him pull the arrow out, it was one of yours, he tried to hide the fletching in his hands but I saw it."

I said nothing. On the walk back, we took turns with the boar balanced between us, upside down on a thin pole between its tethered legs. Usually the return trip of a successful hunt is boisterous and filled with bravado and chatter but the others were oddly silent. They must have seen or guessed what Keer knew. Okla had stolen my hunt. I walked behind, not sure what to do about the new development. Would a guest claim such a crime? Would the Bog-shepherd clan send us off in shame? After all, Okla was the little brother to one of the wedded men and the son of a council member. Who was I? A traveler, sheltering from enemies in Lan's house. I decided to let Okla have his prize but it boiled in my blood as we came into the village with the boar and the others praised him for the perfect shot.

I slunk off and washed in the stream, scrubbing with sand. Copperman came down to join me and we sat silently, watching the sun burn red against the evening clouds.

"Rabbits?"

"No, I missed them all."

He frowned. "That is not a good day."

He looked at me keenly. "What is troubling you?"

"Nothing…everything."

He waited.

"It was my pig!"

He raised an eyebrow. I told him about the hunt, the story spilling out as fast as I could speak. My hands shook from the retelling of it. When I was done, he nodded.

"Wise. You did what is right. Being a guest has its own set of rules. Okla must have known how much trouble we would have both been in if you had claimed such a crime against him. Not many boys would have had the strength to keep quiet about such a thing. Does anyone else question it? They must have seen the arrow."

"Keer suspects it."

"Let us go and see how this comes out. Say nothing and stick close to me."

In the village center, the fire pit held a deep bed of roasting coals glowing white red in the center. The boar, being a fresh animal, needs to be eaten the day it is killed. They had burnt away the foul thick fur in the flames and scraped it clean. It rested, strapped on a long pole between forked stakes, high enough from the coals to cook slowly. Clear fat dripped and hissed into small bursts of flame in the great bed of coals. I have always marveled at the death of creatures, their lives ended with an arrow as easily as mine could be. Do the Gods reward them for their sacrifice? Does a boar or a bear or even a rabbit look upon death with the fear that we do? Do they see all humans as evil? The bear would have eaten us with no confusion, yet I had watched its carcass float down the river with infinite sadness. I have always been haunted by the creatures I kill. But of course this was a silent torment that others could never know about. A hunter can show no emotion about such things. Yet here I was, up against a lie that risked our very safety and my heart hurt for a roasting boar.

I sat at the edge of the circle and hoped the others could not guess my thoughts. The twins sat cross-legged next to Lan and Sola; they looked at me with questions I could not answer. I hung my head slightly as Okla described the hunt to the gathering group. A wild boar was a rare delight and not many in the clan had taken one. Okla was playing to the crowd, pacing back and forth, describing the hunt in all its details. Me loaning him one of my arrows. Him fighting off his fear to make the shot from behind the felled tree. He was perfectly humble in his bragging, describing the shot as a lucky one. The others, enjoying the smell of roasting pork listened to the story, especially the father of Okla who egged him on with sighs and laughs. Suddenly Lan spoke up, loudly so that everyone could hear.

"Why did you borrow another's arrow?"

"He insisted," Okla said, pointing at me. "He is a guest, I could not refuse. Perhaps the Lake-people take pride in their arrows, I know nothing of their customs. It was a good arrow for the job."

Lan nodded. "And you shot from the fallen tree, that begins the main trail of the oak forest?"

"Yes, I told you," Okla said, becoming defensive.

"And Copperman's son sat on the oppisite side of the trail from you?"

"Yes," Okla said. "A bad choice but a man does what he does and it is not my place to question it."

Lan stood and faced Okla. The others grew silent except for Okla's father who puffed out his chest and walked over to stand beside his son.

"This is his hunting story Lan. What right have you to talk over it?"

"Because this story smells of deceit." The crowd became dead silent.

Okla pointed to me. "Ask the lake boy, he will tell you what happened."

Everyone looked at me.

"Tell them!" Okla continued. "Tell them about loaning me an arrow!"

Lan spoke before I had to answer.

"He cannot speak against you. But your lie is evident to us all. That boar was shot in the left shoulder." He pointed to the arrow wound on the sizzling boar. "If the boar came towards you from the deep forest and you shot it from the fallen tree facing the main trail, you would have shot it in the shoulder on the other side."

The others cried out in surprise. The evidence was indisputable. "Your fellow hunters were too cowardly to point it out to you but Keer and Koor told me that suspicion was in the whole group." He looked from one hunter to another.

Okla looked afraid. "Well, we both shot and there were boar running in every direction, it could have been his shot I guess. We both had the same arrows."

"No one believes you anymore, Okla. Go and wait. The council needs to decide what comes of this."

Okla's father looked at the wound in the boar and back to his son in growing disgust. Then he looked at me. He cleared his throat.

"Okla has been spoiled, it is my fault. On behalf of the Council, I apologize."

The hawk

Councils are dangerous. They vary from clan to clan, generation to generation. Copperman told me that five or six old men in a bad mood can be more dangerous than a band of warriors. I did not understand what he meant until I saw the Council of the Bog-shepherd clan punish Okla. They sat in a small circle, speaking low over a fire, close enough to the village to be seen but not over-heard. This had a strange effect on the others, who went about their work quietly, whispering their guesses about Okla's fate. He was made to sit with the Council, completely silent while they debated. To me this seemed punishment enough.

Copperman was getting restless and I could see by his pacing and his checking and rechecking our equipment that we would be leaving soon. There were small fires spotted in the hills, two nights passing. Lan sent scouts who found hidden fire pits and camps, brushed clean, invisible to all but a seasoned tracker. The forest warriors were back. Lan and Copperman spoke of it often. Copperman wanted to know everything about them. Even the smallest details. I knew what he was thinking. If we met them, he hoped to have an advantage with knowledge. He told me that an enemy you do not understand has the advantage. That night, he told me to sleep with the thoughts of the painted cave in my head, to remember clearly every painting. The next day, he brought out the Ink-scar bundle and told me to follow. We sat in the clearing next to the creek and unfolded the tools.

"Now, before thinking too hard about it, tell me the first painting from the cave that you remember."

"The hawk."

He smiled. "Interesting."

It was a small image compared with the deer and bear and I had only noticed it on the second day. Black and carefully detailed with its wings spread over as if it were flying.

"Why do you think this one came to your mind first?"

I mulled it over as he arranged the needle and began to grind up the ink. "Because it was on the ceiling of the cave!"

"Yes it was…and this means someone wanted to put that one above all others. Anything else?"

"Um…" He waited.

Suddenly it came to me. "It was from underneath. Like it was flying over us."

He nodded. "You could see a fish in its claws."

Now I could see it as I had then, lying on my back, gazing up at the bird's belly, head sideways to show its fearsome beak, fish pierced through with talons.

"How do you think they might have gotten up those slick walls to paint it?"

"A high table I suppose," he said as he pulled his thin cloak over his head. His body was a tale in itself, cross-cut with whip-scars from his youth in the mines, etched with ink-scars on the wrists and shoulders, long, healed cuts and scratches from a hundred journeys, nut brown on the forearms and neck, fish-belly white torso. He sat and rested his right forearm on a log. With a thin twig, burnt at the tip, he traced the hawk. I helped him remember certain details, the way the fish turned, the angle of its wing tips.

"Start!" he said, "and do it well."

There is a thing that happens when something needs to be done. Somehow you simply make it happen. If I had done my first ink-scar on Keer or Koor, it probably would have been a good start, a decent first attempt. But this was different. I needed to make it perfect. And so I did.

Copperman never winced as the flint-needle tapped in and out of his flesh. I began with the outline, and, as the bird began to take shape, more memories of the original came back to me: one twisted feather, the number of long tail-feathers (five), the light point of the curved beak with dots for nostrils; everything came with the focus. Others began to gather, watching from a polite distance, then sitting close. Moon curled around my feet as I worked but I barely noticed. I began to fill in the wings in rows and rows. Sola brought water and wiped sweat from my forehead. The work became itself; nothing outside the hawk existed. Just my breathing, Copperman's blood in droplets, and ink dripping from my own wrist. How long it took I did not understand, until the day sun became evening dusk and Copperman took the needle-stick from my aching hand.

"It is done," he said.

"Yes but some of the feathers…"

"No, it is done. It is done well."

He looked more weary than I did and the others led us back to Lan's house. Copperman coated the hawk with a thin layer of boiled sheep-fat and then fell into the deep sleep that always accompanies an ink-scar. It took four days for the hawk-scar to heal and it was the talk of the clan. Of the many, many designs I have done since, this was the very best. Copperman allowed me to make a small scar for Keer and Koor (lines and dots of black after the ancient designs Asha had brought from her world), each on an opposite wrist, and they were a relief to make after the detail of the hawk. Keer shook me with delight after his was done.

"Now you can tell us apart," he said.

Koor suddenly frowned. "But what about our plan to someday trade wives!"

The verdict

And so came the morning of Okla's punishment. The full body of the Bog-shepherd clan gathered in a big circle, all families from elders to children sat in grim silence. Lan huddled with the half dozen other Council members, whispering from one to another. Okla's father stood reluctantly before his son. He broke the silence, startling me with the strength of his voice.

"For the theft of another's kill…for shaming a guest before all the clan, Okla will have the chance of redemption by journey. He will follow the Lake-men, Copperman and Copperson, to their destination, guarding them with bow and life. He will humble himself in every way, gathering food and water, keeping night-watch, he will see the Lake-men back safely to their home in the mountains. He will make the dangerous journey back alone."

Here, Okla's father sighed and gazed at his son with a sadness that hurt the chest to look at. "If any harm befalls the Lake-men while under Okla's watch, he will not be welcome back into the Bog-shepherd's clan." His voice trembled slightly and he walked away from the circle. The council-elders looked exhausted from their days of deliberation.

Copperman muttered between clenched teeth. "I thought they were punishing *him*?"

Copperman slowly shook his head, barely able to contain his disgust. "The bluestone brings fortune, but somehow…somehow it always takes its fee….I should have made a life moving goats from grass to grass."

That next morning Okla stood waiting at the edge of the bog, rucksack against a knee, bow strung and ready, arrow quiver overfilled with twenty or so arrows. He had on far too many clothes and looked ready for a winter trek. I do not know what he thought our mountains were like in the late summer but I hoped we did not get the kind of weather he was expecting.

I did not like leaving. These new friends had in a few weeks become important to me and there was every reason to expect it would be years, if ever, that we would see them again. I tried not to think of the warriors from the forest as I held nose-to-nose with dozens of villagers. Moon whined and pulled at my bootlaces; she could tell it was time to go and dogs are curiously unafraid of travel.

Keer and Koor stood awkwardly back until we were almost off. Then they came up and without a word between us grabbed me hard and shook me back and forth. They had their father's eyes but their mother's warmth. Keer held out a necklace for me. It was the bear-teeth strung perfectly from a band of braided sinew. Koor gave Copperman his necklace, the same but with the bear's claws. I stood taller with this around my neck. Sola came out with an extra bundle of bread-cakes, small and hard, mixed with ground nuts for travel.

She held me so tightly I could barely breathe. "Your mother will be proud to see you."

I felt tears well up as she crushed me against her chest. Lan called out:
"Gods alive! Let them leave before the winter sets in." His eyes shone with the same laughter as when he first greeted us.

And so we were two different men than the stragglers that arrived to the Bog-shepherd clan: clean clothes, proud with jewelry, fattened up on goat's cheese and mutton, well armed and secreting the weight of a season's smelting of raw copper.

But then there was Okla. Copperman walked past him as if he were not there and he began to follow. We walked without looking back as is the proper way to leave friends. They called to us until we were out of sight, heading up the northern trail away from the dark forest and the rock-strewn hill towards green distant mountains and our precious lake and family. We walked up along a gently rising ridge with Okla following doggedly. Moon fell into step, glancing back at him from time to time and growling low as if to warn us that we were being followed. Her cheerful trot made me laugh, she seemed to be the leader of the journey. Copperman set a leg-burning pace and I wondered if it was from the desire to get home or to punish Okla for his very existence. I also wondered how the chunky Shepherd-boy would handle the climb when we got to the high country. By mid-day he was so far behind we had to stop or risk losing him altogether. I sensed it was a hard choice for Copperman. Okla finally came up to us, breathing heavily from the unfamiliar weight of his travel pack. His family must have sent him with half their belongings. He dropped the pack heavily and gulped down half his water-skin. He stood before Copperman.

"Do we have any…." Copperman charged to his feet and grabbed Okla by the scruff of the neck. "You are a tick on the tail of our dog's ass!"

Okla cringed and suddenly seemed the boy that he was. Fifteen years old, away from home without a friend in the world. I suddenly felt sorry for him…no I pitied him. It is a strange sensation to pity your enemy. It makes your hatred seem small and evil. I could no longer hate him, if I ever really did.

Copperman pushed his face up next to Okla's and spoke slowly, enunciating every word. "You *will* keep pace! Do not speak to me unless it is to warn of danger. Eat little and drink less. If we make it safely to the lake it will be a gift from the Gods."
Copperman released his grip and sat back down, dark eyes staring out at the grasslands below. Okla looked at me helplessly. He opened his mouth as if to speak, thought better of it, and busied himself with arranging his pack. Soon Copperman was up and walking.

The fires terrified me. Little specks of light that grew closer each night. By the third night we were up on a saddle between mountains and the fire shone behind us like a low flickering star.

"They follow and lead at the same time," Copperman said. "They know we can see them but come no closer. Sleep. We leave by high moon."

Okla groaned and sank deeper into his sleep-robe. I curled up around a warm dog and drifted into fitful dreams. I awoke to Copperman heaping wood onto the night coals. He edged the fire pit with a thick log that would slowly slide into the flames as they burned down.

"See?" He said to the night. "I can also lie with fire."

With the blaze dancing in the fire pit we marched off, blindly at first but the full moon rose and shone blue haze on our trail, giving us the powerful sight of distant snow tipped peaks. Walking at night with a full pack is dangerous and I knew we would not do it unless things were desperate. Copperman hissed at us if we snapped a twig or scattered a stone down a slope. This was no longer a journey, it was escape. The moon had shifted halfway across the sky when we saw our fire, far below, go suddenly black.

Copperman sighed deeply. "That was an all-night fire…they have put it out. They are closer than I thought. Must be several small groups. Come let us speak to them again."

We found an open space on the edge of a flat-topped hillock and set camp. It was as open and unprotected a place as you could find. I almost asked "why here?" but managed to hold my tongue. As we searched for good burning wood, Okla whispered to me. His tone was humbled and his voice held no contempt in it.

"I know who follows us. You are hunted by the Forest-people." It was the first he had spoken to me since our departure. I nodded. We were united by danger.

"He has a plan, just do as he says and we will get through." Okla nodded. Copperman called to us for kindling; he had a new fire already crackling from the embers of the one we left below. Fire is strange that way, I thought, living from place to place, bearing children, born new, raging at times, slowly dying out or killed by another, only to grow and form new life. Fire follows families, eats with them, listens to their stories. Fire, consuming and creating, hating snow and rain, breathing in and out with the wind. I have even seen fire eat a hillside clean of trees and that fire came as a great spark from the wet sky to touch a single tree. This was the work of the Gods and yet we could master it and become Gods ourselves by the striking of two rocks. I wondered if the Gods strike stars together to send us fire through the sky, and if so, why did it only come from a wet sky.

These strange wonderings usually came to me at the most troublesome times. Times when I should be thinking about immediate things like 'would the forest warriors kill us tonight?'

Okla and I ran down to the small fire and were instructed to stack it high until flames rose into the night. Our pit was on a rise facing out towards the trail we had walked. Easily visible to those below. Copperman seemed oddly relaxed. He set up his bedroll next to the fire and stretched out to sleep. I could not imagine sleep. Neither could Okla. We sat, bows out, arrows notched.

"Put them away," Copperman said. "These warriors will not be taken by a man and two boys with bows. We will wait for them and welcome them as guests." We did as we were told and spent the next hours till dawn scanning the shadows.

Ghosts

Sometimes a thing you think you see is not what you see. When this happens, the first reaction is to simply stare, frozen and confused. When the bush I was staring at in the early dawn began to move on its own, I simply looked at it. Then several other bushes shifted and began to follow and more shapes that were rocks and small trees rose behind them. I squinted and grew suddenly dizzy. Moon raised her hackles and I gripped her hard by the scruff of the neck. She seemed to grasp the danger and crouched low. I slowly pulled her into my lap and held her muzzle.

"Do not...move!" Copperman whispered. He was speaking to Okla who had dozed off under his hood. He woke to the order and froze as I had, looking out in confusion. In the clear quiet morning they made no sound. Moving slowly, like clouds drifting along the grassy hillside, the forest people emerged from all sides, two dozen at least, each hidden by small branches, streaked with ash and mud, tufts of long grass extending from their clothes, boots, hoods. It was as if they had grown from the earth to take form.

I glanced at Copperman who sat cross-legged near the dead fire-pit. He was shirtless in the cold morning, un-shivering and calm. He looked as unearthly as the forest warriors, as out of place, as impossible.

They crept in towards us as we watched; it was like a slow attack. They could see us watching them but for some reason they kept their pace, stopping from time to time. I think they were showing us how hard it would be to hide from them, proving their superiority. Or maybe it was the ink-scarred warrior sitting bare-chested, weapon unstrung, as calm as a snake sunning on a warm rock. Were they afraid? Confused?

One grew close enough for me to see the details of his face, eyes glowering from behind the dark smudges of his mud-painted face. He came within five paces and stood upright. The others stood as well and moved in quickly now, lining one behind the other in several rows. They were short and thin, the muscles in their arms showed a life of activity. They were all warriors, some adults like Copperman, some almost as young as I. Their hair, long and straight, was shaved on the sides and slicked back with mud-fat, their clothes merely folds of un-tanned deer-leather. Stranger still was their lack of beard; unlike the Bog-shepherd clan, they had only thin wisps of beard that made them all smooth-cheeked. It was unusual to see the features of a full-grown man without a beard. I could smell wild game, bear-grease, and the unmistakable sweat of fear.

Their weapons were long thin spears tipped with small, poorly formed flint-shards, many broken and reshaped into flat blades like scrapers. They carried little, only water-skins and small bags, slung around their shoulders and tied down to waist-belts with leather straps.

The lead warrior stood before me and held up his spear. He pointed it at me, the tip within arm's length. Okla, sitting near me, shifted and the man pointed his spear at him. Copperman was silent and I glanced at him. He smiled warmly and motioned with his arms for them to sit, treating them like a hungry guest at a friendly camp. They turned, spears pointed, and slowly circled us. One of the younger warriors bared his yellow teeth like a wolf and shoved his spear at Okla; a few others began to shift and balance their weapons, preparing to throw.

Copperman spoke suddenly, loud and commanding like a wedding ceremony or council announcement.

"I am Copperman and this is Copperson and Okla."

The effect was immediate and surprising. The warriors startled back like sheep from a dog's bark. They did not understand our tongue, this was obvious, but they responded to Copperman's voice with respect. He gently reached to his pack and slid out a thin dark roll of leather;

his trading blanket. He began to speak in the most simple trade tongue as he arranged small trinkets onto the blanket: beads, flint-points, the bread-crackers from Sola and several small copper blades.

"Come," he said. "Let us see what you have brought us."

There was a long pause as the warriors faced us, spears up, but Copperman had singled out one of them and continued to speak in trade-tongue, looking only at the one warrior who seemed to understand. He was round-cheeked like Asha and had some other blood in his ancestors; it was obvious from his eyes, green and gold flecked, while the others' were dark brown. His hair had a reddish tint like that of the Bog-shepherd clan and its crinkly texture fought out of the mud and grease. He was the only one with a beard, though it was short and I thought he must have trimmed it. He spoke to the others, telling them what Copperman had said; they, in turn, spoke to him.

"You.." he said. "You... have...steal the forest Gods."

Copperman thought long and hard before answering. "I gift forest Gods, gift Forest people."

This was spoken among the warriors. A younger warrior, carrying a club made from an oak limb, lunged at

Okla and smashed it down near his foot. He jumped up and the spears threatened till he sat back down, feet tucked in huddled terror.

Moon snarled and writhed and I had to grip her with all my strength. They were afraid of Moon, I could tell, and she could feel their fear. If she broke free they would surely kill her. Finally the one who spoke trade-tongue asked Copperman "What gift?"

Copperman raised and exposed his forearm to the warriors: the ink-scar, black lines against his cold, pale skin. The hawk holding the fish, spread out at them in unmistakable clarity. Watching them as if from their cave ceiling.

"Forest God gift," Copperman said.

Now it was their turn to see something that could not be real, their turn to freeze.
Copperman motioned with his hand to the trade-blanket, then pointed to the big warrior standing forward. "Leader? warrior?"

The man paused. The translator angled his head down and gestured to a slightly smaller man behind him. They spoke and something about the way the words had to bounce back between languages slowed the forest people in their fury. This was fascinating to them. I could imagine them saving it in their minds to tell later to their people over a night fire. Our strength was our ability to confuse and amaze.

The leader, a squat older warrior, had long, healed scars on his face, running from his right brow over an opaque eye along his cheek down to a mangled upper lip. His teeth were gone where the scar ended. He held his hand up and the warriors made way as he came forward. He said something in Forest-tongue and tapped his spear against Copperman's knee. Copperman nodded and looked at the flint spear-tip near his face, then reached down and picked up one of the fine spear-points from the trading blanket. He held it up to the tip and shook his head, then reached down to exchange it for an even better one. The others watched fascinated as Copperman rustled into his pack and retrieved his finest black glass flint point. Feathered razor sharp and gleaming in the morning light, it had the thinness of a leaf and perfect symmetry, narrowing down to a fluted stem for mounting. He smiled and nodded. "This is leader's point," he said.

The others murmured as this was translated. Copperman reached up to the spear and removed the end of it: a short shaft with a hollow cup at the base. This way the tips were easily changeable during the heat of a hunt. If one breaks you simply pull another from your pack and fix it into the front of the spear. A bit of pine tar keeps it secure. The benefit is that you can remove it to use as a knife. Copperman removed the spear tip, and, with his scraper, began to shave away the sinew bindings. The warriors looked at their leader, who seemed at a loss as to what to do about this. Deftly, Copperman wriggled loose the poor flint-point and fitted the gleaming spear point into the gap. Once secure, he wrapped it tightly with the fresh sticky deer-sinew. This done, he fitted the point back to the end of the blunt spear-shaft and aimed it back at himself. The forest leader grunted in admiration at his new weapon.

Copperman motioned for him to sit next to him, and, after a moment's hesitation, he set his spear against a rock and sat. Copperman pointed to himself, "Copperman," he said. The man nodded. Tapping his chest "Saar."

Copperman pointed to the scar on Saar's cheek. "War?" He turned his head sideways, "Wolverine." Copperman showed his shoulder claw-marks. "Bear." Saar nodded appreciatively, then murmured with respect at the bear-teeth necklace around Copperman's neck. "Brother," Copperman said. "Now we trade."

And so we sat, next to the old ones, the Forest-warriors while Copperman traded them bits and pieces for our lives. The trade-blanket became the focus of the group as we sat gathered around. The warriors started a rare day-fire and we huddled in the early fall chill of a clear morning. Once they sat down, Moon relaxed and even allowed the warriors to touch her fur. They traded us strips of dried meat and fresh marrowbones from an elk for beads and blades. Okla gave five arrows for a badger-skull, bleached white, and a leather-braided rope to wear it with. I had a round bead of flattened copper no bigger than a pinky-nail and this traded for a small, well-used roll of sheep-fur.

Slowly the fear receded. Copperman finished trading by closing up his trade-blanket and putting on his cloak. The others spoke in low tones. The translator seemed desperately tired from the back and forth between us. My legs ached from sitting so many hours but I did not dare stand and risk setting them off. The tension seemed to wear on the warriors and their friendly demeanor was turning back to aggression. One of them kept trying to trade for Moon and my refusal did not seem to convince him as each new item he offered came with more insistence.

As Copperman stood and began to arrange the packs for travel, the translator said to him: "You come with us, to forest."

Copperman turned his head down in a solid no. "We trade, now we go home."

The leader spoke. "We bring back God thief."

The translator tried to explain, struggling to come up with the words: "Not home unless God thief...broken."

138

Copperman turned to me, suddenly understanding. "They cannot go back without revenge, their people will not let them...."

He took his knife and cut the palm of his hand, then handed me the knife. "Do the same," he said.

I did. It is hard to cut yourself on purpose but I was used to the ink-scars and managed. Okla struggled and finally I did it for him with a short flick of my flint knife. Copperman went from warrior to warrior and touched blood to their spears; I did the same and Okla followed, until each warrior had been bloodied. They were confused into silence. Now Copperman spoke loudly again, as he had greeted them.

"Blood on weapons. Forest-people happy."

The leader understood. They could return with the enemies' blood on their spears. They could finally go home. They did not have to risk killing a friend of the Hawk-god or his children. With a shout of victory they raised their spears and began to move off. The one who wanted to trade for Moon looked at her and said something; he had tears running down his face as he moved with the others down the path they had come. They disappeared into the scrub of trail and suddenly we were alone again.

"Get moving!" Copperman said. "Now, before they think better of it."

We were moving on stiff legs up and out from the foothills. We had survived an attack from the Forest-people and came out with three small cuts and a few trinkets. Okla spoke to Copperman with great emotion. "I will never forget this day!" he said..."Never!"

Home Trail

The journey home is never as long as the journey away. I could feel the pull, as day after day, step following step, we carried our fortune towards our waiting families, the endless motion pulling the land under my feet, as if I were moving the earth beneath me, dragging the mountains towards me. Thoughts of mother and sister Tau and even longings for my annoying little brother… I would never again mind if he pulled my hair to wake me or snuck food from my plate. I would give him food until he grew red cheeked and healthy. I would work hard for my mother and protect Tau from the boys who teased her. Flowing warmth and soft memories moved me under trees and over rocks towards the lake of family waiting.

If Copperman felt any of this he did not show it. His days were protecting two boys from any and all harm. During one rest, as he went from the trail to find a restful place to sit and relieve himself (It seemed as if older men took great pains to find the right log to sit over for this daily process.) I took the opportunity to lie down for a few minutes' rest. I moved his rucksack to make space and startled at its weight. At least twice what Okla and I were packing. Had he really carried this burden so far? I wanted to offer to carry some but knew he would never allow it. His rule was: 'each man to his own goods.' If you cannot carry it, you do not need it. Okla, who (like I had suspected) suffered greatly on our steeper climbs, lay in a heap, like one fallen from a great height. In the handful of days, he was already leaner and better winded.

"This is a fine resting point," Copperman said, his voice jolting me from my musings. He looked at the angle of the sun, then down to a fold in the bare hills a few hundred paces below. A V-shaped forest of pale birch angled up the slope to a small cliff of crumbling boulders. "There is a spring at the tip of that little forest, where it meets the rocks. Take the water-skins and your bows...We need some fat meat and some roots for the high country."

He began circling stones for a fire-pit. The pit looked large; we would stay the afternoon and rest through the night. The marrowbones the Forest-people traded us were cleaned hollow and Moon gnawed at the bones desperately. She always found small food on the trail as we walked: a dead lemming, grass, bugs of any kind, but I did not like how thin she was.

Suddenly Okla was upright and stringing his bow. Thoughts of food have an invigorating effect on hungry boys and we stepped down from the new camp towards the trail like nimble goats, thrilled with the weightlessness of missing packs. We were a team now, sneaking along, leather slippers whispering against the short dry grass. The birch forest was larger than it appeared from above, fifty paces wide, narrowing to a point. We crept among the dark trails within the labyrinth of white trunks, their patches of stripped bark reflected a mere scattering of light. The breeze drifted towards us down the slope. Anything hiding here would not smell us coming. I could see Okla from time to time as a flickering shadow keeping pace. There was scat from several animals: roe deer, and red deer, rabbit and marmot; this was a place where low-land animals came up to and high-land animals came down to. However, the forest was empty, save for some dry-ish juniper roots, which I pocketed, and three small birds' eggs I saved for Moon. We met at the point of the forest and Okla shook his head. Dinner would be a disappointing snack of the last of our bread-crackers and cold water. We found the spring, a small pool among the rocks trickling into the earth, the top of a small river that fed the forest below. I sighed and the slight sound caused a clattering of small stones from above us. We raised our arrows and stepped back a few paces to see three surprised mountain goats on a ledge above us. We fired and they disappeared. I could not tell if we hit anything. Then we saw two of them galloping straight up the rock-face, with the speed other animals can run on flat ground. There was no trail for them, just seemingly smooth rock. But up they ran. Then the unmistakable sound of hooves kicking above us. It was no small feat to climb to the ledge. There, snow white, was a very fat young male with short curled horns.

It was a perfect hit. Okla's arrow extended from its neck, broken in half from the fall. I climbed up and pushed the creature off the edge and it landed next to the spring. I climbed down to rejoin Okla and we nearly danced with joy and hunger. I clapped him on the back of the head and he smiled.

"We can say it was yours...if you want," he said. I could tell he meant it.

"No. Take the water skins to Copperman and tell him you shot a mountain goat. Then we will see how hard he has to work to hide his joy."

Okla laughed and it was good to see him walk proudly back towards camp with the heavy water-skins. I began cleaning the goat and Okla returned soon with Moon barking by his side. I had to give her a piece of trimmed belly-fat to keep her from fouling her fur in the goat's offal. It was a struggle for us to carry the gutted animal up the slope and when we came near camp Copperman even dared to leave his laden pack unattended to come down and heft it up the trail. He was all work, ordering us around as we hung the goat, skinned it and flayed meat and fat from bone. The only thing that gave away his pleasure was the light in his eyes. We had food enough to get home on.

Okla spent the afternoon happily scraping fat from the inside of the white goat-fur. He tossed Moon each piece and she sat next to him, head down, tail twitching in anticipation, obediently awaiting each morsel.

Liver, heart, soft meats were the main course; goat was tough and, Copperman said, 'good for smoking.' We found some juniper to add to the low fire and smoke dried the meat, travel-style on flat rocks set atop hot coals, dusted with ground juniper-berries. We slept in turns, so one was always awake to turn the slow-cooking meat. Large leg-bones, scraped clean, would last days and their fat marrow would sustain a man on long walks. I saved several ribs for Moon to gnaw on over the journey. Moon ate the eggs and huge amounts of meat, then finally lay on her side, belly swollen, breathing contentedly.

I awoke to Copperman sitting, watching the mountains above us. "Do you recognize that peak?" he said, pointing to a mountain peaking out between the layers of rising earth. Suddenly I did. We had crossed it the first day. "You will need your mother's boots," he said, "and the bear leggings. It is a late return and the snows have begun."

"Have you ever come across them this late in the season?" I asked.
"Yes," he said. "Later than this. But the clouds decide the seasons and men have to follow. Let us not test their generosity." We gathered our things, swept clean our fire

pit, tossed the bones over the cliff-edge and carried heavier packs up along the trail. I focused on the distant peak. "Hello friend," I said. "Hold on a bit longer, we are on our way."

No rest in the high country

Mountains rose into other mountains, blocking our way. Copperman knew the paths and guided us along the tops of ridges, sometimes so sharp that a valley began on either foot. Here lived the winter Gods who watched the green pastures below with envy. They would throw boulders down in frustration, sending them like a game of hop-rocks; a day's walk in a matter of seconds. I looked down at the remnants of mountain tantrums and understood their frustration. It was cold and gray along the ridges; snow, old and rotten, would give way and sink us up to our waists. Okla, unused to the snow-traps was caught often and Copperman cursed, dragging him out again and again. We sought alternate trails up into high country, perilous walks beneath loose boulder-fields. He said whole clans had been wiped out on these journeys by rockslides.

Three days after the mountain goat and we were on the base of our own mountain, the back side of our lake. The wind whipped cloud curls from its peak and we sheltered in a cave to wait the proper time to cross. We slept the afternoon. Wood was scarce and we only used fire to cook the food, huddling around the small coals wearing every scrap of clothing. I was happy now for the Forest-warriors sheep-roll to sit on, Okla shared his new goat pelt with Copperman as a sitting-pad against the hard cold ground. We ate well on goat, roasting an entire back leg Okla had half smoked. In the cool of the mountain air it had stayed as fresh as if it were newly killed. Moon lay, warm in her thickening coat, and patiently chewed the leg-bone to pieces. I admired her as my family would: a beautiful long-limbed pup, growing day by day, strong teeth, fearless, proud. She would be ready to mate in the spring, if I could find a good solid male worthy of her.

I could feel my family waiting for us, Tau and Mother watching the mountain each day, hoping, worrying. The next day was the same, high wind buffeted the mountain side and we slept and ate. That night there was only the smallest of fires, broken shrubs that flared hot but left little coals. Okla and I were growing into friends, laughing and even teasing each other. We spoke into the night. He said that the late mountain-pass was dangerous together; alone it would be impossible. He would have to make the much longer journey across the low country if he was to get back home. This thought seemed to terrify him and he lay awake that night I'm sure pondering his fate.

The next morning well before light we woke and began our assent. The wind had settled to a cold breeze and we moved briskly to warm up the legs. A fog drifted down the mountain and in the dark we had to follow Copperman's shadow against the white fields of snow. Soon, the shadows gave way to dim morning and we were puffing plumes of breath, rising out of the fog and into blue brilliant light. The way showed clearly now, worn smooth by many journeys; old sheep-scat and boot-marks kept us on our track. It was comforting to walk in others' steps again. There had not been any travelers for some time as the boot-prints were crusted in by ice, faded by blowing snow.

We reached the saddle by midday, Okla squinting, covering his face with his hood, suffering from the white reflection of sun and snow. There was no rest in the high country; we were sweating and it was either walk or find your burial place. I lost track of time and began to daydream, mumbling about fish and porridge until Copperman snapped me to my senses with a cuff to the back of the head.

"This is no time to go soft!" he said. "Wake! Find your friend and get him moving."

Okla had fallen behind and was sitting on a rock, resting. I went to him and dragged him up, telling him about the bodies littering the saddle. He seemed to understand but walked far too slowly to get us off the mountain by dark. Copperman made him take the lead and ordered him forward, shouting insults to shift him.

The descent was a knee-shaking trail, winding downward like a snake slithering from a high branch. I envied Moon's four-legged ability to snake down with it. Okla and I took turns, falling and helping each other up and Copperman, grim-faced, followed, driving us like a shepherd. As we neared tree line he had us look back up. A snowstorm crawled across the peak, obliterating everything above us. A few hours difference...a slightly slower pace...it was too horrible to think of. We drove ourselves on, the storm, a deadly weight, beginning to press down. And then we saw it: the lake, small, but growing as we walked. Soon I could make out the lines of water behind afternoon boats, fishermen I knew, bringing back the catch. As evening folded we were stumbling along familiar trails. I carried Moon around my neck and her head draped in sleep across my shoulder. Okla staggered forward as if sleeping on his feet.

"Heads up, Boys. Walk tall!" Copperman said. Dogs barked and children shouted. My mother cried out and ran up the trail to meet us.

Home.

Comfort

Our little home! I savored every detail, sitting in my favorite spot on my old deerskin bed-pad next to the cheerful stone fireplace. Okla lay back, already asleep in the guest corner near the front entrance. He had gulped a mouthful of water and dry bread, then curled up on his goat-skin, using the sleep-robe as a blanket. Covered from head to toe, he snored lightly. Copperman sat in the low seat of the man of the house, shaped by hay into a chair, padded with furs and blanket. He surveyed his home with a keen eye. Mother cooked, arranged and talked all at the same time. She had a lot to tell and I listened intently with Tau (who had grown lovely and taller in one summer), sitting behind me, fussing with my hair. Little Brother and Moon lay at my feet. He held her around the neck and she tried helplessly to shake him off. He clung like a little tick and I could already tell he thought she was his. My promise to tolerate his pestering was already beginning to wane. But, he was here and Tau and Mother. All near me like a fine happy dream.

Mother spoke about the neighbors who would leave their bones about, drawing rats into the camp, and their children begging food and hanging about. About visiting traders who were unhappy to find Copperman gone and had to leave without his wares. There was gossip from the Council who made plans for allowing two new families to move in and half the clan wanted to allow it and the other did not. It seemed that this kind of thing happened every year, a new family would arrive and the homes like ours near the lake would fight their acceptance while the homes up the valley wanted them in. Mother said it is all 'fishing and goats.' The more families with goats or sheep meant shared labor among the shepherds. The fishermen who fended for themselves, saw the new families as competition for net space and more mouths to feed with each catch. Mother said this would always seem like a problem until a few seasons after the new families moved in. Then everyone would forget and the new ones were just part of the clan. Fishermen need sheep and shepherds need fish.

I smiled and Copperman looked over at me; he was smiling too.

" No one needs copper," he said, "but everybody wants it."

She looked at us and cried out. "My men are home!" She slapped her legs and chest to shake off the fear of the last weeks.

She sent Tau and brother to bed and we ate the porridge she boiled from clay bowls. There were chunks of honeycomb in the bowls and goat cream. It melted the last of the ice from my bones. Okla did not know what he was missing. With the kids asleep, Copperman took from his pack a leather roll. It clanked lightly as he rolled it out on the floor: Gleaming pale-red copper. Dozens of blades, the two axe-heads, and egg-sized chunks to hammer into any shape you could think up. She whispered.

"Gods and fire... it is ...it is more than you have ever brought back in a season...it is...."

Copperman slowly folded it back. "It is two seasons worth," he said. "Next summer we stay home."

She began to cry with relief and they blew out the oil-candle, covered the fire with the flat stone and crawled into bed. I dozed off on familiar blankets as they whispered and did what parents do when they think their kids are asleep.

On the lake

I was a stranger again in my own village. Others whispered and stared as I walked around the collection of daub-and-wattle huts. The splendor of the Bog-shepherd clan made me look with fresh eyes at our shacks and huts. The new families had collected birch logs and peeled them clean for the frames of their new homes. They were scrambling to finish them before the first snows crawled down from the mountains. The others, undecided about the newcomers, simply watched. I remembered the house-building party with shame. Why were the others not helping? I asked Copperman about it and he simply said, "If you want to help, help, if not shut up about it." I decided to try but the new family regarded me with suspicion and declined. Copperman shrugged when I told him about it.

"This is not our way. If the others want help, they will ask and then they owe us a favor in return. The Lake-people do not want to owe anyone anything. They are proud about it. If the snows come early others will help. They are not so proud as to let themselves freeze. The Bog-shepherds had to work together to survive. We have more than most villages here and this makes us selfish. This is why I want nothing to do with the Council. It is all about who lives where…as if they really have any power over such things."

He spat into the dirt. "If you want work, collect wood with your friend. He needs to contribute as much as he eats."

I found Okla sitting near the lake, watching the boats with fascination.

"I have heard of floating fisherman but I never thought I would travel far enough to see them," he said, as if all of his dreams had come true. He seemed mesmerized by the comings and goings of the boats, men standing on the thin bows, using long poles to move about. "Let us get some firewood," I said. "And then I will talk to Hanit, he owns a big boat. Maybe he will let us use it if we help him clean some fish." Okla's eyes lit up. "If so, then I will really have some stories to bring back home."

Hanit was an older man with the sun-weathered face and work-swollen hands of a lifetime fisherman. He was short, thin as a water-reed and could tell by the color of the sky the comings and goings of far away storms. He regarded Okla with a gap-toothed grin. "Never been on a boat," he said… "This is a sad life. This must be healed. On with you."

Okla slid into the boat and sat, thrilled to be floating in a hand's depth of water. Hanit threw back his head and laughed. "Crawl to the center before you swamp us." His boat was long and wide, ribbed with patches upon patches of birch-bark and black pine tar.

"It is the boat I learned on as a boy," he said proudly, "built by my father." Okla hunched down low and I joined him, balancing out the boat on the back seat. The seats were simple, flat boards, worn shiny by decades of sitting. Hanit never sat as far as I had seen him. He always stood in front, peering into the water like a fishing-crane. The boat creaked with our combined weight and Hanit reached down to toss out some of the ballast-stones lining the bottom. Soon we were well balanced and Hanit told Okla to keep still and center. Then we were off, sliding along the shallow reed bed and into the lake.

Okla never said a word, just whispered to the Gods as we glided out over deep water towards the small island a few hundred paces from the village. I enjoyed this view, our village nestled at the base of the steep valley, stream running down the hill and spreading out into our bay. The mountain trail we had traversed stood out now and I could not quite believe we made it all that way. The sun gleamed on the snowy peak, revealing nothing of its treachery. The wind carried snow in delicate curls over the ledge. On the lake, it was warm enough to relax in our thin wool skins.

Hanit stopped to retrieve a fish-trap in the shallows near the little rock island; it was marked only by a floating knob of wood, the size of my fist, and I wondered how he knew where they all were. (Hanit had at least twenty such traps around the lake.) Nobody would dare steal fish from another's trap but fishermen kept their places a secret nonetheless. It was a show of trust to pick one out in front of us but I doubted if Okla understood the complement.

He pulled up the trap from its cord, a funnel of reeds woven together with spikes like teeth across the entrance. Hanit explained to Okla how the fish swam in searching for the smell of his bait, in this case a pike-head, and then could not exit because of their shape. To prove his point he upturned the trap and out spilled five or six grayling, a delicate trout-like fish with a colorful fin on their back. These were my favorite fish, white and sweet; they smoked well and peeled from the bones easily.

"Have a few," he said and I chose a small one. He laughed and tossed two more to me. I plucked a reed from the shallows and wove it through their gills. Okla reached his hand into the water and let it glide as we poled back to the village. I knew what he was doing, as I had done it myself in his village; he was gathering memories carefully, feeling them, tucking them in his pocket to bring home. I hoped he would get there. I hoped Keer and Koor would welcome him. I would talk to Copperman about it. I would find a way to let them know that we were friends now.

"Have you ever tasted Grayling?" I asked him.

"No never."

"Well, tonight you will."

Hanit's apprentice

Hanit and Okla spent many days on his old boat and I understood after a time or two that they were happy together and I was suddenly the guest. I busied myself with other tasks and left them to their quiet water. Okla quickly learned the methods of fishing and could flay the bones from Grayling and prepare them for smoking as deftly as anyone of us. I could hear them speaking (as water carries sound far better than land) and thought that maybe someone so young sent from his village by the Council would have a heavy heart and I could think of no one as kindly and wise as Hanit to share a burden with. Mother was quietly concerned about the houseguest that had now been here two weeks. She watched the clouds with trepidation. Finally she broached the subject over dinner.

"Okla...what are your plans? What of your family?"

He stared silently into the fire for a while. Copperman, usually the leader on subjects as important as this, simply gnawed on a section of lamb rib, cracked it open and began to fish out the marrow with a twig he kept for this purpose. Tau, who was always the peacekeeper, offered Okla a clay cup of rose tea and shuddered. "Cant travel now...it is near freeze," she said, as if this settled the matter.

Mother waited.

Okla nodded. "It is time I left. I will walk the river in the morning to the low valley, then follow the grasslands until..."

Copperman inturrupted by flicked the rib-bone sizzling into the coals. "We would find your bones by the trailside scattered by wolves." He selected another rib and began to toast it on the fire.

We waited. He looked Okla in the eye. "Spring is sooner than you think. Hanit says you are a good helper and he has some heavy work ahead to prepare the boats for the freeze. Also there is ice fishing and a new smokehouse to build. You will be his apprentice this winter. There is more than enough space in his home now that his daughter has moved out. If you have a mind to learn, he has much to teach. Also, there will be time for the Bog-shepherds to worry about you. If you came home soon you would still carry their decision with you...but if they think you are a winter's dead then they will rejoice when you return. You will be a man reborn and your people will welcome you."

Okla sagged with relief. He smiled broadly. "Hanit will let me stay with him?"

"It will be better than feeling like a guest near our entrance. There you will be a worker in his own place. In the spring he can take you by boat to the far end of the lake to a trail that follows the mountains' low ridges. A week, maybe ten days, and you will be home in time to help with the lambing."

Okla turned his face away and tried to hide his tears.

"We will gather your things in the morning and help you settle in." Tau hugged Okla, beaming. "See how everything works out?"

Mother gave Okla an extra bowl of night porridge and three smoke-dried plums. She would have her home back now and Okla did not seem to mind if the porridge came from guilt. He would live the winter at least.

The Pack

The few dogs in our village were a straggly batch, mixed from different encounters with travelers dogs into a Lake breed that I was not too proud of. Moon stood out as a taller, sturdier creature and the others were openly jealous. She had come into her first heat and I kept her, whining with confusion, tethered in the house, as the males circled and howled in frustration near our door. Mother found her whining unbearable but Copperman backed my decision. She was still young and it would be safest to wait until she filled out before coupling her.

I had a plan and when I told Okla about it he liked the idea and said he would help. There was a smaller village across the water, a much smaller clan called Elkhorn who lived near the waterfall in the forest. They had been lake-people generations ago but for some reason they gave up their boats and moved into the forest. They were secretive people who rarely visited, living on the rich forest plateau a few hundred paces above the lake. I began to ask Copperman innocent questions about them, as he had traded them tools for the special maple grown in their area to build our roof frame. They were forest-keepers he said;

they would trim and prepare trees for years cutting some, letting others grow. They selected certain trees and built fires at their base until they fell; they would hammer in fire-hardened spikes of oak to split them. The end result was square planks of hard wood. They would trade these to the Lake-people in trade for fish and lamb. And we would pull them behind boats back to the village. Many older Lake-homes were framed with these boards. Copperman said they were tough negotiators who had everything they needed and, as such, drove a hard bargain. They were also a warring people who had a battle every generation or two to keep others from taking over their land.

"Why do you want to know so much about them?" he asked.

"No reason, just curious."

"It would not be because of their fine dogs, would it?"

I realized it was useless to deny it. "Is it true that they are bigger and faster than any of ours?"

"Smarter as well, not as rugged as the Bog-shepherd-pack, but more fit, like small wolves. Their coat is thicker."

I groaned with envy. "And you want to make a trip across the lake and face the Elkhorn just to have Moon mated?"

"Yes," I said

"And I suppose your friend is in on your scheming?"

"Yes."

"Good. We will need Hanit and his boat. Our clan has the worst pack I know of. Some new blood will do us good."

"Plus I can trade the puppies."

Mother sighed. "You are your father's son, that is for sure…but one of the pups belongs to your brother."

I cringed but knew a good deal when I saw one. "Okay, a pup for the pup and the rest in trade."

I liked having Okla around; he was the only boy my age in the village; the others were either a few years older (in which case they were already married or seeking a woman) or a few years younger. After the summer of wild risk and adventure I found their games and plans hopelessly boring. Okla had been through real danger and I trusted him to handle himself when we were out trekking. The journey home was so intense for both of us that living the simple life of Lake-people seemed desperately dull.

Copperman worked on his tools and spent time preparing the house for winter and trading for the dried fish and mutton we would need. There is no end of small jobs to do in the month before the first big freeze: Leather door-straps to repair, cracks in the walls to re-mud, new grass mats for the roof, bone-needles to shape; the list was neverending and I found it all tedious, and—I am ashamed to say—undignified for a young man my age. I suppose this is the lesson for all boys: when their blood boils for adventure they must learn patience to settle the chores of every day life.

Medicine

Tau had spent the summer learning the clay-trade. Each day she would walk the hour-long journey to a creek that had soft rich red clay. She would carve out a chunk and wrap it in wet moss, then heft it back to camp. She would mix it with some dry crushed pieces of broken pottery (this hardens clay, she said, and I made a mental note to bring a few pieces for our next copper kiln). I watched her delicate hands as they curled and smoothed thin jars, cups and bowls. A few other women in the village worked with her and a blind woman we all called Gentle-mother guided her as to thickness and shape. Gentle-mother was bent with age and it ached her to kneel, but her hands were smooth and strong from a lifetime of clay-work.

Tau and the others would build a clay fire once a week or so; they would fill their dried work with beach-sand and then cover it all with the smallest kindling, careful not to crush the pottery with anything heavy. A fire of kindling soon hardened the clay enough to pour hot coals from another fire over them until a pile of red coals could be heaped with small wood. The women stood, red cheeked with heat and determination, as their fire smoldered. This was an all-night affair, with women taking turns, resting and tending the fire. The clay would be so hot it would have to wait until the next day to finally uncover. Buried in the sand were pieces of the earth transformed, fifteen or twenty pieces from each woman. There were always a few that did not survive the fire; these would be broken up and shared out to use as grist for the next batch.

Tau's specialty was holding-jars, sturdy strait containers with matching lids, sealed with bees-wax; they could hold fruit and flour fresh for months. They looked plain but were very difficult to make properly. Gentle-mother seemed pleased with her progress. One of the young men from the new Goat-herd families came often to see her work, and, though she ignored him, I could tell that she liked the attention. I reported it to mother who told me to mind my own work and to stop pretending to be in charge. This was infuriating. She would ask me about gossip and then accuse me of meddling when I brought it to her. I began to envy Okla his bachelor life.

One morning, Copperman told me to get Okla and follow him; he had found a good use for Tau's jars. We followed him a short walk (after our journey every walk seemed short,) into the dense forest and away from the trail. We came to a broken maple, swarming with fat, lazy bees. He was clever to find a hive as they were sought out by every member of the Lake-people. Unlike fish or fruit, trees or sheep, the beehives were fair game to all. We built a smoky small fire and in the chill of the early morning, the bees seemed almost uninterested as we drizzled them with rising smoke. We used wide sheets of birch-bark to catch the slabs of honeycomb as Copperman pried them from the side of the tree. I had been involved with two other honey raids and then I got stung silly but this time I received only three or four small stings. Copperman faired as well with a few bees managing to penetrate his many layers of clothing. Okla, ducking in and out to grab new slabs of honeycomb, did not receive a single sting. We left a good section of the hive so the bees would have food for the winter. I wondered aloud why they worked so hard and saved so much more honey than they needed to survive. Copperman answered: "Do we not all do the same?"

It is true. I had seen dogs bury far more bones than they would ever remember to find.
It is in our nature I guess to store up treasure. Even the bees.

On the way back, a bee climbed from under the comb that Okla carried and stung him on the back of the hand. He yelped and I laughed; but, as we came nearer to home his hand swelled. By the time we made it to the house his arm had nearly doubled in size.

Mother saw the hand and went pale; she had seen this before. " Run!" she said. "Get the elders, quick!"

Okla sat down, still holding the honeycomb and looked at me strangely. "I cannot swallow," he wheezed. "I feel strange."

I turned and ran. The one who would know about such things was up moving sheep down from the high pastures. His wife was grinding einkorn-flour when I came up, babblling, gasping for breath.

"Bee sting! Arm swollen. Not...swallowing...one little sting and ..."
Wordlessly, she gathered a few things from her hut and followed as I ran ahead. There was a crowd near Okla, who they had moved outside. His shirt stretched around the swollen arm and he sucked in air with shallow wheezing breaths. His hand had pillowed out, fingers puffed up, face going gray. His eyes rolled around and he mumbled something to Copperman, who knelt beside him, talking soothingly. Copperman called for a knife and used it to slice away some of the tightening shirt from the arm.

The Medicine-wife came up, puffing as hard as Okla; she shouldered through the crowd and pushed Copperman aside. With a rip, she pulled Okla's shirt open and examined the swollen arm. "Cold water!" she yelled. Not from the lake, from the little ice stream." Several bystanders ran for water-bags. "Basil!" she shouted to three girls. "Armloads of it." Tau joined them, sprinting towards the trail. "Here, hold this!" she said to me, raising Okla's arm. "You, get a water-skin, the biggest you have!"

169

Soon, bags of ice-cold water came down from the creek, followed by armloads of basil. Someone handed her a large water-skin. She used a flint knife to slice it open at the top. "Fill it!" she yelled, and they filled the skin with the creek water. She slid Okla's arm into the cold water up to the shoulder. "Change that water when it warms up! We need that arm cold!"

I liked her way of taking control of the crowd. If she felt any panic, she did not show it. "Grind that basil!" she said. "Who has honey wine?"

Nobody answered. "If anyone has honey wine left and they keep it hidden, then may the Gods choke them with the next sip!"

Someone ran for their hut and returned with a dusty jar. "I was saving it for the first freeze."

She poured sips of the wine into Okla's mouth. He choked but she kept at it till he managed some of the wine down. The owner looked sadly at the amount spilling down Okla's front. "It is good wine..." Copperman silenced him with a glare.

The Medicine-wife was soon joined by her husband, who had seen the commotion from the hill. He nodded at her methods and began to grind up the basil leaves on a flour- stone. He pushed, stuffed and poked the pulp into Okla's mouth ordering him to chew and chew. Okla vomited and the man nodded and began the process again.

"If he can vomit he can breathe. That is a good sign."

We changed the water again and again, surprised at how much heat the arm produced. Okla dozed off and the Medicine-wife slapped him awake. Their methods were apparently to abuse the poison out of him. We all paced and fretted as time ticked by. By the third soak Okla's arm had stopped swelling and by the fifth or sixth it seemed slightly smaller. He complained of a headache and the Medicine-man nodded. "If he can complain he can breathe. That is a good sign".

Hanit came in with his boat and when he saw Okla hurt, he fell to his knees and wept as it were his own son. "Get him out of here!" Medicine-wife said. "This is a healing, not a burial." Mother guided Hanit away from the gruesome scene. I did not know what to do but I had to do something, so I ran with bags of water until they were lined up next to Okla and I was told to stop.

"How long has it been since the sting? "Medicine-wife asked.
"Noon sun," Copperman said. "Maybe earlier."

She looked at the angle of the sun and nodded. She pulled the arm from the water bag and smiled. It had shrunken considerably. "Good. Now put him on his belly on the low raft and hang his arm in the lake. Keep him eating the basil-paste. Tonight, wrap the arm in basil and keep it higher than the rest of him."

She and her husband wandered back to their hut and the others slowly retreated back to their lives. The man with the honey-wine reached for the jar, looked at Copperman and said, "Let the boy have the rest."

We carried Okla to the lake and rested him, face down, on the raft the children swim from. He dangled his arm and groaned loudly. He was breathing well again and his face had turned from blue to pale. Hanit sat next to him and coached him through the misery. That night, his arm was nearly back to normal size. I helped Hanit set him up on piles of furs, resting his arm on a short three-legged stool. Tau wrapped the arm with strips of cloth and more basil-paste.

"Thank you", he whispered. ..."The next time you go on a honey raid...I think I will just wait for you to come back with the honey."

"Or you can just stand back and shoot the bees, one by one, for us."

He smiled weakly. "One thing for sure...I never want to see another basil-leaf in my life."

The idea

Okla recovered quickly from the sting; he had nothing to show for it but a deep fear of anything buzzing. He would start at flies and gnats, jump from a falling twig and run flat out from anything resembling an actual bee. Within a week, the frost calmed him down. It would be a long winter before he had to worry about bees again. His work with Hanit took over his mind and he spent some time with Medicine-wife, learning her cures, in case it happened again. He offered her the ibex pelt but she declined and settled for a jar of honey.

I spent my days learning the art of preparing copper. Copperman gave me an almond-sized chunk to work with and I grew to love its infinite possibilities. I would hammer it smooth and flat then shape different medallions from it. He gave instructions and criticisms and I folded it into a lump and re-flattened it. With each working the piece became more malleable and shiny. I made earrings, beads, a tiny blade and a dozen other objects from the same piece of copper. I began to gather a collection of my own tools, different thickness of deer antler tips from the mountain elk, a deer with a very hard horn. Also a series of leather work-pads, each shaved to a different thickness. I would place these under the work and hammer out dimples and ridges in the jewelry. There were other tricks like grinding up quartz into a fine powder and rubbing it with fat into the rough side of a leather strap. With this, I could sharpen a blade shiny enough to shave off hair from my arm. The coming cold made my fingers numb and I understood that the season was soon over. For reasons he would not explain, Copperman would never allow metal work inside a house.

"It is hard on a marriage," he said, and I understood this was the only answer I would get. Reluctantly I set aside the copper (hidden in a hole in the back of our hut) and began to contemplate a long winter. The dog search, delayed by Okla's near death, was off for the winter. Hanit had spotted the first crust of ice and called a halt to the season. Boats, dragged up on rails of logs, lay upside down around the high watermark of the beach. Moon entered the mating phase and again I had to deny requests from the villagers who wanted to mate their dogs with her. It was getting difficult to explain without insulting them and I understood that the excuse of her being too young would only hold out so long.

The first big freeze came all at once with a storm dropping knee-deep snow. The wind howled for days and when it left, the lake had been transformed into a white field. Beneath the snow, thick ice formed. Within a week we could walk on it and Hanit began the ice-fishing season. Ice fishing is probably the most boring thing a human can do. It required sitting for hours, under a tent of skins, staring at a wide hole in the ice. It was a two-person job; one would dangle a shiny piece of stone on a string, dancing it up and down, and, the other held a spear with many tips pointing out like fingers on a hand. When a large pike came in to check the dancing stone, you only had one chance to plunge the spear into the water. It might be all day to get that one chance and if you missed it, that was your day. Some of the pike were as big as a man's leg and if you got a big one it could feed ten people.

There were usually a dozen tents on the ice during a windless day and we all took our turns, whether we wanted to or not. Okla and I usually went together, dragging the tent on a wooden platform out to the shallows near the little island. The tents were heavy but they slid easily on the curved planks. I thought about the planks and their ability to move heavy objects across the ice.

"Okla!"

"Hmmm?" he said, staring into the black hole in the water, spear arched and ready.

I danced the shiny stone and pondered how to explain my idea. "This is not too cold in here is it?" He looked at me and shrugged. Cold was not a polite topic during the winter.

"Well, I was thinking about this ice tent. If we had logs across the bottom and sleep robes, well, we could be in here for days if we had to."

He looked at me curiously. "What are you thinking?"
"We could make a bigger ice tent and good planks and it could go wherever we wanted to on the lake."

He nodded. "I guess so….but why would you want to?

"Moon goes into heat again in a few weeks. When she does, I want to take her to the Elkhorn-people and get her some real pups. They will be worth ten of our mutts."

Copperman always said that if you want to do something new to you, find someone who has done it before and you will save a hundred mistakes. Okla and I had never made anything of any size from wood, but I knew who to talk to: Hanit's brother, Dol, many years younger and different in almost every way. The main boat-builder of the Lake-people, there were few things he did not know about wood. Dol was as surly as Hanit was kind, his body, thick and muscled from his chosen trade, his brow furrowed from so many years of disapproval. Dol had never married, never shown any interest in family. He was the one least likely to bring a wedding gift or help out a neighbor in trouble. He never seemed to pray or show reverence during a ceremony. He would shuffle his feet and seem to count the time until he could leave any public event. Dol was known far and wide as the one who found a family half frozen and lost in the woods and charged them a trade fee for guiding them to the lake trail. "A service is a service," he had told the Council when they met to debate the incident.

"Why would we ask that old goat for help?" Okla asked. "I tried to help him push his boat up the bank and he shouted at me; 'keep your hands off my boat.'" I laughed. "He probably thought you wanted to charge him for the favor. For one, he is the best builder on the lake. He hates people so he is not likely to tell anyone what we are up to. And three, he will not offer to help us for free."

Okla looked at me as if I were touched. "Think about it." I said "When someone helps someone else they cannot stop telling everybody else about it. But if an adult charges boys for help they should offer for free, they will not want to tell a soul."

He pondered this. "You are clever. Very sharp."

"You get a puppy to take with you to the Bog-shepherd's clan if this works."

His eyes lit up. "So let us waste no time. Moon's next heat will last two…three days. We need to be ready to move at the first sign of it."

We finished our work-chores early the next morning and walked to the outskirts of the village. We found Dol at his bachelor's hut, a small shack that resembled a workman's shed with tools hanging or leaning from every available space, pungent with the smell of smoked fish and wood-smoke. Funnel-shaped fish traps hung from the ceiling along with bushels of reeds used for weaving and repairing the traps. There were coils of line with stone weights, ice-fishing spears and flash-lures, which hung down from the ceiling beams like spiders from their tail-strings. I noticed some of the flash lures had detailed carvings of the minnow's gills and fins.

"So this is what a big pike sees before the spear hits him," I said. Dol grunted. And continued his mending. We waited. He rudely ignored us but this is what I expected. Finally he set his work down. "Whatever my brother wants to borrow the answer is no."

"We have come for our own selfish needs," I said, and he looked up, finally giving us his full attention. "We want to build something that has never been built before and we need it to be a secret."

"What does your foolishness have to do with me?"

I held out my hand. I had flattened the copper beed into a small boat-medallion with a hole where the ore-locks would be. The hole would fit a necklace-string. He paused. This was far more than help with a project would warrant but I had hoped his greed would keep him from any modesty. I was right. He held the necklace-boat and murmured. "It is well made. From the loot your father gathered on his travels, I suppose". He sneered at it. "What do you think this buys from me other than my secrecy?"

"Your advice and the use of your tools and back workshop." I pointed to the back door leading to his shed. The workshop extended from the back of his shack as a long board shelter to work on boat parts during the long winter. Through the winter we could hear tapping and scraping from Dol's workshop. "Plus we will need some spare wood."

He spat into the dirt floor. "You ask a lot." Then he looked down at the medallion. "Some of my older tools, perhaps, and small wood, for a few days."

"For two weeks", I answered.

"Well," he sighed, rubbing the smooth copper-boat with his fingers. "I do not know." But I knew he would never let the shiny object go, once he had a hold of it.
He hemmed and hawed for nearly an hour, bargaining over the size of the project, the time and the wood we needed. Finally I said; "We have to start today if this will happen in time."

He shook his head. "If you do this thing and die, I would never…never…"

We waited as he shuddered. I was almost moved by his concern. "…Never be able to explain it to the Council. So after you go, I never saw what you made and have no idea about your plans. If you die on the lake it is not my fault. Agreed?"

"Agreed," we both said. Now he handed Okla a poorly made hand flint-axe. "Go get five …no six, straight, limbless birch as thick as your calf. And bark them before you bring them back. Also, two ash saplings the same thickness. Make them young or we cannot bend them."

We nearly ran from his shack out to the woods before he could change his mind.

The deal

Dol soon warmed to the new thing we were inventing. We began with a square frame of straight, green branches, big enough for both of us to lie down on. For the bottom sliders we used a method Dol called locking. It involved carving a notch halfway into a piece of wood and then the opposite into the other piece. The result was hammered into place with a round stone. The two pieces of wood held together well and we bound them with cord (we used so much cord that Okla and I spent half of our building-time braiding). The top of the platform was a wooden A-frame like a hut. We bound skins and leather to make the cover and had to use every scrap of cloth we could find to fill in the gaps. More braiding and sewing. This was all in addition to our house-chores of wood-gathering; and, as the locals were doing the same, we had to go further and further afield to find decent wood.

Mother and Copperman hardly noticed my absence as they had their own chores to do. But Little brother certainly did. He would follow me and I had to do something to keep him quiet so I gave him a job to do. He had to watch Moon, never let her out of his sight. I told him if he saw her behaving in a mating way he needed to tether her inside until I got home. He asked what he would get if he did this job and I almost said 'a good thumping if you fail' but instead I said, "Her first puppy."

This was all it took and Moon could not make a move without him on her trail. Okla had more trouble finding time to work, as Hanit needed him for ice fishing and many odds and ends. We padded the floor of the ice-home with pine boughs and hay, covered with Okla's mountain goat. I began saving food for the journey, storing up scraps like a squirrel.

The pups became an obsession. The local dogs a constant threat. If Moon came into heat it would only take one of the Lake-mutts a few minutes to ruin our plans. She hung with the pack whenever she could and this was the life of a dog. I could hardly keep her inside. And Dol would not tolerate her or any dog near his place. Dol had many fine ideas for our moving tent. He had us polish the bottom slide boards with sand and then grease them to slip on the ice. Also, we curved the ends up so they would not catch on the snowdrifts as we moved forward. We had a bundle of hay at the back end for Moon to curl up in and a slit in the front of the furs to enter and exit from. There was even a clay candle-cup hanging from a curved vine to give us a small light. A small heating fire would be nice but the risk of catching the hay made this impossible. If the tent burned we would be on the ice alone.

But what of Copperman? Would he approve of this venture? Certainly not. We had to find a way to be gone without trouble from him or the Council. I lay awake nights, working out plan after plan but he was too smart to fall for the ideas I had. Then the opportunity rose before us like a gift. A hunting party formed by the men to bring back deer for the winter smoke-racks. This happened every year and most of the men in the lake joined. Copperman offered to lead the hunt and picked ten other main hunters to join him. I was a proven traveler and Okla could shoot as well as any of the adults but there were bigger, stronger men who had been on long hunts and it was no surprise when Okla and I were not among the chosen. I had to pretend to be sour about it and sulked around half-heartedly the day they were preparing. Inside, I was dancing a wedding-dance. They would be gone five, six days at least.

Moon was not in her heat yet but by my calculations it was any day now. We would have to risk it. I told Okla to tell Hanit we were going for a short hunt of our own. Just a few days close by at the nearby ridge. There was a camp there and it was common for boys to try their skills on shorted hunts in the fall. The deer were scarce and it was understood that this was a test of bravery more than anything else. Hanit was confused as to why tested travelers like Okla and I would bother but he was generous and allowed Okla to go. My mother, tired of my fake sourness, was more than happy to have me and the dog out of her hair for a few days. She packed us extra food and a few blankets and a skin of water with blackend sour-berries in it. As easy as that, we were ready. The morning the men left at early dark, we followed them to the edge of the woods, bid them God's luck and then slipped down the trail to Dol's hut. The slide-tent awaited. And Moon whined with anticipation. She knew by my mood that we were off on an adventure.

Dol did not even wish us good travel, he merely grunted. "This stays quiet. When you pull that contraption from my shed our deal is complete."

"What deal?" I said and for the first time ever I saw him almost smile...almost.

Ice Walkers

We pushed the slide-tent out over the ice, surprised at how easily it moved over the hard-packed lake. It was a heavy thing. Dol had complained about our choice of season. Green wood was twice as heavy as cured wood and our build had nearly half its frame from green ash and oak limbs. I guess it weighed more than Okla, Moon and me put together. On the ice however, its weight moved effortlessly. We guided the little house out along the edge of the lake curving away from the village, and I only hoped whoever saw us would think we were desperate ice-fishermen going out to new grounds after pike. The morning fog obscured our view of the village and we moved quickly. Moon sat like a child on warm furs, facing outward at the entrance. She sniffed the air and I wondered what she smelled that we did not: perch buried in the snow, deer scat, dead rabbit carried across the lake on the light breeze. The world was a series of smells to Moon and this was the best way to travel. Carried forth on silent feet.

I knew from Copperman's stories that the Elkhorn lived beyond sight on the far side of the lake. We had all seen the ridge they lived on but boats were not permitted near their bay. They were known to shoot warning arrows at fishermen whose boats drifted too close. Hanit said it had happened to him twice, once on purpose when he sneaked over to drop a few fish-traps, and, once years later when his boat lost its pole. He had drifted into their area and as he put it, 'Arrows came down like rain.' He said they landed around him but none hit the boat. "If they wanted to they could have had me like an injured doe." But they listened as he called out about his pole. The arrows stopped and he was allowed to land, cut a quick pole and retreat. "Worst thing was I never saw em...not one. Just arrows flying and arrows stopping."

We moved quickly, covering enough ground that by full sun-up we were beyond sight of the village. The sun made the snow-covered ice white and mid-morning found us sweating in our undershirts, squinting with hats over our eyes. The lake's edges blurred in the shimmering heat and it felt like the world was a white, flat plane. The mountains seemed smaller and distant. Shadows circling the lake. It was perhaps more beautiful than any view I have seen before of since. Golden sun, white world, dark green surroundings. Two late snow geese looked up surprised as we came up to them. They did not spook until Moon shot out of the front of the tent. She was almost upon them when they raised the alarm, squawked and rose, wings high. She ran right into the middle of the two and slid slowly, legs running in place on the slippery ice, right past them, teeth snapping at nothing. They flew off, offended, as Moon slid and scrabbled, humiliated, back to the tent. We laughed as she climbed back to bury herself in the hay. Dogs feel shame to rival any human hunter and Moon did not show her face until the noon sun began its decent over the far peak.

The wind began to blow against us and with it, stinging snow. Our easy slide became a struggle; sometimes, during a heavy gust, we lost ground and had to hold on not to lose direction. As dusk came, we were in the dead middle of the lake, far from sight of any people, and the wind began to build. There were rocks sticking up from a sunken island and we wedged the sliders against them. Okla had the clever idea to dribble water against the outside of the sliders and they froze solid against the lake ice. We kicked snow against the edges until they were stuck solid. As darkness changed the white to a blue glow, we climbed into the tent, tired, happy, and exhilarated by our secret mission. I had saved a hot coal (wrapped tightly in green bark) from the night fire, but, as sometimes happens, it had gone cold. As blackness approached, I tried my hand at flint sparks. It is one thing to start fire outside on a fine day in full light but another to try it in dying light crouched in a tent.

We wanted flame for the candle lamp hanging from the ceiling, not for warmth but for comfort. Man wants to control sleep, not have the Gods force it on him. This was the value of fire. I could not control the sparks and this made me frustrated which made my efforts less effective. I had blisters on my fingers when I finally gave up sending sparks into the bundle of dead coal.

I sighed; "Well, we have blankets and dog enough to keep warm." "Yeah," Okla said. "We do not need it anyway." Suddenly, a red shine in the coal-bundle glowed. We breathed on it until it pulsed and smoke reached my nostrils. What a glorious smell is smoke when you want fire. It took time for the coal to finally produced a tiny flame. Okla held a dry straw to it and carried the little flame to the cloth string extending from the little hanging candle. The beeswax and fat lit high and we were in a little square of light on the middle of a dark lake.

Every new flame is a small victory. In the yellow glow we arranged our tent, Moon in the middle and Okla and I wrapped in layers of fur, warm already. We drank from our water-skin, ate dried bread-crackers and smoked sheep, pine nuts and finished it off with several dried whiting, eaten whole, crunching the bones happily. We picked our teeth contentedly with pieces of straw. Moon gnawed pieces from a frozen deer-leg. It was lavish to feed a dog so well but I wanted her to look healthy for the Elkhorn. I kept the leg frozen so she would not eat it in one go. She seemed to like the challenge, sometimes growling at the hardened meal.

Okla had not even asked me about the plans. It was a journey, it was dangerous, he was ready. Simple. This was a friend. I had no more copper to offer as a gift for the Elkhorn but I did have something almost as valuable. I showed Okla and he whistled as I unwrapped the ink-scar equipment from my pack.

"Do the Elkhorn have any ink-scars?"

"I do not know. Maybe they will want to start."

"If not," Okla said as he dozed under his sleep-robe. "We might be praying to the Gods for our bows."

We had left the bows behind so as not to seem threatening. A trade-visit should be empty-handed and open. But it was an unknown. Okla snored (as he always did) sleeping easily. I lay awake for hours listening to the growing wind. I blew out the candle and curled around warm Moon. "Soon you will meet proper dogs. Your only job is to come into heat soon." She pretended to sleep but I know she heard me.

The long lake

I dreamed I was a hawk, like the one in the cave, flying over the path we walked hunting greenstone. I saw Copperman and I from a great height; we were slow humans and I was a swift creature of the sky. I flowed along the air, pushing forward with my wings, covering the distance to the cave, over the forest up the rocky slopes and then down to the Shepherd bog. I saw everything in fine detail, the roof of the new house we helped build, the twitching tails of their dogs, a teacup left on a table. Everything sharp and clear. I turned my wings to follow our path back when something happened to the air. It grew thin. I began to fall. No matter how hard I flapped my wings I kept falling, the feeling in my stomach of uncontrollable downward motion. I jolted awake to the sound of strong wind. For a moment I was confused as to where I was, and, in the dark, the bed was not too different from mine at home. The feeling of motion was still with me. Then it struck me. We were moving.

"Okla, get up!" He jolted at the sound of my voice and we both scrambled to the front of the tent. In the pale of the half-moon, we could see the lake sliding by. The wind had somehow dislodged us from the rocks and now it was pushing us quickly. What direction we were moving I could not tell, or how far we had gone; all I knew is we had to stop. Moon whined at me and I wanted to whine back. I had no idea what to do. Okla put his foot out of the tent and tried to hold it to the ice but it had no effect. We both put feet out and they simply slid along with the tent. We spun and drifted like a log on a river, captives to the wind's directions. For how long I do not know. We talked about climbing out to try to hold the tent fast but neither of us wanted to risk slipping and being abandoned on the ice.

The tent shuddered to a stop on a shallow snowdrift. We lay, gasping, listening to the weather howl across the lake. At first light we ventured out from the tent. The storm had faded to a flat stillness. Morning fog. We sat and waited until it lifted. We found ourselves up against the snowy bank of a peninsula I had never seen. After some time, we realized that we were on the right side of the lake but far past the Elkhorn ridge. We had traveled farther sleeping than we had the whole day before. Ours was a long lake, stretching farther than I could see and if it were not for the cove catching us like a hand catches a leaf, we might have slid past it and out of sight forever. We ate a handful of cold food, drank the last of our water and began the trek along the lake's edge towards the Elkhorn. Moon was acting strange and I realized she was coming into heat. This put new energy into our feet and we drove forward into the morning.

"Be patient!" I said to her, as she curled into the furs. "There are mates waiting."

It took half the day to get there and once we were there, it was not clear how to proceed. The bay showed signs of use, a few ice-holes well frozen over and some blood from fish around the snow. There did not seem to be any main trail, just dozens of small trails entering the woods towards the looming ridge. This was a problem, as everybody knows not to approach a village unannounced from a side trail. We dragged the tent-house up into the snow-bank at the edge of the lake and secured it with a few large logs. Okla wanted to hide it in the brush but I wanted to keep things as open as possible. I set out a few beads on a string, dangling on a branch near the tent. A camping gift in case the others found it and wanted toll. Okla looked at the beads skeptically. I agreed it was weak toll but sometimes the gesture is enough. We put on our daypacks and bedrolls, picked the trail that looked a little bit more worn than the others and began.

Water is a problem in the winter and you get just as thirsty walking as you do in the summer, only streams are frozen over. Our water-skin was near empty and we shared sips with the last of it. Moon had no such trouble. She chewed snow happily and romped ahead and behind like the pup she still was. I looked at her with such pride. She had filled out strong and sleek. Her fur gleamed silver gray with patches of black around each eye and one dark streak across her forehead. Ears sharp and raised when hunting, folded back for a friendly hand. She had hardly fought with our snarling pack, choosing to run in a short circle and then nip savagely from behind. It had been a good strategy as the mutts soon learned that a face-to-face fight is nothing compared to a nip in the balls. How would she be around new dogs? Bigger and stronger dogs. I worried as I walked... (Copperman always said it was a weakness of mine.)

The trail was snowed over but tracks, faint and numerous, appeared as we neared the base of the bluff. Above us a cliff of stone, edged with trees, showed the plateau of the Elkhorn. Moon found an open stream and drank deeply, the water clear and shockingly cold. It hurt my head as I drank it too fast. I froze fingers, trying to fill the water-skin. I held it up to Okla and he reached for it when an arrow flew from the trees and pierced the skin. I dropped it with a start. We did not dare move. Moon looked at the dropped bag leaking and seemed uninterested. She licked at the water as it pooled around the icy ground. I could see no one in the trees.

"Hello!" I said in trade tongue. "I am here to trade. Friend. We are Lake-people. I am Copperson, son of Copperman of the Lake-people. This is Okla." I tried to remember Okla's father's name. "Okla son of the Bog-shepherd clan."

There was a long pause, then a voice came from somewhere among the trees. "Are you lost, Copperson of the Lake-people, or are you simply foolish?" The voice was a strange dialect but perfectly understandable Lake-language.

"We have come to trade," I said again but this time without the trade tongue. "We have traveled far to see the Elkhorn. We do not mean to trespass. We have left toll with our tent by the lake."

"We found your tent and your 'toll'," he said. He was closer now and we still could not see him. "Six beads would not pay for you to stop to piss in our forest."

I thought hard. "I have another gift to offer."

Long pause. "A fine arrow," I called out. "It was sent from the Gods and caught by my water skin. I will trade you this arrow for a short talk. That way we can return home, having at least seen the Elkhorn with our own eyes."

Okla looked at me and cringed, waiting for the next arrow to pierce our skin. There came a laugh not twenty paces away and a figure appeared through the trees. He was tall, a full head taller than I and very lean; he had a hawk's crooked nose, long black hair under a rabbit-skin short cap. His thin beard was reddish. He was Copperman's age, maybe older and appeared strong in his gait. I reached

195

down and carefully pulled the arrow from our empty water skin. The stone-point was a thin blue leaf from a flint I had not seen before, as finely made as any I had ever seen. I held the arrow out and the man came up and took it from me.

"So it is true. Copperman of the lake did buy a son from the high mountain folk. I can tell by your clever tongue that you are his boy. But you are not as smart as he. He would never leave trinkets for the Elkhorn. He would know enough to wait at the lake until we found him. If it were another than I that spotted you, the arrow would be sticking from your head. But I am soft-hearted."

He examined Okla like a buyer pondering a sheep. "Bog-shepherd clan? I have never met one. You are far from home."

"Yes, I came with Copperman and Copperson to live at the lake."

"Are you a servant?"

Okla bridled. "No, I was their guard."

"Hmmmmm." The man rubbed his beard. "A guard without a bow. A trader who comes baring only a handful of beads. And a dog." He knelt and Moon, ears back, greeted him like an old friend. He rubbed her fur thoughtfully.

"Well, at least I trust one of you. Come let us see if the others are as gentle with trespassers as I am." He turned and strode off at a quick pace. We followed.

The Elkhorn

The trail up the Elkhorn plateau followed the cliff-base through dense pine and short oak-shrub. The trail near a clan is usually worn clear of brush by locals hunting wood and gathering water. Wood of every kind is useful at one time or another. The trails near the lake are stripped bare by men making tools, children chasing each other and women gathering berries and digging roots. This trail, however, was unmarked. It could have been the path to a long abandoned village if it were not for the many boot-prints marking the snow. Our guide (I had failed to ask his name) marched nimbly up to a crevasse in the rock and slid into it. We followed and found ourselves on a trail up and into the very stone itself. It was a trail well mended along a crack in the massive stone, nearly strait up in places, with handholds of stone and wood. We half walked half climbed, sweating with the effort. Moon scrambled and I had to lift her to Okla and at times carry her over my shoulders.

The man disappeared ahead of us and in the half-light I wondered if this was a kind of trap he had set, then, decided that if he had wanted to kill us he could have easily done the job with his bow below. It was a strange feeling to be sheltered from the sky and wind in the split of a stone cliff with a dog on my back, but there was one direction to go and we had little choice but to climb. My arms were twitching and legs burning when we emerged into the sunlight again. We had climbed only halfway up the cliff but the trail curled smoothly in a half circle around the far side of the plateau. I set down my dog and stretched. Below, we could see the frozen lake and I understood why they had spotted the tent. I could even see the feint drag-marks through the snow, marking our arrival.

He was sitting on a rock waiting and when we approached he began walking again. The trail still climbed but we could walk comfortably again and soon we were up off of the cliff and level in thick rich forest. The trees were bigger here, sheltered from the wind. There were huge maple and fat strait beech and ash, with plenty of space between them. The snow was thinner here and I could see burnt stumps of smaller trees rising black through the snow. So it was true: the Elkhorn farmed their forest like wheat. They had cleared the brush and burned the smaller trees, leaving the large ones to grow even larger. Birds and squirrels called to each other, warning our arrival. The tall trees blocked the noon sun and dampened the outside world; there was no forest like it anywhere near the lake. We walked for a few hundred paces and suddenly the forest thinned to reveal a village of perhaps three dozen heavy log-huts, surrounding a long central structure, the longest building I had ever seen. Four or five times the length of a normal home, its sides made from tall trees flattened into square beams, it stretched out the length of a tall tree, and rose tall enough to stand and raise your arms in. It had a triangle roof with the top beam extending from the front with carvings etched into it. The roof of the long hut was decorated with elk skulls facing out like so many skeleton guards. The sight chilled my blood.

A group of men and women were working with hand-axes to de-bark a large maple log. They stopped as we approached and at least a dozen large dogs came towards us, barking and snarling. Our guide held out his hand at them and hissed. They stopped short of us and growled, hackles raised. They were truly fine dogs, every one of them. Dark and thick furred, they looked like well-fed wolves, longer snouts than Moon, wide shoulders and long ears, pricked up at us as if they were on the hunt. One of them moved forward at us and the man, surprised at its disobedience, hissed again and stepped towards it intently. It backed away and he looked at Moon. "She must be in heat for him to disobey me. Hold her in your arms." I scooped up Moon and draped her over my shoulders as others came up to wrangle their dogs. They looked at Okla and me with curious eyes but said nothing.

"I did not ask you your name," I said.

"Gahn," he said. "Follow me closely. Do not speak until you are asked to by the Council."

Gahn led us to the long house and the others gathered in behind us. He opened the door, a single slab of wood on thick leather hinges. He closed it behind him, leaving us at the entrance. I looked behind us at the Elkhorn men, women and children. They said nothing.

Okla whispered to me; "These used to be Lake-people?"

I looked at them: they were taller, thinner and darker than us; they had lighter colored eyes and the men all had reddish beards and dark hair. The women were rounder than ours and their high cheekbones and light eyes made them lovely to look at. Only there was no welcome in their eyes or their demeanor. Their dogs circled and whined, desperate to greet or fight or mate. The occasional hiss kept them back.

The door creaked open and Gahn leaned out. "Come," he said and we entered the long house. Inside the building was even more impressive. There were maybe twenty, sitting on furs and deerskins. The walls had windows made from deer-hide, scraped so thin they glowed from the light outside. There were smoky candles and fat lamps glowing from spaces on the walls. And skulls of every animal hanging from the roof beams. A large fire burned in a stone chimney against the back of the house and drying elk-ribs and haunches hung from twine above it, smoking in the rafters. The place was rich with the smells of cooking and rendering. Steam rose from a huge clay pot, bones bubbled in rich broth.

Despite my nerves I craved the hot food in that pot. We nodded to the others who set down their projects (sewing and carvings); they stood to greet us one by one with a long unbroken stare. Then we sat near the fire and an old woman spooned us our large bowls of the bone and meet stew. Boiling broth has so much fat and marrow that it takes a long time for it to cool enough to eat. Okla, who could eat coals from the fire, began slurring happily but I had to blow and sip from my spoon, desperate to get the food into me. I turned to give Moon a cracked deer-rib but Gahn shook his head and I realized it was taboo in one way or another. I sucked the burning marrow from the bone instead. The others watched us eat as if it were of great interest. It grew warm and I began to unbutton my tunic but again Gahn slightly shook his head and I stopped. Finished, I set down my bowl and waited. The healing stew heated my body and I began to sweat, realizing how cold we had been out on the ice. Gahn began to tell the Council about our arrival, that we had left a strange tent on their shore, tramped into their woods unannounced and drank from their stream.

One of the elders spoke with a gravely voice. "Are they hunting?"

"No weapons, only small flint knives." "Did they leave toll with their shelter?"

Gahn held out the string of beads. Another grunted and pointed to a clay pot near one of the skin windows. He opened it, revealing a pile of beads from bone and various colors of clay. He broke the thin string and let my paltry offerings drop one by one in to the pot. He closed the lid.

"They say they are here on a trade journey?"

An older man with a huge gray beard and nearly bald-headed turned his head to one side with suspicion. "In the snow season? How did they plan to bring back the wood? How did they come around the lake so far without bows or proper equipment?

Why did they not wait for us to come down to them. And this toll? Is it an insult?"

Gahn laughed. "I think they are boys on a testing journey. This one is Copperson, son of Copperman of the Lake-people."

The old one raised his eyes to me. "I see none of him in you. This is clearly a lie." I could feel the anger rising in my blood. "I am my father's son." I pulled back my sleeve revealing my ink-scars.

Another elder nodded. "I remember Copperman of the Lake-people had similar ink-scars." They sat silent for a long while.

"Yes then, Copperson. You have something to trade? Bring it from your pack."

I opened my pack and brought out my tools, trying to keep my hands from shaking. I unwrapped the skin, revealing the ink-bowl, ground bluestone and ashes and spare needles. "I make ink-scars. Copperman, the only master of ink-scars, has trained me. I have brought a gift to the Elkhorn."

I pulled a patch of calf-leather from the bag. Onto it I had made an elk sideways, horns out and head up. One of the elders took the patch of cloth and studied it near the flame of a candle. He handed it around. "It is a fine painting. But ...I do not understand what you want to bring us."

I thought of how to explain. "I can make ink-scars...of paintings. I have made a hawk on Copperman's forearm. If there is one in the Council or a warrior perhaps who has fought bravely and earned an ink-scar...I can put an elk like this one on his arm."

They were silent for a while. Then the elder said, "Give us time."

Gahn led us out to wait in the cold (which seemed even colder with the glaring Elkhorn clan which had grown, dogs and children circling. After a time, we were brought back in and the old one spoke.

"We have one who wants the elk ink-scar on his arm." It was Gahn himself, sitting, sleeve rolled back. "He will take over as the head of the clan when I am no longer able." I looked and realized that they were father and son.

"But first...what do you intend to trade for this?"

I breathed deeply..."I want to breed my dog, Moon, with your finest male dog."

There was a short silence. Then a burst of laughter. Loud belly laughs. They howled and slapped their thighs. I looked at Okla and he shrugged. They laughed long and hard as if this were the most humorous thing ever spoken. "Dogs?"

Gahn gasped for breath. "This is about Dogs? Ha Ha hooo...." He wiped tears of laughter from his eyes. "Oh the Lake-people are strange folk indeed. You can have as many as you want. They make so many we have to cast their pups to keep them from eating everything. Dogs? Are you playing a trick on us?"

I did not know what to say. "The Elkhorn will give you your dogs. There will more to be rid of next spring. I expected meat, wood,...but dogs?" They began to laugh again. "So set up your tools and let us begin."

I gathered candles and we sat by the bright fire. I did not know whether to be relieved or insulted but I looked at Moon curled at my feet. I promised her a mate and I had found it.

Okla ate three bowls of stew before I finished Gahn's ink-scar. It looked far better than the outline on the leather. Its horns were slightly larger than I had planned but this seemed to please him even more. He never flinched as I tapped the needle into his flesh. When we were done and I wiped it with goose-fat it looked clear and proud. The bleeding was light and he went out to show it to the crowd. I could hear murmurs of approval.

We slept, warm in the longhouse, and awoke to a different group than the one that greeted us. They gathered around, asking questions and offering us snacks and drinks. Even the dogs were friendlier, sniffing apologetically up at Moon, who I kept on my shoulders for the time being. By dinner we met with the whole clan, crowded into the longhouse to hear stories about our journey. I described our copper-hunt and visit to the Bog-shepherd like Copperman had, leaving out certain details, Okla froze as I came to the story of the hunt but relaxed as I skipped over his stolen kill altogether. I said that he came to see the lake world and would return in the spring. Gahn told them about our search for dogs and they laughed again at our foolishness.

The longhouse was a public place, unlike a home; it served as a kind of open kitchen, work place for sewing and carving, a Council room and (judging by the reverence given to the elk-horns within and surrounding) a sacred place of prayer. It had many rules and Gahn guided us kindly with a nod or turn of the head. In the longhouse you could not have a dog, unless there was a special situation like our visit. You could not sit on the warm skin-seat on the left side of the fireplace nearest the far exit. This was a place for the dead to visit from time to time. Near it, on a small stool, was a candle-lamp and a bowl of seeds and nuts and a clay cup of water. A guest should not shed his clothing in the longhouse, a clever rule that no doubt prevented long visits. Sleeping there with full cloak was uncomfortably warm and they burned extra wood to talk with us long into the night.

Anyone who broke village rules could be banned from the longhouse for a season. Gahn said few had ever broken the rules twice as the longhouse was such a comfort. He confided that he had, as a boy, eaten the food set out for the dead and had been banished for a winter moon. He would listen near the windows on cold nights to others talking and laughing around the warm fire. The memory still haunted him.

I asked Gahn about the Elkhorn reputation for war and he nodded. "There have been many who have tried to take this plateau from us. They have all failed. Twice I have fought to protect the plateau. They come from above and we shoot them off the trail. They come from below and we roll rocks down upon them. They will never take this land from us...never!"

"Who are they?"

"The Grass-clan came to pretend to be friends and then in the night they killed many and left. They came back the next year with fifty warriors in number. Perhaps three escaped our arrows. The River-clan traded us ten maple square logs and lost them in the current. They wanted us to replace them or return our trade and anger brought out insults against our Gods. They came with a hundred and the fighting lasted in the forest for three days. Their bodies litter the woods. We remain...but enough of war talk, let us eat"

Okla asked the others about their incredible skill with a bow and earned many proud smiles from the complement. "Tomorrow we will show you."

The next morning we gathered our things and prepared to depart. I let Moon run around with the dogs and she had chosen a mate, a fine dark-furred male, young like her but broad and healthy. She chased him in circles and they wrestled and rolled in greater frenzy until they both suddenly seemed to know what to do. The mating was quick and the others watched with mild interest. Moon turned and snarled at the male, who jumped back confused, she sniffed her tail and snapped at the next male who approached, but then in seconds they were all running around and play-fighting as if nothing had happened. I wondered why humans and dogs were so different about mating, why it was a hidden thing with so many rules with us, and a minute of play for a dog. The male followed Moon around and snapped at the other males who tried to mate her. Maybe it was more complex than I thought for dogs too.

Okla had challenged a boy our age to a bow competition and the others gathered to watch. This was of far more interest to them than dogs in heat. They set a walnut into a knothole in a rotting log. From the many arrow-holes in the log I could tell this was a common target. The soft wood would prevent the arrows from breaking. The boy handed Okla his bow and an arrow. Again, the Elkhorn had a different method of fletching their arrows than the Lake- people or the Bog-shepherd. The bow was a fine curved piece of ash with bone carved at each end to hold the string. The string had a nest of wool, built up to the size of an apple near each end. I had never seen this before. Elkhorn arrows had two single feathers opposing each other, tied with a single hard strand of sinew at each end. The target arrow had a blunt flint tip. No point in ruining a fine flint arrowhead during practice.

Okla drew the bow, surprised at its weight, and I could see his muscles strain as he struggled to draw it fully back. "Do not shoot through the log, Okla!" Gahn said and the others chuckled. He was strong, I have to admit, and managed to steady his hand. The arrow released with a soft hiss and struck the log, a hand's length from the walnut. Okla smiled but the others seemed saddened by his failure. "It is not easy to use a strange bow," Gahn said, as the boy took his bow back and fitted an arrow. He shot quickly and the arrow landed just shy of the walnut, nearly dislodging it. Okla and I gasped at the amazing shot. The boy shrugged and Gahn took his bow.

"I cannot watch this display, it is hard on my digestion." Gahn drew the bow back and launched the arrow, shattering the walnut. The others murmured in approval. "How?" Okla demanded. "How does this happen? I am considered the best shot of my age in the Bog-shepherd clan and I might take twenty tries to hit a walnut from fifty paces."

Gahn shook his head. "Look now and see what is possible. There down the trail, do you see the white birch that becomes two in the middle? It is head high where it splits." I looked at the tree a hundred paces, maybe more. "Yes, we see it."

"There is a strip of bark hanging down from it." I could see the bark-strip the size of my hand, folded down, dark against the white bark. Gahn drew the bow and arched his back slightly, the string buzzed and we watched the arrow waiver and disappear for a second, before it sank half its length into the fresh birch, pinning the piece of bark against the trunk of the tree. Now the others cheered with us.

Gahn nodded at the boy and handed him back the bow. "With a war-bow we can hit a man in a boat from three hundred paces." I did not doubt him. "What about the string? Why do you have the wool pieces?"

"They dampen the sound. Otherwise a deer can spook before the arrow hits."

I had experienced this on failed hunts before.

"I want to learn," Okla said.
"Live with us for a while and we will teach you." This was not a real offer but I could see Okla tempted by it. His bow skills were his pride and this test had humbled him.

"I can tell you how to get closer," Gahn said. "Do not try to hit the thing you are shooting at. Try to hit something a few paces exactly behind the thing. This way you have a line for the arrow to follow." Okla thought hard for a few seconds then nodded.

"Can I try again?"

The others had wandered off to their tasks but a few still watched. Okla drew the bow focused, then shot. His arrow hit very close to the others and he smiled. "This is a great gift," he said. "Thank you."

Many followed us along the trail to the edge of the cliff. They offered us small food for the journey and welcome for our return. One of the girls our age came up to me with a string of dried blueberries; she put it around my neck and reached in with her nose. I had no choice but to rub noses with her. "I will miss you," she said, then turned and walked from me without waiting for a reply. This was fortunate, as I had no reply. She was a soft-cheeked girl with fine eyes and I vaguely remember her staring at me during the visit, but why would she miss me? I felt my face blush red. We nodded to the others and made our way to the cliff's edge.

Gahn and his father whistled to the dogs and chose several to follow us down. They had no trouble scrambling down the cliff but again I had to carry Moon who could not find her footing on the down slope. We reached the forest floor and Gahn and his father began to walk carefully. We followed and spread out among the trails, meeting up and branching off. This was their way and I understood that anyone that managed to arrive unnoticed by their guards would have a hard time finding the cliff entrance.

At the lake's edge we found our sleep-tent as we had left it. Gahn and his father grabbed our shoulders like long friends. Gahn's father said: "Copperson of the Lake and Okla of the Bog-shepherds, you are welcome traders. Always come and wait in the open for us to find you." Gahn bared his sleeve to show his healing ink-scar. "Come with your father next time and bring your tools. There is much to trade between us. But now," he pointed to the dogs, "choose three and do not be shy, they were well earned."

I looked at the six dogs sitting obediently; Moon's mate was not among them. They were the pride of any village, wealth beyond measure for a boy. I nearly made the mistake of declining the generous offer, but remembered Copperman's rule with gifts. Unless it is their daughter, always accept an offered gift. Especially if it is from a member of the Council; to refuse is a great insult.

I chose three fine dogs, two males and a female. Gahn nodded with appreciation at my choices and then tied each with a strong cord and handed me the leads. They turned and walked away wordlessly; in minutes they were gone from sight. We slid the tent from its place and out onto the ice. The dogs whined nervously and pulled at their tethers. We had no choice but to send them into the tent.

It was a fine, windless day with full sun, and as we drew away from the shore and out onto the white ice we could see the Elkhorn gathered on the cliff-face, watching. We raised our arms and they did the same. Suddenly an arrow came from the air and landed twenty paces away. Then came laughter, a form appeared, it was the boy who had beaten Okla in the target-game. Okla grabbed the arrow and called out, "Next time!" The boy laughed again and then faded back into the woods.

Crows

The unaccountable site of two boys pushing four dogs across the ice drove the day-crows mad with curiosity. They appeared and vanished in a squawk of black wings; they circled and dropped, swooshing past the tent entrance. Each time they did, four heads would appear at the entrance, barking up at them. It was comical at first but soon became intolerable. Circle, swoosh, bark, circle; swoosh, bark; circle, swoosh, bark. Okla and I tried to wave them away but waving away crows is as foolish as kicking water up a hill.

"If I only had my bow," Okla said, and I laughed long and hard at the image of him losing his arrows in the sky. Every boy has tried to hit a flying bird and every boy has searched for the arrow never to be found after the venture. The dogs were beginning to snarl at each other and the crows (who I think are the only other creature with a sense of humor) came in closer to enjoy their mayhem. I finally opened the tent and shouted the dogs out onto the ice. There was little snow when we reached the lake's center at mid-day. The dogs scrambled out and dropped to their bellies onto the ice, useless legs spread flat in the four directions of the world. Moon, to her credit, ran in place for a several heartbeats, claws clicking and clacking against the wet nothing the blue ice offered her. She dropped as well and tried helplessly to regain her footing. Okla and I stared down at four helpless dogs and the crows laughed. It took some doing to rejoin the dogs and the tent but soon we were off again with the barking and circling.

Animals have no trouble with repetition. Perhaps this is why they live a simple life. A sparrow is content to fly from wormgrass to her nest a dozzen times a day for a spring season. Fish will sip mosquitoes every day all day and never suffer for it. But humans cannot handle anything of the sort. The mind grows weary after the same story two nights in a row, or the same meat, meal after meal. Even fine weather wears on the spirit if it comes relentlessly. Soon you will pray for a good thunderstorm to break the boredom. I could simply not listen to the crows anymore.

We stopped and snacked on some of the Elkhorn meat. The dogs lost interest in the crows and vice versa as we opened the packets of food. I thought about this a bit. The crows were always around after our fishing trips, fighting over the freezing fish guts we left behind. Crows are smart and they only bothered to come when we were finished with a catch. These crows must think we were wandering home from a fishing trip and were waiting for us to clean our catch. I looked at our food.

"Do not even think about it!" Okla said, mouth half full of delicious pemmican (meat and fat ground with barley into a salty paste). I looked at the leather parcel with three fistfuls of the food in it. I had an idea. With the dogs and Okla sniffing out and whining I took half a handful and spread it out on the ice. Then I sprinkled water over it and watched the thin layer freeze solid. The food was trapped in a skim of ice. I left a few crumbs on the top so they would get a taste and work to get the rest.

We left and the crows, half a dozen now, descended. We listened to them fight over the pemmican and moved on. Soon their squawking echoed far behind us then disappeared. How many hours they worked to get the food I can only imagine.

As darkness approached, the wind began again and we slept in turns, the dogs outside, curled in a circle of themselves like a giant bear made up of four sections, on a single blanket. This was good for them, I thought, to become a pack before they meet the Lake-dogs. The next day we awoke to the crows standing patiently near the tent. I left them some frozen food in the ice and they did not even wait for us to move on before pecking away at the offering. They left us in peace for the remainder of our journey.

By midday we could see the outline of our bay and near dark, as the other fishermen pulled their tents to the shore, we simply followed them in, taking care to be far enough behind to avoid any questions. It was unnecessary: the ice fishing takes such concentration over such a long time that those emerging would not notice if their mountain had vanished. Thoughts of a warm fire are the only thing on their mind.

Okla and I halted at the edge of the Lake village. "What do we do now?" he asked. I had no answer. I had been so focused on the trip I had no plan for our return.

"We could say we found the dogs on our hunting trip." I turned my head to the side.

"The elders would smell that lie from a hundred paces."

"We can say they were a gift…" he shrugged. "My last lie to the Council was the worst day of my life," he said. "I cannot do it again."

I remembered the meeting with a shudder. "Okay, we go in and tell all and face our luck, good or bad."

We tethered the dogs and parked the tent near the boats. As it was darkening by then, our arrival went mostly unnoticed; a few looked from their doorways and stared long and hard at the two boys with three new huge dogs but they did not come out to check. It would be the talk of the village by morning.

Mother smiled and laughed at our return but froze in her celebration when she saw the dogs. "What is this?" She looked at me and saw right through the whole trip. I had been up to something, and, whatever it was, she did not like it. Okla excused himself to leave for Hanit's house and I said, "Hold on, you have not chosen one yet." His eyes lit up. He did not even pause in his choosing. There was one large male with black ears that he had paid particular attention to on the journey. He punched me in the chest, nodded to Mother and led his new dog away.

I came in, relieved that the men were not back from their hunt yet. Little Brother jumped up and ran to Moon, who licked his face. Then he came over to the Elkhorn dogs who eyed him skeptically. "Get used to it," I said to them and pointed down. The dogs lay obediently near the fire as Little Brother fawned over them. Now he had three dogs and life was complete. I sipped pine-needle tea, watching him as Mother heaped the fire and heated lamb-stew in the blackened clay pot. How good to be a child I thought: your biggest problem deciding which dog to play with first. I had complications to unravel. Mother served the stew and waited until I had finished two bowls before asking me about the trip that resulted in extra dogs. She was not pleased. Her displeasure grew with the telling of the story and her eyes glowered by the time it was done.

"So it was not enough to risk your first summer out among the dangers of the wild. No, you had to seek out death on the ice and among war-clans. Do you wish for your little brother to be the only son in the house? Do you long for your sister to give your funeral song? And you return not with game or even a single fish, but with two extra mouths to feed."

"I can trade them for anything we need," I said.

"In the summer, maybe, but the winter is not time to trade. There are few who ever feel they have extra when they examine their larder in the winter."

Of course she was right. Trade usually comes when the spring gives the promise of new food and those who have extra dare to part with it. I slept with one failure-dream after another; falling through the ice, getting shot by arrows falling from the sky, lost in the woods, all mingling together. Some sleeps leave you needing rest and I awoke exhausted. Mother and Little Brother and the dogs were out and I could hear voices near the main trail. Copperman and the men were back, dragging frozen limbs from half a dozen deer. I watched them from the door and dressed quickly. By the time I joined the others there was a crowd around the hunters, helping them hoist their burdens down to the center of the village. A pole hung between Y-limbs, displayed the meat and it had been a successful journey. Everyone would eat well for weeks from it.

Copperman, who had apparently already heard tell of my journey, did not look at me when I approached. This was not unusual, as he was exhausted from the journey and always took some time settling in before he would speak. This seemed different though. He avoided eye contact altogether. The dogs were noticed by all and the way the others looked at Okla and me, they knew we were responsible for their surprise appearance.

There was business to deal with first. The head of the Council, Enoch, announced the kills and praised the hunters in turn for their work. Copperman had taken one himself and assisted in another. There were fourteen deer and one elk, all but five of them were huge examples. The meat, sectioned in haunches and rack of ribs, were hung and then chopped into smaller sections and handed out by family, until the hunters were taken care of. The rest was handed out until every family had meat. The fishermen complained and the shepherds complained and even the hunters' families complained over the size of their portion. I remember Copperman talking to Mother about the inevitability of this fight.

"The only way it is fair," he said, "is when everyone is angry. We are wolves and if left to it, we would kill each other for an extra deer-rib. The Council has the worst job, they make the wolves share."

We carried our portion to the house and Copperman ate well, drank tea and looked at the day-fire for an hour in complete silence. He finally stirred and Mother and I prepared for his verdict, but then he mumbled something and fell silent again. Neighbors came by, one by one, to visit but Copperman waved them away. He was not to be rushed. Finally, when I thought I could take the silence no more, he sighed. It was as out of place as if he had howled and Mother and I looked at each other.

"Let me see if this is true," he said, his voice gravelly from the long cold journey.

"You and Okla went to the Elkhorn on a sliding tent to get better dogs...and it worked?"

I nodded. He laughed. "Good. This will make the best dinner-story ever." He crawled over to his bed-furs and lay back. In seconds he was asleep.

Council Blues

That night Copperman awoke hungry. Over Einekorn mutten stew I told him everything. He laughed at my dealings with Dol and there was appreciation in his laugh. He sat upright, excited by the tent sliding in the wind and our awakening to strange shores, and he shook his head when we were walking into the Elkhorn trails unannounced.

"It is a wonder you are alive," he said. He remembered the Elkhorn longhouse and Gahn and his father. He was happy to hear that he would soon become the leader. I even told him about the girl who said she would miss me. He whistled. "They are lovely creatures, the Elkhorn women." Mother scowled. "Why did you not take one of them then?" she said and looked hard at him for an answer.

"Because I did not want a roe-deer, I wanted a lynx!" She smiled, then turned her gaze to me and the smile faded... "There are plenty of fine girls here...no need for searching out wives in other places."

"Who said anything about wives?" I said.

223

I continued the story and when I got to the part about the crows, Copperman's eyes beamed. "You are clever, you must share that one with the others. A hundred years from now no one will know about the trip to the Elkhorn but everybody will know about the trick with the crows." Our door opened and Okla called in. "The Council wants to see us."

"So here we have it," Copperman said. "The old men want to pass judgment." His eyes went dark.

We followed Okla to the center of the village. Copperman looked at the fire of whole logs. It lit the excited faces of those gathered. He sighed for the second time that day. "They plan to spend some time on this."

There were four large logs lying flat, ends touching. They provided seats enough for most of us. The fire in the center gave off yellow heat and I thought to sit near it but realized that I would not be an observer in this meeting. The others came in as word spread. The Council waited, already seated in their long robes and rabbit-fur hats. The seven older men gazed out at the murmuring clan. They held their hand up for silence.

"Okla of the Bog-shepherd clan, Copperson, son of Copperman and Dol boat-builder, stand forward." We moved into the center of the square near the fire. Dol shuffled, mumbling and sour. Okla looked strangely calm and I understood the difference between standing for an action and lying about it. I decided to remain as calm as he was regardless of the outcome. We waited. Finally our clan-leader, who was simply known of as Old Father, rose and shook his staff, knocking it three times on a stone.

"Tales of travel and trade have come to us. The Elkhorn are our reluctant partners in summer trades. You have put this partnership at risk with an unapproved visit. What do you say to this?"

I found my voice. "We have done this. Okla and I but Dol had no part of our trade, only the building of the sliding tent. Okla and I are the leaders of the journey and will stand together for it."

The Council spoke low to each other. The others sucked in breath with a sharp hiss. Old Father lowered his hood. He seemed to struggle with how to proceed with accused who admit everything, and argue nothing. Finally he said; "Why...why did you risk such a thing?"

"I wanted to breed my bitch Moon with big, strong, smart males. The Elkhorn have fine dogs like the ones we have traded for. Okla came as a companion and has received a big male dog in payment."

The others spoke among themselves but I could hear their questions in my head. 'Our dogs are not good enough for Copperman's family?'

"Tell us then," Old father ordered. "And do not leave anything out."

I began the story again and realized something about the telling of a good tale. It grows better each time. This is not to say that it changes; the facts are there, and in the same order, but the details are the teller's to bring forth or subdue. I understood the need for humility and emphasized our failures and underplayed our successes as luck. The crowd clung to each word and I knew they were memorizing it. Copperman was right about the crows, a point of fascination to the ice-fishermen among the group who had enmity with the birds. To make friends with the crow: This was big; the dogs were small game in comparison.

The finish of the Elkhorn story came with smiles and nods. Old father tapped his stick on the rock for attention. We fell silent while the Council sat and whispered among themselves. It was a long stand, suffering the gaze of the whole clan, watching the fire slowly eat itself. Finally Old father spoke.

"There are rules!" He said, hitting each word slowly and clearly. "They have been broken! Dol, your part is without fault though you fail to surprise us with your greed. A copper necklace for some green wood and advice? This is lean trading, but within the rules. As for the two boys. Your trade was based on greed greater than Dol's. You wanted to improve your own wealth… but your foolishness had in its heart a flaw. By bringing male dogs with you, your plan to breed and sell the pups will result in fresh pups for every female in the clan, for you *will* allow anyone who wishes to breed their bitches with your Elkhorn males. By spring we will have a strong pack and your own pups will be worth no more than theirs."

The crowd nodded at the wisdom. The Council rose and one by on kicked chunks of snow on the hissing fire, signifying the end of deliberations. The crowd relieved at the quick resolution, disbanded, leaving me and Okla standing alone near the bubbling coals.
Okla waited until they were gone before snorting and spitting into the fire pit.

"Remember when I said you were clever?…I take it back."

We sat together as young men do when their plans for wealth suddenly dissolve. Dark and gloomy. Sour at the world. Our only comfort was sharing the failure together. Then I thought of Moon, belly growing puppies, and the bed place for me at home.

"Could have been worse," I said. Okla nodded. "Tell me about it…The good thing is we do not have to watch the bloody hounds every minute to keep them from the bitches."

"True." We sat near the steaming coals in silence, our faces burning and our asses growing cold.

Deep down into the Cloud Lands

It begins with a wide sheet of thin cloth, carefully wrapped around the waist, then the shirt of slightly thicker wool, head and arms draped with it. The leggings (mine of rogue bear and Copperman's of mountain goat) tied by straps to a waist belt. Then grass-stuffed moccasins. A middle cloak of softened, scraped doe-hide. The main cloak is heavy elk, stiff and cumbersome. A leather fire-kit belt wraps it all tight. Then three hats, the lining (made by Sister's nimble fingers) of padded lamb wool, pulled to fluff and five times too big, then rubbed in hot water and lye soap over a round rock until it has shrunk to fit my head. This followed by the over-hat of rabbit, tied snug down with scraps over the mouth and nose, topped off with the cloak hood separate but of the same elk.

And finally we could leave the house. Dead winter has within it a few pockets of weather so cold that it hurts the teeth and subdues the heartbeat. My mittens of raw lambskin, stuffed with dry grass, were as stiff as wood as we walked the trail away from the lake village. Bows were slung over shoulders with an extra long leather thong to accommodate the bulk of our clothing. How we would ever remove our mittens and pull an arrow with frozen fingers I could not imagine but we needed to get food this day and there would be nothing that grows that the winter rabbits, hungry deer and hoarding squirrels had not already taken. The wooded trail along the lake was barren white, but also foggy dark, giving the naked trees the look of the standing dead. Gray and empty. This is how the winter felt and I wondered how, as children, we laugh and play in the winter gloom. Wondered why now it sunk my emotions so completely. Adulthood comes with more burden than freedom. I plodded in this dark mood behind Copperman, who finally turned and peered at me through the eye slits of cloth. The eyes behind the hood glowed.

"Gods and fire! Are you hunting or carrying a corpse to burial? Wake up and hunt or go home and shiver."

I nodded and focused on the game that was not there. We covered good distance that day, and further the next, and the next. Other hunters were following other trails with similar results and we would see them dragging their feet on the evening return. There were sheep in the village, huddled in their pens, but only just enough to ensure the lambing season next spring. The smoked fish were thinning out and the houses that had them were saving small chunks for the children. To make matters worse, Moon was fat with puppies and breathing heavily. She needed better food than bone scraps to milk them when they came out. The Elkhorn dogs were thinning but healthy, as Hanit had stored away a small mountain of frozen fish heads and tossed a few to them each morning. They would have been good hunting dogs under normal circumstances but this cold was the kind to kill a dog who runs after game. Their paws get frozen so thick with clumps of snow and ice that they seem to be wearing snow slippers. They had to stay with the family and I envied their job, sleeping with little brother to keep him warm.

An entire moon cycle of deep cold: this had not happened in my lifetime. The others spoke of the last time it happened. Cold bodies need more food, especially fat meat, and by the end of the freeze many of the Lake-people had died from the cold. One whole family found frozen in their homes. This is when the Council decided on the share hunts each fall. Families with food left could not bear the guilt of their neighbors twenty paces away, dead from lack of food and firewood. They died before asking. That is the Lake people.

On our fifth hunt, Copperman fell feverous and we returned early. His upper side tooth pained him and I had to remove it. There was a method and if it was not done, the blackening tooth could kill a man as cleanly as an arrow. The medicine woman came to assist, I tapped the tooth out with a small antler tip (teeth are stronger than one would think) and it smelled rotten and infected. She packed the hole tight with dried mint powder. I had never lost an adult tooth before and from the groans of pain I could tell it hurt like fire. Copperman drank the last of his honey wine and huddled by the fire with all three dogs around him.

I dressed the next morning and fetched Okla. We worked the same trails but with more intensity, Okla managed to kill a red squirrel and I could tell he had been practicing the Elkhorn technique. We stared at the squirrel, both wondering without saying, how many it would take to feed a village. He thanked it and stuffed it into his back pouch. On the route home, the darkness came slowly and I dreaded the thin soup of bones, boiled twice already and half a squirrel. Would they even have any flavor or fat left in them by the time Moon got them? There were two fish left and I knew we would be down to Hanit's fish heads soon. My mouth began to water. Things were bad when Hanit's rotten fish head soup sounded good. A snarling echoed ahead and I thought, 'how did the dogs get out? And what were they up to in the deep cold at dusk?'

The sound came from near the lake's edge and Okla and I jogged there. At first I could not tell what I was looking at, four dogs fighting a bear; but it was bigger than a bear; it was a kind of deer or short-horned elk but many times as big; it had two perfect round horns coming from the side of its massive head. Its body, thick as a maple log, dark brown and rippled with muscles. It stuck out its fat red tongue and bellowed, a sound that rattled the very air around us. Steam poured from its nostrils and rose from the heat of its exertions. Its assailants were not dogs at all but full-furred black wolves, six of them, circling and snapping. They had managed to tire the beast out in a chase—that was clear. It was breathing heavily and wild-eyed with rage. The giant creature out on the ice was trapped by the slickness of its hooves. It stood on a circle of snow, ten paces across and whenever it tried to leave the patch, its hooves skidded and slipped until it regained the snow. The wolves were also tired from the chase and they panted and took turns moving in on the hindquarters of the creature. They were in a stalemate. The wolves who would easily take down an elk in the same situation could not seem to make any headway on a full-sized male like this creature. I thought of Copperman's descriptions of animals where he came from as a child but this was a new animal to me and I was as stumped as the wolves.

"We should get the others," I said, but Okla shook his head, "It is getting dark soon, and this thing will escape the wolves if he gets to the shore again. They will not take him at night here. Look, they are thin and almost done in anyway."

He was right, the wolves were suffering as we were from the long deep cold and in normal times would never waste energy on unwinnable battles. As we watched, a wolf jumped in to grab the creature's nose and with a shake, the beast flipped him up and pierced him with a hook of his horn. The wolf fell and crawled only a few paces before dying. The others howled and renewed their attack but the frenzy was short lived. One of the wolves sat back and whined.

"Let us hunt," Okla said, and I, feeling like a coward, moved on trembling legs behind him. The wolves looked up confused as we slid out on the ice towards them. Wolves are an enemy of people only when they compete for a kill but these wolves were too intent on the big beast to bother about our presence. The beast ignored us completely and stamped at the dead wolf as the others darted in, and spun it around time after time. When we were close enough for a shot, Okla drew back and I understood our situation.

"Wait!" I cried. "What happens when the wolves smell blood…see it fall? Then we will have their full attention." He pondered this. "Gods alive, we have a mountain of food in front of us and we cannot take it!"

I thought of Mother and Sister and Brother and Copperman with a bad tooth and Moon, puppy heavy. I chose the lead wolf and fired an arrow. It hit cleanly and the others attacked the dying wolf, as hunters are prone to do when confused. Okla fired again and another wolf hit, snarling, caused the pack to attack each other and the air around them. The three remaining circled twice and then turned tail and fled. The beast turned to face us and Okla and I both fired. We both missed. I shot high and Okla's arrow bounced harmlessly from the brow of the huge head.

It bellowed a charge and came forward. It is a tricky thing to notch an arrow when you are terrified and it took several awkward seconds for us to manage; meanwhile the monster made ten paces, head down, giant horns swinging. Its legs slipped on the shiny ice and it went down. As it tried to rise, we both fired at its exposed neck. It rose, arrows pinned on either side of its neck; it faced us and bellowed. Blood began to spill from its neck in a growing pool on the ice. It slipped and fell again, tried to rise and then lay back, grunting heavily. The thick ice groaned under its weight. We watched, new arrows ready, but it was over. The beast bled out and finally slumped its great head with a crash. The wolves howled from their position a few hundred paces away.

Darkness was coming heavier now and the outline of the sky showed against black mountain shadows. There came distant shouts and specks of light from the trail. Dogs barked furiously. They had heard the commotion at the village, and as the others approached, the wolves flicked into the woods, leaving half their pack behind dead on the ice. Our people arrived, twenty at least, Hanit and some shepherds and a dozen main hunters, the pack of dogs among them. They cheered the creature on the ice and the three wolves. The dogs licked blood and there were claps on the back and congratulations.

My head began to spin and I stumbled away to vomit water and nothing into the gray snow. I have never liked killing and the vision of those bodies on the ice forever haunted my dreams.

As the others dragged the creature and the wolves over the snow towards the village I asked Hanit what beast it was. "That, my boy, is a great Urus. I have only seen two in my youth but none as big as this. The cold must have brought him from some far away land."

I asked about Copperman. "He is healing as expected from the empty tooth, and your Moon is doing well..she now nurses six fine pups!

I wrapped my face with the cloth and stinging tears froze into it. Six fine pups…and meat to feed her with.

Fat

We were main hunters now, Okla and I, without ever suffering ceremony. The Council announced it while we stood, shoulder deep in freezing gore, cleaning and skinning, handing our impossible slabs of meat and lard to the hungry villagers. One creature would feed us all for several weeks. There was not wood or temperature to have a big fire feast; it was the work of twenty just to flay and separate the meat family to family. Okla and I each received a hastily skinned wolf-pelt, rolled and already frozen solid, and choice portions of the giant Urus: Fat, slab of liver, heart, haunch and ribs. The dogs received offal and the promise of marrow-bones to come. The Urus' head, weighing as much as a boy, was taken to Hanit for skinning and preparing. The Council announced it would be placed on a post at the Council-fire at the very first thaw of spring. Everyone envied Hanit and Okla, who would no doubt feast for days on the meat around that giant head.

As for the wolf-meat, it was forbidden for humans to eat, but we all knew better. If the cold held, we could always take from the frozen haunches and say it was for the dogs. I did not care about the new status of main-hunter, it had no place in my heart. I only wanted to finish the job while there held strength in my fingers. It was dark two hours when I stumbled into the hut. Mother, who had already been down to the kill and back several times to fetch meat, had a bubbling stew in the biggest clay pot, and a wonderful, wasteful fire dancing bright flames up into the stone chimney. Sister jumped up and hugged me, then sat me down and began washing my caked arms with lye soap in a bucket of luke warm water. The water burned my numb fingers and as she washed I stared delighted at Moon, who curled around a mewling blob of wiggling pups. Their eyes were closed and each fought to attach to a swollen nipple. They would fall off and she would nuzzle them back into position. There were five and I looked at Mother, who smiled.

"There has been a lot of warm water and soap this day."

"Hanit said six!"

"She lost one...it was gone long before it was born. This is the way it works with pups, always at least one...good thing too, five will eat enough as it is."

Moon whined at me and I moved over next to her, patting her gently. Little Brother sat scowling, ignoring me in the corner. I laughed. "Why is there an angry badger hiding in the corner?"

Little Brother slapped his hand against the floor. "I want to hold him." he blubbed," his chubby face already red from crying. He pointed to a black and gray spotted puppy suckling at a nipple at the back. "Moon bit me." He held up a finger with a reddish fingernail. I laughed even harder and said, "Well we are all just hoping for your recovery from such a savage wound." He began to cry again. Copperman rolled in his sickbed and waived a hand at the boy to stop. I went to Little Brother and picked him up, walked back to the fur-seat and wrapped him warm in my arms. "Soooo, you have already picked your pup, huh?"

Mother sighed. "He picked it as it came yelping from the womb. We had to banish him to the corner to keep him from grabbing its legs and pulling it out. Moon barely nipped him but he has been in a state over it all day."

"Be patient Little Brother," I said, bouncing him until he smiled. "It will be a long winter. You will have an important job, you will be… the house main puppy trainer."

"Will I?"

"Yes, I have just decided. It will be your job to follow their every move and tell me what they do and how they behave."

"Main puppy trainer?..." He lisped. His fat face opened with a huge gap-toothed grin.

Copperman rose as Mother began to ladle stew from the pot into wide bowls. His right cheek was still swollen but not as much as before; his color seemed better as well.

"Did you bring any liver from the beast?"

Mother showed the slab of liver on the cold plate in the window. His eyes gleamed. He nodded to me. "Slice it small," he mumbled. Copperman hummed with contentment as Sister sliced the soft liver into cubes and spooned it raw into his hot stew.

The deep cold lasted two more days and then slid down off the lake, pushed south by a warm, descending mist. The forest seemed to take a deep breath and village life resumed. Copperman ('healed by that liver,' he said) took to his feet and began his ceaseless quest for things to do. I think the house full of puppies drove him to outside tasks. I spent my time with Sister and Little Brother, mending tools and playing games and sleeping late and early. Soon they opened their eyes and Little Brother, with strict instructions on gentile handling, could finally hold them. He only had two hands and it was comical to see him desperately juggling them all at once. Moon seemed happy for the rest from the relentless feeding.

Days went by softly, and soon the light began to stay longer in the sky, the nights began to lose their bite. Thick snows came and went, providing rabbit-hunts and the occasional deer. Okla and I attended a few hunts and were fine with driving the deer along a valley, our main-hunter status secure. The other boys asked Okla to teach them the Elkhorn method and we all enjoyed the target-games, even Little Brother with his tiny bow managed to hit a target or two. He would be a good hunter some day, I could see it in him.

Sister spent more and more time around a certain man, who was trying to build up the courage to ask Copperman permission for marriage. I felt sorry for him. Copperman is hard enough to handle as his son. For an outsider to approach him...I could not imagine. Sister would watch at the door each morning until her suitor Gy would come up with an excuse to stop by. We all knew what they were thinking: a spring wedding and everybody in the village had small bets on Copperman's answer to his eventual question. I lived with the man and I would not hazard a guess. He, who missed nothing, never gave the slightest hint that he even noticed the courtship circling his own home.

I was out with a few other boys after the day's chores of clearing snow from the draining trench (a job we all hated but had to do before the thaw) when Gy approached me. We had spoken a few times but never alone and I found him to be a quiet, likeable fellow; short black hair, he was typical of the visiting shepherds, darker skin and thin features. They had come, family by family, over the years and built their homes farther and farther up the hill until there seemed three equal camps in the Lake valley; shepherds up top, hunters in the middle and fishermen lining the shore. There were even special ways of speaking that separated us, descriptions of plants and weather, typical to each profession. The shepherds were silent by nature, slow to fight and uncomplaining; the hunters were as hunters are everywhere, louder, braver, and always competing. The fishermen were the base of the tree, solid and prosperous.

'Sheep and deer come and go,' they would say, 'fish are like the rain and snow, wait around a few days and they will come to you.' The fishermen (Hanit excluded) had a smug manner, like they knew the others were fools for choosing other professions, like they all shared a private joke. When a fisherman died they would take his body out, wrapped in thin cloth, to burial bay and sink him with rock weights into the depths. No fisherman other than family ever attended the ceremony. Anyone fishing too close to burial bay would have terrible luck the next season. The Council, made up of two members of each discipline, oversaw the sharing of fish, mutton and game. Disputes were settled by the Old Father and no one dared ever challenge them.

So Gy wanted to talk to me and I could guess what it was about. He shifted from foot to foot, cleared his throat and said: "Your um..father, has he mentioned anything about how he feels about...me or your sister um...and...?"

I could not watch his misery any longer. "Ask him!"

"Yes," he said... "He is a great man though and I..."

"He is the most frightening man I know," I said. "Think of it as a bravery-test, like a night out alone in the woods or an ice-swim from one hole to the other."

He nodded but I could tell he had no idea what I ment.

"If you ask him and he says yes, I will give you an ink-scar on your ankle for bravery."

He laughed but then frowned. "She is better than I am," he said.

"She is fine but she wants you to ask for her... I can tell. Show her you are not afraid and she will want you even more."

He squared his shoulders and suddenly walked with purpose towards Copperman, who stood with his hand axe contemplating an alm log that needed limbing.

Gy stood and, as is the custom, fell on both knees and spoke his request to Copperman's feet. The marriage request must be made in public and the others stopped their work and looked at the spectacle. Copperman gave the request the long pause required and then reached down to pull Gy up by the shoulders. He turned his head to the side and smiled. The deal was done. There would be negotiations later, of course, and then the Council would make the final decision but this was merely formality. Gy and Sister would me married in the spring. The Council would be thrilled with the connection between groups, as it prevented conflict. And I had an ink-scar to plan: Perhaps a shepherd's curved-staff or the eight lines of good health. Gy came back to me, bright-eyed and breathless.

"Soon we will be brothers," he said. He shook me by the arms and laughed. Soon we will be brothers."

Gods and children

Mother changed when she heard the news of the wedding. She first cried, then hugged Sister, and, then they spent hours and hours talking about the ceremony. They whispered a lot as well and it seemed that men were unwelcome in those conversations. Little Brother, usually clinging to mother's shirt like a squirrel to its branch, suddenly found himself plopped on the ground.

She had plenty of time before the ice came off the lake, more time than anyone would need to plan a wedding ceremony, but Copperman said it was a mother's way.

I began spending more and more time at Hanit's hut with Okla, mending fish-traps and carving bone-hooks, braiding line and generally organizing for the first spring fishing trips. Hanit was a wealth of information about almost anything, and, unlike most men, he actually liked talking. Okla and I would sit on the oak plank-bench, dogs and pups at our feet, and sip pine-needle tea. Hanit would offer the dogs a few fish-heads to wrestle over and then we would each choose a small task to fiddle with. Okla or I would start up where we had left off the day before. We were onto the Gods these days and Hanit knew every ceremony and why they mattered.

"The thing about the Gods," he said, "is that they see us as little children. You do not protect your children from small dangers or they will never learn. You test your children so they can gain pride from success. If the Gods shot every arrow true for us, we would soon complain that the game is too heavy to carry home. If the game walked into the village and asked to be shot, we would soon complain that they needed flaying and cooking. Man once had things this way and the Gods grew tired of our complaining, so they said to each other, 'let the children hunt and carry for themselves, let them find their own trouble and we will watch how they manage it.'"

"But what about the dark Gods?" Okla asked." Do they not give us enough trouble that we need help from the high Gods?"

Hanit spit into the dirt and rubbed it out with his foot. "It is never good to speak about the dark Gods…" He leaned in close… "But they never move of their own accord. They need people who are willing to do what they want. The Wolf and Axe are such people."

I had heard whispers of this clan but wanted Hanit to tell me his version. "Wolf and Ax?" I said. "Who are these…traders?"

Hanit raised a shaggy eyebrow. "These things I tell you...they are not to be repeated. The Wolf and Axe are takers. They neither grow food nor hunt, they care for no animals and sew no clothing. They will not suffer the presence of children, and only keep women for a time to use as crude men would do. They come at night upon a village and kill the warriors and children. They offer safety to a handful of young men like the two of you, and the rest flee or die. They spend a time in the village until everything is eaten, then they burn the homes and leave with the new young warriors."

"Wait!" Okla said. "Why would young men band together with men who killed their people and burned their village?"

"By keeping them from food and water and sleep until they are weak and delirious, then slowly they reward them for subservience with bits of food and sleep. After a few months a boy becomes grateful to his captors for the smallest favor. Within a year they do not even remember their old life. They will kill to be accepted by the Wolf and Axe. And they will have to. They have ceremonies of battle within themselves and the winner gets a wolf-skin to wear and a battleaxe of ironwood. The loser dies. This way only the strongest make up the clan."

Okla shook his head. "I would wait until they were asleep and kill them one by one."

"I am sure you would," Hanit said. "But they would see your mind and end you."

"I need to train the dogs," I said, "to warn us of their approach."

"Yes, dogs are good, but not always enough. There has been no sign of the Wolf and Axe since I was a boy. Perhaps they are gone forever. But I fear not."

"Have you seen them?"

"No," he said, "but I have seen their work. Came upon it with my father in the middle boat.   Before the Elkhorn moved from the Lake-people, the Wolf and Axe came upon a band of Lake-people not an hour's walk from here and took their small camp, twenty or so, killed them all, took their skins and fish, lived there for a moon. When we arrived there were human bones and smoking ruin.   We found a boy tied to a tree stump, he had been beaten and abused, he did not talk or even look at us, so we carried him to the boat and brought him back. We took him in to our family."

"Dol?" I asked.

Hanit cleared his throat... "Yes, Dol. A band of our own were so afraid that they went to the other side of the lake to where they knew it would be safe. They became one with the Elkhorn. Half of us stayed here. But this is a long ago tale and I can see I have tormented your minds with the telling of it."

Hanit rubbed his forehead. "Me and my stories. Let us speak of lighter things."
We tried but the conversation drew quiet and we worked away at our little tasks with trembling hands.

The Southern trail

The pups were a joy to behold. There were four other bitches in the village full with pups and with the bounty I knew there would be lower price for mine. But I did not care. I only wanted to keep them all and Copperman told me he would chuck any I did not sell into the lake to prevent them from eating us into starvation. I knew he would not but decided not to test him. As soon as the pups were ready I sold them all but Little Brother's, a spotted male he called First because it beat the others out of the womb. Also it was his first dog. First was a good choice and he learned from Moon and the two Elkhorn males I named Point and Blade. They were full-blooded hunters and the two together could back down a wild boar. Add Moon, who could guide them with a growl or a short bark and we would be a hunting pack.

Okla began to get a distant look in his eyes and I would find him staring down towards the valley's edge and the invisible path towards his Bog-shepherded clan. I tried not to think too much about it but it was coming, sure as the spring thaw. We made the best of the time we had, hunting or lounging at Hanit's; the old man doted over Okla as his own son and I knew he suffered as I did over the coming spring departure.

Gy brought gifts each day for Sister; I do not know how he found the time between preparations for the lambing in the spring but each morning we would open the door to find a little bundle: A wooden necklace carved in sections so that they clipped together in a kind of chain, butter, flour, smoked lamb. For ten days straight, he left a single bead that, when finally stringed together, made a fine red necklace, red being the color of courtship. I had to give him credit, he made the other girls in the village dream of their own courtship and the single boys cringed at how much work they were in for during their courtship.

The night the wind started, we knew the winter was over; it was a warm, wet, powerful wind and the cleansing rain that came with it pounded down over everything. We all lay awake listening to it washing a winter's ice from the roofs in a few hours. Warm rivers ran through the paths between houses, cleaning out the dog shit and rotten snow; mud gushed down and we could see a dark patch as it flowed over the ice on the lake. By morning the lake was half open, murky water lapping like hungry tongues against the jagged edge of the ice-shelf. More wind and rain kept us inside the whole day. Children ran out and came back soaking to report on the lake's progress. By dusk I dressed, cloak fur-side in, to repel the water. I stood by the lake, amazed at how big it seemed now that it was dark again. Ice floated in dying plates, bobbing in water and breaking against itself. The wind pushed it back against the far side in a clump. Mud ran down the side of the mountain and shoved back at the incoming sheets.

Hanit joined me, smiling his toothless grin. "That will be too gritty to fish till the mud settles," he said, "but boats hit the water soon." He had seen this process forty or fifty times, but he seemed like a child looking at new freedom.

"Open water," he said and raised a hand to the sky..." Open water!"

So Okla and I went for a final hunt, just the two of us, and the dogs. We needed meat to add to the wedding. I challenged him to a squirrel and rabbit competition. There were many out now, racing around after the long freeze. I set five traps and Okla seven snares, then we moved into the thick forest and hunted for hours, enjoying the warm sun on snowless ground. I took the first two rabbits and then Okla hit three squirrels in a row. There was a small roe deer that we missed by a mile in our hurry to get an arrow off before the other. We sat near a stream cleaning the game and toasting livers and hearts, tiny snacks but all the more delicious for their size. We talked about our adventures from the trek with Copperman to the Elkhorn and the great Urus. Then I asked him what I had been wanting to ask him for weeks.

"Why do you not stay and find a Lake-girl to marry? We will have so many more trips and hunts."

He looked down. "I have thought of this often. Hanit would have me stay as an apprentice if I even mentioned it…but I cannot." He pulled his knife from its sheath and began carving at a green stick for no reason. "I want to show my clan that I am a man now, want to show my father that I am strong and can be trusted. Want to show my mother that I am alive. I need to step into my old home with a dog and an ink-scar."

I looked at him surprised. "Of course, you cannot leave until you have an ink-scar. I will prepare one soon."

"No, brother…Copperman wants to do this for me. He has a plan. Tonight I will receive it and when it has healed, Hanit will take me across the water."

I could feel resentment at Copperman taking this from me, but immediately saw the truth to it. When he returned home with an ink-scar from Copperman, it would be understood that he had been truly brave and completed his task.

"Let us go check the traps," I said, kicking out the little fire. There were seven rabbits and three squirrels between us. Not bad for a wedding. Added to the deer, smoked fish and a fresh sheep, we would have a fine feast for Sister.

That night near the big fire, Copperman marked Okla with the outline of the skull of the great Urus, copying it from its perch on a pole near the fire as the Council had ordered. It was a very fine ink-scar, not too broad or deep, with hair-thin lines for the plates where the skull connected. It would heal quickly and I would lose my brother Okla to the southern trail.

I held a candle while Copperman worked and steeled myself to the coming days.

A hundred small gifts

Sister had become a very fine woman. I could see her, waiting for him in a garland of white hill flowers and she was red-faced with wedding anticipation. She wore the usual dress made up from layers of wool cloth in various colors, stained blue from various berries, red from the lime tree bark and black from the black sheep wool. Gy arrived wearing more clothes than was needed for such a warm spring morning but it is the costume of the shepherds to show their wealth. He had a fine hat of lynx that must have been the pride of his family. Mother gasped as she saw them together and I imagined she had thought of the event many times and now the happening was as she had hoped.

Full sun was a good omen on a wedding and the yellow light bathed the clan as we walked slowly behind the couple up the small hill to the wedding peak. There, overlooking the lake, we saw the boats lined up side by side to honor the ceremony. They cheered from their boats, the calls echoing across the water. We cheered back. Old Father raised his staff for attention. He gave a warm wedding speech, short on warnings and long on good wishes. An eagle flew a wide circle over the ceremony and

Old Father stopped his speech to honor it. We watched as it circled three times before rising to its perch on a high tree. This was good fortune indeed and he ended his speech with a call to the eagle to watch over the couple all of their days.

We raced down the hill to build the feast fire. Like the Bog-shepherd, we made our feast before the couple's house, a small but sturdy structure everyone in the village had a hand in building. Okla and I had gathered flat stones to shape the fireplace and I liked the idea of Sister cooking over a fireplace that I helped build. The couple went into the house alone to do what couples do when they are finally alone on their wedding day. We gathered in front of the house and built a good crackling log fire. We prepared the meat and foodstuffs for the feast. There were deer-shanks and ribs, rabbit and various birds, roots and grain-bread, pots of honey and goat's milk butter.

Each family has their own tea recipe with as many variations as one could imagine and these were put out for sampling. It was a kind of contest reserved for ceremonies. The teapot that needed replenishing most often was the winner and envy of the wives of the clan. Recipes were a closely guarded secret and no one but the owner was allowed to clear out the empty pot to protect against snooping among its contents. Mother and Sister had a mixture of no less than a dozen different ingredients, including pine needles, (for bite) inner pine bark (for sweetness) ground barley (for warmth) lime leaf to add sharpness, and five different dried and powdered roots they would disclose not even to me. They made big batches of the dry tea every spring and every fall and kept it in a large jar to portion out each morning. (When I traveled, Mother's tea was what I missed the most.) Others were equally complex and the competition was high.

Okla and I sampled tea after tea while we watched over the roasting meat. The clan was perhaps a hundred strong at the wedding-fire that day with the fishermen back from their boats. Everyone had washed and wore their best clothes. Hats of every fur and style mingled in front of Sister and Gy's new home. Children held a wrestling contest and I judged the event that, as usual, resulted in more than a few tears and howls. The men played a game of rock-rolling and Okla joined in, fighting helplessly against a rock nearly as big as he was. The hunters laughed and jeered him good-naturedly. Rodik (the biggest man of the Lake people) rolled the boulder easily and won the match…then proceeded to roll it down the hill and into the lake. No one could match his strength but I admired Okla for even trying.

As the meat and tea steamed and we all grew hungry, we watched the door to Sister's house with growing anticipation. I worried that they were unable to join as couples (it has been known to happen) and if not, the wedding would be postponed while Gy went through several rituals to prove his manhood. I did not know what these rituals were but hoped for Gy's sake he would not have to endure them. Finally the two emerged smiling and red-cheeked. The elders approached them and the crowd hushed. Old Father whispered questions to the married couple. He turned and addressed the clan.

"Gy of the Shepherds and Tau, daughter of Copperman.....are now married."
The crowed cheered loudly. The feast was on.

It lasted the day and into the night. One by one, presents were brought forth. Okla and I had scraped and treated the wolf pelts from the Urus-hunt and they were well received as gifts. Hanit gave them a long thin trade-stick carved with outlines of many fish along its length. They could bring it to him whenever they needed and he would give them a fish and break off a piece of the stick with a carving on it. Copperman gave them each copper rings, carved with flowers and patterns. Even Dol brought a gift of a bone fish-lure and length of string to dangle it from. A hundred small gifts make a fine home and by day's end Sister and Gy retreated to their new home and closed the door to another cheer from the crowd.

Mother's tea made it to the final rounds but Medicine woman's tea was judged the finest and she made a large pot to finish the party. Mother was too happy about the wedding to let the tea affect her. "Besides," she said, "it would be rude to give the bride's mother a tea victory when she is already so fortunate." Then, for no reason, she began to cry and Copperman led her home to her first night as the only woman in our house.

Hanit and Okla sat with me over the dying fire, picking meat from the last of the ribs. "We will go tomorrow," Hanit said. "To take Okla to the southern trail."
I said nothing.

"I will bring you along, but only if the wind is down."

The next morning, still dark, we loaded the boats with Okla's equipment and his Elkhorn dog. Those awake waived or called out as we poled the laden boat out from the shallows. I did not speak, not a word the entire trip. Okla stared forward, already home in his head. Home to big houses and loving family and a summer of wheat and lambing. He would hunt his own trails and it was not fair that I would not be with him.

A trip to the southern trail is a long boat journey but far too short for me. As the sun rose, we made good time with Hanit rowing his expert light pulls of the oars. Before long, we were pulled up to the sandy bank where the trailhead began near dark woods.
Okla and I looked at each other but knew not what to say.

"I will come see you." I said weakly.

"You have a home there whenever you want," he said.

Hanit raised Okla's pack for him, gripped him by the shoulders, looked him in the eyes. "Strength boy." Okla nodded. "I have in the parcel of your pack, ten dried fish-heads, and ten smoked trout. Also a clay pot. Use small fires. Boil one fish-head and one smoked trout each day. Do not stop to hunt. Hunting takes time and you need to walk and nothing else. The dog will find food along the trail as dogs do but you need to cover real ground. Drive hard! Avoid other travelers. Make yourself small, do not allow the dog to leave your side. Sleep hidden and walk early and late. Sleep in the middle of the day…well hidden, remember."

Okla nodded and the reality of the journey he was about to undertake seemed to suddenly hit him.

"You will see your family soon and the Gods will smile on you."

Hanit shook him gently, then turned and walked to the boat. I did the same and pushed us off into the water. I turned and watched as Okla walked with his dog into the woods and disappeared. I did not cry but the hollow in my chest hurt beyond tears. As the boat glided back towards the Lake village I watched the place Okla had been and prayed loudly to the Gods, calling out. "See him safely to his people! Guide my brother home!"

I could hear Hanit breathing heavily as he drove his sorrow into the oars, each stroke pulling us farther away from the one we loved.

Clay

The slick earth-slime feel of it: rich and pure-red.
I kneaded it with my hands, squeezing it between chapped
fingers like a child playing. Sister said you had to make
friends with clay and talk to it, asking gently if it will hold a
shape, then bake it slowly and evenly like good bread. I
cursed it between gritted teeth, slapped it on the ground in
frustration, and burned it in fires until it shattered. Sister
laughed and treated me like the clay she mastered, coaxing
me into the new skill. I labored at this woman's work
despite the looks of distaste from the other main hunters.
Of course, the hunting went on, and, despite the absence of
my friend (I could not even say his name the first summer),
I managed to find enough game to maintain my status. But
the clay-work had a secret meaning. I had dreamed it one
night: a tall copper kiln with four tubes. It would require
great effort, enormous amounts of fuel, but the return
would be a white heat that could melt copper from the
bluestone at many times the speed. If we found a supply
like the one in the cave, I wanted to make sure we got to it
before bears and wood warriors got to us.

I described the new oven to Copperman and he mulled the idea over for days before setting me to work with Sister. I made tiny versions of the oven and kept them well hidden. After six or seven tries, I managed to make a small working version. Sister seemed tired and moody and it was Mother who first guessed that she was carrying a child. Gy strutted around proud and nervous. I imagined what it would feel like to become a new father and decided it was not for me. Not at all. I would be free to hunt and travel to any village, stay as long as I wanted and return with wealth. Gy was now responsible for two others and who knew how many more would come. I gave him the ink-scar I promised, eight short, fat lines along his left wrist for good fortune. Others asked for ink-scars and Copperman warned me to be very selective, or the whole village would have them and with each new ink-scar the next would be slightly less valuable. At the same time he said; 'make sure you do enough each summer to keep your skills up.' I tried to keep a balance and stopped at ten that year. Enough to have honey and smoked fish and a jar of good beads for trade.

Between training at the ink-scars and copper-work with Copperman, clay with Sister and hunting with the dogs, the summer pulled me forward. I did not let my mind wander to the Bog-shepherd clan. It was a dream I did not want to have. I fished some mornings with Hanit and he was as unwilling to speak of it as I.

Falling

The late summer was as warm and gentle as any I could remember. The broad leaf trees that had huddled, skinny-dead in the winter, were now fat with moist leaves, brilliant lime green in the full sun. We were mostly a naked clan in the summer; unlike other clans, the Lake-people had no thoughts to dress other than weather. Hot days after a prosperous spring meant lazy parents dozing in the shade trees as children wallowed in the mud and then swam themselves clean. The shepherds, of course, never took off their clothes. (Copperman told me that this was the way of shepherds everywhere he traveled.) They worked the same summer and winter. Their sheep, however, stripped down by hours of back aching toil with flint blades, ran from the sheering shed, jumping and bouncing like happy weasels, their heavy burden lifted.

The hunters stripped down and lay like snakes soaking up the heat as if they could save it up for the long, dark winter ahead. And the fishermen for a few weeks every summer became fish. I could see their heads bobbing and then a white bottom as they rose to dive. They had games to test their strength and I joined them. One involved throwing a white stone into the deep water and diving down into the cold layer to retrieve it. I would panic as the air left me and my ears would ring from the weight of it all. The children of the fishermen could swim as soon as they could walk and nothing was as frustrating as finding the stone at the bottom of the lake only to have an eight year old swim under you and grab it first. The test of any true swimmer was the island. A boat would follow as you swam from the shore out to the island (at least three hundred paces) around it and then back without stopping. I awoke the morning of the hottest day of the year and decided it was my time. Hanit was serious about the undertaking, clucking his teeth at my age.

"At your age…You should have made this swim several summers back." He was full of advice as I dropped my clothes into the boat. "Have you eaten?"

"Just a half loaf of bread and a bowl of porridge."

Hanit stopped and glared at me. "I need to know these things!" he said.

I understood he was in no mood for jokes. "No, of course I have not eaten."

"Good. Anything sore or injured? Your head is clear?" He meant; was my nose blocked which could be a problem during a swim.

"Clear as the sky," I said anxious to get started.

"OK. Ask the lake!"

I looked out to the lake and said loudly, "Can I make the island swim…please?"

He pursed his lips at my lack of conviction but then a large fish splashed out in the calm water and he nodded at the sign. "Begin," he said, "and keep slow and steady."

I slipped into the lake and felt the thrill of cool water against naked skin. The water was so clear that I could see small fingerlings darting away as I slid over the shallows. The water smelled like summer. I drank a small amount as I swam, thinking how nice it must be for a fish never to be thirsty even once in its life.

Hanit had a system that worked well to guide me to the island as it was so low you could not see it as you swam. He would tap his oar once for me to angle right and twice to angle left. This way I did not have to waste energy raising and searching. The first few hundred paces were easy; this was the danger, feeling too certain of your strength. The lake below sank here, deep and the dark blue beneath me, shimmering with shafts of light that shifted with the shadow of my body. They seemed to reach into unimaginable depth.

"Steady!" Hanit shouted. I could see and feel the swish of his oars and looked up to see him thirty paces from me. Under water he sounded only a few feet away. There were other sounds as well: my labored breathing, my hands sucking air with each stroke, and my increasing heartbeat. Swimming is a mind game and I began to think too much. Giant pike that were fabled to take a hand from a swimmer: we all knew it was not true but looking down I could not help but imagine. Or the dead rising white from the depth to drag you down, I knew Hanit was watching me closely but what if something.... Suddenly, I spotted a light patch and startled, sucking in water. I rose and coughed, then realized it was the island near me and I could see rocks and patches of sand in shallow water. The thought came to me that I could stop here and ride back with Hanit but he tapped his oar and I began to swim again. Tap tap tap. I swam a wide circle around the tiny island and soon the white bottom fell to deep blue again.

Halfway back I began to panic. The deep pulled at me and I began to swim hard to fight it. My lungs burned and I could taste the bitter blood as I gasped for air. "You are close!" Hanit called and I knew he was lying. This is what you call to someone who is in the midst of a struggle and it never helps. A warm breeze picked up and began to lap little waves of water into my mouth as I rose to breathe. One deep breath sucked in only water and suddenly I could not swim. I choked and gasped again only to suck more water. I could see Hanit thirty paces away turning the boat and I could see from his movements that he knew I was in trouble. I also knew he would not be able to turn the boat around and get to me before I went under.

The panic of drowning is unlike any other emotion. The body shudders and wants one thing and, though it is so close, the air I needed rose above me out of reach. I climbed an invisible hill that slid out from beneath me until I could no longer climb. And slipping, over and over, I finally fell, watching the light of the sky grow dark. In seconds, the fear of death and the desire for air changed to a need for sleep.

For a short time I joined the dead at the bottom of the lake that children would fear when they swim, and then something hit me on the chest. Hanit's long oar dipped down from the boat. I looked at it for half a second, confused and suddenly it made sense and I grabbed it. He gently pulled me up like a giant pike and as I began to fade, he had me out. Hanit must have pulled me into the boat because I had no life to help him. Soon I was folded over the edge, coughing out water and sucking in pure sweet air. I retched and retched, each time more water would pour out of me. Hanit cursed and slapped me on the back until I thought he was trying to beat the death out of me. It worked. I finally flopped to the boat's floor and began to breathe. We drifted silently as he watched me for signs of what he called second drowning. As a fisherman, he had seen wet dead bodies many times before and some who come back only to die half an hour later on dry land. He made me stand and raise my arms a hundred times before declaring me alive and rowing us back to shore. I crawled from the boat and walked on trembling legs to the little family beach. I lay back shivering and naked, drying in the sun as Mother and Sister arrived and began to shed clothes.

"Was it a nice swim?" Sister asked, looking out at the lake.

"Yes …perfect." I lay for the rest of the day, coughing occasionally.

Finally Hanit came over and sat near me. He chuckled. "I suppose you thought you would succeed at everything?"

I thought about it. "I guess I did."

He shrugged. "You are a Copperman, and a main hunter… Leave the glory of the island swim to the fishermen." I thought about this, breathed in the good air around me, and suddenly felt better about everything.

New tools

We made things. This was our life and the things
we made came from our fathers' fathers. Spike-sticks to dig
roots with, which were always carved from a slightly curved
box tree-staff with one of its roots still attached, heated
slowly in the fire until it blackened hard. Bows were ash-
limbs, scraped flat on the string side, round-side facing out.
Drinking cups came from the rounded knobs that grow on
older birch trees, slowly hollowed out with burning coals,
smoothed clean with a round stone and sand; clothes,
fishing-spears, knives, houses, all knowledge-gifts left by
those who came long before us. But I wanted to make
things in different ways and this made for some spectacular
failures and much confusion from the others. They thought
me slow-witted and though I had grown up among them,
the Lake-people often spoke to me as if I were newly
arrived.

'A bow-string is woven from red-deer buck,' they
would explain as I wove elk and roe deer sinew into
different patterns. Or; 'a skin scraper must taper at the top
and use black stone…you are not even using the right angle
to scrape with!' It was often the old women who were the

worst, holding the old ways in the respect they held the Gods. Often they were right but even when they were not and my new method worked better, they had no desire to try.

I had seen three different clans and each had their ways of making nearly everything. Why not use what we found to make our own clan stronger. The Forest-people made terrible spear-points but were far better at stalking and disguising themselves; the Bog-shepherds' houses were clearly better and their clay-work would rival Sister's (if not in style, then in durability); the Elkhorn used methods of bow-hunting that made ours sad in comparison and their long-house would be any Council's dream. And they all knew, (whether they had seen it themselves or not) that these things existed; yet, each clan held their own methods as if to do otherwise was an insult to their fathers and mothers.

I found Copperman retouching some arrow-points with a tool made from a short pointed stick with a red deer antler-tip wedged into it. I slumped down next to him and watched, always fascinated by how little he had to work to get the results he wanted. He sat cross-legged with a thick patch of hard-backed leather over his left thigh to protect from the sharp slivers of flint that came off the points. He used his shoulders rather than his wrists to press slightly on the thin black point. He would press with his fingers on the back of the arrowhead as he worked with the retouching tool to find just the right angle. There would be a clicking sound, barely audible and a flake would drop from his hand. The flakes that fell were long and thin. This was masterly. My points were good but never clean and perfect like his. After a bit he sighed and set down his work.

"What?" he said.

"I…I am tired of people asking why all the time. Everything I do is questioned as if I were insulting the clan with the making of anything."

He laughed. "If you do not want to insult the clan with your every action then become a shepherd, or a fisherman. Follow their methods. Marry soon and raise children who you can teach these methods to."

I thought about this for a few seconds. "I would rather wander the woods like Asha and trade puppies for beads!"

He nodded. "Then hide better when you try new things and stop complaining. We have a winter to prepare for sooner than you think and if you have not mastered the new oven by fall we cannot use it on our spring journey."

He picked up his tool and began to flake another point when his antler tip, held into the hollow of the tool, crumbled loose. He cursed softly and stood to stretch out the stiffness. There were three other broken antler-tips near him and I realized he had been there all morning. I sat and began to roll the copper bead I carried for jewelry practice. It had been formed into so many shapes it was soft and pliable. I took two stones and began to tap and roll it between the stones until it was small enough to fit into the tip of the retouching tool like a tooth fits into a jaw. Copperman nodded and took the tool, tapping it here and there with a small stone until it was secure. Then he sat down and grabbed a broken point; he held the tool against the edge and shifted his shoulders. Click, a long flake fell into his hand; he held it up to me so I could look at the sky's light through its thinness.

"This place has enough fishermen and shepherds," he said.

One wolf to another

The summer nights were crowded, perhaps even more crowded than the days. Not a soul in the clan wanted to be inside after the winter we had and would sit in the light of the fire and tell stories. Of course, young fathers and mothers were unable to live like the rest of us. They had squawking babies and extra food to store and what about new clothes and a bigger home for the next one in the wife's belly. The elderly chose the comfort of their own beds at night. But the rest of us made the most of it. If the full moon added its blue gaze, we would let the fire die down and stay awake all night, marveling at the ceiling of flickering little lights above. Were they sparks from the great fire of the Gods? The moon, one of the God's eyes? Or the night, a cloak that they covered us with and the moon just a hole in its fabric?

At times a flash would scar the sky and we would cry out in delight (the first and loudest to call out would have a small favor from the Gods for their appreciation). Often our calls would be answered by our dogs who yodeled delightfully, backs curved, muzzles raised, putting their whole bodies in the cries. Wolves, who used their howls to find each other from mountain to mountain, would answer the dogs with haunting high-pitched howls. I often wondered if a wolf alerted another who alerted others further and how many mountains it could cross. Would my cry at a star eventually wake the wolves from every land? And how many lands could there be? From Copperman's stories there were more lands than there were people in our clan. These thoughts would spiral and I would have to breathe slowly until the dizziness passed.

Copperman was right: I did think too much. But the softness of the summer nights always won over and I would fade to dream and awake to birds and yellow light to find half the clan still asleep near the cold fire. I began to gain height and muscle that summer, seemingly at once. I was smaller than others my age and Copperman said the mountain people who brought me were small in stature. The growth spurt was welcome and I found I could now wrestle and occasionally fight with the other hunters my age.

Mother extended my clothes with scraps until finally giving in and making a new set altogether. I did not need them much in the warmth but new leggings and moccasins were finally necessary. She and Sister spent a week on my winter clothes and boots. I reluctantly began to prepare for the coming of fall and decided if it had to come, I would be ready for it. I made twenty fine arrows and Copperman said it was time for a bigger bow. I was secretly nervous.

A bigger bow is hard to draw back and its power makes it hard to hold steady. We searched for two days to find the right limb for it, an ash-branch as thick as my forearm and slightly taller than I. We felled it carefully and barked it, dabbed the edges with pinesap to prevent it from splitting, then wedged it between the branches of a tree. Bent slightly and exposed to the sun it would slow dry and hold that shape. After a few weeks I began to shape it with a hand-axe. It was nervous work. There were no flaws allowed in a bow. A single knot or tiny split could result in a shattered bow that winter and the end of a hunt.

Copperman explained in detail how a bow should be made but left me to carry out the task. A man should make his own tools so if they fail there is no one else to blame. This was the first time he had referred to me as a man and so I worked intensely to prove him right. This bow would be the finest he had seen. My work, however, became overzealous and by the time I had finished, the elegant curved bow was slightly too thin at each tip. "Slightly" is as bad as completely for a bow and I understood I needed to find a new blank and begin again, hoping it would be warm enough the next weeks to dry it before the fall rains began. Then I remembered Little Brother's toy bow. He had split it by using it to chase the other children with and Copperman had been very cross with him about it. I had fixed it by wrapping wet sinew around the split and when it dried it was flexible and the tiny bow shot better than it had before. On a new unsplit bow the method might make my bow stronger. I traded two fine arrows to a hunter who had taken two roe deer for all of the deer's sinew. I spent the afternoon slowly, tightly wrapping the new bow-tips down along the thin ends with the sinew until each end was wrapped a full foot length down with many layers of sinew. When it dried it was hard, shiny and flexible.

Copperman found me stringing the new bow. "What happened here?" he asked. I told him the situation and he frowned.

"An experiment with a bow can lose you an eye or break your arm."

I waited.
"Begin slowly. Small shots."

I notched an arrow and pulled back slightly. The arrow shot twenty paces or so but the bow seemed solid. I tried again and again with longer pulls and the bow hummed gently as it released. You could tell if a bow had a crack by the sound during release. A good bow made little sound. This was a great bow. Copperman tried it and I cringed as he pulled back to the full extent of the bow's capability. An arrow shot through the anthill we were using as a target and sunk into the roots of the tree behind it. It was a broken arrow but a fine success.

"When the others ask about the sinew, tell them it is for decoration."

Winters waiting

The fall came on so gently that the Lake-people were fully prepared with honey, extra dried meat and firewood stacked head-high behind each house. The shepherds enjoyed the extra weeks of green grass and the sheep needed little tending. A wolverine came down and took several lambs but we were unable to shoot or trap it. Hanit said wolverines were of the dark Gods' making and hunting it was foolish, but the shepherds offered a spring lamb to the hunter who took it. Why was Okla not here with me for this, I thought? He would never let the opportunity pass.

Hanit pleaded with me not to hunt them and I was happy for the excuse. I knew what the little wolves were capable of and did not want to put the dogs to that test. One of the elders remembered a wolverine and two of its half grown pups chasing a brown bear from its kill. I did not think they were evil. After all, a lamb must seem like a weak deer to a wolverine. Would we pass up a fat meal that did not know how to run or hide? I spent my days hunting small game instead, training the dogs, who knew enough now not to run for rabbit and would instead crouch down, tail straight, when they smelled game.

There were game-hens among the trees and we used a special arrow with a rounded end to hunt them. The arrow was fletched with many big feathers and would fly hard and fast for thirty or forty paces and then the big feathers would slow it down quickly. This way we could shoot at flying birds without losing our arrows. It was the perfect practice for my new bow and by the first snows I could hit nearly one out of three flying birds.

One journey I had taken three birds and was stalking the fourth when a shadow appeared in the trees. It galloped along the bent trunk of an enormous oak and at first glance seemed like a giant weasel. It saw me and stopped, rose on its hind legs and looked down. Its hackles rose. The dogs, who always spotted or smelled things before I did, had already frozen. They trembled with excitement, waiting for me to shoot. I looked at the wolverine and it looked at me. Its shaggy brown pelt glistened with dark oil and its oversized claws gripped the tree-bark. It was no bigger than one of the dogs but its paws were huge and menacing. Its eyes, small and yellow, sat in a broad, flat skull; it bared its teeth as it sniffed the sky for my scent. We held our gaze for the longest time before it turned and scrambled up the tree and into a hollow space inside the trunk. I could have easily shot it. Could have marked the spot, ran home and brought back hunters and a pack of dogs to smoke it from its hollow den. I could have saved the shepherds several lambs and earned one for the spring. For reasons I cannot explain, I left the wolverine in its secret home and spoke of it to no one.

The snows settled softly over the mountains and life took on the usual patterns of sleep, small games, sewing and carving. We hunted in groups from time to time but the smoke house had plenty of dried, cured meat hanging and the ground did not freeze solid until late. The ice formed slowly and Hanit was desperate by the time ice fishing began. I could not join him. Simply could not ice fish without Okla. I taught Little Brother (who was driving us to distraction with his questions and restlessness) and he soon joined Hanit on his daily treks. They used our ice-slide and I noticed others using various methods of curved slides on their new sleds. Fishermen have it so hard that any new idea is accepted and incorporated. They also used the trick with the crows and enjoyed watching them from a distance rather than having them pecking at the tent covers. They spoke of it as if it had always been the method and seemed to have forgotten who told them about it. But I knew that they knew and this was a win in its own right.

Hanit, who missed Okla perhaps more than I, began to teach Little Brother about the fishing trade. 'He has got the gift', he said, 'never gives up until he gets his fish, right?' Little Brother was a stubborn boy and if the pike did not show, would sulk home. When he did get a fish, however, the whole clan had to hear about it. As Hanit's eyes were getting tired from years of focus, he let Little Brother mend nets and weave line.

When Little Brother announced he would be a fisherman, Copperman nodded.

"This is good," he said. "A family needs different skills. Sister is a potter and shepherd's wife. She brings meat, wool cups and bowls. If you bring fish and we get copper we always have something to trade."

Little Brother was happy with the deal. I wondered how happy he would be when he was fourteen and we were preparing to travel off on adventures, but let things lie. Besides, I liked fish as much as anybody and the dogs were strong on Hanit's scraps.

The sun turned as it does and began lighting the sky longer each day. Copperman fed up and I began to do the same. We needed fat on our bodies for the spring journey. As the months went by, he began to get that restless preparation I remembered from past springs. I began to feel it too.

By the first thaw, I dreamed of nothing but the journey. Copperman refused to talk about our route and I could only guess that it would not be back to the forest cave. We would not steel from those Gods twice. He mumbled in his half sleep and I tried to listen in for clues but got nothing. When the ice cracked and drifted apart I knew the time would come soon. Unlike the first time I knew the hardships we would endure. And like any young man, had already cheerfully dismissed them.

The wet, warm breeze rotted the last of the snow around the lake and Copperman asked Mother to make us marrow soup and strip fat from the belly-meat to add to it. I watched him go into the smokehouse with a rucksack and his antler-handled black flint knife. He came out some time later and used the blade to mark what he had taken. It was our system during the winter between hunts. The smokehouse was the size of a small hut and could hold six or seven deer at a time, hanging from tethers on the roof beam. In the summer, small fires were kept up to keep flies away and the meat would turn hard and glassy from the smoke. In the winter it kept out scavengers.

A long stick of greenwood wedged into the earth stood near the entrance and each family had a mark. Ours was three dots and a circle. Others were similar. The clan was represented by a complex series of dots, circles and X's. Next to your family-mark you would make lines for how much meat you have taken. It was determined by meals: The amount of meat, fat or bone marrow a person would eat for a meal. This was a complex system, made even trickier as main hunters could claim half of their hunt and the Council needed to claim none of what they took.

There were different methods of trade for fish and sheep and Copperman had always said the Council earned all they could eat for the endless disputes based on who took what and how much. Copperman held the belief that each man should hunt what he needed and trade or give the rest. This was my only disagreement with him and I kept it to myself. I thought the clan would fall apart if we did not have trade rules to keep us working together. We would become three clans in one village, fighting each other for scraps every winter. We were a wealthy family with trade goods and copper and a main hunter and a potter in the family. But what of Hanit? Or the medicine woman whose husband was sick these days? How would they fare over a hard winter? One thing I agreed with him about the smokehouse was the Council's share. They earned every bit of it and I would never want the job, no matter how old I got.

I went to the marker-stick after Copperman left it and could see twenty fresh lines next to our family's mark. My stomach sank with the realization that he had loaded the pack. We were leaving the next day. I walked (with Moon at my heels) around the village, thrilled and terrified by the coming journey. After dreaming it for months, it seemed to appear from nowhere. I found my way to Sister's house and she greeted me at the door with a smile. She looked peachy and red cheeked, heavy with her coming child. She brought me in and heaped a fire with good thick branches as you do for an honored guest.

She had a game that she shared with Moon. She lay her down and pointed to the floor until Moon rested her head. She put a cloth over her eyes. Moon whined with excitement as Sister walked around the room with a sheeprib, talking out loud about where she might hide a tasty rib. She clanked and rummaged around as Moon whined, until hiding the rib behind a chair under a fur. 'Find it!' she said and snapped her fingers. Moon leapt up and rummaged around the hut, searching the smell of it. When she found the rib, she bounced around with joy and sat with it between her paws, chewing in triumph.

I admired the home Sister and Gy had built: Two deerskin windows, scraped so thin you could see the golden light through them. Low chairs lined with sheepskin and good thick furs on dry hay sleep-mattresses. Shelves on one wall displayed her many clay vessels. I picked one up, a lidded jar. I felt the smooth, thin, even walls of glassy clay, burnished near black with ashes and decorated with patterns around the rim. The lid, fitting perfectly with a thin layer of beeswax to seal it.

"You will master them one day," she said. "Most of my best ones are already traded away and my hands itch for the thaw and the first new batch of the year. It will be difficult to work with a young one hanging from my chest." She smiled at the thought. I nodded, knowing that

Copperman and I would be gone when her child was born. She looked at me for a moment and her smile faded.

"You are leaving, are you not? I could not answer. She sighed.

"I can tell because Mother has been tight-lipped and short these days. She hates it when he goes. And now you as well...it is not easy on a mother. When?"

I did not answer. "That soon?" she said. "Well then, stay with me today. Let us go up the hill and see Gy. We can bring him lunch."

I helped her carry the food up the wet hill a few hundred paces to the sheep who were muddy and burdened with the winter's coat. They ate in a ceaseless desperation, searching the earth between snow patches, yanking last years old grass up from its rotten roots. Gy was with another shepherd, holding a sheep while a third trimmed the muddy, shitty wool from its backside with a tiny flint blade. Half of the sheep had white clean backsides and the others were dragging tails of filthy wool the size of rabbits. This is what they will do for weeks I thought and shuddered as Gy wiped his filthy hands on some grass and then rose to send the new white butt into the flock.

He raised his hands as we came up and I could see how he looked at Sister, and how she looked at him. Always a fussy girl, I marveled at her welcome of the muddy hands that patted her belly. This was love, I thought. If anyone else ever reached a muddy hand to Sister they would have it slapped away. Gy might as well have had a hand full of flower petals as far as she was concerned.

"I felt him kicking," she said. "All morning. Wanting out already."

Gy reached in to touch noses with me. "Brother!"

I realized he was proud of his new family relations and wanted his other shepherds to see the connection. I understood the need here to fit in and for an outsider, he married well.

"Brother!" I answered loudly. "How many..."I almost insulted him by mistake and stopped myself..."how many of them do you have left to clean?"

I had begun to ask how many sheep were his but unlike hunters or fisherman who loved telling the number they had taken, shepherds never spoke of the number of their sheep. They kept a secret count that only they knew and outsiders who asked were insulting them. Sister knew how I had almost failed but Gy and the other shepherds did not show any signs of it.

"Oh, three more day at least," Gy said. "There are some lost in the ridge and we will get them down before dark."

We sat and spoke of sheep, eating bread and mutton-fat with last year's chestnuts ground into a paste. Sister had a warm jar of tea and I realized that she had changed her recipe slightly from Mothers. . "Chicory?" I asked. "Juniper root?"

She smiled. "Not telling"

"No wonder Mother has been short and tightlipped these days!"

Sister stood and threatened me with a nasty lamb tail and it felt like we were children again. The shepherds laughed as she chased me around. She was too fat to catch me and we ran short circles on the muddy hill, Moon chasing us barking.

"Stop it, you children," Gy said. "The sheep."

We had startled them and they galloped up to the hill. Gy shook his head. "There goes the afternoon. Hunters and Potters. Hopeless. Away with you."

Sister apologized and kissed him. The shepherds trudged towards their work as it ran further away from them. We giggled as we walked down the hill.

"Are they really doing that all day?"

"Wait till lambing," she said. "They work all spring. Night and day."

"This is a way to make a living?"

"You are one to talk," she said, and I remembered what I would be up to the next morning. Suddenly lambing did not seem so bad.

The origin

The silence of pre-dawn. The sharp black lines of branches. Copperman's shadow a few paces ahead, kicking away clumps of ice, slipping and falling our way up into new territory along the north mountain trail. I had secretly hoped we would be heading back over the Western mountains so that we could visit at the Bog-shepherd clan. I knew we would not. Copperman forged ahead and I thought too much until the sun warmed the edge of the sky pink, then poured, liquid hot, over the lip of the western ridge mountains, turning the lake below into rippled honey. All other thoughts were suddenly gone. We found a flat rock with a clear view down, sat on our elk-skin cushions and watched. We drank from the tea (still warm) Mother had filled our water skins with a few hours earlier. We sat for a while looking at the lake as it changed colors, the long shadows of the night slowly shrinking back into the earth.

Copperman looked strong in his bearskin, his fur hat, leggings and elk greatcoat. His beard had fine gray streaks and his eyes shone as he looked down at the village. I wished I could make an ink-scar or medallion to capture the image. He was never happier than on the hunt for bluestone and his thrill became mine. What would we find? Would the new oven work with only the two of us to fuel and fan it?

I squinted down at the edge of our village to see houses so tiny they looked like pebbles. Sheep were flecks of fluff moving along a brown, patched hill. I could just make out Sister's house; ours was lost among the others in a clump of structures near the lake. Breakfast fires lifted smoke from chimneys, thin lines that caught some higher breeze and joined in a drift over the lake.

Copperman savored his tea, swishing the last of it in his mouth as if to keep the flavor for the long days of cold water ahead.

"Sister has changed her tea mix." I said.

He nodded. "I supposed she would. And no matter how good it is your mother will not like it. This is the way of mothers and daughters."

He pointed down to the shepherds who were following the sheep, dark dots following white specks. "Most of them will never see their own village from above."

As the light grew, I could make out the rock-face of the massive cliff beneath the Elkhorn clan. I could even see the line along the left side that was the climbing trail I carried Moon. I reached down to scratch Moon behind her ears and realized she was not there. She had whined and sniffed the air as we walked away that morning. There had been plenty of times that I left her home for short walks or boat trips but she could tell this was different. I felt dishonest and cruel as I turned my back on her and walked away. There was no discussion with Copperman about it; he would not have dogs this trip and gave no reasons for the decision. 'You would miss your puppies,' I told her. 'Stay and keep Mother safe.' I did not cry as we left but it cost me not to.

We sat on the mountain ledge and watched the sunrise for much longer than usual; unlike the western ridge, this trail climbed slowly and not nearly as high. We did not need to exhaust ourselves and this was a welcome realization. The western ridge looked white and untouched and I wondered how we had ever crossed it. The lake from this angle looked much longer than I imagined curling out of sight to our left.

There were other smaller clans along the great lake but we rarely saw them. A hawk screeched far overhead and I thought of Copperman's ink scar. I wondered if the hawks knew they were also a vision kept on a mans skin, if this endeared them to him and him to them.

"I would like to be a bird so I could visit all the other clans," I said.

Copperman shook his head. "The reason the Gods did not allow us to fly is because we would only spy on each other. If we could see everything the other clans were doing we would become jealous and it would lead to theft and battles. Hawks only eat what they need. They deserve to fly. We do not."

I peed off the cliff and then shouldered my pack. "How can I stop thinking too much if you tell me things like that?" He began to laugh loudly, but I did not share the joke. I thought of nothing but flying for the rest of the day.

This became a drab trail, bleak and treeless. We rationed the food and water. Rain had not come to this place yet and the patches of snow were too dusty to want to melt and drink. Copperman had a method of cleaning bad water and though it took time we had to do it here. After a long search, Copperman found a suitable tree, a sapling birch, sheltered from the wind enough to grow straight. He used his copper-axe to gently split its bark lengthwise in one long cut. He used his fingers to reach in and separate the bark from the tree in one long tube. That evening we stuffed the dirty snow into our water bag, a young goatskin scraped clean, tied at the legs and sewn tightly. Then we hung it over hot coals, high enough to keep it from burning. We packed the hollow birch bark tightly with dry grass and topped it with a handful of cold charcoal we had removed from the fire. When the dirty snow melted we poured it through the tube. As the water ran through the tube, the coals and the grass held the dust and clean water slowly trickled into the other water-skin.

It was a laborious process and it took three melts to filter one full water-skin. The result was pure and clean. We emptied the tube of its dirty grass and coals and kept it for the next day, and the next.

We moved slowly through the foreign landscape. We were not yet above tree line. The wind-swept slopes held stunted pines, curling back their branches as if recoiling from the relentless weather. Rockslides were a problem here. A single miss-step would send head sized boulders bouncing down the ravine. Mountain goats scrabbled away from our approach but never close enough to even bother stringing our bows.

On the fifth night we came to a rock-strewn valley. There were trees here and a creek running along grassy patches. And huts. Copperman stood staring at the little village. He rolled the wispy ends of his beard with his fingers and marveled at the sight.

I looked at the surroundings. We were in a basin, like an ancient lake that had drained, leaving behind a few giant boulders along a craggy bottom. The trees surrounding the valley had been harvested clean. A man-made tree line began several hundred paces from where we stood. It made a wide, dead circle around the village. They had taken what was closest. A lazy way of tending the forest. The Lake-people would never fell the near trees, for the wind, water and snow would have nothing to stop their movements.

A few dozen huts littered the valley: poorly made shelters, mainly branches and skins. Above the basin, I could see the mouths of three caves a few hundred paces apart.

My stomach sank. This was where I was born. The Mountain-people had returned to the shallow valley. I became dizzy with fear.

"Why did you bring me here?" I said.

"Because there is bluestone beyond it," Copperman said. "And because you have always been afraid of it. You are Copperson. These mangy rabbits are nothing to you. They belong to this mountain like fleas belong to a dog. Look at their homes. Look at the land they claim. For you to fear them is a like an owl frightened of lemmings."

The villagers came from their huts and began to walk towards us. I had to fight every step not to turn and run.

"Steady!" Copperman said. "You have faced down Elkhorn and forest warriors. Do not fear them, pity them."

I squared my shoulders and felt the fear turn to something far more horrible. Hate. Pure molten hate. The

Mountain-clan, who had sold me, came out to greet us with bits of food and cups of creek water. It was fortunate we had not strung our bows. I would have shot every arrow. Copperman accepted a cup and small chunks of bread and smiled. At that moment I hated him too.

The Look of Them

How can it be that humans born of the same earth could be so different in their manners, their methods, their appearance. The Forest-people had been filthy, smaller and darker, but with a dignity and ability that made them equal in any battle. The Bog-shepherds were heavy and strong; the Elkhorn hard and clever. Of course our Lake-people were too familiar for me to even judge. But all other peoples I had encountered held the dignity of their clan.

The Mountain-people had none. They were lesser in every way. Weak and short-limbed, many with the bowlegged walk of past hungers that weaken the legs for life. They were poor builders from the look of their homes. Their children, glassy eyed and pale, looked out mutely as we approached. Where was their fascination? Children of clans usually need to be scolded for pestering new visitors. Small faces peered out blankly from half open doors. Women, thin as reeds, held babies up to empty flaps of breasts. Had the Gods forgotten this valley?

Three young dogs came out to meet us and they, like their owners, cringed and followed meekly. I suppose my hatred of these people was petty and immature. Ignoble for the wealthy Copperson and main hunter. But hatred is often fear, and more than anything I was afraid. I saw myself in every boy there, and understood my near death was not in surviving the avalanche as a newborn, but in escaping the very clan that bore me. I could be that boy with the clubfoot from an early break, using a gnarled stick to support his walk. I could be one of the hunters who sat salivating as visitors ate precious chunks of bread his children needed.

A girl my age with a curled lip, missing most of her teeth, sat near me, a hand on my leg. She nodded at every bite I took. She smelt of mold and wet fur. We ate slowly as they watched and then drank a cup of silty water. I remembered the dusty taste and knew there must be an ice wall in the mountains above feeding the little creek. I could feel its cold breath. Who would winter here?

There were perhaps thirty women and children and a dozen hunters sitting around us waiting for the elder to come out. He was older than any I had ever seen. His hair aged down to a few white strands, his arms (sticking from furs patched a hundred times over) looked like skin-wrapped bone. He had an injured eye, pure white and the other milked over with cataracts; he walked with help to the center of the clan and they lowered him down onto some sitting furs next to us. He cleared his throat several times and addressed Copperman in a voice so low and gravely that we had to lean in to hear it properly.

"If you have come to trade, we have little to offer, unless it is a ceremony for good luck for your journey. Or do you seek a wife for your young man?"

He peered with his faded eye at me and then back at Copperman. The question hung in the air for so long that I wondered if Copperman would answer at all.

Finally he said. "You found a way back to your valley. I did not know there was a trail to this place that did not pass our lake."

The old man smiled. "I remember that voice. The aggression and arrogance of it. Yes, Copperman of the Lake-people. We finally came back to the sacred valley. The world below had little kindness or welcome for us. We passed the lake at night. As we had nothing to trade we thought not to disturb you."

Copperman nodded. "This was a kindness. I notice the new sheepskins on many of your hunters. You must have had some good fortune on the trail."

"All fair trades I can assure you," the elder said.

I remembered the sheep thought taken by the wolverine during the summer. I looked at the skins on a few of the main hunters and recognized a certain quality to the wool. Patches of black among the well groomed white. Gy and his men cared for their sheep and fed them up, then these thieves snuck them away in the night.

"So how did your foundling fare?" The old man asked.

"Oh the babe?... He died that day. He is not to be spoken of."

"Hmmm...." The old man squinted at me. I felt my skin crawl with loathing.

"And is this your son? He is not the size or shape of you."

"I am Copperson," I said. "I am a main hunter. If you have questions about me, speak directly."

The old man chuckled. "He has your arrogance, insulting us with our bread still in his teeth."

The others stood. One of the hunters with a new sheepskin on his back stepped forward.

"Is this a trade visit? State your business here. We have given you the kindness required and you insult the elder."

The old man raised a crippled hand and waited until the others sat back down.

"This is Copperman of the Lake-people. Let him tell us of his journey and I will decide the nature of his intentions."

They sat but the hunters fingered their weapons and the air of welcome changed around us.

"Bluestone!" Copperman said. "Bluestone is what we seek."

Copperman slid the copper axe from his pack and the others marveled at its perfection. He held it up for them to see. "The one who leads us to bluestone will have a fine copper knife blade in return. If it is on the Mountain-clan's territory we will bring meat back when we return for the trade."

The mood changed again. Copperman pulled a small copper blade from his pack. He handed it around. Each hunter held it then passed it reluctantly to the next. This was Copperman's way and a good trade technique. Many in this clan would have never held a blade like this before and might never again.

The elder waved us away and we retreated while he spoke to a small group of main hunters. They were gesturing excitedly and I knew the decision was not if we could use the land but how much they would want in return.

The elder approached us and motioned for Copperman to speak to him privately.

The two walked along the rock creek and spoke lowly as the rest of us watched and waited. The girl with the split lip sat, clutching my leg with both hands. Her hair tangled into clumps, her wrist-beads made from bits of pinecones and rough twine. She could have been my sister. My cousin. My wife. I wanted to run and not stop until I swam in our cold lake, scrub with sand and ash to wash this place from my bones.

Soon Copperman returned and rubbed noses with the elder, signaling the completion of a deal. A hunter motioned us to follow him and began walking the trail through the village and up the narrow slope towards the mountain. Finally we were on a trail out of sight of the valley of mountains. We walked until dark, stopped at a rest-camp and lay out the bedding. The warrior slept near his own little fire a hundred paces ahead. He was thrilled to be our guide and thoughts of the copper blade no doubt kept him warm that night.

Copperman built up the fire and wrapped tight in this robe. He said nothing but looked at me from time to time. I could not speak to him. Finally as the fire dyed down to embers he looked at me directly.

"Are you not going to ask?" His voice trembled with emotion.

I said nothing.

"I told him, told the elder that I brought you here to face your dark Gods. I told him that he was a fool. That you were a main hunter. And if they ever came near the lake again we would slay them all as sheep-thieves and sink their bodies into burial bay without ceremony. If we find bluestone we will smelt it here and bring them two deer in return."

Copperman banked the fire with a log, and lay back to sleep. As quickly as it had come my hatred of him left. Not from what he said but from the emotion in his voice. We had not come here to face my dark Gods, but to face his. He needed them to know what his son had become. I slept long and deep; drained, empty, exhausted. Separated from the past. Dreaming of nothing.

A hidden loathing

Once I had gone hunting with Okla and we came upon a red-deer stag a hundred paces into the first trail. It had run up to where we stood and stopped, turning sideways to sniff the markings from a doe in heat. Too focused on mating to see us twenty paces away. It stood ignoring us as we drew arrows and fired, hitting it in the neck and chest. It ran past us back down the trail and we found it within sight of the village. The morning had barely begun and the hunt was over. I struggled to understand why this perfect hunt had been so unsatisfying. Neither Okla nor I ever spoke of it over the camp fire.

I thought of that deer the morning of our hunt for bluestone in the mountain valley. Our guide, a main hunter named Aro, walked us to a shelf of bluestone that had broken from a cliff like ice cracked from a glacier. It was next to the trail and splintered like misfired pottery. Not quite as pure as the bluestone from the cave but still beautiful against the gray stone it rested on. It looked naked and out of place among the rubble. Copperman handed Aro the copper blade he had promised and he nearly danced with joy as he held it. Copperman told him to keep it covered with a thin smear of oil by rubbing it against his nose and forehead from time to time. He even helped him find a good fine grained sand-tone with no cracks or ridges in it and taught him how to sharpen the blade with it.

The blade was more for status than use, but sharpened properly it would clean a fish or trim a green arrow from an arrow-bush. Copperman told Aro to fetch anyone with strong legs who wanted to earn beads in trade for cracking and carrying the stone to the creek. The main hunter ran childlike down the trail and I watched him rubbing the blade against his face as he went. He wanted it to shine when he showed the others.

Copperman stood on the shelf of bluestone. It was as high as my waist and twice as long as a man. The place it had fallen from, a dark line against the cliff above us, probably held several times as much but could never be reached. "This has fallen in the last year," he said. "Judging from the plant growth around it."

I felt no thrill in this treasure, just waiting for us in the open like a dead fish in a net. Copperman sighed. "Do not be fooled. We were alone in the forest with your first find. Here we have to deal with human greed and we have to be on our best game if we want to get copper back to the lake. The more we melt the more they will want and the less power we will have to keep it. People who have little will risk everything for a little more."

We found a small creek, the start of the runoff from the high glacier. The water tasted even more silty and cold enough to cause a headache if you drank it quickly.

"There is nothing dangerous in it!" Copperman said, as I winced at the taste.

"I have enough to plan without nursing you along."

I had so much dark emotion over the place that every sense rebelled against it. There were many times on previous journeys that I would have been overjoyed to have steady running cold water. I squared my shoulders and began the task of building a stay-camp from the stunted trees near the creek. I found a fine slab of green flint and a small hammer-stone. Sitting cross-legged I began tapping small flakes from it and eventually had a smooth edge on one side. This was my favorite part of the job, choosing the angle and speed of the hit. A bad angle or too much force would result in a shattered crumble of flint (and probably a stone splinter or two in the hand). I remembered Copperman's technique, breathed slowly several times and then, without thinking, simply struck.

The sound of a proper axe flake is a sucking sound, like a foot in mud as the stone peels apart from itself. This was good. I held a shining leaf of flint the size and shape of a child's foot. Thick enough to grip well in one hand and thin enough at the end to sharpen. With a smaller stone I chipped feathered flakes of stone from the cutting edge until it was sharp enough to shave hair from my arm (the true test of good sharp flint). Then dulled the back half by rubbing the coarse stone against any sharp edges.

There were many large flint slabs here, a quarry worthy of a few days travel for any clan. I wished I could bring it all back with me but if we were lucky there would be weight enough for our packs in the weeks ahead.

I could hear Copperman's determined hammering as he sank wooden stakes into the cracks in the bluestone. I began setting camp, cutting green branches and arranging them in a shelter. It looked as bad as the Mountain-clan's huts and the curved branches were impossible to lay flat against each other. In the end I had to settle for what looked like an upside down bird's nest, piled high with tangled branches. I cleared stones from our sleep spots and layered in armloads of fresh pine boughs for mattresses. It would have some effect in keeping us warm but if rain came we would be huddled, steaming near a high fire.

By evening a line of perhaps a dozen villagers came, each carrying slabs of bluestone. I told them to pile it near the creek. We slept that night to the sound of the gravel sliding along the edge of the silt creek. The next morning the same villagers showed up, including the girl with the split lip. She had a new necklace, a single red clay bead around her neck on a thin sinew string. She smiled and I smiled back. She was strong and during the day she carried as much as the men. By day's end she had three beads on her necklace.

As the pile grew I began the search for clay. Not abundant here. We found little marshes holding a clay of sorts but nothing useable. Finally by the fourth or fifth day, men came with blocks of good red clay. They must have traveled far to find it as it had hardened like stone on the journey. Copperman rewarded them well and I began building my new oven. I wet the clay and kept it moist with a bed of wet grasses. I sat for hours working it, kneading it like einkorn dough until my fingers were raw and chapped. I built a fire and began rolling the long snakes of clay, one slightly shorter than the next, until the giant beehive began to take its form. I made spaces for the extra air vent and built up a dense mound of grass as an inside mould to keep it from collapsing.

I had to use every lesson Sister taught me. It is one thing to work with a full belly in the warm space next to your own village; quite another thing to create with hunger biting your guts and desperation waiting a hundred strong in the valley below. The villagers came and went, always friendly but there was a strained quality to their kindness. A groveling that belied a hidden loathing. They would accept our beads and foreign magic for a time but their appetite would not be satisfied with trinkets from the wealthy.

They carried the bluestone as if it was theirs and were far too eager to see its possibilities. The bluestone had been dismantled in head sized chunks, stacked near the creek and then re-broken into fist-sized pieces. The hunters did not know exactly what we were up to; this was obvious. A few of them thought sorcery made the stone into copper; others thought copper came from the sky and the bluestone a trade with the Gods for it.

Copperman did nothing to dispel either theory. He carefully portioned out the trade beads until the last of the stone was cracked and piled. He handed out a few extras to the hardest workers and I noticed the new leather string of beads, eight or ten, that the girl with the split lip had. She had washed her hair in the creek and combed out the clumps with fresh pinecones. I had not noticed her eyes before; they were green flecked and wild. She was thin but strongly built and every time she walked near, she found a reason to touch me, a hand on a shoulder, a brush against my feet. She could speak but with the missing teeth her language was barely recognizable. Once I cut my hand slightly against a stone and she rushed me to the creek, rubbing it with cold water. Then she found nettle-root, crushed it and rubbed it into the wound.

Copperman called her Little-Asha and gave her several jobs around camp. The day came to send the others back to their village he asked her to stay and assist. I understood his reasoning. The hunters would watch and learn our ways, begin to make the copper themselves some day. Little-Asha was an innocent who could help without risk to us. Also she had a gentle way about her. I was happy for the extra hands and even happier for the privacy away from the main hunters and their questions. They were off with their trade-goods and we were left to our work.

Firewood was a three-day job, scrounging the hills for every dry pine branch and pinecone we could reach. The surroundings were becoming familiar and I did not want them to. Did not want my mind holding this place. We were along a small creek at the foot of a hillside, beginning a long, flat plateau between the high mountains and the rock valley of the Mountain-clan. Game was scarce and mainly consisted of marmots and rabbits, low on fat and hard to hit among the rocks. I lost many arrows and Little-Asha constantly replaced them, coming in with bundles from arrow-bushes and tipping them with antler-points, simple points made by splintering antlers and rubbing them into shape against a large flat sandstone. Not very effective for deer but perfect for small game, as they were tougher than flint against the rocks. There were no fish in the shallow creek lakes pooled around the mountain. The roots and pine nuts were never enough and I understood why the Mountain-clan were small people. My weight, gained over the summer, dwindled and I could already see ribs where there should be meat.

Nights, Little-Asha slept out near the fire under a thin deerskin, worn nearly furless. I watched her near the fire and thought of my warm sleep robe. I rose one night and watched her sleep. Copperman grunted and I looked over to see him in turn watching me. He slowly shook his head and I lay back down. Of course, he was right. I knew well enough what resulted when robes were shared, even if I knew not how it was practiced between husband and wife. What could come of her sharing my robe and bed? And would I take her as a wife? Would I leave her here carrying a child? Also, she was of my clan by blood. This was never good and there were rules among all peoples about who among a clan can share a child. All of these things I knew well but still there was a cold girl and I was warm under a robe, not ten paces away. Troubled thoughts burned in my body all of that night.

Rains threatened but never came. I smoothed fresh clay over the freshly fired oven and mixed it with chunks, fired and hardened from the day before, to strengthen it. I made two tubes from the only arm length straight branches I could find, wrapped them in clay, fired them and cleaned out the charcoal from inside. Copperman spent these last days arranging the spot near the river, firewood stacked in easy reach. Little-Asha came and went; she brought small food with her, bread crackers from einkorn and pine nuts and shreds of deer. She slept near our fire and once in the night she came over to me and tried to crawl into my robe. I shook my head and she pulled again at my robe. It took all my will to send her back. Copperman, only a few paces away and no doubt listening for such activity, grabbed a branch from our shelter and snapped it against the ground in warning and she scampered back to her place near the fire. The next morning she was as sweet and helpful as usual as if my rejection never happened. A Lake-girl would have refused to speak to me for a summer at least but life had a different meaning here. It takes food and shelter for hurt feelings to have an effect.

Copperman came to me after she left for the village. He examined the new oven and nodded. "Strong and big. Half as big again as last year."

"We have a problem," I said. "We need to send them off for more clay." I had only just realized my error that morning. With the size of the oven and the clay needed for the extra tube there was no clay left to make moulds.

Copperman shook his head. "Do you think we would spend days crafting jewels and blades here? They would watch and demand most of it. Or simply kill us in our sleep. No, we will make large pieces and bring them back to the lake to work in safety. This is how they did it when I was a slave. A round bowl in the wet sand will be form enough for our needs. Have you noticed Little-Asha getting bigger? She is eating well. She has new leather slippers and some of those beads on her neck are not from us. She is spying and telling them of our activities. This is why she would join your bedroll. The elder's plan no doubt."

I thought about this betrayal and suddenly it all made sense.

"Do not look so surprised. If you were her, would you do any different. These are days of plenty for her. She is well fed and important. We are the outsiders here and she owes no allegiance to us."

"She works against us...why do we allow her to stay?"

"Because she will help us survive. We are using her far more than she is using us." I did not understand it at all but trusted Copperman in matters as complicated as this. He said we should rest the day and eat most of our rations. That afternoon we sat near the small fire when Little-Asha came up to join us. Copperman told her that we were fasting and praying until the next day. Then the others should come the next night to see us trade for metal with the Gods. She left excitedly with the message. As soon as she was out of sight Copperman leapt into action.

"Now we begin and every second we save, is copper in our packs!"

Melting earth

Copperman's meticulous nature had become mine and I understood that night the importance of our methods. There were five elements needed to make copper and we had them laid out before us in abundance. Wood, water. Fire, earth and air. We had the wood stacked on one side of the clay oven and a small mountain of bluestone on the other. The small creek near camp had risen, as ice creeks are prone to do as summer builds. Copperman checked its path and said we had the night to work before water rose to cover the camp. He hoped it would let us do our work as the pile of bluestone would take an extra day for the two of us to move.

He began piling firewood and pinecones into the oven and I carried a small flame on the tip of a twig from the little fire in the pit to the pinecones in the oven. The day before I had found a chunk of twisted pine so filled with pinesap that it dripped. My hands still smelled of it. I put this on top of the pinecones and fire leapt around it, liquid sap filling the oven with white flames. In minutes the pinecones were gone and we began stuffing the oven with solid chunks of wood.

We each had a deerskin sewn into a funnel like a half-finished water bag. The pointed end went into a tube of clay that fit into one of the air vents in the oven. Lifting the open end of the deerskin filled it with air. Closing it again with a quick snap trapped the air inside it. Leaning down on the bag while holding it closed pushed air down the tube and into the oven. It was delicate work, like milking a goat. The air would not be forced; it had to be coaxed. We had practiced this together at home and now we fell into a rhythm. The trick was to begin pushing air into the oven at the exact time the other had finished. In this way there was never time for the fire to cool down. It takes only a few seconds to lose the white flame needed to melt bluestone. We had to keep our bellows wet inside to prevent sparks from the fire burning the leather.

Copperman was impressed by the new oven; it glowed in minutes and ate wood like a hungry child eats porridge. After three fills, the pinecone coals lay in a deep bed at the bottom of the oven and the heavy wood chunks we dropped into the fire nearly burst into flames. I took a small lump of the last of our wet clay and packed the exit tube shut with it. This was tricky. The exit-hole had to be sealed well enough, but not so well that we couldn't unplug it without breaking the whole oven. We began to drop chunks of bluestone into the fire and a gentle mist began to fall, a summer wet that makes hot work even hotter.

The sky was so wet it began to press down on us and made the world small and stifling. I wanted a cool breeze but the day held dead quiet, save for the puffing exhale of our bellows and the angry in-breath of the fire.

For or the first time we were equals in labor. Copperman made a bowl-shaped depression in the sand in front of the exit tube and wet it with a handful of water. We had burned through four refills of firewood before filling the front of the oven with bluestone. Now we worked frantically, stacking wood until it balanced on top of the oven, then bellowing air until the clay walls glowed in the evening's fading light.

There is a smell when the copper begins to melt, the smell of an oven at full fire, a dusty, dangerous sensation that warns the world. Within the white-hot oven stone is becoming liquid. Copperman had seen ovens shatter at this heat and liquid copper splashing out to burn flesh from men's legs. I kept pace with my bellow as he moved quickly around to the front and tapped a pointed stick into the clay plug. With some effort he managed to knock it free. For an agonizing moment, nothing happened. He poked around into the fire a few times and then wet metal poured golden red out of the front of the oven and filled the bowl-shaped mould to the very top. Three or four axe head's worth of copper in one melt! This was more than even Copperman could imagine. He smiled up at me like a child, his eyes lit by the furnace of the clay oven.

He gently skimmed dark lumps of charcoal and slag from the top of the copper with the pointed stick, and, like burnt milk, it folded away, leaving shining red beneath. We let the fire die down and rested, holding our hands in the cold creek. The bowl of copper cooled in a short time and we poured water from our bags over it until it steamed itself out. Copperman was thrilled with the quality. He said the color of the stone led him to underestimate its content. This was as pure as the cave stone, maybe better.

We cleaned out the charcoal and slag from the oven as best we could with sticks that burned as we used them. Then, after a few bites of food and deep gulps of water, we began again. The dark night expanded as we breathed into our fire and over the next hour we burned through half our wood and melted another bowl of copper. We rested after that letting our hands (gone numb from heat) soak in the cold creek. We ate the very last of our food, six deer ribs, a lamb thighbone and several strips of dried mutton. I knew this was both to build our strength and to lessen the load we would carry.

Copperman, who never rested during a rest, went through our packs, leaving out anything we did not need to survive. This was difficult as everything we carried we desperately needed. He cast aside extra flint, a small sand stone to sharpen his axe, our water filter tube, anything to off balance the great chunks of copper that would weigh down our escape.

We fired the oven again and Copperman picked out the best stone for the melt. As I worked the fire up he tossed the rest of the bluestone into the creek. I could hear them splash but the night was too black to see into. The last melt was the hardest. A light rain began and there was no way to keep our wood dry. The chunks steamed in the oven and big wet drops hissed against the outer walls.

It was greed I guess that pushed us into that last drive, burning the wood down to the last twig. The melting point was close; so close, but we were exhausted and sweat and rain poured from my forehead as I raised and pushed air into the never-ending hunger of the fire. Copperman, possessed by the metal so close, jumped up and began dismantling our shelter, smashing chunks with his axe and tossing them into the fire.

I drove the bellows and he filled wood and began again, until the smell of melting came, dusty through the growing rain. The walls glowed dangerously and I smelled burnt hair a few seconds before my bellows burst into flame. I jumped back as the air itself burst from the bellows, singing my forearms. I ran to plunge them into the creek, only to fall, face forward into the water. The creek had risen during the night, climbing up right next to the clay oven. I nearly fainted from the shock of the cold after hours of sweltering heat near the fire. I was in ankle deep water but the current was swift and threatened to sweep me down with it into the blackness.

I crawled from the crumbling sandbank towards the glow of the fire and Copperman's shadow kneeling before it. He was skimming the top from our fourth bowl of copper.

"How bad are your arms?" he said without looking up from his work.

I checked them with relief. "Pink but not blistered. The water," I said. "It is almost on us."

"Burn camp," he said. "We need more light."

I took a branch from the half-toppled shelter, lit it in the dying fire of the clay oven and set the shelter alight. Soon our small world was bigger. Copperman poured water from his skin into the freshly smelted bowl and plumes of white steam rose from it. In the growing firelight I could see the creek, grown to a small angry river, only paces away, eating chunks of the soft sandy bank as it climbed.

"The rain!" Copperman shouted over the sound of the water. "It almost won!"

He used a stick to roll the steaming bowl from the sand, pouring the last of the water onto it. He handed me both water bags to fill. "You are already wet." He held onto me as I stepped again into the river. Anyone who has tried to fill a water skin in the night in a glacial river will understand my frustration. Water surrounding me, pouring onto me from above, freezing me from below and shaking me from the ground with its pull; water everywhere but inside the bag.

Copperman pulled me back up and looked at the empty bag. "What were you doing out there?"

I was too cold to answer. He grabbed a bag and crawled on his belly out to the edge of the river. The bank collapsed and he slid in over his head, came up spluttering and fought back out of the wet sand. He had lost the water bag in the struggle.

"Gods!" he shouted.

As the rain faded, we stood, shivering and slowly drying near the dying fire. The stars flickered overhead and it grew colder as it does with a clear sky. We packed in the last of the firelight and then huddled in the circle where the shelter had been. The ground was hot enough to thaw us out as we waited for morning.

A wall of ice

We moved out into the very first gleam of light, marching up and away from the growing water. The creek had not only swollen but separated into three other smaller creeks. To our fortune, they were small enough to cross and fill our water skins in. We had three water skins left after Copperman's mishap, and, though they seemed heavy, they would diminish soon enough. Looking down from the short climb, our camp was a burnt smudge in the morning haze. It was already half sunken into the gray river.

The rain came harder and we climbed slowly, following no trail. Copperman began walking hidden-steps. It seemed pointless in the rain but I followed, stepping in his footsteps, as we moved from rock to rock, avoiding any dirt or mud, circling around bushes or grasses that might break and reveal our passing there. He looked down to the camp often, half crumbled into the rising river. He stopped me with a hand twice on our climb, once when a doe stepped nimbly across the water and again when a fox darted around the empty fire, searching for burnt bones in the rubble.

The river was a dark, straight line, snaking down the valley, branching off into smaller creeks. Once he stopped and sank into a crouch and I followed. We watched, legs cramping, until I saw what he did (his eyes were better at than men half his age). It was Little Asha, sneaking along the small ridge just above camp. When she found us gone, she gazed around, uncertain, then, began to run back down the valley. We watched until she was out of sight and then he motioned for me and climbed hard, ignoring the hidden-steps.

We had a short time before she would warn the others that we had fled. I could feel the weight of the copper in my pack, sagging and rolling awkwardly; its cold crept through the leather and into the small of my back. Copperman had twice the weight and I wondered if it was a burden to him. Mine felt nothing like treasure, and I was tempted to throw it down the hill to slow the pursuit of the hunters.

The higher you are the better you can hide. This was the rule, hunting or running. Of two opponents, the one on higher ground has the advantage. This was the reason the Elkhorn made their home on a plateau. If nothing else, they could throw rocks down upon invaders. But this was the opposite direction from home. Our packs were heavy and we could neither eat nor drink the copper we carried. By high sun we were above the last of the small trees and against the great ice wall. I had never seen one before though they were above all camps if you walked far enough. This one was crumbled and a deeper blue than I knew existed. The sun sank into it, illuminating layer after layer of ice. Copperman said it was older than the memory of men and older even than the rocks that it shoved aside on its slow crawl.

Rain clouds hung below us, obliterating our view of the mountain valley. A river, encouraged by the sun, gushed from a deep cave on its belly, and another smaller river ran from its very top, a hundred paces high, and misted out over its entrance into a colorful rainbow. I forgot everything as I watched it, mesmerized by its splendor. I wanted to follow the river into its belly and see what was hidden there. Small chunks of ice fell from its upper edge, crashing down to the river below. They floated along to join the eternal flood. We rested for a good time looking upon it.

"There are animals in it," he said.

I waited. "I hunted along its edge years ago, and there are bones of animals great and small that reveal themselves as the ice melts. Animals I have no explanation for."

"Do they live in the cave?"

"No, they are from another time…their bones crumble as you gather them. But there is told of hunters who have found great animals whole and have eaten them in times of hunger, giant beasts many times the size of your Urus, fur so thick it was axe work to get to the frozen meat. I do not know if this is story or truth but the one who told me was an honest man by nature."

We watched for a while longer, letting the full sun warm us. We made tracks up to the ice wall, so close the waves of cold made a temporary winter in its shadow, then we followed our steps in reverse, walking backwards into our own tracks.

"They will think we made the journey onto the ice wall. The path leads to the other side of our lake," he said. "They will not follow us there as the cracks in the ice are now uncovered and few men could make it safely to the other side. They might think us dead."

We circled around the ridge until we were some distance from the original path. Then we waited. By afternoon they came; a tracker with eight or ten main hunters following. We could not make out individuals but I'm sure the hunter with the copper blade was among them and Little Asha was obvious as the small figure following them many paces behind. As they moved up towards the ice wall trail, we went down the way they came.

It is very tedious walking up a trail seeking tracks, but fast going the other way. The trail melted before us as we jogged down it; in the afternoon light we were back within sight of our camp though it was now gone under the river.

"If our plan was to mislead them, why did we hide our footprints on the way up?" I said.

"To slow them. Also, if the path were too obvious they might suspect trickery."

We took the route above the rivers and by evening we were before the three caves, the caves they had taken refuge in as my mother lay curled about me in the valley below.

We saw their torches as they returned, beaten and defeated, no knowing we were in sight of them, never expecting us to be in their sacred caves.

That night was a sleepless one. I could not even rest, ever expecting a shout and a rush of torches and spears. I could hear Copperman lightly snoring as I took watch. The cave, dry and perfect at its entrance, must have had many paintings of interest and sacrifices within its depths. But I would never see them; we arrived at dusk and left well before first light.

Floating

Hunger has different effects on people depending on their nature. Okla had rage hunger and it kept him dark and angry. He said his father had the same and it was a curse in his family line. He would become argumentative until the first big bites of food and then he softened and became himself again. Mother seemed unaffected by food or the lack of it; she went about her work the same in times of lean or fat. Sister was the same. Copperman slowly hardened in times of hunger like the point of a wooden spear cured in the fire. I had been hungry often enough to recognize the signs of its effect on me.

I walked the trail in the dark, feeling my body lift slowly just off the ground. I would float and drift lightly, euphoric, as if watching myself as a stranger. I did not carry hunger; it carried me. If I stumbled, it was a cushioned fall. I would smile slightly and even giggle, struggle to my feet and begin again. The stars waved to me and the trees spoke softly, whispering my name. I could see well enough in the half moon and Copperman kept a pace he knew I could manage. I wondered how fast he walked alone as he always had to slow his pace for the others with him. The day came suddenly as we crossed a sloppy marsh and climbed a small crest of stone. Bright sun woke me from the slow hungry dream of night walking. Copperman rested his back against the rocks, taking in the sun on his face.

"How was your sleep?" he asked and I laughed. "Do you think they have followed us?

He thought about the question longer than I liked. "No," he said, "but it would be foolish to ignore the possibility. If they have, and we are not clever, we would lose more than the burden in our packs."

The water was gone from the three skins and we found a clear slick coming from cracks in a rock face. This was safe water as the earth cleans it. Water in pools held belly sickness and a traveler will spill his food from top to bottom from its effect. We filled the skins from the trickle of clean water. I saw something white in the bushes and scrambled in to retrieve six small eggs. My fingers shook as I cracked one gently against a rock: Pure, clean eggs with yellow yolk. I drank it down in one sip. Copperman smiled and took his three, cracking them expertly between thumb and forefingers. A trick I have never mastered. This was pure food and it needed no cooking, though we would normally rest them in sand over coals to harden them for travel. He drank eggs gratefully and I felt the happy blur of hunger change over to sharp focus. I liked the dream better.

How far had we come? What was the way home now? Copperman took deep drinks from the rock slick and then pointed at the bushes near him; there were two more grouse nests. We each ate as many eggs as we could from the surrounding nests, and, with every egg, the hunger subsided until I could eat no more.

"We will climb down," he said, pointing to our left at a steep slope. "It is not the easiest path but one they will not suspect."

Walking down hill is harder than climbing and the legs shake as you drop. Despite its dangers, the way down from the mountain clan was more satisfying than any other I can remember. Each step down brought us closer to the lake, and, as its edge came clear so far away and seemingly directly below us, I felt the strength of my Lake-family connected to it. Soon the path became a cliff and we used hands and feet to navigate the drop. Stones dislodged from time to time and we watched them tumble and bounce out of sight. This is how we would drop if one of us fell. I had power from the grouse eggs and climbed fearlessly from one ledge to another, holding cracks in the stone, gripping roots from stunted trees. A few times we seemed stuck until Copperman found alternative routes. He had done this before and was full of advice as we climbed.

"Make one foot secure before using the other," he called, or "slow is secure, fast is loose."

By afternoon, the lake was so close we could smell it, sweet mud and water lilies, rising in the warm breeze. There was some question as to our making the lake by nightfall and Copperman had to abandon his caution, urging me on. A night, crouched on the side of the mountain, would be cramped and sleepless and rocks sometimes fell from above as the heat of the morning sun awoke them to fall.

I began to fade as the evening came on and with the very last of our strength we made the final descent along some deep crevasses. Flat ground came with a jolt and I nearly wept I was so grateful to feel it on my aching feet. We stumbled the short path to the lake, and, though it was far from home, it was familiar and welcoming. We lay under a tree on the sandy bank and Copperman flicked with his fire kit but to no avail; even he was too weak to start a fire. We lay under our sleep furs, back-to-back, and dreamt hard and deep with the sound of the lake lapping at our tired bones.

Blood brothers

The spark clicking stones of Copperman's fire kit did their jobs early the next morning. It was still chilly but the cloud-covered sky held the warmth against the earth and the day would be a muggy swimming day. I had thought of little else on the journey. Heavy wealth in our packs and dark spirits following and all I could think of was a clear cool swim. The fire wanted to cook food that we did not have and I sat near it warming my hands. I found a small round pebble and sucked on it like a child does when he is hungry. My stomach was not fooled. I could find a few crawdads in the nearby creek but this might awaken a hunger that a few tastes of crawdad would not comfort.

Copperman took the two crude bowls of copper from his pack and one from mine as well, hefted them in one hand with effort and smiled at me. I tried to smile back but they were nothing to me. I wondered for the first time if this was a life work to follow.

He scowled. "What? Is it not lovely? Is it not perfect?"

He set them down and glared. "Never in your life will you take such a treasure! Never will you see again such a perfect melt!"

I shrank back from the tone in his voice. He stood and paced. "You are young! Maybe too young to understand so I will tell you once and you will remember. This…" he grabbed the largest bowl, held it to the fire light, its reddish sheen dulled by the layer of sand melted into it, pitted and strange.

"This was taken from the land of our enemies, smelted in their very presence and then it disappeared from their grasp. We slept in their cave and left with two winters' worth of trade goods. With a dozen main hunters and a hundred arrows we could not have taken such a victory. And our enemies…make no mistake, they were our enemies…have no idea how we took what we took…they do not even know if we were successful or if we died on the ice wall above them."

He sighed. "This will feed our family and repay the sheep stolen from your sister's husband."

I nodded. "I think I understand. It just seemed so…"

"Ugly?"

"Yes, it is ugly."

His eyes gleamed at the chunk of raw copper in his hand. "Soon we will make it beautiful."

There was a noise I recognised, the frendly hollow clonk of a wooden pole clanking the side of a boat. We spotted two small fishing vessels far off. We called to them and they turned, poling over the flats towards us. They had day-bread, still slightly soft from the morning's cooking, and skins of warm tea.

I did not recognize them but Copperman did: the father Ebal and son Ebalno from the far side of the lake. We traded on occasion with them and the father remembered me from years past. We were on the farthest north end of the lake and the people there were much the same as us, only they had a small village, perhaps two dozen. They lived on fishing only and had no connection with the hunting and shepherds in our clan.

The boy, a few years younger than I, wanted to talk about everything and as he did his words stopped and repeated often. He was friendly and desperate to be liked. He was what some called young minded. I had met their like a few times before, short round faced and chubby hands. Excited, he showed me the fish traps and how they needed to be set with bait; his father patted him gently.

"Now, Ebalno, I suppose they know this already," he said. But the boy would not be satisfied until he explained their work in great detail. From the way he repeated everything I could tell this was how it had been explained to him many times over. He was tedious with explanations but also extremely happy and his good mood and wonder at the magic of fish traps cheered me up. When he began to explain it all again his father laughed loudly and said

"Now it is told, now it is all told."

Ebalno thought about this, and then settled down, his job done. We ate everything they had for lunch and drank all of their tea; it was rude but impossible to resist. They must have known how hungry we were as they checked a few fish traps near by and came back with seven fat perch for our lunch. We made no mention of the reason for our journey and they asked for none. In the day's heat I swam, rested and swam again, and again, until the knots in my aching muscles relaxed. I slept the day away, vowing to never journey again. That night we were invited to their village and it was with no small relief that our packs were taken in small boats and we in another to the very end of the great lake to the grass flats that held the small Lake-clan's houses.

The houses were made of thatch and thin straight birch, peeled and grayed from the sun. They stood out from the lake's edge and rested like the Bog-shepherds' housed on posts driven down into the mud bottom of the shallow water. They were not near as sturdy as the Bog-shepherds' houses but trim and finely crafted.

Ebal's house swayed slightly and creaked fearfully as I climbed up to it. The others had their boats tethered between structures and they came out to greet us, walking nimbly from boat to boat until the whole clan was gathered like a floating tribe in a dozen boats around us. We sat on a ledge jutting out from the house and greeted them one by one. There were too many to remember their names but I could see a similarity to our clan. The language was the same with a slight dip and rise, a sweet sounding dialect I wanted to remember as it gave a certain music to our tongue. They were slightly built from a diet of fish and their lean muscles were covered by thin cloth.

The smell of bug root drifted around among the smoke of small fires which they kept in wide clay pots. As evening came, the warm air held swarms of gnats and mosquitoes that rose from the wide, weeded shallows. They offered us bug root and we split it and rubbed it around our arms, necks and around the hairline.

Copperman sat, shoulders square, and spoke loudly about our journey, weaving in and out of the tale without a mention of copper.

'We were on a spirit quest,' he said and as he described the high mountains he gave amazingly detailed

335

descriptions of the plants and animals we encountered. The Lake-folk were fascinated and I listened carefully. This was how to earn your fish and bread. Many of them shouted out questions and Copperman was happy to answer them as it made the story longer. We dined on smoked pike and eel, grilled trout and small cakes called whitebait, made from hundreds of whole, tiny minnows rolled in Einkorn flour and sizzled on a greased clay plate over coals. They seasoned everything with the small onion weed that grows around quiet coves. I could not eat enough and my hunger brought sighs of sympathy from the mothers in the clan, who refilled my plate until Copperman motioned for them to stop.

His story went into the night, describing the swamp water and our need to make a water filter from the hollow bark. When we got to the ice wall, Copperman said:
"But now my throat is dry, Copperson will describe it to you." All eyes turned to me and I froze for a few seconds, then began. It is a skill to tell of a strange new thing so that others may see it. I summoned everything I had and told of the great ice wall, remembering its blue and its power to move huge boulders like pebbles, its cold breath pouring out clean from the cave in its belly. By the time I had finished the others were faces in the light of their torches clicking their tongues in appreciation.

Ebalno cleared his throat. "Do...do...do you know how to bait a fish trap?"
I could see his face looking at me eagerly.

"No," I said. "Tell me!"

In the days that followed, the dark journey melted away, as pain from all journeys eventually does, leaving behind the adventure of it all. There were many friendly faces to meet and, in the way of small clans, questions to answer. These were quiet folk and not many travel to the end of the lake to trade fish. I followed Copperman's example and answered the questions with as much information as I could. They saw me not as a boy but as a well-traveled main hunter and the stories from the Elkhorn, Bog-shepherd and Mountain clan won me meal after meal.

There were two girls near my age and for the first time ever, I had females fighting for my attention: One, a dark-haired girl with caramel colored skin, and one, a pale creature with light reddish hair. The women of the clan kept close eyes on us and rebuked the girls if they became too physical with me. The water was the one place they could not follow and the girls made the most of our swims, pulling my arms and wrestling me into a state of torment. These games fooled no one and soon—far too soon for my liking—the women would call us back for one reason or another. I would have chosen either for a wife in a moment for my childish longings but Copperman took me aside and explained the situation. If I were to choose one, she would have to come to our village and my wanderings would be set aside for the wedding and house building and the

337

trappings of adulthood like children (which he guessed would come soon after). I wanted a girl to wrestle with (I wanted both of them in all honesty), but a wife? children?

When Copperman announced our departure the next morning, I was more than ready to go. The small clan was so happy with our visit that they gave us each a shell necklace, delicately carved with the fish sign of the Lake-clan. This meant we were members of the clan now and their elder told us that we were always home on their side of the lake. The girls were miserable at my leaving and each kissed me right on the lips, despite the scolding of the mothers. Ebalno was the most stricken by our departure. He cried loudly, his mouth open in grief. And the others never thought to scold him for it. It was his way and his tears nearly made me cry with him. I took a piece of flint and made a small cut on the meet of my hand where it meets the thumb, just enough to draw blood. Then I handed the flint to him. His father whispered to him and he dutifully made the same small cut on his hand drawing a single drop of blood. We gripped hands together. "Now we are blood brothers," I said. "We are always connected and your enemies are mine." He smiled broadly and held the hand up for the others to see. They cheered and clapped Ebalno on the shoulders. Copperman nodded to me and I could see this had made him happy. We entered the guide boat and the others stood as we poled across the shallows and into open water. Copperman took some herbs from his pouch and rubbed them into my tiny cut. He gripped my arm.

"This cut was a bigger gift to their clan than any I could have given."
Ebalno and his father followed our guide boat for most of the morning, reluctantly turning back and calling best wishes over the water until we were out of sight.

Never draw your bow on her

Our home landing came with the welcome of most of the clan, joining us first with a cheer from Hanit's boat. He rowed over to join us and others came, dropping their fish-traps. We poled over shallow water towards our familiar bay, looking as beautiful as if it were dreamed up from a starving traveler. Smoke filtered from at least four smoke houses with fish and game plentiful during our absence; it drifted across the warm water to tempt me with tantalizing scent of sage and dripping fat.

There were naked children calling and some even swimming out to greet us, holding the side of the boat to drift with us. Copperman laughed at their splashing games, rowing hard to drag our boat with them attached. The women gathered first and then the lazy, main hunters stood from their places of rest. Others on the hills, shepherds, stopped what they were doing and struggled with the choice of tending their sleepy flock or joining the ruckus. Soon they were dropping their daypacks and jogging down the hill.

As we came within a few boat lengths of the harbor, I saw Mother; she was looking at Copperman and her face glowed like a teenage girl. Her man was back and as she searched his face, he smiled and nodded. This was man and wife, the ability to ask and answer a question without speaking. She had asked him if he had found enough copper to stay the summer and he had answered; enough for the next summer as well. All in a look. In that moment I understood that having a wife (some day) was a good thing, maybe even a great thing.

She searched me quickly and it was a mother's look to see if I was injured, holding myself on two good legs, no scars, skinny but that could soon be fixed. I was not part of this communication; she saw and all was good. This happened in a matter of a few seconds but told everything. She splashed into the water and grabbed the bow of the boat. With everyone attached, they lifted the boat half out of the water and dragged it up to the sand as if it were an empty shell.

This was a different kind of homecoming. We were a few days healed and full of energy; there was no need to let us sleep or rub tired feet. Copperman had never come home before the threat of first snow, and as such, most were usually too busy with winter work to pay that much attention. Now we were back to summer heat and Copperman had a story to tell. The elders announced a feast day. These were rare and the others jumped at the occasion.

This should be explained; there is always...always something to do. It is the Lake-people creed. If a child ever makes the mistake of saying that he is bored there will be a dozen tasks thrown at him. This is how we thrived as a people. It is the work law of any people. As such, it is the job of the Council to pick certain days as feast days: Longest day of the year, a wedding or birth of a first child. These days, the only work allowed are jobs necessary to facilitate the feasting. It is then everyone's job to stop working.

Women sent children to gather wood and roots, nuts and fruit, fill water buckets. They made tea and built up the fire in the main fire pit. Families gathered small delicacies, Clay jars of honey and honey wine, bowls of pine nuts and baskets of mushrooms; the hunters brought out a fat doe and some twenty game hens that had been smoking for days. Copperman and I, as the feast day recipients, were set in the cool shade of a curly maple, near enough to the fire to watch the food sizzle but far away enough to escape its heat.

We drank Mother's tea, so familiar that I nearly cried to taste it. The others had to wait for the food but Mother brought us bits of meat, crispy fat, and handfuls of nuts and thin sliced roots, crunchy and raw. She sat at Copperman's feet and rubbed his calves, they were so happy with each other that I could tell they really just wanted to be alone. Soon enough they made an excuse and disappeared into the house.

Little Brother was out hunting with Moon and her two pups, and I watched desperately for their return. After an hour or so I heard that familiar bark and saw Little Brother, proudly carrying a small rabbit. Next to him was a blue-gray fluff of a dog, my Moon. She saw me from a hundred paces and ran so fast that she knocked me over from my sitting position, howling and licking my face at the same time. She was turning herself inside out to nuzzle and wrestle me, her tail wagging so hard it swung her body back and forth. I was happy for the next hours with her in my lap and Little Brother, full of his own stories and wanting to show me new tricks as if I had been gone a whole season.

Moon guarded my every move; if I stood to walk anywhere she would hang so close I would trip over her. I was not going anywhere without her if she had anything to do with it. Soon the sun relented, giving in to a warm hazy afternoon, the feast was ready.

Mother and Father returned, looking happy and disheveled and I knew what they had been up to. If they were happy my world was happy, and finally came Gy and Sister. Gy had slain a lamb for the feast. They arranged it on a spit next to the fat doe and there was barely enough room to cook over the great bed of coals. This was to be a feast where no one left hungry. I was offered honey wine but, remembering the headache that was its cost, I stayed with my mother's tea and drank it the whole evening. The clan gathered, each and every one: Five dozen at least, some two dozen main hunters, two dozen fishermen and the small shepherd clan. They had brought blankets and bedrolls for the small children; we were going to feast long into the night and the cloudless sky promised a showing of stars to keep us company.

The elders gave prayers and thanks to the Gods of the water, air and land for the bounty of the last weeks. The main hunters had never seen such plenty, red deer, roe deer, rabbits and grouse were thriving in the soft season, and warm rain had food-bearing plants of every kind in bloom. The medicine woman had filled her jars with dried herbs and was teaching two of the children to gather extra for the families. Two of the families who specialized in honey had found a string of hives within walking distance and we would have wine to trade. Sister would have traders for as many jars as she could make.

And now Copperman and Copperson had returned within a few weeks of leaving with tales of copper and conquest in the mountains. This was a summer of reward after a few lean years. Gods to be thanked.

After their speeches, Copperman rose, and, despite the heat of the fire, donned his great-robe. He held his copper axe as he spoke, gesturing with it. I could not recreate his story. Suffice it to say that the one he told the little Lake-clan, fine as story as it was, paled in comparison. For the first and only time he told of our trek, leaving out nothing.

As he took me to the mountain clan, many gasped and grumbled at the cruelty of it; then when the sheep-theft came clear, there were shouts from the shepherds, overcome with rage. When we smelted the copper, he drew out from the pack the slabs of metal, one by one, and they shone in the firelight. Our trip to the glacier brought gasps of disbelief and when we finally slid down the mountain into the welcome arms of the little Lake-clan, they cheered and laughed, loving my new blood brother Ebalno. Several fishermen, including Hanit, wanted to go there to meet them and thank them for the service.

Copperman said there was to be a disk of copper to the shepherds for each stolen sheep and they cheered.

'And what of Copperson, what has he to say of this?' I stood, moved by the tale as if it were new to me.

"I ...I have stood, bow drawn, to the wolverine thought to take your sheep. It lives in the maple-wood behind Two Rocks Creek. We have found the real sheep-thieves and taken our revenge. I ask the main hunters to never draw your bow on her. She stands for those we falsely accuse."

I do not know why the wolverine came to me suddenly then and there. The shepherds frowned and the main hunters looked astounded at the request. But we had avenged the clan against theft and this was a reasonable if not unusual request.

The Council nodded and the top hunter, a muscled squat man named Aral, looked at me with a gleam in his eye.

"I have seen her. The tree she lives in, the cubs she feeds. If she keeps to her ground she will never see one of our arrows."

"So it is done!" the Head Council said. "Now Copperman will take his game and we will begin."

This was an honor that came with complications. Take too much and you are greedy, too little and you insult the tone of the feast. Copperman pondered the roasting doe and took a worthy slice with his axe from its haunch. Mother placed it in our clay platter. Then he took a foreleg of the roasting lamb, handfuls of roasted roots and a full game hen. The others cheered and joined in to the taking.

I will not describe the night of feasting: Little Brother on my arm, Moon at my feet, Sister draped around me. Some joys are too perfect to suffer examination. Suffice to say that I was truly happy and for the first time in my life, truly full.

Winter baby

The summer was an eating, swimming, lazy working season of plenty. I found each day merging with the next, and often spent the warm nights next to the main fire outside with the others my age. I had friendships with them all and even a few short-lived romances with a girl or two but nothing beyond kissing and cuddling on a late night. The Lake-clan had rule upon rule about sharing a sleep robe and to take things too far was to risk expulsion from the clan. The girls were not wives for me and the friends were good company but not like my lost brother Okla. I thought of him often and saved the best stories in my head for when we would meet again.

I gained all the weight back by fall and settled into winter with a strange longing for the snows. They came late and gently; the ice coming over the lake was not set for walking until the days were well dark. Hanit had grown dependent on Little Brother's help with the mending and making of fish traps and equipment. His eyes struggled with small knots and close work. Copperman had been to visit Hanit several times during the fall and they had made an agreement. The large open space of his fishing hut was suited for project work and Copperman arranged a space for us there during the days. We had a bank of candles along one wall and a low table of thin split oak stable enough for copper work. This way, Copperman could break his rule of no copper work during the winter and mother could keep the home she wanted without the tapping and noise of it in her head all day.

Hanit had a window facing the weak morning sun and it was made of scraped doeskin so thin that the light came through for our work. It was on a square frame and could be removed and replaced with planks during heavy cold. I settled into the work of transforming our copper slabs into trade goods. Sister made a large heavy clay cup and we fired it many times over to strengthen it. We worked with granite spikes to hammer the copper bowls into chunks (no easy task) and Copperman put the chunks into the heavy clay cup. We made a small kiln using flat stones to make Hanit's fireplace into a smelting oven. We used clay to fill in the cracks and the top was a large thin flake of silvery stone of the type we often used to cook flatbread upon. Oh, the difference when you have food and shelter and good company and most of all: Time.

We worked slowly and deliberately. Little Brother ran errands, getting the things we needed: Fire-wood stacked neatly against the far wall, the ashes ground fine in a grain bowl, pure silky clay to make delicate molds with. We set up the bellows on either side of the fire and arranged half a dozen full water buckets. After many days of preparation the smelting began. Little Brother's eyes gleamed with excitement and I remembered the magic of watching the first copper melt. We made things properly this time and Copperman was right, it was beautiful now. The fire pulsed and the others in the clan knew something was happening, but Copperman kept a fierce guard and visitors would receive an eye glaring through a crack in the door until they left. During our days of melting only Mother or Sister Tau were allowed to enter to bring food. Hanit sat basking in all the excitement; he fiddled with fishing equipment and kept Little Brother in check.

The firing grew so warm we had to open a board at the back of the hut to let the winter in and were grateful for the icy air swirling around the shack. Copperman was in his element and had the intense joy that only came from copper work.

"We should only melt in the winter," he said. "I cannot believe it took me so many seasons to discover it."

We heated the cup of copper chunks until it gave way to liquid. It took far less effort to melt the pure metal then to extract it from heavy rock. We let Little Brother work the bellows a few times but it is hard to keep pace and he soon tired out. I had made tongs from a thick wet green wood branch by splitting it half way and then tying it well with braided string. When the first pot melted well we extracted it by dipping the tongs in water and then reaching in like a two-fingered hand. The green wood smoldered but held fast as I pulled the cup of red copper out. Copperman mixed in a handful of ashes and stirred it into the thick liquid with a thin stone spike held in a small tong. Our hands chapped and we had to re-apply wet clay to our hands and arms often.

After mixing ashes into it we re-melted the cup then poured it into a square clay dish Copperman had greased with mutton fat. It was fine to see the eager faces surrounding the shaking cup as we poured the copper into it. When it had cooled enough to handle, Copperman dipped the clay dish into cold water and the copper block slipped out. Copper, perfect and red on the top with a black layer of ashes and sand, stuck to the bottom. A sharp tap with a stone and the bottom fell away leaving pure shining wealth.

We all held it, marveled at its weight and purity. This happened for days until all three bowls were melted, mixed with ash, re-melted and then poured into forms. Finally the delicate work could begin. The amount of firewood we went through those days would keep a family warm for a winter.

We arranged the clay molds on Hanit's long low table: Blades of different sizes, many medallions and an axe head. Each made by carving out two halves of a clay block and then sealing them together with clay slick. The tops carved open to funnel the liquid down into their shape. It took only one day to melt the pure copper and pour the molds and by the end of that day Copperman called a halt to our work. He stored the molds at the back of Hanit's hut and we went back to our lives.

Mother, who had lived like an only child for so long, enjoyed the family again and no doubt Hanit was happy to have his home alone. I hunted with the dogs who had grown lazy in my absence and managed to take grouse and many snow rabbits and a very fat red deer doe. The woods were bright in the winter sun and the fresh air cleared my lungs of the long smoky work of smelting. The hair on my arms grew back (unlike Copperman whose arms had been burnt hairless so many times it had long ceased growing back).

After weeks of rest Copperman brought us back to Hanit's hut to detail what we had made. Breaking open the smaller medallions first, we found our work to be clean and the disks of copper the finest I had ever seen. We began the slow gentle art of jewelry. Each copper disk was greased with mutton fat, wiped clean and then engraved by using a set of tools made mostly from red deer antler. The tips are hard enough to press an outline into the soft copper. Once an outline becomes clear (a boat or snake or hawk or even a woman, large hipped and well breasted) the antler would trace with pressure over and over until it showed clear. Using a small crystal stone we would tap it with a wooden hammer on the top to punch a hole to string a leather necklace cord through. This was lazy work and we did it on the mornings when the sun came through Hanit's scraped doe window helping the candles light our work.

Little Brother was thrilled with the arrangement and the chance to sit for hours every morning with his three favorite men. He tended to talk too much and Copperman would sigh then scowl as Little Brother asked Hanit question after question until he finally stopped and turned to face Little Brother with a blank stare. The questions would stop for a while until the silence grew too much and he would start them again. Once Copperman sent him to do random chores in the snow as a punishment.

Hanit, who was patient with Little Brother, admonished Copperman. "Be gentle! Boys have empty heads and it is our job to fill them."

Anyone else who tried to speak to Copperman like this would have paid dearly for it but Hanit had Copperman's respect more than any of the elders.

He shrugged, "Possibly...possibly you are right, but he scratches the back of my temper with his babble."

Hanit snorted. "You were deprived of parents at his age, and raised by the whip and the cane. There were none to listen to your questions. He is your blood and deserves at least as much patience as the medallion you hold."

Copperman looked down at the copper disk half engraved with leaves and flowers. I held my breath as he set it down and went out to retrieve Little Brother. They returned and Brother, sniffling, sat down at the table.

"OK," Copperman said looking at him. "What do you think of most often? What do you want to know about? Ask and we will tell you."

Little Brother thought about it for a while. "How do you kill a bear?"

We talked into the afternoon about bears and wolves and even the great Uris. Hanit sat back tending the fire and re-filling the candles and teacups. We did not make any trade goods that day but it was good work nonetheless and I saw a change in Little Brother afterward. He asked fewer questions and worked harder at his bow skills.

We hunted at least every other day, usually in the morning dark and usually with a group of main hunters. I hunted the maple grove from time to time near Two Rocks Creek and found the tracks of the wolverine but never saw her. There were often tracks near hers of a smaller wolverine and it made me happy to know that at least one of her cubs survived. Once I found half a roe-dear carcass dragged up a tree and knew she had made a kill. It was not good to be prey in the maple forest.

That winter I taught Moon's pup to stop chasing rabbits. It took some effort until Moon understood my meaning. She taught him by snarling if he began to give chase; smaller than him, she was the boss and he soon learned. With the two working together we managed to take deer and even a large she-goat where the big trees gave way to the mountain trail. I had to take enough game to keep my status as main hunter and the others, full grown men, watched closely and kept tally of what I brought in. If a main hunter failed to keep up with the others, he would be voted out and his privileges would suffer at the smokehouse. My inclusion was in a big part due to Okla's genius with a bow and the others suspected this. Now he was gone and I spent more time with the copper work and clay work and even ice fishing. (The main hunters teased me about it.) I was spreading myself too thin and would have to choose soon. Copperman laughed at my worries.

"This status is more of a worry than a blessing. It is like becoming a member of the Council. A way for others to determine your actions. Do away with it. Deny it. I take as much game as any but do I ever seek main hunter status?" He snorted and spit into the fire. "I would deny it if it were offered. The same with Council membership. Or, Gods forbid, Council chief. All of it is men deciding what other men should do. Would we hunt any less without the rules? Or fish less? It is all bird-shit in the water."

Hanit, Little Brother and I took to using our ice sled not only to fish from but also to gather and drag wood. This was helpful as his fireplace burned day and night and one sled of wood was the same as ten trips by foot for the same weight. Little Brother's dream was to spend the night out on the ice in it like Okla and I had done on our Elkhorn journey. After weeks of begging I relented. Mother packed us too much food and Hanit even gave Little Brother a ceremony, asking the lake for its approval to sleep on it.

It was his first real adventure from home and we pushed out across the well-traveled ice, past darkened circles of used ice holes, speckled with scales and blood of pike and perch. As the sun faded we anchored only a few hundred paces from the home. He watched the lights of candles and smoke from chimneys, shivering at their great remoteness. It was his first night away from home and as we covered the front of the ice hut with its deerskin door, he nearly whimpered in the dark. I had carried a coal in a bundle of tight moss and let him blow it to life, light the beeswax lamp and hang it on the little holder above us, giving off a flickering faint glow against the skin walls. I thought of Hanit's words and began to tell him stories about the cave in the woods with the paintings.

We lay, wrapped in heavy skins, talking late in to the night. Moon curled between us, gathering heat from both sides. I slept and awoke to Little Brother's crying. The night had grown dead quiet and windless.

"What is it?" I said.

He sniffled, "The dead are coming up from graveyard bay. Trying to get into the hut. Listen."

I waited, then the ice whined and groaned before giving off great cracking sound deep in the lake, like a giant log splitting. We could feel the shudder of it.

"It is just the ice. It cracks. You hear it when we ice fish. You have even seen the cracks move through the ice. Besides, the dead keep watch and guard us from intruders. They want nothing with our tent, and Moon would warn us if there were any real danger."

Moon licked his face as if to reassure him but each creek and groan beneath us made him cry harder.

"Do you want to go back?" I said, "and explain to the others how you grew afraid and could not sleep from the village?"

He shuddered..."No, I am brave enough...I want to stay."

I slept again and awoke to him shaking me. "We made it to morning!"

The sun was a brilliant white as we pushed the short way back to the village. To hear him speak of it to his friends, we were near death's door and lucky to survive it.

Mother made us Einkorn porridge with extra honey and dried berries, fussing as if we had come back from a great journey. I crawled back into bed and Mother let me sleep until long into the day.

Sister gave the village a new boy that week. Fat and squealing, he was named Gyson and I was the first to hold him after Gy. This is the way with uncles, a privilege I had looked forward to. But new babies are loud and puffy and purple, wriggling as if the way you are holding them is never right. I looked into his face for recognition but he merely blew bubbles and grunted.

"He looks nothing like you," I said to Sister as way of a complement but received only laughs from them all. I was his uncle and would be second guardian, though he would probably want to chase sheep for a living like his dad. Still, he was strong and his cries gave great promise, Mother said.

She clutched him as if he might escape. Sister was nearly unaffected by the event and unlike some, she was already walking around and eating porridge and tea and shreds of mutton. The problem was her milk. The baby would not drink it and the first day she held a nipple to its mouth without result. Sister complained of pain from the milk wanting to release and by nightfall the medicine woman came. She tried half a dozen teas and herbs for Sister and rubbed little Gyson with sheep fat from head to toe, then rubbed it off with soft moss. Still nothing. By morning the family had changed from celebration to despair. He would not feed and Sister squeezed painful drops of milk into his mouth only to have him spit them out.

Adults can go weeks without food but a new baby must eat soon or perish.

It was Moon who finally saved him. While we were fussing and Sister lay crying in a corner exhausted and delirious, Moon found the baby's face in among the layers of furs and barked loudly at it. The baby startled as Moon began to lick furiously at its mouth. We all moved in to stop her when we saw the baby's mouth begin sucking at Moon's flapping wet tongue.

"Quickly!" Mother said and we moved the child, Moon still attached at the face, over to Sister's heavy, hanging breast. The baby began to suckle and Sister took notice.

"Ouch!" she said and cried. "It is eating...it is working."

Twice, the baby stopped suckling and we lowered him to Moon, who barked and licked it back to attention. Within a few hours the fears were over and Gyson burped and fell immediately to sleep. Gy knelt down and buried his face in Moon's fur. We left the pair in their fine home, Moon attentively at their side.

War

Little Brother saw them first, with his friends, fishing the ice near home. A line of figures walking the far side of the ice, like slow geese dotting the white expanse. They were beyond calling to and something about their movement caused Little Brother to leave his fishing and alert the others. We came from Hanit's dark workshop and squinted with a dozen others at the sight. When they were abreast of the village, they stopped and watched us watch them. The dogs, eyes far better than ours, saw the strangers, sensed our apprehension and began to bark. Though they were far away they must have heard, as sound travels a flat lake as far as you can see. The travelers stood still for a time, then gathered in a tight group. Copperman stared intently.

"They are talking about us now...men certainly...from their movements."

The strangers began their trek again, walking in a line along the far side of the lake in the direction of the Elkhorn ridge. Copperman told Little Brother to find the Council and tell them to gather the clan.

Little Brother nodded.

"I saw them first," he said. "I spotted them. Is that good?"

Copperman had the look that meant he was too lost in thought to answer foolish questions. Little Brother ran to find the Council. I wanted to ask but waited with the others near the main fire-pit. Copperman began loading the fire with wood until there was a 'meeting–fire' stack. He told me to run and gather green bows from the trail and I knew this was serious. By the time I returned with an armload, the fire rose, flames head high. I piled the soft branches over the top and black smoke rose in the clear noon sky.

"They will see it and know that we are alert and gathered," he said. I did not know whether he meant the shepherds or the distant travelers.

The Council was not as concerned as Copperman was and even sour at being brought out from their warm homes. The lead elder looked as if he were roused from his bed and he rubbed his eyes and huddled in his robe.

"This is Copperman's meeting and he will say…what he needs to tell us."
The other three Council-members looked at Copperman, who said loudly.

"There were two dozen, maybe three. Crossing the ice near Funeral bay. They were not traders. There were no women among them, and their dress and manner concerned me."

The Council spoke to each other as more and more of the clan gathered. Sister and Gy came down, she with Gyson wrapped in a baby-roll of lamb's wool.

The elder spoke: "So travelers were spotted from such a length that they could not even be determined, and as they passed, they stopped for a short rest. Is this the situation we were gathered for? They did not come to trade and so we set a smoke fire to draw them?"

Copperman glared at him but said nothing.

"Well, perhaps this is an emergency for a copper-trader but not the rest of us."

Copperman breathed deep as he does when dealing with a child's foolishness.
He spoke clearly and measured his words carefully.

"If they were traders, they would have come directly here and received our hospitality, or at least gained permission and left trade goods to cross our land. If they were a clan moving, they would have had women and children with them. If they were hunting, they would not walk, single file, across a game-less stretch of ice. Tell them

362

what you could see with your child's eyes," he said to Little Brother. "You were closest. Were they carrying anything?"

Little Brother froze like a doe hidden in the tall grass. We waited.

"They were carrying bows and heavy branches across their shoulders, like this." He took a branch and rested it over his shoulder.

"These were warriors, carrying bows and clubs, crossing open space, single file to hide their tracks. I have seen this before and it means battle."

The elder raised his head at Copperman's tone.

"You have seen this clan before?"

"I have seen their type. They are heading towards the Elkhorn clan, our brothers and distant kin."

"We do not know where they are heading. They are strangers who keep to themselves. As for our land, they have shown no sign of hunting our forest or staying as guests, therefore, they owe us no trade toll. If as you say they travel to the Elkhorn, they will negotiate with them if they stay. From what we know of the Elkhorn, they are more than capable of dealing with travelers without our intervention. The only rule broken has been broken by you,

Copperman, by signaling the clan and inviting notice from the travelers with your smoke fire. Put it out now!"

Copperman frowned at the order.

"Is there anything else for the Council to attend to?"

The question hung in the air and was distinguished with the whoosh of cold water against hot coals. Copperman walked away as bucket after bucket billowed steam around us. The others grumbled and seemed separated by opinion. Some said Copperman knew trouble when he saw it and others said he was the trouble and wanted to stir a battle with strangers for nothing.

That night, Copperman was angered and pacing. He gathered our winter's work, the portion of medallions and small blades from the largest of our copper slabs, and buried them deep in a hole at the back of our house under blankets and straw. Then he spent the evening working on arrow-staffs, stored and bound straight. I joined him in his work and Mother fretted as she cooked us smoked roe-deer haunch and dried herbs stewed with marrow-bones. Perhaps she thought this dish, Copperman's favorite, would soothe him.

He ate without pausing in his work (one of his many strange talents) and by high moon, he had a dozen new arrows wrapped with flint tips and fletched with crow feathers. These were of the heaviest staffs and the crow feathers were unusual. They were battle-arrows and the flint tips were broad and sticky-sharp. He loosened up his bow by flexing it back and forth over his knee dozens of times before stringing it with his heaviest woven string. Finally, he sat back and sipped a cup of hot tea.

"If they come it will not be tonight. They saw our fire and heard our dogs. It was good that you brought bigger dogs into our clan," he said. "Dogs are a menace to a raiding party. The dogs sleep out these nights. I have to convince the others to do at least that much. We will go into the woods at first light and into the high country. If they are on the move we will see them or evidence of their work. Sleep now and pack light for the morning. We will cover a lot of ground."

He slipped out and I guessed it was to convince the others to shed the comfort of their night-dogs to guard the camp. I do not know when he returned as I was deep into bad dream sleep. I woke to him nudging me. It was crisp and hours before light. I dressed quickly and followed him out. We left Moon's pup, our male, large and more powerful than Moon but still puppy-minded. He tried twice to follow but Moon understood our meaning and growled him back to his place on old furs near the door. If strangers came, he would alert the others.

We moved at a slow jog, sliding across the iced-over trails, until we came to a steep rise and Copperman turned and climbed the unused trail, following through the fresh snow by memory. I had grown a bit soft, as happens during winter but the urgency of our task drove me to keep pace. By first light we were high above the lake. The sharp, clear morning held windless and we had to shade our eyes with hat-fur until the morning sun grew high enough to melt the mountain's long shadow. Then we saw it. Smoke trails above the Elkhorn ridge. One of them rose with a spark of flame at its base. It was much larger than any signal fire. In the snowy winter, this was no feast fire.

"Who are they?"
Copperman spat into the snow. "Takers."

Fear clung to me then. "Wolf and Axe?"

He scowled. "So Hanit told you the stories. We are not supposed to speak of it but this is what happens when no one speaks of dark forces. Do you think the Council has the blood to protect us with their decisions? They have grown fat and lazy with new shepherds and abundant game. Our main hunters have never seen battle, and the old ones who have, are told not to stir fear with their tales. Hanit knows. He should have told his stories at every feast. Now this is at our feet and our hunters have no idea how to protect themselves. Remember the party that came to greet us at the Bog-shepherd clan with their spears and dogs?"

"But the Elkhorn are a warring tribe, they can shoot a walnut from fifty paces. They are hidden atop a cliff. Surely they can defend themselves."

"The Takers think of nothing else but war every day. They feed on it, hunt villages like we hunt deer. They have ways. Perhaps there were others meeting them from the other side, perhaps they came at night. Come!"

We jogged the trail down and made the Lake-clan by mid-day. Again, Copperman lit a signal fire and the others came.

Copperman wasted no time with formalities and spoke before the elders all arrived.

"There are fires from Elkhorn ridge. They must have been attacked by the party we spotted yesterday. They might have succeeded. The Elkhorn are fierce and far more prepared than we for such an attack, but until we know we have to ready ourselves. If these are Takers, if they are 'Wolf and Axe', they will use what they find and then come for us."

The Elders were divided; some wanted Copperman reprimanded for another unauthorized gathering and the others wanted to follow his plan and prepare. In the end they retreated to discuss the matter.

Copperman addressed the others in their absence, (another violation of the rules).

"While they sit drinking tea and chewing ginger root, the enemy are fighting our kin. Gather your weapons, mend them, make as many war-arrows as you have staffs for. use crow-feathers to fletch them with. These are the arrows of warriors and will let them know they fight a prepared clan. Keep the fire stacked high. They will come at night. Dogs need to feel our plan and guard the houses from the outside. Each house needs a spear and a woman who will guard the door with the sharp point of it. Children need to know where to hide if they come and hunters need to spread out in all directions with an eye to strangers, even one walking alone. There are tricks too many to count used to take a village. If a single stranger comes, he will be a spy asking for shelter, observing our number and readiness. This is their way. If a stranger comes, welcome him in and we will show him what his clan should expect."

The others livened with his speech and by evening, most of the clan were making plans to protect ourselves. The Council gathered us without fire for a short declaration. They would follow Copperman's advice, but only as a precaution. They had little choice but their anger towards him was obvious in each and every look. I began to worry.

If we were attacked we might all perish; if we were not, the Council might have had enough of Copperman's meddling and expel him and us from our home.

Night came and I waited, bow next to my bed, listening for the slightest sound. 'Okla would be outside,' I thought, bow drawn. I wished I could tell him that the Wolf and Axe were real, that our Elkhorn were in trouble. He would be braver than I; he would give me strength. Night stretched into morning with nothing stirring but the fear and the waiting.

Lie after lie

For three days we waited. The main hunters kept watch in turns and there are few tasks as hollow and grim as sitting watching the dark, bow across your lap, startling at everything that stirs in the night. On the fourth day, the village settled back into normal life; main hunters relaxed their watches or skipped them altogether. Copperman made stackes of spear points and shafts; he gave one to Sister and an axe to Hanit, a flint slab fixed with resin and sinew into a light formidable weapon the older man could swing without effort. If trouble came, the children would hide at the back of Hanit's work-hut under grass mattresses and old furs. Hanit fretted about his boats stranded by the frozen lake. If the thaw came, he and the other fishermen could explore the lake and spy on the others.

We talked of taking the ice-sled out to the Elkhorn but we would be easy targets and there would be no hiding or running from the Takers out in the open. Also, the Elkhorn would certainly shoot first if they spotted anyone approaching after an attack. I thought of our friends there and what they must have endured. What of the girl who kissed me on the cheek?

I went to different lookouts with Copperman each morning and we searched for signs of men. On our fourth day we found footprints, coming upon our main trail from the lake. These were brushed over by a pine branch but Copperman found traces of two men's leather boots and the branch hidden in the snow a hundred paces up the trail. We followed them back towards home in a flurry of new snow. The clouds showed signs of more to come and we were lucky to see the new tracks before they were buried under.

We moved cautiously, Copperman leading on a second trail parallel to the main trail; it was smaller, maybe fifty paces, and used to hunt deer and other game that shared the trail with us. Now our game was human and I found the hunt exactly the same, even the thrill, as we followed and began to hear the men making their way towards home. The difference was that deer cannot shoot back. We stopped often and joined the main trail as the two forms were within sight of the village.

"Stop!" Copperman called with a booming voice.

The two men, dressed in shabby clothes and furs of every kind, stopped and we could see they had their bows slung over their shoulders. There were no other weapons to be seen. They turned and stood calmly as we approached, bows drawn. I tried not to shake as I held my aim at the man on the right. He was the larger of the two. They were fully bearded and around Copperman's age. The large one smiled and he had a set of white teeth that glowed from the darkness of his beard. The other smiled as well and held up a hand.

"Friends!" he called. "Trade, food."

His trade tongue was clear and easy to understand but had a vibration, a tongue roll that extended the R's. I had not heard this dialect before and decided they were from a far away place.

"Hands together!" Copperman said and the two followed his orders, holding their hands clasped in front of them.

Copperman and I approached and I was shaking with fear and excitement.

"The young one…fear?" said the smaller man.

"Fear is dangerous," Copperman said as he approached them. He undrew his bow and slung it over his shoulder. Still holding the arrow in his right hand, he took out his copper axe and held it up in an attack manner. The men cringed, their eyes widened at the axe and I understood this was Copperman's method. The copper gleamed and they were impressed and afraid.

He took their bows as I held aim at them but my arms were tired and shaking.

Copperman noticed and nodded to me. I gratefully lowered the bow and I could see them both looking at the war-arrow, its huge, black flint and even blacker crow fletching.

"What is this?"

The voice came from our main hunter who held his bow from the village side of the trail.

"Strangers," Copperman said. "Trouble."

The men shook their heads fiercely. "Not trouble, friends. Friends, friends."

"We will see," Copperman said.

We led the men into the village and the others who saw called out until there were two or three dozen gathered. The Council came and set a day-fire.

The two men sat, surrounded by the suspicious Lake-clan, all holding weapons. They ate smoked pike and flat bread, drank cold tea, warming themselves near the great fire. When they finished the food, Copperman gave them another serving from our own share, dried sheep and leftover porridge from the breakfast.

The elders seemed confused as to Copperman's plan and their fears must have overcome their dislike of him, for they pulled him aside and asked him counsel. I watched as he spoke low to them, then they returned and the elder asked the men to tell us of their journey and reason for being on their land.

Their story:

It was in trade tongue and spoken mostly by the smaller of the raggedy men. The large one simply smiled at everyone and said 'friend' so often that the smaller man finally motioned for his silence. The large man smiled at this too but there was anger in his smile and I thought that he was not a man who often accepts silencing by another. The smaller man, who said his name was Tun, told of their journey along the lake in search of game. He said there were a dozen of them who saw us from the lake, days earlier. Main hunters from a southern clan called the Quetek; they were hunting Ibex and decided to stop among the cliff dwellers across the lake and trade furs for food and basic goods. Their numbers were fired upon and all killed, save the smaller man and his companion, who ran across the frozen lake. As the only main hunters left, they wanted to ask for a few bites of food and shelter for the night before returning to the Quetek with the news of their fallen hunters. They wondered how their small clan would fare with the main hunters slain by the cliff warriors.

As this part of the story slowly unfolded, the large man with the gleaming white teeth put his hands against his great beard and pulled at it, weeping at the loss of his brothers. After this tale the elders had counsel with Copperman and the men were asked to stay with us as guests for the night. They would be given small provisions for their journey home.

The men were grateful and knelt down to put their faces to the earth of the Lake- clan for their kindness. As darkness came, the others followed us to our hut and we were left inside with the strangers. Little Brother was sent to Hanit's for the night.

The meal Mother made according to Copperman's instructions, was a good portion of our week's rations: dried root stew and Elk-bones, stewed until the marrow softened. Cup after cup of tea.

The big man stared at Mother as she cooked and the smaller man's tongue, loosened by the food and comfort, spoke more and more fluently as the night wore on. He had questions about everything in the clan and Copperman answered with lie after lie. It was wise to send Little Brother to Hanit's to keep him from contradicting Copperman's stories.

I had to admire his genius as he told of our own war, not a year earlier with the Elkhorn, how the Lake-clan was attacked and the Elkhorn tried to take our copper. They were nearly successful but for the main hunters, who had been away, came back to fight them off. He said we had lost four of our best and taken nearly twenty of theirs before they retreated. Copperman told this as he sharpened and cleaned his copper axe and began to flake and prepare a spear point from black flint.

Tun nodded at Copperman's skill and said it was obvious that he was the tool-maker for the clan.

Copperman laughed. "I am perhaps third or fourth best. The Lake-clan make and trade weapons for all the peoples of the lake." He said that after the Elkhorn attack, we had armed every man and child with weapons that were not to leave their huts to prevent another assault and that even the women are good with a spear.

Moon stayed by my side and her pup curled against the legs of the big bearded man, who reached down from time to time to feel his fur.

"The dogs are good here" Tun said.

"Yes, they do their job. It is time to put them out now," he told me and I sent them both to the front of the house.

"You do not use them for warmth?" the big one said, and he surprised me with the first question, as it was worded well and pronounced with a better dialect than Tun had.
Tun glared at him. Copperman did not appear to notice this and nodded, continuing to speak to Tun.

"No, they are more needed for their guard than their heat. You are lucky you did not come at night, or there would have been them to greet you instead of me and my son."

"You came upon us just in time," Tun said.

"No, we were warned of your approach by the northern lookout. They saw you join the trail and as there were only two of you we decided to wait for your approach. It is wiser to come to a new village by the open lake so there are no ugly surprises."

"We were lucky to find you," the big one said.

"Why lucky?" Copperman said. "You saw us not three days earlier"

Tun shook his head. "We thought this village was closer than it was, we…got lost."

Mother was visibly uncomfortable with the visitors who made our home small and cramped, crowding the entrance. She drew herself into her sleep robe at the back of the hut and pretended to sleep. Copperman put a new chunk of wood into the fire and half buried it in the ashes to keep it burning slowly.

"Sleep well," he said, "for your long journey tomorrow."

I did not sleep one wink that night; neither did Copperman. As the two men lay curled near the fire, snoring loudly, I could hear Moon's pup whine from time to time; once he even scratched at the door before Moon snarled him back to his pile of old furs. After some hours Mother began to snore gently. Copperman slept under covers and I could tell he had his axe in his hand. I kept my flint knife gripped in my right hand until it cramped.

At first light, the men were roused, grumbling and bleary eyed. Any attempt at civility was gone from the bearded one who licked his lips at Mother as she made a quick breakfast porridge. Copperman was as friendly as he could be, happy to help the men and even giving them gifts of dried meat to travel with. The main hunters followed the men to the edge of the lake trail and waved them off.

The minute they were out of sight Copperman gave orders. He sent two of the best trackers to follow them and watch where they left off. The Council met with Copperman and he told me later of their discussions.

The men were not of the Quetek; this was sure. Copperman had met the Quetek several times and they were Einkorn farmers and sheep folk from the south, a dozen days walk. There was not a scrap of sheep's wool on our two visitors, nor did either wear any of the Quetek's hair-beads and their ears were not notched at the right lobe as a Quetek main hunter would have had. Finally, the Quetek spoke no trade tongue and Copperman remembered using only hand-language to trade with them. He guessed the poor lie was due to the fact that the Takers probably did not bother to infiltrate the small clan and had killed them in a single raid. The two had clothes from many different clans upon them, their trade tongue was far better than they pretended, and Tun had a bracelet from polished Elk-tooth that must have been taken from an Elkhorn warrior. I remembered Gahn wearing such a tooth bracelet and shuddered.

Copperman had hoped his lies would have their effect but unlike his dumb companion, Tun was sharp-eyed and Copperman doubted that he believed all of the stories.

It is good there was a snowfall to block out the sight of our Shepherd homes in the hills as they would be the first to be attacked. I thought of Sister and Gy who would not win a bow fight with a child, and little Gyson.

"Why did we not kill them?" The main hunters wanted to know, "when we know they were enemies."

"Because what they carry will be tales of our weapons and power, our alertness. Perhaps they will see us as a wolf pack sees a bear, not worth the meat for the danger of its claws."

If there was any question of Copperman's warning, it was gone now. The Council saw their comfortable life as vulnerable now and wanted any advice Copperman could offer.

That night, the trackers came back. They saw the men cut across the lake at the far end towards dusk. They were heading back to the Elkhorn ridge.

Far from their grasp

The battle raged on. We could see it from our village as bands of warriors walked across the ice, single file, sometimes a few, sometimes two or three dozen. From our vantage point on the mountain lookout, we saw three different fires that week over the Elkhorn ridge. The Council had concerns about our supply of food and hunters, who were already tired from watch duty, had to spend more and more time from home to keep the village in game. It was fortunate that the good weather held.

After two weeks with no sign of the Takers, life relaxed. It was not normal, would never be normal again, as we all watched for strangers and slept with weapons at our sides. Copperman hunted on the mountains mostly alone and I knew he was searching the hills for signs of the Elkhorn.

One morning, while pushing the icehouse out towards the little island with Little Brother and Hanit, I spotted something dead on the ice. A white deer I thought at first; then walking closer, I saw it was a naked body, curled up on the ice as if huddling for warmth. The skin was thinly haired and pale blue in the morning light. Little Brother screamed that it was one of the dead come up from Funeral bay through a hole in the ice. I thought it was an Elkhorn warrior left for us to find as a warning, but Hanit recognized the form and knelt before it. Others came and they too knelt and wept.

It was Dol, his thin hair ringed his bald head, frozen stiff and gleaming with ice crystals. The expression on his face was one of serenity, as if the ice were a warm blanket next to a fire. We left the others to guard him from the crows who were gathering overhead. We traced his path, barefoot traces were rare to see in the snow and it was as if we were tracking a wild animal. The tracks wandered back to his little fishing-hut and we found the door open and his clothes placed neatly among the disarray of his hanging lures. The coals of his fire were still slightly warm. Hanit sighed, then began to weep openly.

"They finally killed you," he said to the ghost of Dol in his shack. "After so many seasons, the Takers finally ended you."

Dol had embarked on 'the walk of death', as some have done when they are too old or sometimes happens if a family member dies and the grief comes too heavily. When a mother loses a child, the elder women keep watch to prevent a mother, delirious with grief, from walking naked into the dark. The word that the Wolf and Axe were back must have driven him to unbearable despair.

We sank Dol's body into Funeral bay that day; it was impossible to dress the frozen body but I noticed the boat medallion still around his neck and was glad of it. We wrapped him in his sleep robe and tied stones around the body to sink it deep. We were armed and nervous, aware that the Takers might be walking that trail. Their path was visible as a single line. It took some time to chop a hole in the ice large enough for a wrapped body. Dol sank slowly, face ghostly pale against the black well of water.

The burial was an act of bravery and the defiance tempered the main hunters, gave them strength. As we waited watching, the ice froze thin over the hole; soon it would be a darkened patch of ice and after the first snow it would disappear completely.

Suddenly there came a shout and we all turned, arrows drawn, as a figure approached. It was Kadal, the father of the boy Okla had practiced arrows with. Kadal had blood smeared from a wound on his scalp; he limped and carried his bow with empty quiver over his shoulder. I ran to him and called his name and the others understood he was a friend. They gathered his things and I helped him, arm around his shoulder, over to our ice-sled. Though he was injured, he smiled slightly as I lowered him into the blankets.

"This is the walking house you came to us in. I have wanted to sit in it ever since…have wanted to…"

He slumped and I thought he was dead. Then he opened his eyes and reached feebly for his bow that was not there.

"It is OK now," I said. "You are with the Lake-clan now, we are friends." He tried to focus and then fainted again.

"Hurry!" I shouted. "If he lives we will know all."

We ran the entire trip, pushing the sled ahead. Dol, keeping watch behind, now sleeping under the trail of the Takers. Safe. Alone. Far from their grasp.

Kadal's story

Kadal lay in the large, single-roomed hut of the medicine woman. She had never seemed happily coupled with her husband and now that he was gone, she had done very well for herself as an Only. The room was as large as our own hut and with only one person's belongings there; the space seemed twice as big; our equipment as travelers used up far too much of the room in our houses. She had set up her husband's old skin and hay mattress in the center of the room near the fire, as a sick bed for visitors or the dying; she had spaces over the rafters of her short ceiling, stacked with trade goods, jars with markings in black that I guess only she would know. And two good windows of scraped skin to let in light, also a patch of roof that could be pushed up in the summer to let in the direct sun and air the place out from death's vapors.

There were smaller jars Sister had made for her that she kept dried herbs and roots in and a rounded stone and pounding stone, worn down from countless grindings. She was partial to seed remedies and would spend hours picking and separating them from certain plants. A day's work might result in a single spoon of the tiniest yellow fire-seeds.

It was from this that she made Kadal's poultice. Ground fire-seed and bear-root, boiled with fresh hay until the water boiled out, leaving a hot paste. This was applied, still hot, to Kadal's three wounds, and he groaned as the paste sizzled against his skin. The bleeding did stop and the paste hardened over the wounds like boat-tar.

The pain certainly woke Kadal up and then Medicine woman gave him quiet tea, a bitter mix of plants known only to her. I had needed it only once when a fever caused my head to suffer terribly. I hoped Kadal was experiencing what I did that day. The mind settles and the limbs grow soft as if they weigh more than the heaviest stones, then the pain stops and becomes warm sleep. Only we did not want Kadal to sleep.

The others waited outside and Copperman addressed them from time to time on Kadal's progress. As night came, warriors were sent to keep their watches and they made me promise several times to remember the story he told in detail. I promised and felt a sense of pride to have men treating me an equal, asking rather than ordering.

The last weeks my childhood had dropped away and the others could see it. This is the time I became a man. Kadal was a friend and I was the last of our clan to visit the Elkhorn. We stayed with Kadal as night approached.

I enjoyed watching Medicine woman at her work. She had long ago lost any sympathy to pain and could cut, poke or burn away an injury with the detachment of a wife preparing a dead grouse. This was her wonder, her perfection. Detachment. I wondered at the skill. If there was one above Copperman to go against the Council with impunity, it was Medicine woman. If she took extra meat without marking, or found and kept an entire beehive without adding her portion, who in the Council would first complain? If they did, would she refuse to treat their piles or rotting teeth? Would she slow slightly in stopping the blood from a slashed hand? She earned whatever she took, I thought, as I imagined living in a hut with the sick or dying. If she saved Kadal, I decided to make her a copper medallion for the skill.

He sweated and shook until the quiet tea took hold and then he smiled at me.

"Kadal, you fought well," he said and tears welled his eyes. "You took five men with as many shots. Kadal my warrior son, my best and your …"

He drifted off into sleep and Copperman put his face in his hands for a moment.

"Why did he call me Kadal? This is the tea confusing him?"

Copperman shook his head. "Kadal has a first son of the same name. He would be about your age."

We waited through the night and I slept in my clothes as Medicine woman kept the fire high and lifted the roof tiles a few times to clean out the air. At first light, we roused Kadal and she fed him strong tea of some other magic. He was stiff from his wounds but there was no fever in his eyes and I knew with some help he would live. She washed his head wound with hot water and a sheep-cloth scrap. The hard poultice softened and fell away. The wound was as long as a hand and down to the skull, which showed deathly white as she opened the wound to examine it. It was from an axe, a hardwood, fighting-axe.

She held his head near the candle and nodded. "There is a long scratch in the bone from it. A little harder of a swing and you would have been feasting with the Gods."

"The one who swung it received an arrow in the throat from my son, my son…"

Copperman gripped his arm. "Tell us what you can. We have been watching from but the very nature of the Elkhorn ridge prevented us from helping."

"They are from the dark Gods, this is for sure. They came as friends and had a great wealth of goods to trade. Their trades were generous and we spent two days in the long house. They had flint and furs of every kind and beads from shells of the far away waters. I was taken by the greed of it but Gahn …he was wise and leery of the visit. Three days later, when some of us went for a hunt, we saw smoke and returned to find our long house burning from the roof and bodies with arrows between our houses. We spent our arrows on their shadows in the woods and took several of them but they were baiting us away from the village and soon smoke from another house began. We returned and had to pull arrows from our dead. They hunted us by deceit, drawing us into the woods after them, only to attack from another direction. There were twenty of us down, and we found a dozen more, women and children, hiding in the caves we have for such a reason. Gods' thanks that they were not found but there were two dozen dead, even the smallest children we not spared. We found their bodies split by war axes. Wooden clubs with a flint blade fixed into their blade end. They used arrows soaked in pine tar, set into the fire and then shot onto our roofs. The rain saved many of them but five huts and the long house are now blackened squares."

"Where are the others?" Copperman asked. "Are you the only left?"

"I do not know. They took everything of value, and it was obvious from their tracks that they had left with some of the young boys of the clan. The women they raped and killed. We had gathered and followed them as they left for the mountain trail and we were set upon by guards that waited to ambush us. This is where I got these wounds. He was a scarred and savage warrior. He came in with no fear and a touched look in his eyes. Mad from the battles and shouting in thrill as he swung his axe. That is when my son shot him in the throat. Then he was struck by another and it was a blow to the head ...too great to survive. There were only three or four but the battle was overwhelming. I fought but had to retreat as arrows hit me in the side and leg. I ran...like a coward, I ran downhill until I saw your figures on the ice, recognized the Lake-clan. I ran from battle and my son is gone..."

He stopped and stared into the fire. Medicine woman gave him another quiet tea and nodded to us. We left them to their herbs and my stomach felt hollow from the battle story. These were the Takers of my nightmares, walking my mountains and killing my friends. I thought again of the girl who had kissed me on the cheek. Did she live?

We had to find her and the others. Copperman was already gathering supplies for the ice-sled. Mother cried as she helped pack. Copperman borrowed Kadal's elk great coat, washed from the blood, also his beaver hat.

"The Takers are gone," he said. "We have to save who we can now." The Lake-clan had many relatives, distant as they were, at the Ekhorn. They all gave arrows, bows, dried meat and furs to take and the sled was heavy as we pushed it out onto the ice. We would walk through the night and present ourselves before Elkhorn ridge.

Night shadows

The full moon is intensified on a frozen lake, white upon white, its luminous glow hypnotizes the mind, confuses the heart, and dreams that usually visit at night come despite your open eyes. I listened to the creek and groan as our sliding weight moved masses of ice just the tiny amount needed to crack the lakes great skin. I saw the dark outline of familiar mountains, sharp against the stars and pale sky, and on the ice itself figures moved, shadows just beyond focus, flitting in and out. I asked what they were and Copperman shook his head,

"Night shadows are only your eyes looking too hard at nothing."

But I saw them as they moved in and out, ghostly as mist. One looked like a fox with white fur and it stopped and looked with red eyes before fading at our approach. Another, black as flint, walked on two legs like a man but had a long neck and flowing black hair. There were small creatures that seemed to move in a pack like sheep and gave way as we approached, parting to let us through. Crows swooped and flitted soundlessly, sweeping past my peripheral vision. This was new and my chest cramped with fear. Were they spirits warning me of something? Was this like the great Urus? Something from far away lands?

Copperman seemed not to see them and this frightened me even more. We walked in the growing light until the moon was directly overhead. I struggled against the edges of the sled, pushing it over patches of snow and trying not to look too hard into the darkness. Hundreds of paces would pass and then I would see another form or many in a row. There was Asha ahead and I cried out to Copperman that she was there lost on the ice. He looked where I pointed, and seeing nothing, he stopped.

"When have you last slept?"

I tried to think. I had kept watch the night before and then there was the funeral for Dol...I could not remember. Had I missed sleep altogether? I tried to explain to Copperman that I might have missed a day or two but my words jumbled and I could not string them together. I looked behind him and Mother was sweeping the ice before us to prepare it for supper. I began to laugh and could not stop. Copperman ushered me to the front of the ice sled and arranged the furs over the pile of food and weapons we carried. The he guided me into the tent. I felt the strange movement as Copperman grunted and pushed us across the ice. The moon was so bright by this point that it shone through the skins covering the sled and I laughed at this as well.

"Quiet!" Copperman said and I realized I was howling with laughter.

"Sleep!" he ordered and I pressed my face into the furs to stifle my laughter. The world began to spin and I rested my head against the uncomfortable edges of bows and hard chunks of frozen meat beneath the furs. In seconds I was asleep and the shadows followed me there in dream upon dream.

Copperman woke me by dragging me from the tent by my feet. He slid me roughly onto the ice and crawled into my sleep space on the furs.

"Close the flap! Wake me when they come!" he said.

I sat there disoriented and stiff. From the look of the mountains, he had pushed us clear across the lake, the moon fading, the ridge pale with the coming of morning. He must have walked the night through. I felt ashamed and stood away from the tent sled to pee on a patch of snow. The dark rock-face of Elkhorn ridge rose before us and I gently slid a small sitting fur from the tent as Copperman, already asleep, snored like a bear in its den. I sat cross-legged and watched the dark forest perhaps three or four hundred paces away.

The morning came sharp and dry cold; I shivered from the deep sleep and wondered at the visions of the night. I counted back and realized that it had been two days without sleep before our walk. The fear and night watch of impending battle had thrown me from the natural cycle. I stood and paced, clenching my fingers in their mittens to keep them warm. The morning gave way to day, sunlight greeting the mountains behind us first and then sliding down the mountains, brilliant pink, before moving along the ice. I had never seen it like that before, sunlight as a line that moved across the lake gently towards us. It made everything better. My head cleared, I drank cold tea and ate a chunk of smoked red deer meat rubbed with mint and basil. The visions from the walk seemed distant as a dream and I waited and thought of nothing as warming light filled the lake basin.

Copperman slept until late morning when I saw smoke rise from a small fire near the tree line. I called to Copperman, who rose quickly and stiffly, stood to watch the smoke. He drew out the elk great coat Kadal wore and exchanged it for his own. He clapped his hands three times and whistled three times with an ear-piercing whistle (another skill I had not yet mastered). We waited and several times Copperman repeated the three claps and three whistles. From four hundred paces over ice with no wind the sound was unmistakable and soon two claps and two whistles echoed back from the others. We began pushing towards them and Copperman, somehow refreshed from only a few hours' sleep, looked at me with concern.

"Why did you not tell me you were so long without sleep?"

"I did not know."

"We are warriors these days. A warrior has to know the spaces between sleep and food. Our lives now depend on knowing these things."

I nodded and pushed harder to take the effort from him, and soon we were at the edge of the ice; the sled crunched its runners against the shores sand and gravel and we stopped.

"Now what?" I asked

"We wait."

And so we did until the sun rose high in the sky. At midday we started a small fire and sat cooking pieces of meat much larger than we needed. An arrow struck and shattered against a tree twenty paces from us and Copperman said: "Do not move."

We waited and there came two claps and two whistles and Copperman answered with three claps and whistles. We waited further, then Copperman called, "Elkhorn! We come for Kadal who is injured but alive at the Lake-clan. Come, eat. The Takers are gone from here."

There was a rustle and crunch of footsteps and then they came, a dozen main hunters and nearly as many women and children among them, their bows drawn until they could look us in the eye. I recognized many of them and they recognized us and unbent their bows.

"Come eat!" Copperman said and began to hand them food and supplies from the sled tent. I looked for the dark-haired girl among them but she was not there.

We emptied the sled tent in minutes and they set guards to watch while we cooked meat and handed out bread. There was a spring near by and the others went with water-skins and returned to warm the water in the bags near the fire. They were a straggled crew, many of them nursing wounds, and the skins of the warriors were stained with blood they had not washed. They ate frantically and Copperman handed out small portions of food, warning them not to eat too fast or the food would harm their long empty bellies.

We did not speak much until everyone had eaten and drunk, warmed themselves near the fire and dared to believe they had food again. They were nervous and never set their weapons down, eating with one hand, always looking to the woods like deer feeding and startling at birds and squirrels in the trees. One girl, not half my age, held a flint knife and pointed it at me, flinching as I reached to her with a handful of flat bread. They were numb with fear and

Copperman told them over and over in a soothing voice that the Takers were gone now. After they ate, one of them I recognized as Gahn's son Rahl told us what had happened.

The Wolf and Axe came as friends, two men, one small and wickedly smart and the other huge and bearded, came to trade and brought many fine things to offer as gifts. The trade went well though Gahn suspected them and only allowed them a day in the long-house but offered them no shelter for the night. They left and were escorted by main hunters to the edge of the Elkhorn territory. The next night, arrows (dipped in pine-pitch and flaming) came down from the sky. They burned against the roofs of the long-house. When the Elkhorn began fighting the fires, the takers came from the dark like wolves, their faces painted fearfully in red and black. They struck with hardwood war-axes and the dogs were upon them but to no avail, as they struck them artfully. Though the main hunters were at them with their bows and took many, others came from above and below. There were a dozen bodies from their clan and twice as many Elkhorn scattered about in the light of the blazing long-house. They retreated and then struck again at first light. Their archers were nearly as good as the Elkhorn but their main strength was in the speed of the assault. Men from all sides came at once with no thought to life or limb and as one fell another would come over him without pausing. Another dozen of theirs fell and perhaps that many Elkhorn, the elders were dead and weeping women held dead children. Gahn took the opportunity to gather the remaining clan and retreated into the forest on hidden trails set for such a purpose. They went towards the secret caves, perhaps two dozen, carrying what they could grab and as they went. The Wolf and Axe came in again behind them, a few fell but the rest gave way as they retreated. That day the Takers moved in to the Elkhorn village. They could be heard shouting challenges and then came the smell of the bodies of the dead being burned in a great fire.

One who they found later, the little girl with the flint knife, said they stripped the bodies of the Elkhorn and their own and set them into the smoldering great house and set wood atop of it until fire leapt into the sky. The Takers stripped each and every house of its belongings and set them into a pile, then began dividing them. The girl watched this and hid within sight until she was found by Elkhorn hunters days later, nearly dead from hunger. Gahn and the others spied as the Takers sifted through their belongings, spears, arrows and blades went to the warriors who had made the first attack, clothes and furs went to those that they fit, food, the winter's supply, roasted in wasteful amounts.

There were women among them who were spared but these were used shamefully and in front of the others. Gahn had to fight the urge to attack then but he would die surely and the sacrifice would achieve nothing. There were four boys who were kept tied and those were prisoners to become new members of Wolf and Axe once their spirits were broken to their ways. Gahn gathered a few men, including Kadal and his son, and they kept watch on the Takers as they finished their work of cleaning out the Elkhorn village.

As they left, some three dozen (not including their captives), Gahn's party tracked them. When they came near the trail on funeral bay they began a trail upwards again, this was when Gahn's men attacked, hoping beyond hope to save a few of the prisoners. They took several of the Takers but were overpowered and Kadal was hit as was Gahn and the Elkhorn had to flee. They were still hiding in the caves fearful of the return of the Takers and were grateful for our gifts.

I listened to the story as if living it myself and it left a pain in my stomach.
Copperman nodded and pondered the situation.

"It is as we feared," he said. "They are on the high trail and will be over the mountain soon."

Gahn's son Rhal was a fine man a few years older than I but with the posture of a leader. He had taken responsibility for the clan and he listened to Copperman's counsel.

"You have to go back now. The Takers are gone and if you let fear keep you in the caves you will live as refugees. I have seen wandering tribes before and they soon perish, soaked up in other clans as servants or beggars. This cannot be the fate of the Elkhorn. We will follow you back to your village and stay for some days to help prepare for the winter."

They were divided; half wanted to come to the Lake-clan with us and half wanted to return home. Copperman said that we would not arrive to the Lake-clan with two dozen to feed and house; the Council would only offer a night or two of shelter and then maybe a family or two would take in a relative but the rest would be winter bound and begging from clan to clan. The Elkhorn were either gone and scattered or they would rebuild.

They heeded his words and after much debate among them they agreed. It was terrible to see such a proud people reduced to the group that we followed, up the icy dangerous rock face and through the tall tree forest. We came up the trail and I began to see the signs of battle, arrows shot deep into tree trunks, a missing mitten, footprints and drops of blood in the snow next to the trail, and then a body. The Elkhorn gave a cry as they recognized a young woman. She lay curled around a small tree trunk as if it could hold her to this world. She was pale frozen and days dead; they wanted to bring her but Copperman said there would be time to tend to the dead but now we needed to make fires and gather what we could while there was life. Then we saw the footprints of wolves circled around her and a section of her leg had been chewed away. The others refused to leave her to the scavengers and so they took turns dragging her behind, crying as they did.

There were others as we walked, a Takers warrior with an Elkhorn arrow through his side. The wolves had been at him too and the others spit on his body as they passed it. One tried to extract the arrow but it was sunken into frozen flesh and would never come out. An elder, skull crushed and horrible to see, the white bones of his face exposed. Crows scattered as we came upon body after body, a dozen in all before we found the village. The others cried out in unison as the ruin of their lives spread before them. Half the huts had been burned and the great long-house, the place of comfort for them all, the place of Gods and Council, was merely four posts at each end of a rectangle fire pit. The dead were gone from the main village but we found their bones burnt in the rubble of the long-house.

The Takers were ruthless in their assault but methodical in their occupation; they had left very little of the Elkhorn belongings. Furs were gone as well as all weapons; the smoke-house and perhaps a dozen shelters were empty but unharmed.

"Why did they not burn it all?" I asked Copperman.

"The same reason we take only half of the honey from a beehive. So that seasons later we can return and take again. We are all prey to them and a village, a big hive they risk a few stings to harvest."

He addressed the group. "They will not return now. They are gone and we have work to do if you will live the winter through to the spring."

Copperman was their leader now and the eldest by far. The others followed his directions and fell into the numbing job of clearing out the village. We slept gathered together that night in the huts and the warm fires and exhausted sleep gave the Elkhorn survivors courage. The next day we gathered the dead Elkhorn and Wolf and Axe alike and removed what furs we could salvage. There was no choice Copperman told them: the furs are life and warmth and must be used, enemy-made or not. He explained they were mostly stolen from other clans as the Takers had no skills in the making of clothes. This made a strange sense and the others donned the warm coats in honor of those who they were stolen from.

We made a bonfire in the woods and burned the bodies of the Elkhorn and dragged and tossed the naked bodies of the Takers from a point on the rock cliff that fell straight down a hundred paces to jagged rocks below. The scavengers would scatter their bones by summer. It is a burning energy that drives the grieving; the Elkhorn under

Copperman's leadership, cleaned and picked and arranged for several days from first cold light till the night fires died. The huts were brushed clean and new wood gathered, beads and small trinkets rescued from the rubble and placed carefully at the end of the burnt long-house. Black-handed and determined, they carried plates of ashes and charcoal from the long-house down to the base of the flat rocks it had been built upon. Hunters returned with a fat doe and we roasted it whole, nourishing the others who had not had a warm feast for over a week. Copperman and I hunted and helped wherever possible, and there were more small jobs that I could count.

On the fifth or sixth day there came a clap and whistle of half a dozen Elkhorn. They came yelling with joy to find the others working and small game hanging in the smokehouse. They had escaped the first attack and two main hunters among them led the way to the little Lake-clan at the far end of the lake. Two small children with them stared wide-eyed; families clung to brothers and sisters they thought dead and it was wonderful to see joy and smiles in the Elkhorn village again.

And she was with them, the girl with the dark hair. I nearly cried out when I saw her, unharmed and in the arms of her loved ones. She did not recognize me at first in the chaos, but that night when we sat around the fire she sat near me and said, "You are thin."

I did not know what to say. "The others at the little Lake-clan said you were a great warrior. The boy Ebalno said you were large and broad shouldered and could shoot a wolf from a hundred paces. He said you were blood brothers."

I showed her the tiny thread of a scar on my hand. She smiled, "He showed me the same."

She gazed around at the others, perhaps two dozen now, eating and talking heatedly with Copperman about the plans for where extra shelters should be made.

"Maybe you are a great warrior. You are going soon?"

I nodded slowly, for some reason unable to make the words come out. I had thought of what I would say to her if we found her alive. She went to the fire and found a section of rabbit well cooked and used a sharp stick to roll it onto a flat plate of birch bark. She carried it back to me.

"I looked for you," I said"...each one we found.... I thought it might be you."

She took pieces of steaming meat from the bone, blew on them and then handed me one bit at a time. It was what Mother did with Copperman when she was happy with him.

"You will come back," she said decidedly. "So I will not say good-bye when you leave. I will know you will return and so I will not be sad. If we make this winter, and new houses are built you will come back."

When a warm day came and the others began chopping a large maple for the poles of the next long-house, Copperman said it was time for us to return home. The Elkhorn asked us to stay and were disappointed at the loss. When a clan is small the loss of even two is sorely felt. We promised to come again in boats at the first melt and there would be some from the Lake-clan that would join us to help with rebuilding.

It was with heavy heart that we gathered our packs and walked the tall tree forest towards the rock cliff trail. The girl with the dark hair did not follow with the others and she did not say good-bye or wish us well on our journey. But I found placed in a pocket in my pack her bracelet of red clay beads. It was a love token. I understood that she was right: I would come back for her and the thought kept me warm on our long journey home across the ice.

Taila

The clan had counsel for days and days. After Copperman told the others of the Elkhorn and their battle there was panic among the others. The fishermen were concerned but they had a strange confidence that comes from being water-people. The ice would soon melt and then they were the masters. The Wolf and Axe had no ability on the water and the fishermen could flee or shoot them from their boats. They could spread out and live from their boats if necessary during times of danger. The hunters were worried, but as men of weapons, they were more than willing to fight and fear was not to be nurtured among them as a matter of habit. The shepherds were more than afraid; they were terrified. They had slow moving flocks that the Wolf and Axe no doubt noticed and would come back for; they were soft spoken and reluctant to fight as if they were so connected to their sheep they embodied some of their nature. They held counsel with the clan but also among themselves and the leaders among them wanted to escape, to live in the mountains and move from place to place like some of their fathers and grandfathers had done.

Copperman was silent during most of the conversations and listened, declining an opinion until the third day when the elders begged him to address the clan. This was his plan no doubt, to let the discussions run their course. Now, each and every clan member, having had their turn, would be more of a mind to listen. He spoke as evening approached and the slow logs in the main fire-pit crackled in red coals. He stood tall and his voice carried the comfortable conviction of someone who knows he is right. I swelled with pride to know he was my father and his strength would some day be mine. He looked to Hanit and his group and nodded.

"The fishermen feel safe in their boats on open water... the Wolf and Axe will take them one by one, like ducks on the water, then they will burn the boats and houses."

He looked to the hunters who stood defiantly.

"The hunters feel safe behind their bows. The Wolf and Axe will take them in small groups until none dare hunt for fear of ambush. They will be glad of the smoked meat in your smokehouse and they will be even happier with the sport your wives and children will provide."

The hunters mumbled and glared at him.

"The shepherds feel safe in escape...the Wolf and Axe will find them in the mountains and make a short feast of their life's work, and, of us all, only the young men will be spared to swell their ranks."

The others mumbled and shook their heads. If this was his rally speech it clearly needed work.

"I was raised among men like these, I know how they think, how well they enjoy the killing and power of fear they carry. They call themselves dark Gods and draw joy from the misery of others. They have no place for women and the lack of female thinking makes them more animal than human. Men like these killed my family and, but for the gift of cunning, I would have died their slave or worse, become one of their kind. The Lake-clan have always been a peaceful people, and we will be peaceful again...one day... but now, for a time, we must become a war-tribe and we must join with the other clans to mount a force and hunt the Wolf and Axe until they are no longer a threat."

The elders raised hands as voices called out, for and against the idea.

"Quiet!" the main elder called and the others reluctantly lowered their voices. "The Council will talk of this."

Kadal, who was now very well recovered from his wounds, moved into our house and spent long hours speaking to Copperman about the Takers. Copperman wanted to know every detail he could remember, and it is a wonder, the things one remembers when asked the right questions. It was Copperman's method when asking about bluestone: one would tell him he did not remember the trail and then Copperman would say,

"So there were large birch trees?" And the other would remember that they were oak and from that memory would come a small ravine where a rabbit was taken and then four large boulders and a stream where they cleaned the rabbit and took four trout; and, as Copperman asked and asked, smaller details would come until the map came quite clear. This was his way with the Elkhorn during his stay, and with Kadal, and over many nights we found out methods and routes the Takers must have followed, their ages and manner of attack.

Kadal remembered that a volley of flaming arrows came a few minutes before each attack and that the Takers came from four directions at once and to the doorways first to catch others coming from inside. Kadal remembered that they found some of the dogs, dead but seemingly unharmed; that several of the dogs never even attacked and were slow to move from the clubs of the Takers. Copperman understood the dogs were probably thrown meat with some kind of poison and their lack of warning had much to do with the surprise attack. It would be easy enough for a poisoned carcass of an animal to be left near enough for the dogs to find.

Two days of counsel and the elders announced that there was no other option than to gather warriors and seek out the Wolf and Axe and to fight our battle away from home. This would take a leader of men and Copperman understood his situation. He would have to take on the task he had avoided his entire life and become a member of the Council.

They named him leader of the War Council and the others would follow his advice, as they must any Council member. This weighed heavy upon his mind and he sat near the hearth that night, silently staring into the small flames. He would not eat and his cup of tea sat full and cooling until Mother took it away. I spoke to him but he did not answer and Mother shook her head; he was not to be spoken to.

Kadal and I walked to Hanit's and sat with him, telling stories until late in the night. The next morning, Copperman addressed the clan and made his choices. There were ten men among them who would be warriors and they had to stop all other work until this was over; others in the clan would have to help their families while they were gone. Along with the ten were Copperman and I. Of course he had to have me or the others would not offer up their children to fight. His choices were strange to me; some were as young as I and the oldest was a shepherd

411

who I had never seen hold a bow. Many of the main hunters complained but Copperman had no ear for them or the family of the men who were chosen. None were married, save Copperman, and this was wise.

He sent messengers to the little Lake-clan and a few days later they returned with four young men, well armed and ready for battle. Mother was beside herself with grief and Sister and Gy both wept openly at our coming departure. Little Gyson was fat and happy and it was for him that I was going to fight the Takers. I held him as often as I could in those days and knew he had to be protected. Sister gave me a new sheepskin bedroll and it was as soft as anything I had ever felt.

I had no desire for long good-byes and spent the last day in focused preparation. Little Brother was angry at not being chosen as a warrior and showed Copperman how good he had become with a bow. Copperman was uncharacteristically gentle with him, explaining that he needed to stay with the others to protect Mother and little Gyson with his bow. He gave him instructions on what to watch for and the new job was enough to settle Little Brother in his desires. I remembered my own longing to follow the men into adventure and now longed to be so innocent as to envy this task of ours.

Moon watched our preparations with eager anticipation and I ached with the knowledge that we would be leaving her behind. If the Wolf and Axe killed dogs first in battle, she would be left behind for her own good. All dogs were to stay, and, though we could have used their help with hunting, they would be no good to us in battle. I asked Little Brother to keep her well fed and if he took good care of Mother, I would bring him back a present from our travels.

With warm weather dawning the coming of spring, we left, well stocked and fully armed to make the trek back to the Elkhorn. The clan gathered and we left to the sound of their grief.

Copperman scowled. "They send us off on a funeral march and now I have my work to bring the men into warrior mind." He stopped the group as soon as we were out of hearing from the Lake-clan. He addressed the line of warriors.

"Do you think the Wolf and Axe weep as they walk into battle? Do you think they sob into their collars and think of a warm hearth and loving mother? These are dark forces we march after and until we slay them there will be weeping mothers and dead children from one valley to the next. Put your feelings away! They will not be needed on this journey. Gather the strength and cunning of your enemy and we will use it against them."

The group shed their emotions and at least pretended bravery. I had the benefit of our journey to the Elkhorn and most of the shock of battle death had worn off but now it came back to me as we walked across the ice. We pushed the ice-sled forward and as each warrior took turns, they made comments about the thing's usefulness. It was laden with dried meat, sheep and deer, bundles of hard travel-bread, ground with the last of the season's pine nuts and rosemary, and cheese made into hard lumps by hanging for weeks above the fire to dry. There were bows and hand-axes and other gifts. The hoard would be welcome relief to the Elkhorn and I hoped they were faring well.

We walked the night and Kadal, who must have been weak from his injury, kept pace and worked with Copperman to rally the men's spirits with hunting stories and tales of the Elkhorn's many battles. He also schooled the others in Elkhorn rules and laws to prevent any accidental offense. They listened intently and the talks made the trip go faster. I marveled at the trip's ease, and, it is the way with long journeys that the more often you take the same path the shorter it seems. We walked a nearly moonless night and made the lake's edge my next morning. This time the clap and whistle exchange took place before we had even stopped walking and I was glad to know they had a lookout back in place before the Elkhorn ridge.

Kadal rejoiced at the appearance of his clan members near the lake's edge and there were loving embraces with the lookouts and their long lost brother. Our warriors were stumbling tired as we made our way up the ridge trail and I watched for the girl with the dark hair as we moved through the maple forest. All signs of the battle had been carefully erased by busy hands. Blood stained snow had been swept clean with branches and arrows were broken off from trees and trimmed flush with the bark.

The others rushed out to welcome us and I looked for her. She came from the woods with a bundle of firewood; she dropped them and ran up to me, breathing heavily. Her eyes sparkled with delight and I found myself smiling a foolish grin.

"I have brought you something," I said and handed her a copper pendant on a leather necklace. It was carved with vines and leaves on one side and flower patterns on the other. She put it around her neck and then we simply stared at each other for several minutes until Kadal called to me. "So you have met my niece?"

"Yes…we have met."

He paused and recognizing the emotion between us, made some excuse and wondered off. "Come," she said. "See what we have built so far."

The long-house already had walls waist high and the work must have been enormous to cut, trim, bark and drag trees of this size.

"We are working out our misery," she said. "Exhaustion is the only way we can get to sleep."

"Others were found," she said. "Four children and one who escaped from the Takers when Kadal and Ghan attacked." She pointed to a young man, maybe twelve or thirteen, who was hacking away at the bark from a split log. He worked with a fire I had not seen in one so young before. I imagined what he had seen the days of his confinement.

Copperman called to us and we gathered around him.

"There will be time to counsel and explain and plan but you have worked hard during our absence and we bring gifts and greetings from your Lake brothers and sisters. Let us roast some of this fine sheep and feast and celebrate the building of a new long-house."

They cheered and began building up the great fire as we brought out the gifts from the Lake-clan. For the first time since the battle there were many gathered at the Elkhorn ridge and the mood was high. The girl with the dark hair brought me food as I hoped she would and we ate together, sitting so close our legs were touching.

"I have never asked your name," I said.

"Taila…There are too many names for a traveler to remember them all."

"Taila," I said. "I will remember your name."

I understood that if we survived the Wolf and Axe I would ask her to be my wife.

Training

Gahn returned one morning. He looked half the man I had met, limping, hungry and filthy from weeks of trekking. He slept for two days waking only to eat and have his wounds tended. The story he told was of one long search for the Takers with three other hunters, coming close a few times and then losing their trail all together. They had returned over the perilous rock face and his men died one by one as loose stones and slick ice fell beneath their feet. He had eaten from a rotting ibex left frozen in the crevasse of the cliffs and somehow found his way down the slopes back home. He held Copperman's hand and wept in his exhaustion. His son Rhal would not leave his side. When he found out about our War Council he seemed to gain strength and began to ask the kind of questions a leader would ask. He officially placed Rhal in command of the Elkhorn and pledged as many warriors as they could spare for the battle.

There were great hunters among the Elkhorn and Rhal told Copperman to chose five among them to join his battle clan. He chose them for their strength and also he chose those who had lost all family; it was calculated and wise for those would have the most rage in battle and would leave no wives or children if killed. Five members was a lot to offer for a clan down to a few dozen; but, unlike the Lake-clan, Copperman had no complaints or explanations to make. This was war and we had the complete cooperation from the Elkhorn. He sent two of the Elkhorn to a nearby river clan who agreed to allow three of their men to join us. The war party was now near twenty and they lived among the others but had a new status as warriors. The others gave them extra rations of food and the very best hats, clothes and weapons.

Each warrior had to receive the ink-scars upon their wrist and Copperman and I spent the first several days sitting and tapping ink into their skin. We began first with bow training and Kadal, the best among the Elkhorn, took upon himself that task. He lined up dozens of practice arrows and each man in turn had to hit moving targets. He was ruthless with those who failed to follow his instructions and each of us shot twenty or thirty arrows a day, honing our skills until we could all hit the deer-skin bag hung from a vine as it swung from side to side.

"The Takers are moving in fast and we must be able to shoot three arrows in the time it takes for a man to run a hundred paces full speed."

He trained us by hanging three targets a hundred paces into the thickest forest and one of us would run while the other shot at the three targets, pulling and notching the arrows franticly. The runner had to try to reach the targets before the shooter could hit them. This training was incredibly exciting as we were set into two teams and the thrill and fear of running just ahead of targets, while arrows flew around, made for the best sport I had ever known. There were close calls and once I shot at a swinging target and the arrow skipped off of a hanging branch and flew through the leather sleeve of the runner. We all gathered to see the hole in his sleeve.

Kadal called to us to stop fooling around and begin again. These games served several purposes, as war games must. We became close and competitive; at the same time, we sharpened our skills beyond what we thought possible with a bow, and, after a few weeks, we could hold a run full speed without gasping for breath. The extra food came at the expense of the others, who had to make due with the little they could hunt in our absence, and this knowledge gave us conviction. If they were suffering for our training then we would train with all our hearts.

Copperman began setting obstacles for us to accomplish each day. He would set out a target and we had to sneak to within shooting distance of the target while he and Kadal sat watching for our arrival. At first they spotted us and called out the name of the failed warrior and the mistakes he had made to expose himself. After days where none of us managed the task correctly we came closer and closer. Learning the lessons from the forest people, we clad ourselves with grass and small branches, blackening our faces with soot and mud. Finally after a week of failure, we all snuck within shooting distance and one of the Elkhorn, a young man named Casara, managed a fine shot, hitting the hanging target near Copperman who sat gazing into the woods. He called out Casara's name and we yelled in triumph.

Copperman, who had seen so many clans on his journeys, spent his days remembering their methods. I sat with him, long hours over small fires, as he spoke to me about the different clans. I understood that my part in these talks was to give his mind a reflection and he would speak about weapons and methods of battle he had seen. His plan was to use the best from all clans and he wanted me to help him design a war-bow. Something with enough flex to send a large arrow through the heavy skins that the Takers wore. The bodies found had been shot in vulnerable places like the leg or neck but the others told of arrows hitting Takers directly in the chest and bouncing off. Copperman examined the clothes left by the Takers and gathered together every skin left by them. There was something peculiar about their dress and when Copperman realized what it was he laughed.

He held up one of the strange vests worn by a Taker. It was an uncomfortable elk-skin vest, untreated and caked with dried mud.

"How am I so foolish not to see it at once!" he cried.

He gathered the others to explain what he found.

"They wear them only in battle," he said holding up the vest. He set the stiff garment against a tree and shot it with an arrow. The arrow, shot hard and straight, stuck only a finger's width into the vest.

"It was not muddy by accident," he said, holding up the ugly garment. It was covered with wet clay on the hair-covered side. "When the clay dried it made a coating that helps stop an arrow. These are battle-cloaks and we need to make them for our warriors."

For two weeks the warriors hunted elk. Our training games made us far better hunters than we had been just a few weeks earlier. We hunted as if the elk were the Takers, sneaking up on them without them spooking; we took only the largest bulls. Copperman said the older the better as the skin would be tough and thick. It took five bulls to make twenty battle-cloaks and the meat, though tough, was welcome back at the village.

We made special war-quivers to hold twenty arrows each and spent another week peeling and cutting the bundles of branches. Meanwhile, I worked with the ideas for war-bows. They were shorter than the usual bow and now that the ash trees were free from snow we began cutting and splitting them. I made small bows from every shape and spent days carving and testing them. One branch I had forgotten to stretch between logs to shape, bent back on itself while drying in the spring sun. I found it hopelessly curved and decided to string it anyway. The result was one of those happy accidents that come when you are trying new ideas. The curved bow was the shape of a bull's horns and when strung, it twanged dangerously from the extra tension the curve gave the string. I shot with it and startled at the strength of the little bow. It had much more power than a bow twice its length.

Copperman thrilled at the discovery; the smaller bows would be much better for forest battle as you could move through heavy brush or sneak along trails without rattling a long bow against branches. He said the first signs of us he saw when we trained was the tell tale flickers of bows against branches.

I began experimenting with shapes and within days had a good method of wedging the green ash branches between logs so they could dry in the proper shape. I made three war-bows and tipped them with flexible sinew and antler at each end. Taila had used the elk-bull leg sinew to weave and stretch bow-strings of incredible strength and I shook with excitement and a bit of fear as I strung one of the war-bows and notched an arrow. If a bow fails, it can shatter and ruin the arm holding it. I drew back and shot, watching the arrow disappear into a large ant pile. This was the most powerful bow I had ever held and I could not wait to show Copperman. He tested the bow, drawing it to dangerous length and it held. He smiled and clapped me on the shoulder.

"I knew you would come up with some kind of improvement but this...this is..."he seemed lost for words. "This is a bow to fight the Takers with."

He had been experimenting with the muddy war-cloak, shooting different points into it. There was one thing that would cut through the hard leather and that was a narrow point of obsidian, a black stone, rare and shiny. I had worked with it a few times and did not like its brittle quality. Copperman had made points of every kind but the obsidian, small and sticky sharp, shattered on impact but pierced the tough hide as it entered. He sent the others to the lakeshore, now clear of snow and they searched until they found several obsidian stones, enough for Copperman to make a hundred points from.

The ice on the lake was gray and crumbling now, unsafe to venture out on. I walked to the edge of the Elkhorn ridge and sat with Taila to watch the sun set. I could see our village some clear days, as a smudge of dark against the snow-patched hills. The ice would break open soon and I hoped Hanit and the other fishermen would feel safe again in their boats. I knew the first open water would bring Hanit and others to visit and give news of the home village. Copperman said the Takers would have gone over the mountains and there were other clans they would attack. I knew he would not have left Mother and Little Brother home if he thought otherwise...but how does one predict the actions of the dark forces? I worried and dreamed awful dreams. I worked days until my hands bled, making bows, staffs and arrows until my mind saw them when I closed my eyes. I fought and killed the Takers, each and every one and in turned was killed by each in different ways until sleep was a task to be avoided. The day the ice broke, we all gathered to watch the wind shift great patches of it upon itself. By the next day we saw boats, several of them, like water bugs, twitching their legs across the new water.

It is their lake

There were ten boats in all, bringing meat and bread and more weapons. The families of the warriors were generous and the Elkhorn-clan would be forever in their debt. The fishermen made the unusual choice to bank their boats and join in with the building of the long-house. (It was made clear by Copperman that the Elkhorn needed the long-house to be who they were in the same way that fishermen needed their boats and shepherds needed sheep.)

I clung to Hanit as we made the journey and at first I wondered at his clumsiness, climbing the rock trail that I had grown so accustomed to. Then I noticed the same awkward gait from the other fishermen. Of course, they never climb if they do not have to, and, as nimble as they were, standing on the tips of their boats in heavy wind, they were equally hopeless against firm unmoving rock. Hanit told me that Little Brother was doing a fine job of helping Mother and Sister, that Gyson was smiling at everyone and using his hands to grab at things, growing fatter by the day as a baby should. He said that the Council had everyone on a war-ration so that some of each kill had been saved and smoked hard in herbs for the warriors to carry into battle.

The clan had tightened together and he spoke of an unusual kindness and attention between the three factions.

The Takers had tempered the Lake-clan. He said Moon watched each day at the trail for my return and this made me impossibly sad. He said she was eating well and when this was over we should bring her a male from the Elkhorn dogs to breed with. I had to tell him that Moon's pups were the only remains of the great Elkhorn stock and we needed to breed them up and return with a few for gifts.

The other fishermen struggled their way ahead and were fascinated with the different trees and plants at the cliff plateau. They looked down at the lake and marveled at its shape. Never had they seen such a sight and the overwhelming sense was pride. It was their lake even more than it was ours. They were the original founders before the hunters and shepherds joined the clan. They had built the first post houses far at the end of the lake and then moved to our little cove generations later. They had known no war, and, until the Wolf and Axe came, the only fear they knew was the cold or the high wind.

The Elkhorn gathered to help them carry gifts and we led them to the growing Elkhorn village. Now, with three dozen, there was little room but the extra hands made tree felling far easier. The fishermen were fine builders and the group of us could lift one tree and drag it in one easy walk to its place near the long-house frame. Tree by tree we raised the walls of the long-house; the trees were notched at each end to fit into each other and slick clay old grass and mud packed tightly into the cracks. We sent the children seeking for flint to make new hand-axes and Copperman and I made several each day. In this way, I finally began to match him in some of the axes; the method of striking flakes from a large stone to the right length was usually a morning's work but we now made two or even three in a short sitting. Mother had made her mix of dry tea and the large leather bag of it was more valuable than anything else we owned. It was the only thing we did not share with the others or even speak of. The taste of it was home and we used small pinches to boil jars of it. I found Taila sifting through the leather pouch and when she saw me, she dropped it. We picked up the pieces, saving most of it. She hung her head in misery. To be caught sneaking into other's belongings, especially into another's pack was forbidden and she trembled at the shame of it.

I hardly knew what to say.

"If you want anything of mine I will give it to you," I said, "but why…?"

She turned and ran from me and I sat pondering the petty crime, wondering at her strange behavior. I thought to ask Copperman but he was busy and he might think badly of her if he knew. I sought out Hanit and pulled him away from his work for a talk.

He listened to the story, slowly nodding.

"So this Taila, she is fond of you?"

"Yes"

"And you feel the same?"

"Yes, very much."

"And she has never tried to steal anything else that you know of?"

"No, I never thought she was the type. I want to ask her to be my wife."

"Hmmm," Hanit said. "Do you think she knows your thoughts?"

I nodded.

"Well, if I were a young girl wanting to be the wife of a young man, I would want to make the tea mix he is used to. And this recipe you cannot ask. So I would probably sneak into the tea-pouch and try to learn it secretly."

It hit me in a wave of relief and then sympathy

"But Taila is so proud… what do I do?"

"Hmmmm," Hanit rubbed the gray fluff of his thin beard. His eyes, red from a lifetime of staring into water and sun, sparkled with humor.

"I would take a small sample of the tea and give it to her without speaking of it. She will know that you understand her meaning, which is hardly an offense, hardly a crime, but do not ask her to explain."

I did as he said, taking a bit of the tea and folding it up in a scrap of leather. I found her in the woods, furiously dragging firewood from a tangle of dried branches. I handed her the parcel and kissed her on the forehead. We never spoke of it again.

After the weeks of training, the long-house work was a welcome relief. It was labor but mindless, and other than keeping watch in turns, the warriors settled back into normal clan life. The roof beams of the long-house required smaller trees and these needed to be long, thin perfectly straight birch. We searched further and further afield to find each one and the last tree took the entire clan days to find. Limbed and peeled free of bark, the roof beams were white and naked against the light brown of the maple logs. We had split the bark from the long birch and flattened it into strips. We covered the roof beams with the bark, then began making great mounds of mud and grass, stomping barefoot until the mix was sloppy and thick as porridge. We lifted the smaller among us up to the roof and tossed up clumps of the mud for them to smooth onto the bark until the expanse of the long-house shone wet and slick with it. Then handfuls of young long grass were pulled, gently to keep the roots intact, and these were set into the mud at even intervals. With some luck the rains would come softly enough to let the grass grow without melting the mud away. Once the grass took root and spread, their roots would keep the roof together in one large living blanket.

We worked in a frenzy now, half from the outside and half from the inside, attending to every detail. Gahn cried openly as he carved markings into the door-frame one by one. Antlers set upon wooden spikes hung from the top logs beginning the roof. Blankets and sitting logs followed inside and candles lit the interior as they swept it clean of loose dirt with pine branches. Finally the low table set to the rear of the structure was set with seeds, nuts and dried bread for the Gods. An empty chair next to it made the space for ancestors to sit again in the Elkhorn long-house.

That night was a great feast in the long-house and the fishermen, warm in their coats, as guests, told stories near a blazing fire. The Elkhorn would survive the spring now and our long lost cousins were now close family. There was talk of maple trade and visits between the clans. New signals were set so we could always recognize each other from strangers.

Taila was trembling with joy to be in her long-house and I wished I could share her joy but now I had the coming of war between us and the Takers filled me with dread. Not of the death I felt was most likely, but of her receiving the news, of the clans living in fear should we fail, of the return of the Wolf and Axe.

Copperman announced that we would leave in the morning and encouraged the warriors to eat well. The warriors were subdued in the feast, all thinking of those we would leave behind. I looked at them one by one. Were we enough to even challenge the Wolf and Axe? Surly not. But Copperman would not lead us there without a plan.

I looked at him smiling and laughing at the fishermen's stories and wondered. He looked at me and motioned for me to sit near him.

"You think of your own death," he said. "I can see it in you. Stop this thinking and enjoy what we have built, what we have done here, enjoy the love of your girl, eat and drink and sleep tonight on soft furs. It will be a long journey."

"How can we possibly find them with a trail gone half a spring cold?"

"We cannot. But I know of some who will know, a clan with strong connections to the trade routes, a clan who have strong dogs and great warriors!" I felt my hairs raise on my arms.

"The Bog-shepherd Clan!"

He smiled; "I thought that would change your dark mood. You did not think we would face the Takers with only these boys? No, we need more warriors and a few trackers from the Forest-clan. It is good that we found copper to trade along the way, we will lose every medallion by the time this is done."

Wreathed in smoke

The gathering of warriors before the new long-house would have given the Wolf and Axe some pause. We stood clad in our new battle-vests, polished black with ashes, war-bows short and curved back, decorated with hawk feathers, and black bands burnt into the wood, giving the bows the look of serpents. Our modified quivers held twenty war- arrows, tipped with the special battle-points. Some among us held a spear or axe made to fit their personalities, Ailor, a quiet, thin man, made a spear as tall as he, with a wide flint point like a leaf and a copper wire wrapped around its base. Another, Borg, was wide muscled and sturdy from a lifetime of tree-dragging. He carried a club made from the root of a large maple, with its hardened end rounded. He had lost his entire family save his little brother, who had been taken captive. He moved slowly during our exercises but could crush an elk's skull with the swing of his club.

We wore black faces as well, smudged with ashes. Our hair scraped away on the sides by obsidian blades, the top slicked back with bear grease. The idea was from the Otali, a clan Copperman remembered from his wanderings, a warring tribe from the far south. They were fearsome in battle and wore black stripes on their faces and hair shaved at the sides. The effect was not only on those who saw us, but also in our hearts; we felt battle ready and fearsome. Kadal's brother Dune, the Elkhorn medicine man, and the eldest by only a few years, took the new position seriously. He spoke low and chanted to the Gods, scattering burning handfuls of grass at our feet until each warrior stood wreathed in smoke.

"Let them be the fire that burns away the Wolf and Axe!" he called to the Elkhorn Gods. "Let them move through the woods unnoticed and guide their arrows to the enemy!"

He took white clay and rubbed markings upon our faces and Copperman nodded in approval. His men were in order and, unlike our weeping exit from the Lake-clan, this would be a warriors' walk.

Gahn had a drum made from a tree-branch that had grown around and back into itself. Trimmed flat on the inside and outside to make a hoop with tight boar-skin on its face. As he began to bounce a rounded red-deer antler against it, the vibration echoed through the woods. Copperman hefted his full pack and we followed; the packs were as heavy as I had ever carried, stuffed with provisions and I wondered how it would be trekking with them. We walked from the Elkhorn with the clan following until we reached the start of the side trail leading down and around the rocks to the lake's edge. There was a call from the cliff-tops as we walked from sight. It was Taila, who could whistle even louder than Copperman. We all looked up and the others jeered as she waived.

"Your wife needs you to come back and fix the thatch on the roof," someone said and I blushed as the others laughed.

"Keep your breath!" Kadal said. "You are going to need it soon enough."

We entered the lake trail and I tried not to watch as the day brought us to the edge of sight from the Lake-clan, then turned away and down along the river, the river that Okla and Moon's pup followed. We would be to the Bog-shepherd in a dozen days. I thought about Okla and the fine village, and it gave me strength along the strange new trail.

Walking and Resting

Sweating in the hot sun, ashes streaming down our faces, bugs of every kind, excited by the winter's sleep, coming from the weeds and marshes to greet us in swarms, we moved, single file as the Takers did, doing our best to walk upon the others' footprints. We spoke less and less as the trail pulled us downward. We walked until our legs began to give out and then Copperman called a halt. We had practiced setting up a quick camp and Kadal and Copperman barked orders as we scrambled to find enough branches and firewood to protect us through the night. The food we had could never be eaten alone, so Copperman and Kadal sectioned it out, cold smoked mutton strips and something the Elkhorn called walking food, deer fat and ground Einkorn rolled into balls and heat-smoked in twisted strips of intestine. It was hard as husk bread on the outside and when you managed to bite into it, waxy and sour. It did fill the belly and needed no cooking.

We made no night fire, only a few moss smudges to keep bugs at bay, and as we slept packed next to each other, the group snoring sounded like a den of bears. Keeping watch took a small but terrible bite from each night's sleep, as two of us silently went to the location set for us. Twenty paces apart and facing away from each other, we looked into the darkness and fought the urge to sleep. Once Kadal caught a young man named Ilar (one from the little Lake-clan) sleeping against his tree and he silently gathered the others to rise and stand around him. We watched him sleep for several minutes until he woke to fear, then shame as we all went back to our beds. The sight of us all surrounding him must have been awful. We kept awake during watch from of the dread of suffering his humiliation.

The days rolled under us in multiple steps and our packs grew lighter in barely perceptible increments. We passed low mountains on either side and soon our own was beyond sight. There were fields with small huts and each brought a small excitement, as spotters went to see if the Wolf and Axe had been there before us. None had been attacked but a traveler among them had word of villages pillaged the year before in the far west. On the sixth or seventh day we found a small shelter against a half fallen tree in heavy woods. It was made of scraps and nearly upon the well-worn trail. There was a small fire smoldering out in the late morning, and as we approached, a man came from the shelter to greet us. He stopped as he saw the battle dress and black faces. He smiled and held out his hands, palms up, to show he had no weapons. He was as old as Copperman but life had been cruel to him; his clothes were tatters and his footwear held together by strands of old leather. He had a bearded face but completely bald head; without a hat he seemed a ridiculous animal and the pigeon trade tongue was barely understandable to Copperman, the best linguist among us.

Kadal was prepared to march us on but Copperman sat and began to chat with the man, offering him a piece of walking fat. He relished the food and seemed apologetic at his inability to offer us anything in return. Kadal grew restless but Copperman motioned us to sit and he spoke to the man for most of the bright morning as we sat and enjoyed the sun coming through the trees and the weight of the pack from our tired shoulders.

Finally Copperman stood, gave the man another parcel of food and motioned us off the trail and onto a small side trail veering up into an uninviting tangle of small trees.

"Why are we stopping to chat with beggars? Why are we giving our food away? Borg wanted to know. Kadal froze his question with a glare, then went forward to speak with Copperman. We walked through the scratching brush and fought our way across a sliding patch of loose rock until the sun began to set. Near dark we came out of the dense brush to find it connected with a wide, easy trail.

We set camp in a shelter used by many travelers and filled our water bags in a creek near by. Copperman set toll of beads and a copper wire ring into the crook of a tree.

"Two days of travel." he said. "That is what the trader saved us." He looked at Borg. "Worth a few bites of food?" Borg said nothing and that night I sat watch, proud and alert. They would not question his judgment again. The Bog-shepherd clan was so close I could almost taste the porridge and honey. Could almost hear Okla's loud laugh.

As It Should Be

The village waiting for us, white and orderly, well tended and summer busy, thatched roofs and swept paths among and between homes. Dogs lounged in the shade beneath each home. I could see their pink tongues lolling from the wet heat, rising over of the noonday bog. I had to compel myself to slow and not gallop into the Bog-shepherd village like a child. We had scrubbed the black grime from our faces and bathed in a creek, and, as our group of warriors waited, Copperman and I approached the village from above and walked in open sight along the welcome trail, stopping a few hundred paces from the village.

It took time for them to notice us and when they did, the villagers came out from houses, bows and spears out, the dogs sprang into a chorus of barking and snarling. We waited as they gathered and suddenly came a shout from among them. It was Keer or Koor (I could not tell which) who came running and laughing. I ran as well, all pretence of decorum vanished. He nearly tackled me and we clung to each other in such joy that even the dogs lost their guard and ran to greet us. It was Keer after all... I could see only

441

by the ink-scar on his left wrist. He made much of my shaved head and laughed until he could barely stand. The others gathered as they recognized us and we received a welcome as if we were long lost family. We walked into the familiar village center and I floated as if in a dream among the low wooden tables and white clay walls.

Koor came running and greeted me with the same laugh, the same smile, the same joy. If anything, the growing had made them more alike, and, standing together, they were reflections of the other, long hair braided in several bands, skin browned by the sun, taller than I by at least a head. Their mother raised her hands in surprise as we dropped our heavy packs near her entrance and cried for us to come in.

Copperman asked for Lan. She said he was near and she seemed surprised that he had not greeted us. Copperman startled. He called to the group of children.

"Who among you is the fastest runner?"

One of them, a skinny youth, stood forward solemnly. Copperman said,

"I will give you a prize if you can run to the bank of trees upon the hill there, full run." He pointed. "And give a message to our hunting party. Tell them that they should set down their bows and spears in a pile and sit away from them. Tell them Copperman orders it."

The boy ran off with great speed and we all watched him as he flitted like a sparrow down the trail and then up towards the distant tree line. Suddenly, I understood. If Lan and the others were to spot our war party they would not recognize any among them.

"Is Okla with them?" I asked Keer
"Okla…?"

The way he said it frightened me, as if he had not heard the name in years.

"Do you mean Tan? When he returned from the journey, he was given a new name by the Council. He is quite changed and you of all have nothing to fear from him. He said you had become friends."

"I …we have…great friends."

"Quiet!" Copperman said to me as we saw the boy, only a speck now, entering the tree -line, disappearing into it. We waited.

"Foolish not to show ourselves all at once," Copperman muttered.

The others could not imagine what he meant but his intensity gave them pause.

The boy came slowly from the tree line, then our war party, single file, followed by a group of Bog-shepherd hunters. We jogged out to meet them and as they drew into sight, I began to recognize individuals. Our men were unarmed and the Bog-shepherd carried their weapons. The boy's message had come in time. Copperman smiled broadly as Lan, leading the way, held up his hand in greeting.

Behind the group, eyes bright with joy, came Okla (for I could know him by no other name) raising his bow over and over in triumph. Moon's pup, well grown, hackles raised in bravado against the strangers ahead, followed closely at his heals.

That evening as Copperman and Lan spoke low and earnestly. I sat with Okla and listened to his story. He had traveled several days without seeing anyone, hiding from travelers as Hanit had told him to. He found a man living on the trail who shared food and shelter with him. The company (though their trade tongue was poor) gave him courage. I knew from his description that it was the one who had given us the shortcut to the wider trail. He met a woman on the journey but would not speak of it with the others present and I understood it was a secret he kept to tell me of later. Within ten days, he stood, as we had, looking down on his home village. He said the others welcomed him as if he were a new clan member and the

444

Council gave him the name of his father's brother Tan, who had died as a boy. This was the Bog-shepherd way of clearing banishment. He received no ill treatment from the others and even his mother called him Tan now.

He asked about the Lake-clan and I had so much to tell him that we spoke for hours and hours, only scratching the surface of the year gone past. He was leaner, taller, and I wondered if I would grow taller soon, or ever. He had surprised them all with the new bow skills and stories of our adventures. They did not seem to believe the tale of our ice sled and I promised to confirm it. This pleased him greatly.

To take in a group of two dozen warriors was more than could be asked of any clan and we reluctantly moved to the edge of the Bog-shepherd village into a camp near the place where we took the wild boar. Okla came with us and Copperman went to stay with Lan's family. I was jealous of his comforts and imagined warm food cooking on the hearth but Okla and I had much to speak of and took the first long night watch to speak low into the night.

As the fires died down and the moon hung low in the sky, he told me of the woman and this was the most interesting story of all. He had walked until his legs ached and his food, set out in portions for the journey, was gone days too early. (I accused him of eating the lot in the first day and he did not object enough to deny it.) Then he came upon a small village of perhaps ten huts. A couple allowed him to stay under the lee of their hut with some extra skins as shelter and they offered him a week's food in exchange for his young dog. He declined but thanked them for the shelter. They had a woman with them, the wife's sister and she was kind to Okla. I asked what she looked like and he said she was plump with brown hair and light colored eyes. As Okla slept in the cold evening, she crept from the hut and crawled into his bedroll with him. As he told this, he whispered and looked around for fear the others would hear him. She had taken her dress up and the two had coupled. As he described it, they had coupled time and time again until they were both exhausted; then she gave him some bread and dried venison before sneaking back into the hut. Unrested as he was, Okla snuck away at first light, confused and amazed by the encounter. I could understand his worries. This could have been disastrous. If he were found out there would have been violence from the village men, or worse, a forced marriage and he would have been stuck with a surprise wife only days from home.

"If she had wanted a husband, she would have not have done it in that way," I said.

He shook his head. "She was perhaps lonely, or taking pity on my loneliness. It was the first time I had ever coupled...but I do not believe the first time for her." He described in great detail the methods of coupling she showed him and I understood his reasoning about it not being her first try at it.

"This must be our secret," he said. Bog-shepherds are strict about these things and I never, *ever* want another session with the Council again."

I pledged my secrecy and he seemed happy to have told at least one about his experience. The clan ceased all summer work the next morning and gathered in the bog center among the houses where we had built the pole-house and celebrated the wedding. There were four or five dozen in the open space and those who could not find room, stood upon wooden tables to better hear Copperman's description of the recent events. He told it with great detail and I enjoyed watching his method of story telling, each detail designed to follow the path towards what he would be asking of them. The others listened, transfixed by fear and sympathy for the Elkhorn warriors who listened, heads down, faces too grim to look upon.

Copperman finished with the story of how he almost lost his new warriors to the bog. "Shepherds who had spotted us long before we arrived with bows drawn ready for an attack."

Lan stood forward, his face, usually wrinkled with smiling, held a kind of heavy darkness in it.

"These are not new stories for the Bog-shepherd. Our grandfathers fought and died in the mountains against such evil and fled to the bog to create a safe home for our wives and children. We have seen the stragglers from clans destroyed, wandering the hills naked and starving. Now it seems the dark forces are growing stronger and will soon need more food than the clans of the mountains can provide. Copperman has gathered the Lake-people and the neighboring clans to hunt those who attacked our grandfathers and sent them from their mountain homes. The Bog-shepherd Council will join with him and offer a dozen warriors to his war clan. Those with new wives and those who are only sons will not join."

This left perhaps twenty men who stood forward and a few boys who seemed earnest but were too young to battle. Copperman picked fifteen from the pack and the clan followed as he carried a war-bow and fifteen arrows to the edge of the bog. He chose a rotting log as a target and scratched a mark in its center.

"The ten closest to the mark will join the war clan and follow it until our task is done, regardless of the time or path it takes us."

Okla strode forward and flexed the war-bow, testing its pull and feel. He looked at me and grinned.

"It has the feel of a Copperson bow," he said, and with one long draw, shot the arrow to its hilt in the rotting log. His arrow touched the edge of the mark Copperman had made. An incredible feat for the first pull of a new bow. He shook his head sorrowfully and said to the Elkhorn warriors:

"Hardly worthy of your skills but I will learn it soon enough."

As the others shot the bow it was clear who wanted to go and who did not. It was a well-thought plan, as anyone fearful of battle could miss and pretend disappointment. One who was truly upset by his miss was Koor, who shot clear of the log and complained so bitterly of the misfire that Copperman gave him a second chance. In his nerves, his second shot fell worse than the first and Keer, who had made quite a fine shot of it, put a hand to his shoulder in comfort. Koor turned away and walked from the group, deeply wounded by the poor performance. Lan nodded.

"In a way it is good not to send two sons to a battle, but I wonder that the risk is just as bad either way. Koor will suffer from it."

Lan, as a member of the Council, would not be joining us but that one of his sons went was important. He would not have had the power to compel the others to release their sons to the challenge.

The ten who made the best shots were to begin training that very day and join our group in the woods to sleep. They spent the day shaving their heads on the sides and Copperman and I drew out our ink-scar kits to mark them properly, a job that took hours and hours to achieve. By the last ink-scar I stood stiffly and Copperman groaned, stretching his back from side to side.

"I only hope this was the last of the volunteers we will take on," I said, and he laughed. Copperman always seemed to laugh at the things I said when no joke was intended and I wondered if this was his elevated sense of humor or if we simply kept different humors entirely.

Okla looked fierce with his hair shaved at the sides and could not wait to be traveling with the dark face-paint we would use. For now we kept clean and Lan said we should enjoy as many summer swims as we could before the path takes us into the battle.

We trained the new Bog-shepherd warriors in the battle methods and shot hundreds of arrows daily, making as many as we could to make up for those lost or broken. This was different than hunting and the Bog-shepherd were slow by nature but stronger than the rest of us. Copperman said it was muscle from lambing and building. He made for the larger of them heavy war-axes and they practiced with them against tree branches until they could smash one with a single blow of the axe.

Copperman and Lan went to the woods and left trade gifts and a signal to the Forest-clan. There was one among the Bog-shepherd who was once of the Forest-clan and he knew the ways of communication. They sent warriors the next day to Council and after what Copperman said was the most frustrating Council session ever, the warriors finally understood our desires. They would have no part in the battle but would track the Wolf and Axe for us for a copper bracelet each. These we had but it cost Copperman dearly to see our hard won copper disappearing at such a rate. We had less than half of what we smelted in Hanit's shed.

"War is expensive," he said. "And those we hunt will have nothing of value to take back."

"Perhaps this is good," I said. "If we hunted them for treasure we would become the Wolf and Axe."

He halted wrapping an arrow to looked at me.

"This is the best thing I have ever heard you say. Remember it when we are done with this and coming home."

He began working again and I left him, saying the thing over and over so it would stay in my mind forever.

Following ghosts

Heat. Drawn and heavy in its oppression. Sweat and black soot dripping down the small of our backs. We could not move as insects of every kind the woods have to offer used us as moving homes. We were five days out, following the Forest-clan. It was like following ghosts and any thought of emulating them in our war practice seemed like silly childish games. They were far better than any of us would ever be at camouflage. Even to say following them is a deceit. One would occasionally motion with the twitch of a branch and we would move towards the place only to find him gone. Then ahead, another motion and we would seek that.

"It is good that their wants are simple as a people or they would rule us all"
Okla whispered as he searched the ground where one had signaled. Not a trace in the soft mulch. We were approaching a clan known as the Aloi and it was told from one traveler to the next and finally to us that the Aloi had suffered attack from bandits. This tale was six-days old and Copperman doubted the Wolf and Axe would still be there if it was even them; but, it was a start. Also there were

routes from Elkhorn ridge that could conceivably lead down a mountain pass to the Aloi, who, like the Forest-clan, lived in simple structures, keeping neither sheep nor goats.

Our warriors numbered three dozen plus five Forest-trackers. We were armed fully, packs loaded with weeks of dried food, black-faced and lean; grass and green twigs sprouted from our heads like living hair and most uncomfortably, war vests, still stiff as plates of stone but softening around the underarms and necklines from use. Copperman made us wear them always and the Bog-shepherds had their own version sewn from wild boar leather, hide out, coated with hard clay. They were heavy and as unwieldy a garment as any I could imagine but testing them against arrows showed a protection worthy of their discomfort.

The village of the Aloi hid beneath us barely visible from its roof peaks of small branches topped with animal skins. So different than the Bog-shepherd clan that I wondered how the people could live within days of each other and learn nothing of their building habits. Winter in such habitats must be unbearably cold and yet they had lived here for generations.

I scratched at a mosquito that had swollen with blood and like dozens of its brothers left to enjoy the meal in peace. I watched the mosquito struggle with its load and wanted to catch it and kill it (why do we desire the revenge?);

then, as it flew into a spider's web, I watched a very lucky spider tie up its dinner. This was surely a feast it would find delicious. I thought of the spider laying hundreds of eggs from the meal and its young flying off on threads populating the woods from a drop of my blood, never knowing what they owed a passing stranger.

Copperman woke me from my reveries with a flick on the back of the head. The others were ahead now and my ponderings were slowing me down. I began to crawl; shedding leaves and twigs as I went. From behind, our war party looked like a creeping landscape, and, as one moved, another paused; it was a slow animal method that had become second nature to us all. Kadal, leading, held up a hand and we stopped. After some time, he stood and motioned us to stand. Liberation! Walking upright even with all of our gear seemed free after hours of slow creeping. We gathered to look down at what Lan had seen: Scattered bones, among a long dead fire pit. We were up wind but now the smell of the dead drifted up unmistakably in its sickly sweet warning. I understood what we would find in the small collection of huts, the tale of killing in boot marks and blood.

Keer looked at me with horror. "They killed them…killed them all!"

Had I grown so callous in these months of death? I felt fear and hatred but saw in Keer's eyes what must have been in mine the first visit to the Elkhorn after the attack. I wanted to be as innocent as he again. It struck me that this was part of the war plan. Why we came to a battle weeks too late. So the new warriors could see their enemy by what he does rather than tales that might be exaggerated.

The Bog-shepherd knew some of the Aloi by name, knew of them as friends. They had no trouble in their history, only the occasional trade for cheese or smoked mutton. We spent the day among their bones, packed their remains into the fire pit and covered them with cold ashes. When Kadal and Copperman said we could go, the warriors could not get away fast enough.

That night far from the Aloi village we camped with tiny fires and heavy hearts. The Forest-clan guides came to counsel with Copperman and made camp among us for the first time. They made no fire and ate their strange food silently whispering among themselves. I recognized one as the boy who had held a spear to us long ago. Okla remembered him as well.

"That's him… only grown." he said. "Remember the missing tooth on the right side. I thought he would kill us…then he wanted to trade you for Moon. And he cried, remember? Cried to leave her."

"I understand how he felt." I said.

He nodded. "Leaving Bear hurt me worse than I thought it would. He did not understand why I would go hunting without him."

"You named him Bear?" I chuckled. "Bear?"

"He spotted three on our journey...chased a young one from the fire one night."

"You did not tell me that!"

"A lot happens in a year."

We thought about things for a while and it was like it always is with a good friend: nothing had changed since we looked at the night sky near the lake and fought sleep to tell stories.

"Is it true he said...about them...that they kill dogs with poison and..."

"It is true I said, it is all true."

"The Elkhorn dogs are gone? The parents of Moon and Bear? We have to take these men all from the world. They have gone on too long. Remember Hanit's brother? We have bred up our dogs to give the pups to the Elkhorn."

"We will take the sled across the ice again and bring them the puppies." I said.

I almost told him about Taila but it was too big a tale and I did not know how to even begin it. I thought of her very little not wanting to bring her memory to this hunt, not wanting to hope and hope.

Days of walking and now the Forest trackers spoke to us often, walked among us and then ahead. We were hunting the ones who killed their Aloi friends and the one we recognized walked with Okla, Keer and me, learning trade tongue and teaching a few forest words to us. They feared Copperman and often asked about the ink scar of the hawk on his arm. He warned us to keep the ink scars a mystery and I answered their questions evasively.

The Forest-people carried long spears and small sticks to throw them with. I had seen them before but did not understand how throwing one stick with another made any sense. Why not just use a bow? They had seen our bows and could trade for them with other clans. The Forest boy who spoke to us was named Vu and he showed us the method one day while crossing a field. Tall grass moved in golden waves as the wind slid over it.

The Forest guides stopped us with a hand and then moved forward, the five of them making a half circle. Vu whistled low and fixed his spear not much thicker than an arrow but made of heavier wood and half as long again as he was tall. He turned sideways and held the spear resting in a flat groove along the throwing stick. At the end of the throwing stick was a notch and this fit into a hollow in the back of the spear. He threw high and the spear, fletched loosely with two white fathers, flew and flexed like a long arrow shot from a giant bow. It went up into a high ark and sank a hundred paces away nearly straight down. There were hooves kicking and large red deer scattered in all directions. They were too fast and distant to even attempt with arrows and we all ran to see the doe, speared clean through the chest and glassy eyed. It was as clean a kill as I had ever seen. Vu removed his spear, the flint tip of which had split in the dirt as it passed clean through the red deer.

The Forest trackers began to flay the doe with amazing speed and as they did Copperman dug around in his pack and found a fine gray flint point. He gave it to Vu who smiled showing his missing tooth. He licked the flat side of the point and rubbed it with a thumb to see it shine in the sunlight. He sat and began to trim the bloody sinew holding the old point. With a few twists the old point came loose from its resin and the new point wedged into the v-cut in the wood cleanly. (Copperman was a genius at measuring these things from eye.) Vu wrapped the spear head into place with a wet string of roe deer sinew he kept in his small rucksack.

"Re-tipped with new stone before the game is even cleaned," Copperman said. "These spears would go through a war vest."

"We should make some of them," Keer said.

Copperman shook his head. "It would take a lifetime to learn it and you should start as a child. These would be of no more use in our hands than a bow would be it theirs."

I thought of Little Brother spending his youth with my tiny bows, his arms growing in accordance with the training. I understood.

Hand talking

The common language among us slowly merged into a warrior trade tongue. Signs made with the hand are but few in the Lake-people, but the Forest-clan used them as often as words. The silent methods of talking were well suited to our purpose and we learned them each night around the fire. 'Hand down, fingers moving like legs meant deer ahead. Hand held waist high, fingers slowly waiving was grouse or birds nesting. Fist to the side meant strangers and then the number of fingers that followed out was the number of the strangers. If they numbered more than five, the hands continued to close and open. There were dozens of words and signals soon known to every warrior and we could pass these along from hundreds of paces from man to man as we moved. The Forest guides would lead and with a hand extended from a bush or clump of branches, speaking to us all before disappearing again into nothing.

Kadal set a new rule that talking of any kind was forbidden during slow trekking.
It does not take long to learn hand signs when the voice is gone.

Okla and I incorporated our own secret signs: 'a circle of the right foot, toe pointing' to show each other something funny or fascinating. Still children on men's missions, yet it made our journey separate from the others and gave a few bright moments during days that were otherwise tedious beyond description. Slow movements caused the mind to race and at times (after days spent bearley moving through dense woods), I feared I would jump up and run screaming down the trail.

We came upon a fresh kill, a red deer from the size of the blood-pool and drag-marks. It had been dragged away from the trail and hung from a low branch, skinned with obsidian blades, evident from the flakes around as the hunters had re-sharpened their tools; there was human shit under a flat rock behind a tree and branches newly broken from a dead wood log. Shavings showed how an axe sharpened the points of the branch to pierce the body and gave handles for dragging it. This must have been done the day before or even early that morning as the blood had dried but was sticky to the touch and scavengers tracks showed that the offal was recently dragged away (probably wolverines or badgers from the claw marks in the dirt). This was territory new to us all but the methods were hurried. If a proper clan killed the red deer, they would have simply sectioned it into pieces and carried them to the others to process. This was a few men, maybe only two from the boot prints left, and, they were in a hurry to move the entire deer. The most interesting to the Forest-clan was the leaf marks as the hunters tried to cover the trail with branches.

"Clans do not hide their kills or drag them far from the trail to clean," Okla said.

Copperman nodded. "Men who hide their tracks are worth following."

Mushrooms

Thoughts of tedium were gone now, replaced with the finger twitching intensity of tracking prey. This had the feel of Wolf and Axe and Okla and I held together as we moved; if we came into battle it was understood that the two of us fought or fell together. The trail they left was well concealed and any passers-by would surely have missed it. The Forest guides followed the trail as if it were marked purposely for them.

The day grew warmer as we sifted through a tall stand of birch, arrows and spears out, stopping and starting every few steps. Voices came low from an opening in the trees. They were murmuring but in our silence the words lifted loud and crude over the quiet woods. Borg closest to Okla and me, pointed to three birch trees grown together; he signaled for us to move there and wait, bows ready. He gave similar orders to the others, using signals and gestures. They drifted to strategic points in twos and threes, barely visible shadow forms among the low brush and branches. Soon we half circled the men.

They were Wolf and Axe. Of this there was no question.

Four of them (They had hidden their tracks better than we thought.) sat facing each other, in a shallow depression behind rocks. It was a fine place for hiding their work, built up by some long forgotten clan who set stones atop one another to form crude walls. It was perhaps twenty paces from side to side, flanked by old trees. They murmured at their work, like women sewing on the same blanket, slowly, cheerfully slicing strips of meat and draping them across a lattice work of thin green branches. They were building a smoke rack and probably planned to smoke the meat overnight when the smoke would be invisible and the small fire hidden by the covering of leaf branches.

The red-deer head (small spike horns extending from the white skinned skull) hung low on a maple branch, ten paces from where they sat. They snacked on raw meat as they worked. I recognized the smallest of the four from his visit to the Lake-clan after the Elkhorn attack. He wore the same furs and used a fine obsidian blade with a horn handle to trim the meat. The others, solid and well muscled, were from different origins. They had grown into the same warriors we found dead at Elkhorn ridge: scarred faces and multiple scars along their forearms in patterns like ink-scars but without color. I shuddered to think of how they earned them. They were short-bearded save the smaller man and their hair braded in ropes that tied together in one piece down their back. It was warm work and their furs were folded neatly under them as cushions and their war-vests leaned against a maple stump with their boots set in pairs next to each vest. They wore simple undershirts and leggings with leather loincloths. Their bare feet showed the muscle and callous of men who walked the earth.

I watched them with growing fear; these were not bloodthirsty savages but something much worse. They were as organized and meticulous as Copperman. The strips of meat were evenly sliced and draped in order along the mesh of green wood twigs. Their methods had the efficient teamwork that required no thought. The smaller man was in charge; he would mention things or point and the other three would instantly comply, handing him what he needed or rearranging the collection of ribs into a stack. I considered my Lake-people neat and orderly and the Bog-shepherd clan the height of efficiency, but this was something different. Animal rage we were prepared for, but this...

An arrow interrupted my thoughts. It struck through the red dear skull, pinning it to the maple. The black crow fletching extended just beyond the bone, the short length of the war-arrow gave the impression that it had gone half through the trunk of the tree.

The men froze. Copperman and Kadal stood and we followed them over to the four men, who looked around in wonder at the war-clan who had come from the very air itself. The smaller man turned to Copperman and smiled as if meeting an old friend.

"These are the men who saved me," he announced to the others. "Please, welcome!"

Copperman turned to one of the Elkhorn warriors, Borg, the sturdiest among us who carried a fearsome war-club. "Borg! Raise your club and crush the skull of the next of them that speaks"

Borg, who had lost many and heard the screams of his mother during the Elkhorn attack, had the look of a man who would take great joy in following Copperman's order. He stood forward and gripped his war club in anticipation. The words froze in the small man's throat.

"Please," Copperman said. "Continue making our dinner. Do not let us disturb you."

The men, trembling with fear or rage, looked around unsure, confused. Copperman sighed; he turned to me, "Copperson, shoot the first one who is not preparing meat to smoke."

I drew my bow and aimed it from one to the other, who were suddenly working very fast to finish the work they started. We were silent as they worked and this unnerved them. In short order, the meat and bones were finished and stacked among the greenwood frame. The small fire lit, juniper branches beginning the fine smell of warm food. They cleaned their knives on the grass and handed them to me. I took them and handed them over to the others, keeping the fine knife of the leader who had stayed in my house once, had eaten my food, had tried to betray my people to the Wolf and Axe. I wanted to slice his throat with it.

He smiled at me, almost said something, but glanced at Borg and thought better of it. Their furs and boots were useless to us but we cut them into pads to sit on and tore the rest to shreds. Their packs were better than those of the Forest guides and Copperman emptied them and gave them over to the Forest guides, who seemed overjoyed with these meager spoils of war. Copperman sifted through the contents of the packs with great interest while the men, shivering now in a light evening breeze, watched with growing fear. Twine, medicinal herbs, flint, beads and shining brown trade shells from clams and snails unknown to us. Copperman recognized them and smiled wistfully at the oddities.

"From the shore of my great water to the south," he said. "The long years have forgotten them...I have wondered if they were a dream." He held them up. "Here they are trade. These were so plentiful, we children used them as toys. Thousands of them along the water, every color, every shape the mind can imagine, and each morning the waves brought new ones to us."

He found a bag of leathery flaps in one of the packs, strung together on a long twine. Perhaps three dozen.

"Mushrooms?" Kadal mused, holding one of them between thumb and forefinger...He suddenly dropped it as if it burnt him. "They are ears!"

The warriors who had fallen into a relaxed state drew up their weapons and tightened the circle around the four Takers.

Copperman tossed the string over to them. The prisoners looked down at the vile collection of war trophies as if it were new to them.

"This is why we came!" Kadal shouted. "Some of these belonged to friends and family."

"They are not mine," one of the warriors said. Time slowed as Borg raised his club and with sickening force brought it down upon his head. The sound and reaction was so sudden that we all recoiled from it. The man fell forward, dead before he landed. He twitched a few times and then lay silent as blood pooled around him.

It was the first violent death many of us had seen and the reactions were varied.

I grew hollow in my stomach and staggered back, stumbling, nearly fainting. I fought the urge to vomit. Keer, eyes white wide, raised his bow and aimed it first at Borg and then at the three remaining men in confusion. The Forest guides began to shout and raise their spears in thrill.

Copperman stepped forward and addressed the leader. "Remember this, my men follow orders too. You will speak when we ask you to speak."

The leader nodded slowly, eyes averting from the dead warrior at his feet.

Copperman knelt and took the string of dried ears, we watched as he set the evil necklace around the leader's neck.

"Now you will speak and if I sense you are lying or lacking in use to my war party you will sink like your friend into the soil."

That night we built small fires against the four short walls of the old house and crowded in to tend the smoke rack and listen to Copperman question the men. The smell of smoking meat fought against the sight of the dead Taker and we hungered and sickened from it in turn. The Wolf and Axe had the high language skills that come from roamers. Trade tongue was unnecessary though they had a dialect unpleasant to the ear as if they had no joy of the language (though the dialect of the enemy is nearly always unpleasant to the ear.)

They were smarter than any of us expected; even Copperman was sometimes taken aback by their openness and ability to express their methods. They were hunters and unapologetic about the fact that it was humans they hunted. They had Gods, sure, but these Gods lived in the fire of the storms and wanted them to win battles and rewarded them well for bravery. To die sick and old was to fail. They did not call themselves Wolf and Axe. This was given to them by those who survived, and, as the title seemed to create fear in those they fought, it was a good name; but they called themselves Nagaal. They would not say what it meant.

They did not keep houses or farms ever, or worse yet (in their eyes) sheep. There were a few women in the camp, though none ever came to battle. Instead, wives waited for the Nagaal men to winter in camps south.

"But once we all came from the south," the leader said. "The Mountain-folk are our sheep. We come summers and save up stores and trade goods before going back down." Again this said without guilt or any hint at its darkness.

Once, in the night, the largest of them, who had been mostly silent, could no longer look at his dead partner and with a scream of rage, charged up from his position at

Kadal. Okla, who noticed his agitation, had an arrow ready. He shot him through the chest as he rose and we watched amazed as the man ran into the darkness and disappeared from light, arrow stuck from front to back. Some went to follow but Copperman called them back into the light of the fire. "We will find him in the morning, not fifty paces away." Okla sat and trembled.

Copperman returned to his questioning as the others held arrows notched in case the others tried the same. Two killings in the same night and we were losing our fear of it already. I sat with Okla and Keer, both shaking and silent. I put a hand on Okla's shoulder and he turned to me, pale. "It is not like killing a deer, he whispered…or even an Uris…it is…" he shook his head and fell silent.

By first light the two men, shivering uncontrollably, could no longer speak to answer Copperman's questions. The meat and bones had smoked well and we packed them away, piled the belongings of the Takers onto the fire and let them smolder; then, we peed out the fire, leaving the dead warrior and the red deer skull stuck with an arrow against the tree. I felt for any poor hunter who might wander into the sight.

"The scavengers will scatter his bones," Kadal said.

We tethered the two remaining at the wrists and left the place on empty stomachs. We found the one Okla shot, slumped over a stone, nearly two hundred paces from camp.

Okla stared dumbly as one of the Forest guides tried unsuccessfully to remove the arrow.

"Leave it," Copperman said. "Move on now."

He untied the two Wolf and Axe. "You can return south without anything from the Mountain-folk. Two of the Forest guides will follow you for several days. You will never see them but if you deviate from your trail they will end you. . You have killed their friends and it is with great reluctance that they let you live at all. Warm days might just find you home. There is at least a small chance. If you live, tell them that there are arrows, clubs and spears for any who come to steal from the Mountain clans. Go!"

They stood confused,
"Go. South. Now!"

They ran and Copperman told two of the Forest guides to follow, make their presence known, and, then return.

Mapping

Okla, Keer and I kept tightly together the next day, so close, that Copperman spoke to us about it. He said there were dangers to a war party forming into smaller alliances. We spread out and tried to make friends among those we had not spoken to. I spoke to Borg, whose will had hardened even further after killing the warrior. I asked him if it was strange to kill. He had the look of many in the Elkhorn after the attack, as if he were looking past me to something far away. He spoke without emotion.

"They took five from me. I pledged to my family two Takers for each we have lost."

He wanted to trade me some of his share of dried meat for an ink-scar. I told him I would think about it but I did not. Ink-scars were for bravery but I would not do killing-scars. I told him if he carved a mark into his war-club, others would see it and know immediately what the marks meant. If they were ink-scars, he would have to explain it to the enemy. He liked this and began carving at our first rest. The others knew the meaning. His was the sentiment of nearly all the Elkhorn.

The Bog-shepherd were nervous and wanted to hear stories of the Takers' deeds over and over. They needed to know that what they were doing was real and necessary. The Forest guides seemed happy to be along for the trip; they had no problems with what we were doing and only showed concern when we let the two Takers live. I supposed the loose prisoners would die soon without furs, food or weapons. But Copperman was equally convinced they lived.

"They will find a way, he said. "At least I hope so. They need to guide us to their hornet's nest."
"But they were warned to go south…"
"They will know a fake threat when they hear it. They know we would not lose guides for several days following them. They will circle around when they think it is safe."

That night the guides came back hungry. They showed Copperman how far the men were and what direction they left them. The Forest guides used a series of sticks and placed them into the ground. None of us understood this but Kadal, who had seen it before. He explained it and Copperman's eyes lit up like a fat man gazing at a wedding feast.

"A new method of finding places!"

He gasped and looked around at us to see if we were witnessing the same miracle he was. We looked blankly back, then crowded in to see what the fuss was about. None understood it at first and some never really did. The Forest-clan sat in the dirt and made a series of small twigs into a pattern, then used small round pebbles. Two of the pebbles they called the Takers, the handful of pebbles a few hands' lengths away they said were our war party. They scooped sand to imply a tiny mountain. Slowly, painfully, the idea came to me. They were making the land small so that we could see it like a bird would. We all told distances by describing days traveled and the difficulty of the journey. One might say: it is two days travel west; there is a trail with rocks on the left side into a cliff; then half a day slightly uphill until you reach trees of birch; and, then north until the pines begin small, there is the camp with standing water and bad mosquitoes near. To follow, you had to repeat the words until they stuck.

Copperman laughed out loud and those who had never seen him do this were confused, frightened. 'Was he gone mad from the killing? Squatting with the Forest-folk, laughing at sticks and dirt?' I knelt down to focus on the thing they made and it hurt the mind to take it in. At times I would see it clearly, then it became dirt and twigs and pebbles again. I saw it in my sleep that night, and, by the next morning, I joined Copperman, who sat with me and tried it with our Lake-clan. We made a small lake in the dirt and argued about the shapes of mountains and where the trails went, the space from the lake to the glacier and Mountain-clan. The shape of the lake seemed strange to me but Copperman explained the coves and inlets until I understood he was right. It curved and ran far to the west, getting skinnier to the shallow flats where the little Lake-clan stood on its pole- homes in the reeds. We stacked rocks to build the Elkhorn ridge. Then marked trails leading outward. Keer watched as we played like children in the dirt. I cannot remember ever seeing Copperman so thrilled with anything.

Okla came over to look down on our work.

"What are they doing?"

Keer shrugged. Kadal sat down to join our map.

"They are pretending they are Gods, building the land beneath them," he said.

Copperman shook his head.

"Better than that…we are winning the battle."

Ice from the sky

I dreamed about the hawk again; I was carried naked in his talons, high along the snow mountains, sometimes skimming the jagged peaks with my bare feet. He took me higher and higher. I watched the familiar shape of our lake shrink to a single blue drop of water in the crook of wrinkles that were our mountains. There were more lakes, so many that I lost sight of ours among them. And beyond them, the shore of the great lake of Copperman's childhood. And even beyond that, the curved land where Asha's mighty clan dwelt. It was devastatingly beautiful. We climbed higher and higher still so that the lines of the horizon blurred black and the frozen air escaped my lungs. Above us now was the waterfall of lights, somehow dark behind the growing fire of the sun. And then the hawk, sensing I had seen enough, dropped me, tumbling, spinning, ever falling end over end until the land drew up suddenly to crush me.

I awoke to Borg nudging me. It was my watch and for the first time I was glad to take the turn. I needed time alone with the new dream to remember it over and over before it faded, as dreams do, to a numb feeling in the chest, a flash of memory that only held if you did not look directly at it.

I let the next watch sleep and stayed to search the night-sky hopefully. Mother always said that dreams come to tell you something you already know. If the world I saw in that dream had always been in me, then what other knowledge awaited there? I wanted to tell someone about this but somehow it was not the talk for a war party, or even for Okla, who would make light of it. Then I realized whom I wanted to tell it to: Taila. She would like the story of this dream and when we slept in the same furs I could tell it to her. With this to ponder I sat, bow ready, waiting for the dawn.

That day clouds came in from the south, boiling up into white structures in the sky. We sat, frustrated from the morning's crossing of a river. Alone, in safe territory, a river of twenty paces across would be a short swim and nothing more. A war clan, however, is in danger crossing rivers. If set upon by the enemy, warriors are as vulnerable as lambs, as they struggle slowly across chest deep water, holding heavy gear and weapons. We moved in twos and threes, covering each other with bows drawn, fifty paces up and down either side of the crossing.

The summer rains upstream had the glaciers melting and the icy current numbed our legs. Ailor slipped and tumbled in slow motion for thirty or forty paces, losing most of his gear in the process. He lay, gasping and coughing water as the others traded and arranged dry skins for him and hunted down-stream to rescue what belongings they could. Keer sparked up a small fire. This was all achingly slow work and there was nothing to do but wait until Ailor stopped shaking and could breathe normally. By midday we had crossed no more than three hundred paces. Then the sun dimmed behind a wall of dark cloud.

"Make camp!" Copperman shouted. "Stay-shelters on that slope! Dig in deep...extra roofing!"

He looked at the wall of clouds intently. He rarely raised his voice, and when he did, it had a spectacular effect. It takes a lot of sweat to make stay-shelters for many men. They were also impossible to hide the next day. So far on our journey we had made camp like the Forest-clan; bedrolls against hard ground, small cook-fires atop stones that could be easily scattered, tracks brushed over by pine branches. We worked as a single creature now. Within minutes the wet thump of hand axe against aspen echoed over the hillside like so many woodpeckers. Copperman must have seen hard weather in those clouds; whatever he saw had moved Kadal as well and the two ran from soldier to soldier barking orders and generally abusing our methods.

Okla and I competed, choosing trees side-by-side and fighting to fell our own first. The hillside was a fine place for stay-shelters in a storm. A white, head-high stonewall ran for a hundred paces horizontally along the middle. The wall of stone formed a natural barrier against rain as it would divert flowing water behind it and around either side of the shelters. Against this we built ten shelters by leaning arm-thick aspen against the rock face, then binding thinner branches sideways along the two poles. The result was a small angled roof with enough room for three men to lay side-by-side, with a small fire pit at their heads.

We lined our shelters with thick piles of long green grass and fresh young branches, soft tips inward. Upon this we laid every fur we possessed. The rocks beneath the wall were wedged out with poles and sent tumbling down the hill until we all had a reasonably flat place to lie, (though some had holes that needed filling with many thick sheets of moss and earth). For roofs we stripped large birch of their bark with long slices down and then across, peeling back the sheets in great tubes. These, stepped on and flattened, were impervious to rain and stitched in place with roots from juniper at the corners. It was sweating work, and as we struggled further and further afield for the last of the bark, the sun blotted out from the approaching storm.

Copperman's intensity made sense now and we drove ourselves ahead of the coming weather. I had seen a few storms as foreboding as this one and they were dangerous, even from inside of a well crafted hut. Pity the men who did not finish their roofs in time. We cut extra aspen, luckily plentiful along the base of the hill. These we

limbed and laid upon the roofs to keep the wind from the
bark tiles. Wind came in now in short gusts, pushed ahead
of the rain. With flat rocks piled around the base of the
roof poles, we climbed into our shelters, covering the open
ends with small pine and anything else we could find.

The cloud grew. We huddled in the strange
darkness of day, peering out from time to time. I went out
for one last pee and stood looking up at the massive wall
rolling over our heads now. The sky swirled in delicate
patterns like silt in fresh water. The air smelled dusty and
electric. Then the first flash of lightning pulsed the center
of the darkness and a low distant rumbling followed. The
first big drops began to fall, speckling the white stones gray.
Drops heavy enough to knock loose leaves from the taller
trees below. I darted for the cover of our hut. Okla, Keer
and I had ignored Copperman's warning about alliances and
made our hut together. This day I was happy to have the
company of good friends.

One of the Forest-clan came out from the heavy
beech woods below. (They refused to help make or even
enter our shelters.) He had small coals wrapped in maple-
leaves for each of us. It was a motherly act and so unlike
the Forest-clan that we marveled at the kindness of it. We
had squirreled in a small stack of pinecones and a few good
chunks of long burning wood for the night fires. They
would be smoky and in the summer night, more comfort
than necessity. Keer tucked the cinders in the maple leaf

into a handful of dry grass and blew rich smoke into small flame. Heavy coughing from the shelter next to ours made us laugh. Borg cursed and opened his skin door to let out the acrid smoke.

"Maybe juniper was not the best choice!" Keer called over and Borg cursed us as we laughed harder.

Wind pulled at the side of the shelter now, and rain began to rattle against the birch bark shingles. We waited cross-legged, backs against the rock wall, watching the sloped ceiling before us. The rain rushed down it in growing speed but none came through to us.

"Your father is a seer." Keer said. "Another half hour and the shelters would have been useless. We would have spent a night soaked."

Okla cringed at a lightning strike so bright it showed through the cracks in the door. A heart beat later thunder vibrated the very rocks we leaned against.

There was no telling how long the day lasted or exactly when it melded with the night. We nursed our little fire and murmured curses as the water pounded against the hillside. At one point we could hear the struggle, as a pole from a shelter slid from its hold against the ground and wet warriors fought it back in place. The sound changed from rain beating the roof, to stones bouncing. Ice chunks, large as walnuts, came from the sky, shattering against the stone and punching through the branches of the shelter to leave round dents against the wet fresh bark. One piece came right through the corner of our roof and it was our turn to stoke the fire and re-sew the thing with cold fingers. What would have taken a few minutes in the dry day, took ages in the confused night. I thought of our poor Forest guides: Were they huddled against a tree? Dug into the earth? They were proud of their skills and no doubt spent many nights under a storm…but this?

Lightning began to flash faster and faster until there was hardly a pause between the flashes. And the ice turned once again to sheets of rain. I must have dozed off. The rain had settled into scattered drops and the thunder sounded from remote mountains, comforting in its retreat. The birds, like the Forest-clan, had survived the night in the open and now called out to each other in the pre-dawn. One by one we crept out of our cramped shelters and joined Kadal and Copperman who had already removed the roof from their shelter and were burning damp wood dry against the pit of their fire. One by one we searched for anything dry within our roofs and piled it on until the fire steamed with piles of wet bark. Eventually the drying shingles exchanged dank smoke for clean flame. We stacked a circle of wet bark like a nest around the edges of the fire.

Birch bark has many uses and as a damp fire fuel it has no equal. Our war clan was somehow cheerful, exhilarated even, as if the storm was not something we survived but an enemy we had concurred. The Forest guides came from their beech woods, nimble and alert, joining our fire to toast several squirrels trapped in the ingenious string snares they set at the end of each march. The discipline had them well fed through the journey and we envied them as they munched the half cooked meat. We shared out the small food we had between us.

Copperman surveyed the devastation the storm (and our stay camps) left across the hillside. Jagged tree stumps, branches scattered, wood, reddish wood chips, sodden and fresh, a mess that could not be burned or even brushed away. He shook his head. We have gone from a family of roe deer to a pack of wild boar. You could see our tracks from the far ridges.

"Burn it," he said, pointing to the roofs of the shelters. "The poles too, burn it all in a great heap. Their guides would find it anyway. With a fire pit ten paces across, they will question our numbers."

The smoke rose high into the sky as we piled on a small hill of steaming green poles and snapping pine branches. I had never seen a fire so large and smoky. The Elkhorn had, however, when their homes burned. They stared into the flames, rekindling their rage.

"Let them wonder at the smoke…"Copperman murmured, suddenly smiling.

"Are we signaling them? They will wonder," he said loudly to the war clan. "Are we burning a village? Are we touched? Wondering the woods in madness? They will see it and come to spy…and we will wait and follow. Pack and move, quickly now, up to the hills. Make as many footprints as you can. Come back down leaving no trail and then stomp back up. We will let them think we are an army ten times our size and then let the trails vanish."

The Forest guides watched in bewilderment as we tramped up and then down the rising hill above the rock ledge. After four or five times, we regrouped, breathless, at the ledge, stepped delicately along it, and moved as one line into the beech woods. The Forest guides suddenly understood and smiled broadly nodding to Copperman. This was their world again, signaling and hiding.

The great fire wained, showing itself as a high, thin line in the late morning sky. We circled around, found a vantage point for the guides and then waited. Mid afternoon they came, two Wolf and Axe. So stealthy that we barley saw them stepping among the rocks like Ibex on the hill above the burned out stay camp. They studied the scene before descending into the open, stopping often, looking hard at the heavy footprints.

"They are counting," Kadal said smugly, "puzzling it out."

They followed down to the stay-camp, stopped and stood confused at the array of evidence.

Okla snorted. "What would we think if we came upon a smoking camp with five dozen boot trails and fire pit the size of a hut?"

They poked at the ashes and conversed for a time. I froze as they looked in our direction, then down towards the river, then in the four directions equally.
Finally they stopped and ate and seemed deep in discussion. Three others arrived at the top of the hill and moved down to join them. More discussion. In the end, the five moved down to the river trail and began following it north.

"Are they seeking us still?" Kadal asked.
"No," Copperman said. "They do not hide their trail now. They are heading back to tell the others."

He motioned to the Forest guides and they moved down to follow.

Is it your witch?

Thus began a long slow trek. They were heading to higher ground, the river trail so open and treeless from the heavy use that we could not risk it for fear of ambush. We followed in dense woods, moving until the light failed. The insects were hungry after the heavy rain and we could not use smudges against them, nor was there any bug root to be found. That night, under a warm windless canopy of high weeds, we wrapped into our skins, leaving only a hole to breath from. The choice was near suffocation or a blanket of mosquitoes. I chose to suffocate. Borg, whose bulk made him overheat easily, slept, furs open and let them feast. By morning his face was swollen and grotesque. He rubbed his short stiff beard and spat into the dirt.

"Let me die fighting in the open before I spend another night in those weeds."

One of the Forest guides gathered a handful of pale yellow flower buds and crushed them into a paste. He gestured to Borg to rub the mush on his face. Keer said it could not make his features any uglier and even Borg smiled at this. He rubbed the goo around the bitten areas and after some time nodded. He gathered a handful for a pocket and we all followed suit.

The Forest guides led us to where the men had slept. We saw no evidence of the camp. The Forest guides pointed at things we could not see and nodded. Kadal spoke to them as Copperman searched the place on hands and knees and found nothing.

The Elkhorn warriors were restless from the sneaking. Of us all, they seemed to suffer most from this dainty maneuvering. They were fighters born of fighters and their style did not favor stealth. Ailor, who had not said a handful of words since he joined the war party, smiled and then began to chuckle. We all stopped and stared at him. Keer smiled and began to chuckle with him.

"Ailor…. what is it?" Ailor shook his head and tried to stifle a laugh.
He looked at Copperman. "They look for nothing. Now they have found it"
Ailor nodded to the Forest guides in turn. Copperman began to chuckle as well, growing in understanding.

"Of course…how do you find men who leave no trace…? You look for no traces."

Suddenly we understood. The act of sweeping over traces of a camp not only covers up your own tracks but all others. Deer prints, feint in the sand, rabbit, bird and even mice leave their prints by the hundreds on every space in the woods. By carefully brushing away all footprints from a place, you leave a blank spot that looks untouched by anything. This was the print of a master tracker. We looked at the surrounding area and found deer pellets and footprints, barely visible. And then, as we looked, we began to see what the Forest guides were looking for. It stood out more and more as we examined it. One patch of ground, ten paces from side-to-side, large enough for a small party to camp, without any trace of another living thing.

"From now on we would look as our guides did, for nothing."

"Well done, Ailor," Kadal said and gripped him by the shoulders. "I was beginning to doubt our guides and without that trust the game is lost."

Ailor did not answer but was pleased and stood a bit taller. We stepped again from the trail and followed it parallel for the rest of the day. That night we slept in the crook of an overhang with a soft sand bottom and the next morning we watched the strange early ritual of the Forest guides. Finally, we knew why they carried the rabbit feet and bird claws. They brushed away our tracks with dry branches, flicking the sand perfectly to leave no marks, then reached in and marked a few tracks with the rabbit paws and covered those with the bird claws placing them in twos as a bird would walk. They swirled a small indent where a fox might curl for a short nap, and, reaching in to a small pouch, scattered three small piles of rabbit pellets. One took his water pouch, sipped and spit a perfect shot of water on the pellets. Anyone finding the camp that day would feel the pellets and know from their wetness that a rabbit had been there in the night.

Okla nudged me. "Every time they did that I thought it was a kind of...offering to the their Gods or...I do not know."

Keer nodded. "I feel such a fool."

"Me too, brother," I said. "We will not doubt them again."

I spent that morning thinking of the hundreds of things other clans did that I had thought foolish and pondering how they might be of use.

The figure sitting alone in the woods did not stir as we approached. It was late in the afternoon and we were rejoining the trail, seeking a place to camp when the guides motioned to us. We slowly circled the huddled figure and drew arrows nervously. Was it a trick to draw us in? Suddenly Copperman stood and held up a hand for us to lower our arrows. He walked out into the open and approached the figure, who stood slowly, stiffly and cackled in delight. Then I recognized her, the tattered robe of a hundred different scraps, the tangle of jet-black hair with ribbons sewn into it, the loud trade tongue. Asha.

She was unafraid of the band of face-blackened, well-armed warriors who surrounded her. She pointed over to me and called.

"Dead dog boy! Come…come… you trade!"

The others looked at me and lowered their weapons. Borg nudged me with his shoulder. "Go to her Dead-Dog Boy…your woman beckons."

It was the first time I had seen him smile. The Forest guides vanished into the woods and would not return despite Copperman's signals.

"Is it your witch?" Keer said. "The one who gave you Moon?"

Okla gasped. He had listened to the story a dozen times. "It is Asha, is it not?"

I walked forward and greeted her, rubbing noses happily. She had lost another tooth and one of her eyebrows had a white scar running across it but she looked as wild and wonderful as I remembered. She ignored the others, speaking to Copperman and me as she had when we met her in the woods. The conversation took several hours and the war clan spread out, guarding either side of the trail.

Her language was tedious to understand but Copperman sat unhurried as if it were a summer's day at the lake.

Asha's story: She knew of the Wolf and Axe and sometimes even traded with them. They wanted healing crow root and the tiny red mushrooms that gave visions when dried and made into tea. They traded her furs and beads and none of them wanted to lay with her because she was a witch. She had seen their work in burnt out villages and dead bodies but they had disappeared for many years, only coming back now to hunt the mountain regions. She saw them only that morning, five men walking quickly. They would not stop to trade or even talk. They looked nervous and she had wondered at that. She understood now what made the Wolf and Axe afraid. She admired our war clan and asked if we were going to end the Takers for good?

"Yes." Copperman said.

She shook her head. "It is trade you will cost me, but good to see the dark ones gone." She spoke of it as if it had already happened.

"Do you trade poisons to the Wolf and Axe?" Copperman asked.

She shook her head. "They kill dogs. I will not help them kill dogs."

"You save dogs," she said to me.

I told her that Moon was big now and has puppies as big. She smiled.

"We have to track them now," Copperman said. "We must leave you." He offered Asha beads for her hair. She closed his hand around them.

"Do not track them," she said, pointing to a hill in the northeast. "They stay in the dead homes of the old valley."

Kadal gasped. "They have taken the old Valley-clan?"

Asha nodded. "Killed most, the scattered left are gone south and walked this very trail four days ago. They had no food to trade. Not one piece of dried meat. The Takers are there. Go beyond the rocks and up the steep cliff. It is faster."

We thanked her and were off away from the trail, moving fast into the afternoon.

There was no trail on Asha's short cut, only rockslides and cliffs. It was no wonder the Takers took the open trail. We made no secret of our walking; time was more important now. We walked into dusk and reached the cliff edged Ibex-trail that led up to the old Valley-clan. They were remote and not even Copperman had been there before. Kadal had as a boy and several of the Bog-shepherd said they had distant relatives there.

The old Valley-clan were protective like high clans tend to be. Something about having an overview of the world below makes people distrust it. Like the Elkhorn ridge, the old valley was only a destination, no one went through it on their way to somewhere else.

The Elkhorn among us spread out between the lowlanders, guiding us on the cliff climb. They seemed frustrated as darkness came and we were still climbing. At times one of us would slip and an Elkhorn would grunt as he stopped our descent over the rocks. Borg caught Keer three times and finally said.

"The next time you fall I will only grab the pack from you on the way down."
The two were becoming fast friends and the threat was somehow a kind word from Borg.

The full moon cast its blue sheen on the granite wall; it was bigger this night. I wondered what made the moon swell to such a lantern some nights and shrink to a sliver on others. Sister always said it was a face that turned to watch us and then turned away to give us our secrets. But I could not think of Sister tonight, or the pull home might begin. It had happened a few times on our journey, and, like that first time on the mountain, I felt it as a weight in my chest. Best to leave home where it is on a war journey.

I pushed the thoughts down and focused on the climb. One step and one hand firm, then the next, and the next, and next. We were sweating and gulping for breath when the dark backdrop of mountain curved to show us the top. We were on the middle of three ridges surrounding the half circle that cupped the old valley. It was a bowl shape with treeless mountains to its back and the beginning of tree line at its base. How had Asha known of the back trail? We could see flickering fires, far below and the shapes of huts, men moving and the occasional laugh or curse.

A single dog barked and a woman called to silence it. We looked to each other in surprise. There were women with them, we had been warned, but the thought of it made our attack seem underhanded. We were the predators now, stalking human prey and there were women. Would they fight along side of the men? Would I shoot one? Could I? Could any of us?

Copperman called us away from the view and back to an underhang in the cliff. We huddled there as Copperman and Kadal started a small fire from pinecones and bits of brush we could scavenge. He needed to see. In the small light we made a map of what we could see in the dirt and Copperman and Kadal argued quietly over the details.

"We need more time," Kadal said. "We need to watch and plan."

Copperman turned his head. "And if they leave tomorrow? We will not beat them on a trail, the men armed, the guides watching. But in a camp, in huts, sleeping, we have surprise with us. The dog must be silenced. This is the night. We will stake a man aimed at each hut and when the fighting begins we shoot as the huts open. Use their own methods against them. There might be women, if they come out armed, they are warriors and must be treated as such. If unarmed, let them run and we will help them after."

The Forest guides were excited as Copperman described the plan. They would go first and silence any and all dogs. I cringed at the thought of Moon and choked down the emotion. We would die if we did not do this. If not now, then eventually at the hand of the Takers. Tonight we would be the Takers, and, Gods willing, we would walk away from it at the end.

Now!

Fear weighed me down. I carried it, throat tight, legs rubbery, hands trembling. My kidneys felt watery and I could not pee often enough to keep the feeling down. We sat to eat and I could not touch a bite. Copperman and Lan???? went from warrior to warrior, speaking low to them their individual instructions. Okla and I sat checking and rechecking our bow strings and arrows; we tied our boots with double laces and wrapped sinew in bundles around the laces with knots so tight we would have to cut them free when we were done.

Kadal said there were many a warrior who died from a broken bootlace in the heat of battle. Copperman came to Okla; he told him Borg would be with him on the west side and I would follow the Forest guides and take huts on the east. I began to protest but Copperman would not listen.

"Would I have had Keer and Koor fight shoulder to shoulder? It is foolish to set brothers together in battle. Either they argue or sacrifice needlessly. Keer will stay with me and Kadal in the south. When they retreat down the main trail we will ambush them."

Our hair had grown out some and we were ordered to set it right. We sat with obsidian blades tending each other's hair in the flickering firelight like a group of women. For a short time the only sound was the scrape of blade against scalp until the sides of our heads shined and our hair, stiffened from travel oil and dust, stood like fins. We took ashes from the fire and rubbed our faces black. In profile we looked like angry war Gods. And now we felt it. My throat relaxed and my fear turned slowly to anger.

Copperman gathered us tight and spoke with great emotion. "Some of us will die this night. And all of us will kill. If you fail, the Takers will come again next summer and our clans will live in fear. They will come and it will be our wives and children who suffer."

Borg thumped his war club softly against the ground as Copperman spoke.
"These are the men who keep the ears of our families as trinkets. Steal our children as their own. Burn our houses. Feed on our fear. The Takers have never felt their own fear, until tonight. Tonight we use their methods against them. The Gods will decide who should walk the long trail home."

We tightened our war vests and stowed our packs under the cliff ledge, then covered the small fire with dirt.

We sat a few moments in thought, eyes adjusting to the night, and then, in twos and threes, began our trek down to the old valley and its sleeping monsters.

The trees were sparse and the trail rocky and loose. My task was to keep up with the Forest guides who had spent time with Copperman and Lan ????planning the attack. I hoped they understood the plan and hoped even more they would not disappear before my eyes when the trees thickened. Vu made sure they did not. He carried his long spear as they did from its tip so the branches would not catch as we descended into the tree line. I held the back end of the spear.

Vu was excited as we left the main trail and began slipping through the dark stunted shadows of the trees. The moon began to cast shadows under its blue light and I could see him looking back at me with a huge grin as if to say, 'is this not the best adventure ever?' I nodded and tried to hide the fear growing again with each step. This was bear-attack fear, this was drowning fear. The beginning of the end of everything fear. And still we walked forward.

Sooner than I imagined, far sooner than I hoped, we were within a hundred paces of the village and crawling. One of the Forest guides stopped us with a hand signal and then crept forward. The very slight breeze was in our faces and the dogs had not smelled us yet. We waited for a signal and then crept even slower until I could see the huts of the old valley clan. They were well built and lined, a dozen at least, in a half circle. Their version of a longhouse was directly before us, low walls from stacked stones, bark roofed, and thatched with straw and branches. It was not as big as the Elkhorn's but it could hold ten or fifteen. It had a low door in its very middle, and, in front of this, two dogs slept. I could see their forms curled on furs at the entrance.

Vu nodded to me and I crept forward in agonizing slowness, even in the terror, I felt a need to show well under the gaze of the Forest clan. As a plant grows, I raised, drew my bow, whispered an apology to Moon and her kind, and fired. The arrow hit cleanly and the dog half rose before falling back kicking. The other dog woke and attacked the dying one as dogs often do in their confusion, I fired again and the second dog fell near its mate. There was a growl of anger from inside the longhouse and someone hit the door several times. We waited, nothing more. They must have thought the dogs were quarreling and the following silence froze my blood.

Heart beat pounding in my ears, I drew another arrow and notched it. Nothing. Waiting and waiting. Nothing.

The evening chill clung to the sweat, now dripping down my forehead. I tried to breathe more slowly but the breaths came gasping and I was certain they could be heard from inside the huts. At one point a man came from one of the huts, naked from the waist down. He was like his companions (as if they all came from the same dragon mother): broad shouldered and powerful, scarred with marks, white in the moonlight, from self-inflicted cuts along the forearms. They were the marks on Borg's club. Death counts. Did I know any of the marks on that arm? Were they men I had traded with, the sisters or mothers of travelers I had met? By first light would I be one of the scars on a Takers arm? He snorted, spit loud in the night, then peed steaming from the edge of the hut into the dirt. He looked up at the sky for a cold moment and then we heard the hut door creak shut.

The smell of charred meat from the night's feast and dead coal, pine and maple mingling with the scent of furs and people, and the feint odor of dog and human shit. No clan would use their village so poorly as to shit near their huts. The fire pit in the feasting area near us was far too big and I understood these were their methods. They must have burned the clothes and bodies of the old valley clan like they did the Elkhorn.

I shifted and found that my legs had fallen numb from holding position. I sat flat and stretched out my legs, slowly massaging them back to life. We were near a large maple with a long heavy branch that arched out at an angle up to a small platform of branches, worn shiny by children playing. It was the village tree and the parents had driven spikes into it so the kids could climb up the trunk. It offered a good vantage point. I snuck out into the open and climbed it without thought; like an animal in danger, I suddenly wanted the advantage of height.

Vu pulled at my shirttail as I scampered up the tree but I brushed him off. This was an unexpected advantage; the limb allowed me to grip with my legs and fire into the entrance of the longhouse, but a branch curving up would make a small shield to cover behind when they fired back. I clung with my legs and focused on the entrance to the longhouse until my eyes burned. Then, like a falling star, the first flaming arrow fell upon the longhouse roof, followed by three more, expertly placed along the dry grass of the roof edges. Three of them began to flicker like winter candles, and the fourth, buried too deep into the thatch, sparked out. Another flew to replace it. Nothing stirred as the silent flames began to grow horribly bright in the dark sky. Smoke and small sparks drifted high in the chill air, mingling with the carpet of stars. I followed their paths upward and wondered if the Gods were watching.   I whispered to them for help and courage.

The fire began to crackle loudly but still nothing. I drew an arrow back and aimed it at the door. Seconds crawled by and still nothing. A door creaked open and the man who peed earlier walked out, still naked from the waist down. He looked confused at the flames in his half sleep. A spear sunk into his chest and he sank to one knee, stood again, and raised his head to cry out, but no sound came. He fell, snapping the spear.

Then, coughing and a shout from inside the longhouse. I looked down to see three of our own kneeling, bows drawn and aimed again at the door as it flew open. A man came out fumbling with a bow and a fist full of arrows. Our arrows flew. He tripped over one of the dead dogs and all three arrows missed him only to hit others coming out as well. I drew and fired as he rose and hit him in the neck. He stood and looked with rage up the tree directly at me. He was big, half again as wide as I, and well muscled in shirtsleeves and under shorts. He had dozens of scars along his arms and long red hair tied back in ropes behind his head. He reached out at the arrow and finding its tip, grabbed it with both hands. We both screamed as he dragged it from his neck in one long bloody pull. He looked at me again as I waited (for what I do not know). He stumbled over to the base of the tree and tried to pull himself up after me. This was a warrior shot by a coward trembling in a tree. I cried out again as he slid back down the trunk.

During this, warriors were spilling from the huts and arrows flew from bows still hidden in the surrounding trees. Cries echoed from all sides as the roar of the roof fire grew and sections of the roof fell in on those still inside. The entrance, littered with bodies, had to be pushed through by those inside, and, any who made it out, met with arrows. A woman crawled from a side window and an arrow hit her directly. She was pulled from the space and a boy followed, an arrow sunk into the wood near him and he slipped from the window, fell and ran silently into the darkness.

From my left, Takers with clubs fought Borg and Ailor and Vu. Borg was a wonder with his club. Swinging it low, he took the leg out from under a warrior and with the same swing spun round to hit another, crushing his shoulder. Vu jabbed and parried with his spear. I drew an arrow and shot too low, drew again and this time hit the Taker in the side. Vu rushed in and thrust up with his spear, ending him.

I realized the Takers could not see me as some came under the very tree itself, drawing their bows or swinging their clubs. I shot down onto one after the other, as they spun around confused. Ten paces high and I was invisible. The longhouse was a bright burst of flame now, gathering strength, blowing towards me too hot to bear. Leaves on the branch that held me lit with golden fire and I suddenly stood out as in the noon sun. I tried to slide back down the tree with men from both sides in heated battle directly beneath me.

An arrow (from where I could not see) shot well and perfect, hitting me directly in the chest. It felt as if someone had punched me. I looked down at the arrow protruding from the war vest and broke it off. It had not pierced the clay-covered vest. A hand's length either side and I would have been pierced through. Another arrow hit the tree near my hand, sending stinging bark up into my eyes. I swung under, hung for one terrible second, and dropped down into the swinging clubs and arrows' paths.

The heat was a force against me and also an ally. I choked in the smell of singed hair. Those fighting were cowering back from the flames. I grabbed at my scattered arrows and ran, dodging a swing from a club, trying unsuccessfully to notch an arrow as I fled. Coming around the side of the longhouse I stumbled against bodies along the path. Most were Takers dead or dying; a few were ours. I ran past them in a dream then recognized one of the fallen. Keer! I stopped and turned as a shadow ran towards me. I drew an arrow and Borg called out. "It is me, you fool."

He helped me draw Keer up and then flung him like a child over his shoulder. We ran to some trees and set him against one. He was still breathing but a wound on the side of his head looked swollen and his nose was broken, blocking his breathing.

"Watch over him." Borg said.

He ran back into the fire light and bounced his club against the back of a Taker, an arrow stuck him in the meat of the thigh but it was a poorly drawn arrow and Borg pulled it from the shallow wound and stuck it into the dying

505

warrior he had just clubbed. He roared and I saw his teeth in a broad grin. He was in glorious battle and I suddenly felt the thrill of it. I took the five of six arrows I had left and knelt behind a tree, scanning the paths.

"Live." I told Keer. "We are fighting brothers and you have to live to see it through, to tell Koor…"

More footsteps. Three of them, coming from behind a small hut on the outskirts of the village, war bows and arrows between them. I held my breath as they crept within a dozen paces, then past me to aim at the battling warriors in the fire light. I chose the one at the back and shot him. He grabbed at the arrow in his back with a howl and rolled away. I shot again and the one behind him, hit high between the shoulders, howled and pitched sideways, knocking the third onto his back. The third landed on the war bow with a snap and the bowstring whipped him bloody across the face. He jumped up agile as a bobcat and spotted me kneeling there behind Keer. He charged, shouting a challenge in a language I did not know. I did know his meaning however. He ran towards me as I fumbled to notch an arrow. He was ten paces from me, running full speed with a long obsidian knife drawn from its sheath, when I realized he would reach me before I could shoot. Keer kicked out with a weak leg and the Taker fell and rose again, spinning around, slashing at the air. He raised his long knife over Keer and everything moved slowly, the great knife arcing up. My fumbled arrow, shot wide, bouncing from his shoulder, and then Copperman, axe raised, came from the darkness like a ghost. His gleaming axe sank into the Taker's skull and the handle snapped, sending the two men tumbling onto Keer, who was too slow to roll away. I ran to them and struggled to shift the dead man from Keer. He groaned, opened his good eye and looked weakly around.

"Have we won?" "I do not know," I said.

Copperman stood stiffly. He had a short thin blade tip broken from the Taker's knife sticking from his vest. He undid the vest and pulled it out. The blade had made it partway through and its broken tip wedged into his sternum. I tried but could not pry it from the bone. With a struggle, Copperman took his axe head from the dead man's skull and wiped it on the grass. The sound of battle had grown nearly quiet now, the smoke and flames contained in the square, roofless firebox of the longhouse. A call and rush of footsteps, and then cheering, loud cheering from our men.

The dim morning glow showed the ravages of battle, dark patches of shadow turning slowly to blood; body after body revealed itself in the growing light.

"Did we win?" Keer mumbled, trying to rise. I knelt to help him up and rested an arm over my shoulder.

We walked over to the center of the village and marveled at the destruction our war party had wrought.

"Did we win?" he asked again, bleary eyed. "Yes," I said, then noticed Borg, lying among the dead, and turned Keer away from him to rest him against the wall of a small hut.

Copperman had his shirt off and was working with a stone to bend the knife tip back and forth, with a sigh it dropped to the ground, he picked it up, and, satisfied that it was whole, he rubbed the wound gingerly. Then donned his cloak again and called a cheer to the warriors. They began to gather and cheer together. Warrior after warrior came into the warmth of the dying fire of the longhouse.

"We live!" he shouted. "We live!" I joined in, suddenly washed with elation, thrill, overwhelming in its realization. It was over.

"The Wolf and Axe are done!" Kadal cried from the other side of the village. "The Takers have been taken."

"We live!" I called into the sky. Then, growing dizzy, I stumbled over to Keer and slumped next to him. I watched the smoke billow into the growing light and let the world spin for a few moments.

"Thank you," I whispered to the Gods, then closed my eyes and let sleep take me.

What we found

Four dozen fly-gathering bodies, black tarred with dried blood. Seven of our own. We gathered their belongings in a pile at the base of the singed tree. The bodies of the Takers were too numerous to burn. We lined them up and took the beads, knives and any trinkets worth saving. Their bows were fine and we kept them along with the arrows and some of their boots. Inside the huts were piles of loot unimagined: Some six dozen wolf, Ibex and fox pelts, wrapped tightly for travel. Leather sacks of beads and fine flint blade blanks. Strings of fungus and other medicines carefully dried and packed in thin sheets of rabbit intestine. There were wooden carvings that seemed to have come from distant lands and Copperman said they were scraps in his memory from childhood. The Takers had no doubt brought them along as worship goods. They were packed and ready, there was no doubt.

Kadal praised Copperman's wisdom to attack when we did. They would have been gone soon enough. There were no injured Takers; warriors' rage had ended each and every one of them. Of ours there were five injuries grave enough to need attention and several smaller wounds that

Copperman and Kadal treated and cleaned. I had a deep bruise and my ribs creaked, from what part of the battle I have no recollection. Ailor had a flap of scalp open on his forehead and Copperman used Ailor's own hair on either side of the wound to weave it back into place. Okla and three others were at the trail waiting to ambush the runners and the Forest guides were hunting the surrounding woods for stragglers.

Keer was recovering from the head wound but could not breathe from the broken shape of his nose. Copperman told me to hold his arms and then smiled at Keer.

"You were a warrior this night," he said to him. "Your father will hold a feast in your honor. Your brother will be so happy to see you he will forget to be jealous."

As Copperman spoke he had two sturdy twigs as thick as a man's pinky and twice as long. He slid each into Keer's nostrils and he shook but did not cry out.

"Borg would be proud," Copperman said and pulled up sharply on the two sticks. The broken nose crunched and popped as it came out from its dent in Keer's face. The pain must have been excruciating and Keer cried out and lunged with his hands. I held him and Copperman slowly released the short sticks. The nose, bleeding well, seemed to find its place on Keer's face. He blew blood and slime from his nose and then lay back weeping from the trauma of it all.

"He is breathing from the nose again," Copperman said. "It had to be done."

A few hours later Okla and the others came back, Okla had his left hand bandaged with strips of his shirt and his eyes were glassy and strange. He walked past me and slumped next to Keer. I approached him carefully. This look was on several of our warriors and I remembered it from the Elkhorn attack. The look of murder stays in the eyes. I sat next to him and waited.

He glanced around as if slowly waking from a bad dream. He looked at me for a few moments. His eyes cleared to recognition. I smiled at my old friend.

"I knew you would live," he said.

"I thought we would all make it and then we began fighting and I thought none of us would make it," I said.

Okla stared out at nothing. "They came down the trail so clumsy in the dark it was like shooting lambs, big stupid lambs. They were half naked and crazed and I could see them, fish belly white in the moonlight. I think I killed ten or twelve. The Forest guides were following any who veered from the path. None escaped. I do not think there are any Takers left as prisoners."

He looked around. "Some of them were young and two were women. They had weapons on them but some...I could not be sure. I just shot until the arrows were gone. And still they came. One I hit with two arrows, then he reached me and I hit him with my bow, then the bow broke and we were clawing and kicking, Ilar came up and hit him with a stone and he fell but then he came to his feet again..." Okla looked at me"...He just would not die...He...."

Okla went silent and Keer rose to face him, blood still trickling from the nose.
"Borg is gone," he said to Okla. "He would have been proud of you."

The day faded to dusk with our jobs half finished, our wounds still fresh. We made great, comfortable beds in the huts of the old valley clan, using dozens of furs, each of us collapsing in exhaustion. Sleep, broken by sudden cries from the wounded. I awoke several times, grasping for weapons that were not there, fighting off invisible foes. Night guards watched the trails but there were no enemies left to attack us.

By first light we crawled out to finish our grim tasks. We dragged the bodies of the Takers to the square of the burnt longhouse and brought in wood to stack over them. Great dried logs and branches, load after load. It took half the day to prepare the fire. Two of ours died in the night; Ketal from the Bog-shepherd had a wound unseen under his ribs and it bled out in the darkness. He had been strong and elated during the battle and none knew of the wound. Perhaps he thought it was too small to mention. Like a lost stitch in a water skin it had opened and spilled his life while we slept. Copperman said it would not have mattered if we knew as these wounds from an arrow are beyond our repair.

And Nalo of the Forest clan came in and rested on skins only to stay in sleep forever. He had a bruise on his skull, much smaller than what Keer suffered but somehow far worse. We leaned our dead against the outside of the longhouse walls as guards, bows and knifes in hand, watching over our victory. The sight was haunting and beautiful. It was a fine burial.

The three Forest guides came into the village near dusk. Vu wept at the sight of Nalo and told Copperman of their battle. They had taken a dozen at least, trailing them through the night and into the morning. One, the short bearded leader we held prisoner near the Aloi camp, escaped. They were keeping three prisoners to take home as prizes.

Copperman startled. "Prisoners? Where?"

They pointed to the trail; there were two women and a boy, tethered together at the base of a tree. The war party ran to bring them and this enraged the Forest guides. For a short moment there was threat of violence as the Forest guides raised their spears and some of our men drew bows. Copperman stood between them and I rose to stand beside him. Into the firelight the three bewildered prisoners were terrible to behold. Scratched from head to toe from running through the thorns and branches half naked, they were delirious and shivering. Copperman struggled to communicate with the Forest clan as we all rushed to find furs and water and dried food for the prisoners.

The Forest guides were shaking with rage at the insult and Copperman struggled to understand the situation. This was made worse when the Elkhorn realized the boy was Borg's brother Kae, taken months ago during the attack. Kae saw the body of his brother against the wall of the longhouse and ran to it weeping. The women were cringing under their new furs as the argument raged. Finally, with a flourish, Copperman opened his pack and brought out the last of the trade goods. He held up a goatskin bag and reached in to show the fine beads it held. He offered it as trade and the Forest guides pondered the offer. They shoved one of the women forward and took the beads. The other woman gave Copperman a pleading look. He searched around in his pack and found a large copper medallion with flower patterns around its edges. It had a hole for a leather necklace strap and Copperman unwound the leather cord, cut it and fitted it with a knot. He placed it around the Forest guide's neck. After a moment's pause, the guide smiled and reached in to rub noses with Copperman. The struggle was over as quickly as it began. The guides gathered a bundle of furs, extra bows and arrows and wordlessly left, following the southern trail into the night.

We slept again, this time deeper and safer despite the bodies ripening in the longhouse. Before light we awoke. The war clan was seventeen strong with three survivors from the Takers. Borg's brother Kae, now dressed as a warrior, had shaved his head on the sides as we had and he carried his brother's war club despite its weight. He said nothing and ate with haste and fear, gone savage in the few months with the Wolf and Axe. The others fawned over him. The lost son rescued. He would be the joy of the Elkhorn if he survived the journey home.

The smell of death was overwhelming now and we packed intently in the firelight. As dawn came, we were tightly packed with extra furs rolled and strapped to our backs. There were hidden treasures among the stores of the Wolf and Axe: Three slabs of poor copper that could be re-smelted and purified. Necklaces and bracelets and too many arrows and spear points. Copperman had us each load our quivers with twenty of the best arrows among the pile gathered and we each had our choice of the dozens of fine knives and flint axes. The rest of the arrowheads he carefully trimmed from the arrows until he had a fine heavy bag of points, packed in soft moss to keep them from braking against each other. The rest of the loot, older furs, extra bows and arrow-blanks, bloody boots and each and every war vest were thrown atop the great mound of enemies that filled the old longhouse walls. With torches we lit the sides of the woodpile and watched for a few moments as the dry pile began to grow in flames. We walked towards the south as the flames leapt up and at the edge of the village we stopped and watched the funeral pyre.

We were silent as the shapes of our brothers guarding the last of the Takers, flickered against the stonewall. Black smoke billowed up into the morning sky and I stood next to Keer and Okla, shaking as the fear and trauma of the last few days, the last few months, poured from me. Keer called out to Borg and his brother Kae joined in. Soon we were all calling farewell, crying openly for our lost brothers. Finally as the flames roiled black with the spirits of the dead and we turned away to begin the journey south.

Walking the trail back was a slow brightening, a gentling of the spirit. We no longer had to hide our path, or creep along the trail. Lookouts were unnecessary now and the camps we chose were in open spaces with running water and large night fires. We had furs to sleep well and faces cleaned of dark ashes.

The women were kept near Kadal and Copperman during the nights, as the men, lonely after the long summer around men, began to watch them with more than a passing interest. Copperman coaxed them into conversation and their stories were different than we had expected. One, with black curling hair was very lovely. She was the wife of the smaller bearded leader. She asked Copperman what would become of her and her slave. The younger girl she referred to was my age or maybe younger. She offered her as a slave wife to Copperman in return for her release. Copperman spat into the dirt.

"You have no power to trade. Your slave can come with us or follow you south. In return for your life, you will swear by your dark Gods to tell the southerners of the fate waiting for them in the north."

She held little grief for her lost husband, or the demise of her entire clan. She would not tell Copperman about their lives as the women of the Takers, saying only, "The men always bring a few of us to remind them of their wives back home. We are not shared among them. Men need to at least look at a woman now and then or they begin to crave each other."

On the second day we came upon Asha's camp and found her cold fireplace and scraps of her little stay shelter…and the short bearded leader of the Nagaal, the last of the Wolf and Axe. He lay back as if resting, one of Asha's wooden cups near his hand and black liquid spilled around his hands. He had no apparent wounds and I knelt to look closer.

"Do not touch that cup!" Copperman said. He murmured as we watched him pace around the little camp. "Only his footprints approaching. He sat here...she made him a cup of special tea and gave him scraps of food." He flicked small squirrel bones with the toe of his boot. "He felt strange and lay back to rest a moment...and his spirit slipped from him as she packed her things and left."

The wife of the dead leader screamed up at the dark woods. "You poisoned him! Witch!" He nodded.

"This is Asha's work if ever I saw it. If the Forest guides were still here, they would tell the story in fine detail but that is the raw shape of it."

He took a large stone and placed it atop the poison cup. He stood on the stone and beneath it came the sound of crunching wood.

"Any passing traveler might be tempted to keep the cup and die the first time he used it."

We dragged the body to a near bog and sank it with a pile of stones so that the bears and wolverines should not eat the body and suffer Asha's poisons. We marched on. The widow pale and shaking. She was unmoved by the death of her clan but tortured by the unmanly burial of her husband.

Each day, Keer's face took on a more normal shape, his swollen nose shrank down and his blackened face turned from blue-bruise to yellow. My creaking ribs softened and the wounds of the others healed as they should. Copperman's chest was a problem as the wound grew red and painful under his cloak. There was nothing to do but burn a red hot coal against it. This was my job and it is nothing easy to do. I grabbed a red coal from the fire in the pinchers of a split green branch and the others held Copperman while I pressed it sizzling against the wound. He cursed and kicked me hard against the shins as the others held his arms. I ran back as he swung and kicked out at the others until the pain subsided. Although this treatment was his request, he would not look at me or the others who held him for the rest of the day. The next morning, however, he announced with a smile that the wound was looking better.

Okla and Keer were stepping lighter as we came closer to the Bog-shepherd clan. The last of our food gone, travel-weary, sick of our own footsteps, we came one morning over the short hill and looked down on the Bog-shepherd village. A cheer came from the near field and then more, as families came in a wave. Dogs ran to greet old masters and mothers dropped their work to race across the field. Sol and Lan gathered Keer in their arms and Okla's father shook him by the shoulders and walked proudly, shouldering his pack and gear the last few hundred paces.

"We will have a feast the likes of which the Bog-shepherd has never seen" Lan cried out. "A feast to make the Gods jealous."

Longing drove us

The body carries memory and it is through the body one must heal from trauma. We swam in the heat of the day, naked and delirious, scrubbing clean with sand and soap-root until the last of the blood and death-smell left us. We drank honeyed wine and ate Einkorn porridge and smoked lamb until our bellies bulged. Women tended to every injury with oils and poultices. We slept in the day and night, received as many bravery braids as our hair could hold and moved from house to house as guests.

The widow disappeared in the night, stealing a good knife and a lamb. Her servant stayed and a family of the Bog-shepherd took her in gladly. She seemed so lost and confused that I wondered if she would ever recover from the life of servitude. Copperman said that he had recovered from just such a fate and suspected we would find her as a happy farmer's wife by our next visit.

The celebration lasted for days and days, softening the misery and filling us back up after long hungers. On the third night I slept without calling out in fear. Okla and I began to goof around again, shooting arrows at targets and dunking each other in the river. The play felt cautious at first as if we were not certain of our ability to be foolish after such serious work. Soon enough Keer and Koor were arguing over petty things and teasing each other again. Keer looked more and more like his brother as the swelling reduced but with the slight crook of the nose and the scar over his right brow, no one would ever struggle to tell them apart again. The rest of our warriors went from recovery to relaxation to boredom, as being a guest is a small kind of work in itself. And finally, Copperman announced that we were leaving the Bog-shepherds to prepare for their fall harvest and lamb work. We were going home. My feet ached to begin the trip.

The good-bye was nothing like the kind of pain it had been when Okla left the Lake. We were a ten-day walk apart and now as men who had covered that a dozen times over, it did not seem such a trip. We would see each other soon, deciding upon the winter to meet when he could cross the ice. He promised to bring several dogs for the Elkhorn when he came. And perhaps even a black lamb for Gyson. We left early the next morning and even in the dark, the entire clan came out to call blessings to us as we walked the trail. Strange to walk with the small group.

The Lake called to us each with different longings. The Elkhorn were triumphant and wanted to rest in the new longhouse and tell the stories of our battle. The Little Lake-clan wanted nothing more than the roast fish and green onion cooking they had known every day until our journey began. I thought of Ebalno and how he would love the stories, how he must have hated being left behind.

I dreamed of several things and did not know which pulled me harder, the family watching for our return, Moon at my feet again as I hunted familiar paths or Taila, dark eyed, perfect, tea-stealing Taila. Finally I could think of her again. Longing drove us faster than any of us had walked before, day after day, sleeping little, marching in the red falling leaves, packs heavy with fine furs and hearts full and proud. Until the morning came to show us standing at the water's edge. A boat in the distance raised the call, and by the time others came to retrieve us, I could see the smoke of a signal fire from the Lake village. I set the heavy pack down near the water and knew that loving hands would lift it to the boats and others would carry it to my own house.

Copperman sighed over and over, staring out at the distant boats. "They will ask us to tell it all over and over…and we must. But leave the worst of it out, leave the worst of it where it lay in the ashes of the old valley. We do not need to carry that part into our home."

I thought of this for a while and understood the wisdom of it. From a boat in the lead I recognized Hanit and Little Brother waving; then came a bark, and Moon, nose up, began to howl with joy.

"Now we are home!" Copperman said and laughed as Moon leapt from the boat twenty paces out and swam to the shore to meet us.

Made in the USA
Monee, IL
07 February 2022